**Emine Sevgi Özdamar** was born in Turkey and now
lives in Berlin. She attended drama school in Istanbul and
has appeared in major theatrical productions in Germany,
Vienna, Avignon and Paris, as well as in films. She has
also directed in the theatre and written plays. Her other
books include the novel *Life is a Caravanserai*.

# The Bridge of the Golden Horn

EMINE SEVGI ÖZDAMAR

TRANSLATED BY MARTIN CHALMERS

A complete catalogue record for this book can be
obtained from the British Library on request

The right of Emine Sevgi Özdamar to be identified as the
author of this work has been asserted by her in accordance
with the Copyright, Designs and Patents Act 1988

Copyright ©1998 by Emine Sevgi Özdamar

Translation copyright ©2007 Martin Chalmers

Originally published under the title *Die Brücke vom
Goldenen Horn* in 1998 by Kiepenheuer & Witsch

First published in the UK in 2007 by Serpent's Tail,
an imprint of Profile Books Ltd
3a Exmouth House
Pine Street
London ECIR OJH
website: www.serpentstail.com

ISBN 978 1 85242 932 4

Designed and typeset at Neuadd Bwll, Llanwrtyd Wells

Printed and bound in Great Britain by Clays, Bungay, Suffolk

10 9 8 7 6 5 4 3 2 1

The paper this book is printed on is certified
by the © 1996 Forest Stewardship Council
A.C. (FSC). It is ancient-forest friendly.

This book has been selected to receive financial
assistance from English PEN's Writers in
Translation programme supported by Bloomberg.

Recommended by **pen**

# Contents

# About Badness

by John Berger

*I*t's difficult for me to comment on Sevgi's writing because I love it, and analysing something you love is a daft activity. Of course she's a story-teller, an irresistible all-night story-teller, and late in the morning wakes up telling another story. And what makes her stories so rich and necessary? Necessary because when you hear them, you realise the extent of the emptiness they have filled.

What they offer is often lacking today. I'm not sure whether this is an historical remark; what do you think, Sevgi?

Perhaps story-tellers have always been listened to because they fill a lack. Stories never concur with the official version of events which, by definition, is the version of those visibly in power. The story-teller by contrast is invisible except when telling her or his story.

And the magic of a story is always invisible for it finally derives, not from the story being told with all its described incidents and carefully drawn characters, but from the voice telling it. Is her voice feminine? Immensely so, but often not. She can talk about sex like a man. She talks about dreams like a child. She talks about the cruelty of the existent like a grandparent. Her voice changes age from sentence to sentence. And what is between its legs changes too. (I put it like this for a word like *gender* would never pass her voice's lips.)

The first thing you might think about her voice is that it exaggerates. Yet this is not as simple as it sounds, for the essential difference between information and a story is that the latter always exaggerates! Without exaggeration there would be no stories. Exaggeration begins as soon as feelings are shared.

Stories exaggerate some things and understate others, and it's this which allows the path of a story to go up and down hill. Talking of downhill, Sevgi is, on certain occasions, the fastest story-teller I know. You sit pillion behind her, arm round her waist, and when you corner your knee grazes the ground.

Re-look at the verb *exaggerate*. Exaggeration relates to what is normally said. Exaggeration is to go beyond those norms. When referring directly to reality, is it possible to exaggerate?

In its cruelties, its injustices, its repetitiveness, and its gifts, there is nothing more exaggerated than reality. Governors, ruling class, bureaucrats, moralists, judges ceaselessly pretend that reality is not exaggerated. Slaves, citizens, scammers, know otherwise, and mostly they keep quiet about it – except when they are asleep and dream. This is why stories fill the emptiness created by all the official pretences that reality is not exaggerated

At one moment – towards the very end of the book – Sevgi listens to many mothers crossing the Bridge of the Golden Horn. 'They didn't say anything, but I heard their voices.' And the voices say: 'With these eyes in this blind world we have seen the Day of Judgement.'

The great stories she tells here are all about badness, and about those whom the official versions of what's happening in the world continually fix the label *bad* to.

Her stories are the opposite of what mothers tell their young children. They are, however, what the mothers live with.

They are about poverty, betrayals, disobedience, cruelties, desperation, wild hopes, lies, deceits, vengeance, pain, helplessness, pain again, endurance, cowardice, taking unreasonable risks and fury.

Thanks to her stories the listener learns how the bad suddenly and unexpectedly contains the good. Yet the trick of telling the difference between the two is hidden in each story and cannot be transferred to another.

So there's no golden rule? No, never. If there's a very approximate rule, it's this: As soon as it's big, forget it. Only what is small can grasp what is immense and what matters!

Since their beginning, stories have pretended to take place far away. Faraway and once-upon-a-time are code words for Here and Now. Just as information is the opposite of stories, informers are the opposite of story-tellers. When a story is being retold every word becomes a code-word describing a Here and Now.

And saying this makes me suddenly wonder whether Sevgi's voice is not her whole body? Her whole body throughout her entire life. Her whole body entering the listener's ear! It could be that this contortionist act – funny, grotesque, beautiful, incredible (of course you don't believe it) – is the secret of Sevgi's great story-telling!

Yes, she's laughing – and we join her...

# Part 1

# The Offended Station

# The Long Corridors of the Women Workers' Hostel

On Stresemannstrasse at that time, it was 1966, there was a baker's shop, an old woman sold bread there. *Picasso*

Her head looked like a loaf of bread that a sleepy baker's apprentice had baked, big and lopsided. She bore it on her hunched-up shoulders as if it were on a coffee tray. It was nice going into this bread shop, because one didn't have to say the word bread, one could point at the bread.

If the bread was still warm, it was easier to learn by heart the headlines from the newspaper which was displayed in a glass case out on the street. I pressed the warm bread to my chest and my stomach and shifted from one leg to another on the cold street like a stork.

I couldn't speak a word of German and learned the sentences, just as, without speaking any English, one sings 'I can't get no satisfaction'. Like a chicken that goes clack clack clack. Clack clack clack could be the reply to a sentence one didn't want to hear. For example, someone asked 'Niye böyle gürültüyle yürüyorsun?' (Why do you make so much noise when you walk?) and I answered with a German headline: 'When household goods become used goods.'

Perhaps I learned the headlines by heart, because before I had come to Berlin as a worker, I had been in a youth theatre group for six years. My mother, my father were always asking me: 'How can you learn so many sentences by heart, isn't it hard?' Our directors told us: 'You must learn your lines so well that you can even say them in your dreams.' I began to repeat my lines when I was dreaming; sometimes I forgot them, woke up very much afraid, immediately repeated the lines and fell asleep again. To forget one's lines – that was as if in mid-air a trapeze artist doesn't reach her partner's hand and falls down. But people loved those who carried out their professions between death and life. I got applause in the theatre, but not at home from my mother. Sometimes she had even lent me her beautiful hats and ball gowns for my parts, but when I stopped doing schoolwork because of the theatre, she said to me: 'Why don't you learn your school exercises as well as you do your parts? You'll have to repeat a year.' She was right, I learned only the lines of plays, even the lines of the others I was acting with. When I was sixteen, I played the part of Titania, Queen of the Fairies, in Shakespeare's *A Midsummer Night's Dream*.

> *Haydi, halka olun, bir peri şarkisi söyleyin*
> *(Come, now a roundel and a fairy song,)*
> *Then for the third part of a moment hence:*
> *Some to kill cankers in the muskrose buds…*

I couldn't keep up with school any more. My mother wept. 'Can Shakespeare or Molière help you now? Theatre has burned up your life.' – 'Theatre is my life, how can my life burn itself? Jerry Lewis didn't have a leaving certificate either, but you love him, Mother. Harold Pinter left school for the theatre, too.' – 'But their names are Jerry Lewis and Harold Pinter.' – 'I'm going to go to theatre school.' – 'If you're not successful, you'll be unhappy. You'll starve. Finish school, otherwise your father won't give you any money. You could be a lawyer, you love speaking. Lawyers are like actors, but they don't starve, do they? Do your leaving certificate.' I replied:

*'Adi olmayan cinsten bir ruhum* (I am a spirit of no common rate).'

My mother replied: 'You want to make an ass of me and frighten me as if I were your mortal enemy, and you want to kill me with worry. Perhaps I'm partly to blame, but I'm your mother and I'm going to run out of patience soon.'

She wept. I replied: 'Scorn and derision never come in tears.'
'My daughter, you are so terribly wild and still so young.'

*I will not trust you, I,*
*Nor longer stay in your curst company.*
*Your hands than mine are quicker for a fray.*
*My legs are longer, though, to run away!*

I didn't laugh at home any more, because the rows between me and my mother never stopped. My father didn't know what to do and merely said, 'Don't either of you do anything you'll regret! Why do you force us to speak so harshly?' I replied:

*My lord, fair Helen told me of their stealth,*
*Of this their purpose hither to this wood.*

The sun shone in Istanbul and the newspapers hung outside the kiosks with the headlines: 'Germany wants even more Turkish workers', 'Germany takes Turks'.

I thought, I will go to Germany, work for a year, then I'll go to theatre school. I went to the Istanbul recruitment office. 'How old are you?' – 'Eighteen.' I was healthy and after two weeks I got a passport and a one-year contract with Telefunken in Berlin.

My mother didn't say anything any more, but instead smoked non-stop. We sat in clouds of smoke. My father said: 'May Allah bring you to your senses in Germany. You can't even fry an egg. How are you going to make radio valves at Telefunken? Finish school. I don't want my daughter to be a worker. It's not a game.'

On the train from Istanbul to Germany I had walked backwards and forwards along the train corridor for a couple of nights and looked at all the women who were going there as workers. They had rolled down their stockings below the knee, the thick rubber straps left marks on their skin. It was easier for me to tell from their naked knees that we were still far from Germany than from the signs of the stations we passed and whose names we could not read. 'What a never-ending journey,' said one woman. All were silently in agreement, no one had thought of saying a word, the smokers just took out their cigarettes, looked at each other and smoked. Those who didn't smoke looked out of the window. One said: 'It's got dark again.' Another said: 'Yesterday it got dark like that too.' Each cigarette pushed the train on more quickly. No one looked at their watch, they looked at the cigarettes, which they constantly lit up. For three days, three nights, we hadn't taken our clothes off. Only a pair of shoes lay on the floor and vibrated along with the train. When one of the women wanted to go to the toilet, she quickly slipped on any pair of shoes, so the women went to the blocked toilets hopping comically in someone else's shoes. I realised that I was looking for women who looked like my mother. One had legs like my mother. I put on my sunglasses and quietly began to cry. On the floor of the train I didn't see any shoes that were my mother's. How nicely her and my shoes had stood side by side in Istanbul. How easily we slipped on our shoes together and went to the cinema to Liz Taylor or to the Opera.

Mama, Mama.

I thought, I shall arrive, get a bed, and then I shall always think about my mother, that will be my work. I began to cry even more and was cross, as if I hadn't left my mother, but my mother had left me. I hid my face behind the Shakespeare book.

When the night had come to an end, the train arrived in Munich. The women who had taken off their shoes days ago had swollen feet and sent those who had <u>kept on their shoes</u> to buy cigarettes and chocolate. <u>Çikolata – çikolata.</u>

I lived with lots of women in a women workers' hostel. We said hossel. We all worked in the radio factory, each one of us had to have a magnifying glass in our right eye while we were working. Even when we came back to the hossel in the evening, we looked at one another or the potatoes we were peeling with our right eye. A button came off, the women sewed the button on again with a wide-open right eye. The left eye always narrowed and remained half shut. We also slept with the left eye a little screwed up, and at five o'clock in the morning, when we were looking for our trousers or skirts in the semi-darkness, I saw that, like me, the other women were looking only with their right eye. Since starting work in the radio valve factory we believed our right eye more than our left eye. With the right eye behind the magnifying glass one could bend the thin wires of the little radio valves with tweezers. The wires were like the legs of a spider, very fine, almost invisible without the magnifying glass. The factory boss's name was Herr Schering. Sherin, said the women, they also said Sher. Then they stuck Herr to Sher, so that some women called him Herschering or Herscher.

We had been in Berlin for a week. The Herscher decided that on the tenth of November, the anniversary of Atatürk's death, we should stand up for Atatürk for a couple of minutes at five past nine precisely, just as in Turkey. At five past nine on 10 November we stood up at our machines on the factory floor, and once again our right eyes were bigger than the left. The women who wanted to weep, wept with their right eye, so that their tears ran down over their right breast on to their right shoe. So with our tears for Atatürk's death we made the Berlin factory floor wet. The neon lights on the ceilings and on the machines were strong and quickly dried the tears. Some women had forgotten the magnifying glass in their right eye when they stood up for Atatürk, their tears collected in the magnifying glass and fogged the lens.

We never saw the Herscher. The Turkish interpreter carried his German words to us as Turkish words: 'Herscher has said that you...' Because I never saw this Herscher, I looked for him in the face of the Turkish interpreter. She came, her shadow fell over the little radio valves in front of us.

While we were working we lived in a single picture: our fingers, the neon light, the tweezers, the little radio valves and their spider legs. The picture had its own voices, we detached ourselves from the voices of the world and from our own bodies. The spine disappeared, the breasts disappeared, the hair on one's head disappeared. Sometimes I had to sniff up mucus. I put off sniffing up the mucus for longer and longer, as if doing it could break up the enlarged picture in which we lived. When the Turkish interpreter came and her shadow fell on this picture, the picture tore like a film, the sound disappeared and there was a hole. Then, when I looked at the interpreter's face, I again heard the voices of the aeroplanes, which were somewhere in the sky, or a metal thing fell on the factory floor and made an echo. I saw that at the very moment that the women interrupted their work, dandruff fell on to their shoulders. Like a postman who brings a registered letter and waits for a signature, so the interpreter, after she had translated Herschering's German sentences into Turkish for us, waited for the word okay.

If a woman, instead of the English okay, used the Turkish word *tamam*, the interpreter again asked: Okay?, until the woman said, 'Okay'. When a woman's okay was slow in coming, because she was just bending the little legs of a radio valve with her tweezers and didn't want to make a mistake or was inspecting the valve through her magnifying glass, then in her impatience the interpreter puffed her fringe up from her forehead until the English okay came.

When we went with her to the factory doctor, we said to her: 'Say to the doctor that I'm really ill, okay?'

The word okay also came into the hossel...

'You're cleaning the room tomorrow, okay?'

'*Tamam*.'

'Say okay.'

'Okay.'

In my first days in Berlin the city was like an endless building to me. Even between Munich and Berlin the country was like a single building. Out of the train door in Munich with the other women, through the door of the Travellers' Aid. Rolls – coffee – milk – nuns – neon lights, then out of the door of the Travellers' Aid, then through the door of the aeroplane, out of the plane door in Berlin, through the door of the bus, out of the door of the bus, through the door of the Turkish women's hossel, out of the hossel door, through the Hertie department store door at the Hallesches Tor (Halle Gate). From the hossel door we went to the Hertie door, we had to walk under an underground railway bridge. Groceries were on the top floor of Hertie. We were three girls, wanted to buy sugar, salt, eggs, toilet paper and toothpaste at Hertie. We didn't know the words. Sugar, salt. In order to describe sugar, we mimed coffee-drinking to a sales assistant, then we said shak shak. In order to describe salt, we spat on Hertie's floor and said: 'Eeeh.' In order to describe eggs, we turned our backs to the assistant, wiggled our backsides and said: 'Clack, clack, clack.' We got sugar, salt and eggs, but it didn't work with toothpaste. We got bathroom cleaning liquid. So my first German words were shak shak, eeeh, clack clack clack.

We got up at five in the morning. In each room there were six beds, in pairs one above the other.

Two sisters who weren't married slept in the first two beds of my room. They wanted to save money and fetch their brothers to Germany. They talked about their brothers as if they were part of a life they had already lived when they were in the world another time, so that I sometimes thought their brothers were dead. When one of the two wept or didn't finish her food or had caught a cold, the other said to her: 'Your brothers mustn't hear about that. If your brothers hear that!' After work they wore pale blue dressing gowns in the hossel, made of an electrically charged material. When they had their periods their hair was charged too, and their dressing gowns of electrically charged material gave off noises in the room. When one of the sisters came down from her bed and in the dark, damp early morning put on her shoes, she sometimes put on her sister's shoes, and her feet didn't notice, because the shoes were so alike.

In the evening after work the women went to their rooms and ate at their tables. But the evening didn't begin, the evening was gone. One ate because one wanted to quickly fetch the night into the room. We leapt over the evening into the night.

The two sisters sat at the table, leant a mirror against a saucepan and put their hair in curlers. Both had rolled their stockings below their knees. Their naked knees showed me that the light would soon be put out in the room. The two talked as if they were alone in the room:

'Hurry up, we have to go to sleep.'

'Who's turning the light off today, you or me?'

One stood at the door, her hand on the light switch, and waited until the other had lain down in bed. She laid her head with the curlers on the pillow, as if she were carefully backing a car into a parking space. When she had properly laid her head down, she said: 'Turn it off!' Then her sister turned off the light.

We, the other four girls, were still sitting at the table, some were writing letters. The darkness cut us apart. We undressed in the dark. Sometimes a pencil fell down. When everyone was in bed and everything was quiet, we could hear the electrically charged material of the two pale blue dressing gowns, which hung on hooks.

Ever since I had been a child in Istanbul, I had been in the habit of praying to the dead every night. I first of all recited the prayers, then recited the names of dead people whom I had not known, but whom I had heard of. When my mother and grandmother told stories, they talked a great deal about people who had died. I had learned their names by heart, listed them every night in bed and gave prayers for their souls. That took an hour. My mother said: 'If one forgets the souls of the dead, their souls will be in pain.' In the first nights in Berlin I prayed for the dead, too, but I quickly grew tired, because we had to get up so early. I fell asleep before I had said all the names of my dead. So I slowly lost my dead in Berlin. I thought, when I go back to Istanbul, I'll start to count my dead again there. I had forgotten the dead, but I had not forgotten my mother. I lay down in bed to think about my mother. But I didn't know how one thinks about mothers. To fall in love with a film actor and to think about him at night – for example, how I would kiss him – that was easier.

But how does one think about a mother?

Some nights, like a film running backwards, I went from the hossel door to the train on which I had got here. I also had the train run backwards. The trees ran backwards past the window, but the journey was too long, I got only as far as Austria. The mountains had their tops in the mist, and it was hard to make a train run backwards in the mist. That's where I fell asleep. I also noticed that I thought about my mother when I didn't eat anything and remained hungry, or when I pulled out the skin on my fingers a bit and it hurt. Then I thought, this pain is my mother. So I went to bed hungry more often or with sore fingers.

Rezzan, who slept above me, didn't eat properly either. I thought, she's thinking about her mother, too. Rezzan stayed awake for a long time and turned in bed in the dark from left to right, then she took her pillow from one end of the bed and put it at the other end. After a while she again started to turn from left to right, from right to left. Below I thought with half my head about my mother, and with the other half I began to think about Rezzan's mother as well.

Two cousins from Istanbul slept in the other pair of bunk beds. They were working in the factory in order to go to university afterwards. One had two little braids and deep scars on her face, because as a teenager she hadn't left her pimples in peace, and she had bad breath. The other cousin was beautiful and sent the one who had bad breath to the post office or to Hertie. Once she came back from the post office, and the beautiful cousin forced her to lie down on the table, she rolled up her sleeves, then she pulled the belt out of her jeans and struck her cousin across the back with the belt. The two sisters in their pale blue dressing gowns, Rezzan and I said:

'What are you doing?'

She shouted: 'The whore went to the post office and came back late.'

We said: 'She hasn't got wings, is she supposed to fly? She didn't come back too late.'

'No, don't interfere.

'Don't interfere.

'Don't interfere.

'Don't interfere.'

And with every sentence she struck her cousin across the back, but looked us in the eyes as she did so. Her pupils spun like a light that had gone crazy, like all the other women her right eye was bigger than her left.

That night, as everyone lay in bed, the two sisters with their curlers one above the other in two beds, the two cousins one above the other in two beds, Rezzan and I one above the other in two beds, the cousin who had bad breath and had been beaten suddenly climbed up on to the bed of her cousin who was beautiful and had beaten. In the darkness they pulled the blanket out of the quilt cover, dropped it on the floor and crawled into the cover as into a sleeping bag, buttoned it up and then – buttoned up in this bag – they kissed each other slurp slurp and made love. And we, the other four, listened without moving.

Opposite the women's hossel was the Hebbel Theatre. The theatre was lit up and a neon sign was constantly going on and off. This light also fell into our room. When the sign went out, then from that day I heard kiss voices slurp slurp in the dark, when the sign was on I saw the curlers on the two sisters' heads gleaming on their pillows in the semi-darkness and the two pairs of shoes on the linoleum floor.

Rezzan, who slept above me, never took off her shoes at night. She always lay in bed in her clothes and shoes. When she slept she held her toothbrush in her hand, and the toothpaste was under her pillow. Like me Rezzan wanted to become an actress. Some nights, as the light of the Hebbel Theatre went on and off, we talked quietly from bed to bed about theatre. Rezzan asked: 'Which part do you want to play, Ophelia?' – 'No, I'm too thin, too big for Ophelia. But maybe Hamlet.' – 'Why?' – 'I don't know. And you?' – 'The woman in *Cat on a Hot Tin Roof* by Tennessee Williams.' – 'I don't know Tennessee.' – 'He was homosexual and left school for the theatre, like us.' – 'Did you know that Harold Pinter left school, too?' – 'Do you know *The Servant* by Harold Pinter?' – 'No.' – 'An aristocrat is looking for a servant. In the end the servant becomes the master and the master the servant. Goodnight.' Rezzan said nothing, the rollers of the two sisters gleamed in their beds as the light of the Hebbel Theatre went on and off.

When we got up at five in the morning, Rezzan was already finished. She brushed her teeth and made coffee, a full cup of coffee in one hand, her toothbrush in the other. Brushing her teeth shuff shuff she walked up and down the long corridors of the women's hossel. All the other women were still running around in their dressing gowns, with towels around their bodies or in their underpants. But Rezzan already had her jacket and skirt on. All the women looked at Rezzan as if she were their clock and then did things faster. Sometimes they even went to the bus stop too early, because Rezzan was already standing there. In the darkness Rezzan looked in the direction of the bus, and the women looked at Rezzan's face.

In the morning the Hebbel Theatre had no lights on. Only our women's shadows waiting for the bus lay on the snow. When the bus came and took us, only the marks of our shoes and splotches of coffee were left in the snow in front of our women's hossel, because some women came to the bus stop with their full cups of coffee, and when the bus came and the door opened tisspamp, they poured what was left on to the snow. The lights of the bread shop were on, in the newspaper case the headline of the day was: HE WAS NO ANGEL. Out of the bus window on my right I saw the newspaper, out of the bus window on my left I saw the ruin of the Anhalt railway station, which like the Hebbel Theatre was opposite our hossel. We called it the broken station. The Turkish word for 'broken' also means offended. So it was also called 'the offended station'.

Just before we reached the factory, the bus had to drive up a long, steep street. A bus full of women tipped backwards. Then came a bridge, there we tipped forward, and there, every wet, half-dark morning, I saw two women walking hand in hand. Their hair was cut short, they wore skirts and shoes with low heels, their knees were cold, behind them I saw the canal and dark factory buildings. The asphalt of the bridge was cracked, rain collected in the holes, in the lights of the bus the women's shadows were thrown on the rainwater and on the canal. The shadows of their knees trembled in the rainwater more than their real knees. They never looked at the bus, but never looked at each other either. One of the women was taller than the other, she had taken the hand of the smaller woman in hers. It looked as if at this time of the morning they were the only living people in this city. It was as if the morning through which they walked was sewn on to the night. Were they coming out of the night or were they coming out of the morning? I didn't know. Were they going to the factory or to the cemetery, or were they coming from a cemetery?

Outside the radio valve factory all the doors of the bus opened, the snow came into the bus with the wind and got out again with the

women's hair, eyelashes and coats. The factory yard swallowed us
in the darkness. It was snowing more heavily; the women crowded
more closely together, walked through the bright snowflakes, as
if someone was shaking out stars on to them. Their coats, skirts
fluttered and made quiet noises amidst the factory hooters. The
snow went with them as far as the time clock, with one wet
hand tink tink tink they pushed the cards in, with the other they
shook the snow from their coats. The snow made the cards and
the floor in front of the porter's lodge wet. The porter rose a little
from his chair, that was his job. I tried out my German sentence,
which I had learned from today's newspaper headline, on him:
'Hewasnoangel' – 'Morningmorning,' he said.

On the factory floor there were only women. Each one sat alone
at a green-painted iron table. Each face looked at another woman's
back. While one was working, one forgot the faces of the other
women. One saw nothing but hair, beautiful hair, tired hair, old
hair, young hair, combed hair, falling-out hair. We saw only one
woman's face, the face of the only woman who was standing, Frau
Mischel. Forewoman. When the machines of the Greek women
workers broke down, they called out to her: 'Frau Missel, comere.'
Their tongues couldn't pronounce a 'sch'. When we, our magnifying
glasses in our right eyes, looked at Frau Missel, we always saw one
half of Frau Missel bigger than the other half. Just as she always
saw our right eyes bigger than our left eyes. That's why Frau
Missel always looked at our right eyes. All day her shadow fell on
the green iron workbenches.

Only in the toilet room could I see the women's faces. There
women stood against the white tiled walls under strip lights and
smoked. They rested their right elbow in their left hand, and the
right hand with the cigarette moved in the air in front of their
mouths. Because the toilet had such strong strip lights, smoking
looked like work, too. At the time one could buy a cigarette from
German women workers for ten pfennigs. Stuyvesant – HB.

Sometimes Frau Missel came, opened the door and looked into

the toilet room, said nothing, shut the door, went. Then, as if the lights had gone out, the last smokers dropped their cigarettes in the toilet bowls and flushed the toilet water down. On quiet feet we then went from the toilet room into the factory hall, but the toilet water noises followed us for a while. When we sat down our hair was always a little more nervous than the hair of the women who never left their green tables for a smoke.

For the first few weeks we lived between hossel door, Hertie door, bus door, radio valve factory door, factory toilet door, hossel room table and factory green iron table. Once all the women could find the things they were looking for in Hertie and had learned to say bread, once they had remembered the proper name of their bus stop – at first they had noted the name of the stop as 'stop' – the women one day switched on the television in the hossel lounge.

The TV had been there from the start. 'Let's see what's on,' said one woman. From that day many women watched figure skating on TV in the hossel lounge in the evening. There, too, I saw the women from behind again, as in the factory. When they returned to the hossel from the radio valve factory, they changed into their nightshirts, boiled potatoes, macaroni, fried potatoes, eggs in the kitchen. The sound of boiling water, hissing frying pans mixed with their thin, thick voices, and everything rose in the kitchen air, their words, their faces, their different dialects, the gleam of knives in their hands, the bodies waiting for the shared pots and pans, nervously running kitchen tap water, a stranger's spit on a plate.

It looked like the shadow plays in traditional Turkish theatre. In it figures came on to the stage, each speaking their own dialect – Turkish Greeks, Turkish Armenians, Turkish Jews, different Turks from different towns and classes and with different dialects – they all misunderstood each other, but kept on talking and playing, like the women in the hossel, they misunderstood each other in the kitchen, but handed each other the knives or pots, or one rolled up another's pullover sleeve, so that it didn't hang into the pot. Then the hossel warden came, the only one who could speak German, and checked that everything in the kitchen was clean. After the meal the women took off their nightdresses, put on their clothes, some also put on make-up, as if they were going to the cinema, and came into the hossel lounge, turned the light off and sat down in front of the figure skaters. While the older women sat like that in the cinema, we, the three youngest girls – we were all virgins and loved our mothers – went to the snack bar opposite the hossel. The man made meatballs out of horses – we didn't know that, because we couldn't speak any German. Meat balls were our mothers' favourite food. The horse meatballs in our hands, we went to our offended station, ate the horses and looked at the weakly illuminated Turkish women's hossel windows. The offended station was no more than a battered wall and a projecting front section with three gateways. If we made a noise in the night with the meatball paper bags, we held our breath and didn't know whether it was us or someone else. There on the ground of the offended station we lost sense of time. Every morning this dead station had woken up, people had been walking there who were no longer there. When the three of us walked there, it was as if my life had already been lived. We went through a hole, walked to the end of the plot of land without speaking. Then, without saying anything to one another, we walked backwards to the hole that once had perhaps been the door of the offended station. And as we walked backwards we loudly blew out our breath. It was cold, the night and the cold took our loud breath and turned it into thick smoke. Then we went back to the street again, I looked behind me to see the remainder of our breath still in the air behind the door space. It was as if the station was in a quite different time. In front of the offended station there was a phone booth. When the three of us walked past it, we talked loudly, as if our parents in Turkey could hear us.

One evening the warden, the little Turkish woman, the only one in the hossel who spoke German, said: 'This evening the radio valve factory has arranged a dance with English soldiers.' A bus came for us women and drove us to the British barracks in Berlin. The women sat down at army tables, and the soldiers stood at the bar and invited us to dance. All shared pots and pans were forgotten. This evening we had soldiers. The soldiers danced with us, we returned to our hossel with soldiers' smiles. That night no woman looked into another woman's eyes. The women walked to their six-bed rooms with slow steps and drew back their blankets as if it was hard work to lie down in bed. Some unbuttoned their nightshirts and for the first time perhaps opened the windows of the rooms. During the night snow blew through the windows on to the sleeping blankets, and in the morning we all stood up as wet women. Then all the women very quietly spread margarine on their bread and also ate it quietly, then they lay down on their beds again. The rooms were silent and a woman's face looked out of every bed. Then they gathered in the shared hossel lounge and talked. One had been an opera singer in Turkey. But one day the new opera director in Istanbul brought his wife with him. This woman was not a star singer, but he had microphones set up for her on the opera stage. That was why the singer had come to Germany. Another had met an American soldier in Smyrna, he wanted to marry her, but she had to pay the fare to America herself. That's why she came to Germany, to earn money for the air ticket to America. The third had been a secret policewoman in Istanbul and had fallen in love with a secret policeman, who simultaneously had star parts in Turkish films and secretly also loved other women. The secret policewoman had run away to Germany from these secret love affairs of the secret policeman. Another girl was called Nur. Nur said her breasts were so big that even her back hurt when she lay down in bed. She had come to Germany to work, to have her breasts operated on.

After the dance evening with the English soldiers the warden, the only one who could speak German, took men to her room. Each time she invited a girl to her room in order to be able to say later that the man had been the girl's lover. Soon after that the warden was thrown out of the factory hossel, but not because she had taken men to her room. The women in the hossel received packages from Turkey with Turkish sausages. When the postman came with the packages, the women were in the factory, the warden took the Turkish sausages, hid them under her bed, showed us the receipts from the German post and translated: 'The sausages from Turkey are poisonous, sick. The German post has confiscated them.' But the women found their Turkish sausages under her bed, went to the radio valve factory director with the sausages, and the warden was dismissed.

The radio valve factory directors sent us a Turkish married couple as wardens. The husband had to work in the hossel, his wife became our interpreter in the factory.

Our new warden said, he was an artist and a communist. No one knew what a communist was. In the evening he taught us German. All the women gathered in the shared hossel lounge, after work they didn't put on their nightdresses any more, the figure skating continued on the television which had not been switched on, and we learned German with our communist hostel warden. He sat in front of the women with his Turkish instrument, the saz, and sang a Turkish song in German, which we all knew in Turkish: 'Greet my father, he must pay a thousand lira, and free me from prison.' All the women repeated it. He smiled and tugged at his moustache. Outside, in front of the Hebbel Theatre, the members of the audience were slowly making their way inside, and in the hossel we repeated the German sentences. 'He must pay a thousand lira and free me from prison.'

When the women had difficulty repeating the words they said: 'The girl in the trousers must repeat them, we've forgotten them.' I repeated his sentences. The communist warden said: 'Have you ever acted before?' – 'Yes, for six years.' – 'One can hear that. What parts did you play?' – 'Titania in *A Midsummer Night's Dream*.'

*I pray thee, gentle mortal, sing again!*
*Mine ear is much enamoured…*

He replied:

*I am a spirit of no common rate.*
*The summer still doth tend upon my state...*

*Your name, honest gentleman?*

'Vasif,' he said and tugged at his moustache.

The communist warden told us that he would give the lesbian cousins a two-bed room, so that they could love one another in peace. So the cousins moved out of our six-bed room. First they kissed us all, as if they were going on a long journey, one wept, so Rezzan took her things, and I led the weeping cousin to her new room. Their beds remained empty in our six-bed room. Ever since the cousins had begun to love each other in the quilt cover at night, the sisters who wore the pale blue dressing gowns of electrically charged material had begun to put on their clothes in the morning hidden behind their beds. Not until they already had their coats on did they sit down together on the lower bed, put on their shoes simultaneously, switch off the light and leave the room. We switched the light on again. Although the lesbian cousins were gone now, the sisters continued putting on their clothes hidden behind the beds and said that the two cousins were masons, freemasons. I didn't know what mason meant. They talked about their brothers again: 'A good thing our brothers don't know.' They also said to me and Rezzan: 'A good thing that your father doesn't know that you were sleeping in the same room as lesbian girls.' But Rezzan's father was dead. They talked so much about their brothers and about our fathers that I thought their sentences about the brothers and fathers were weaving a spider's web that covered the whole room and our bodies. I began to be afraid of their brothers and of my father. I was even afraid of Rezzan's dead father. Every time I became afraid I wrote a letter to my mother with sentences like: 'God protects me here with the help of my father – I swear, I shall not do any bad things here.'

At Hertie the two sisters bought suits and washing powder for their brothers and laid these things on the two empty beds of the lesbian cousins. The men's suits lay on the beds, and at night, when the neon signs of the Hebbel Theatre went on and off, the light fell into our room, and then I saw the shiny curlers on their heads again, and the shiny buttons of the men's suits, which lay across the two beds like bodies.

When we three girls, the horse meatballs in our hands, walked on the other side of the street opposite our hossel to our offended railway station and went past the phone box, I no longer spoke loudly outside the phone box, but quietly, afraid that my parents in Istanbul could hear me. But soon a book came into our room, and that took away my fear of the brothers and of my father and of Rezzan's dead father. Our communist hostel warden had a lot of books, which we could read, if we wanted to. Rezzan brought the book into the room – Oscar Wilde's *The Picture of Dorian Gray*. She read this book so much that she became this book, and at night she told me the story. Her head hung down to me from the top bed, I saw her only as head. When the neon light went out briefly, the head disappeared, but I went on listening to the story in the dark. When she told the story of Dorian Gray, she whispered, because the sisters were already sleeping. My body got used to this fear and freed me from the fear of brothers and fathers.

Our communist hostel warden was very ugly and funny. His door was open day and night. Like a messenger of his own humour he walked around the hossel with an expression on his face that made him look as if he were wearing a comic mask, which he wanted to show everyone, in order to make them laugh. His wife came back with us from the factory in the bus and often lay down for a little. She lay in bed, the communist hostel warden sat behind a table, a book in his hand, the door stood open. The women came and went past this door. He did not look at them, but always kept his face behind the book like a laughing mask. He read his book and said to every woman who walked past, 'Good morning' or 'Good afternoon' or 'Good evening,' turning pages at the same time. Sometimes, when he said the words 'Good morning' just as he was turning a page, he said 'Good...' – then turned the page – '...morning.' He and his wife had worked in the theatre in Turkey. Then they had an invitation from a theatre festival. So they came to Germany, performed their play and stayed in Germany. During the day he went to a German theatre to watch rehearsals, the theatre was called 'Berliner Ensemble'. When he was talking to his wife, he said 'Brecht... Weill... Helene Weigel... Helene said to me today... I said to Helene...' When I lay in bed at night and thought of my mother, I also thought of Helene, I practised her name: Helene Weigel. The wife of the communist hostel warden – he called her 'my Dove' – liked me, she asked me: 'What are you doing this evening?' The word evening! I had forgotten that there were such things as evenings. I searched for evening in my head. The Dove said: 'Come to the theatre with us, you want to be an actress one day, don't you?' We went to the other Berlin, to the Berliner Ensemble, and saw a play, *Arturo Ui*. The men in gangster suits put up their hands, there was a head gangster, who stood on a high table. I didn't understand a word and loved it and loved the many, many lights in the theatre. On the streets of East Berlin I suddenly felt a longing for home, for Istanbul. I smelled the air and drew it into me. The Dove told me that in East Berlin and Istanbul they used the same diesel oil.

Sometimes our communist hostel warden walked around the hossel naked to the waist. He was as thin as a skeleton and had hair everywhere up to his neck – like a pullover. When the women saw him, they fetched voices out of their bodies as if *they* were naked and a man was looking at them. He went on playing Turkish songs on his musical instrument, which he sang in German:

*Oh the willows trees of Smyrna*
*their leaves rain down*
*they call us bandits*
*our loves are like the young willows.*

So we learned, even before we had learned to say '*Tisch*' – table – in German: 'Oh the willow trees of Smyrna, their leaves rain down.'

A new life began with the communist hostel warden. Before he came, there had only been women in the hossel. The women searched for their mothers, their sisters or their stepmothers in the other women, and like sheep who on a rainy night were afraid of thunder and lightning, they came too close to one another and sometimes squeezed one another until they couldn't breathe. Now we had a shepherd, who could sing. He gave us books and said: 'Here, I'm giving you my best friend.' One of his best friends was Chekhov. So he was not the only man we had. Other men came into our hossel with him: Dostoevsky, Gorky, Jack London, Tolstoy, Joyce, Sartre and one woman, Rosa Luxemburg. I didn't know any of them before. Some women fetched books from him, which perhaps they didn't read, but they loved these books as a child loves foreign stamps, they loved to have these books in their bags when they got on the bus to the radio valve factory.

When our communist hostel warden spoke to a woman, he always began his sentences with the word 'Sugar'. When he spoke to several women at once, he said 'Sugars'. 'Sugars, go and sit down, I'll be with you in a moment', 'Sugar, here's a letter for you'. The women who loved him also began to address each other as 'Sugar' and 'Sugars'. And so slowly the hossel divided into the women who said 'Sugar' and the women who didn't say 'Sugar'. When the women in the kitchen were cooking with the pots and pans, the pots and pans were also divided between the women who addressed one another as 'Sugar' and those who didn't address one another as 'Sugar'. After they'd finished cooking, those who said 'Sugar' to one another gave the pots to the women who also said 'Sugar' to them, and those who didn't say 'Sugar' gave the pots to those who didn't say 'Sugar'. The women who said 'Sugar' found the evening. After the factory work they didn't immediately go into the night any more. So the hossel divided once more into the women who had their evenings and the women who immediately leapt over the evening into the night. When these women went to bed, the audience was slowly making its way into the Hebbel Theatre, which was opposite our hossel. The others began to draw out their evenings. They bought records, and so Beethoven's 9th Symphony came into the hossel and a hit song: *'Junge, komm bald wieder'* – 'Boy, come back soon'. In the hossel lounge the TV was on in the background, and they listened back to back without a break to the Beethoven and 'Boy, come back soon', as if, were they to remain without these sounds and voices for one second, the evening would disappear from their hands again. It was so loud that sometimes even our communist hostel warden shouted: 'Donkeys, lie down! Donkeys, go to sleep!' The women who didn't say 'Sugar' did, however, use his new word 'Donkey' and now shouted from their rooms to the hossel salon: 'Donkeys, lie down!' We three girls also belonged to the donkeys. Even the morning bus, which took us to the factory, divided into two groups of women. The women who didn't say 'Sugar' but 'Donkeys, lie down!' now sat down as a group at the front of the bus, and those who said 'Sugar' and were donkeys sat at the back of the bus. In the factory, however, everyone sat at their old place. Those who drew out their evenings and so stole something from the night often went to the toilet in the factory, the lens in front of their right eye. Behind the lens our right eye now looked even sleepier than our left. In the toilet room we went on buying cigarettes for ten pfennigs from the German women workers and went to the toilet with the cigarette. When we went to the toilet, we often forgot to take our lenses out of our right eye, so our cigarettes, which we smoked in the toilet, looked much bigger. We smoked inside and nodded off a little. However, Frau Missel, the forewoman, came and fetched us out of the toilet. So slowly, even in the factory, the women divided into those who slept in the toilet and those who didn't sleep in the toilet.

At some point Beethoven's 9th Symphony and 'Boy, come back soon' were no longer enough to draw out the evenings. The women who were donkeys now went out of the hossel. From that day on, the automatic light in the hallway of the house constantly went on and off and the hossel door opened and shut with a loud creak. We three youngest girls of the women's hossel walked along the streets of Berlin to Zoo Station, to Aschinger, and there we had pea soup and no longer the horse meatballs from our snack bar next to the offended station. But we went on talking loudly when we passed our telephone box next to our offended railway station, so that our parents in Turkey could hear us. On some evenings, when we three girls came back late to our hossel room from Zoo-Aschinger and in the night filed our nails with a file, another woman, who was already in bed, threw her pillow at us and shouted at us: 'You'll end up whores!' I went on practising my German sentences, which I didn't understand, at the newspaper display case every morning, and replied to the pillow with newspaper headlines learned by heart:

THE GLOVES ARE OFF
LOOKING COSTS MORE
SOVIETS ARE ONLY ONLOOKERS.

When we walked along the Berlin streets, I was astonished at how few men were to be seen on the streets, even in the evenings there were not many men to be seen. I was also astonished that the men whom I saw didn't scratch themselves between the legs, like many Turkish men on Turkish streets. And some men carried the bags of the women they were walking beside and looked as if they were not married to these women, but to these bags.

They walked along the streets as if at that moment they were being filmed for TV. To me the streets and people were like a film, but I didn't have a part in this film. I saw the people, but they didn't see us. We were like the birds, who flew somewhere and from time to time came down to earth, before flying away again.

We had all come here only for a year, after a year we all wanted to go back. When we looked at ourselves in the mirror, no mother, no father, no sister walked past in the room behind us. In the mirror our mouths no longer talked to a mother or sister. We no longer heard their voices, the whispering of their clothes, their laughter in front of the mirror, so we saw ourselves every day in the mirror as lonely people.

Once we had understood in the mirror that we were alone, everything was easier. So we three girls went to the Wienerwald restaurant on Ku'damm and ate half-chicken. Then I saw Christ. To warm up, we had gone into a church, and there for the first time I saw Christ on the cross. In Istanbul, too, Christ was one of our prophets. I loved him as a child, but I had heard nothing of the cross, my grandmother had told me that as a baby Christ floated alone in a basket on a river. I also loved his mother Meryem.

In the factory we went on smoking Stuyvesant in the toilet and falling asleep there, the forewoman, Frau Missel, fetched us out again, the faulty radio valves landed in the bin. When there were too many radio valves in the bin, we bought perfume, soap and creams from the men who came with suitcases during the factory breaks. We also signed documents, without knowing that these were encyclopedia subscriptions, the money was deducted from our monthly wage. We thought that the forewoman, Frau Missel, would be less angry because of the broken radio valves if we bought the things.

One day we three girls went into a pub for the first time. It was snowing outside. Men were standing at the bar. The men asked in English: 'Where are you from?' Rezzan and I could speak some English, and Rezzan replied: 'From the North Pole, we are Eskimos, our sledges are outside.'

When the other women came back to the hossel at night, they also brought back new addresses from Berlin with them: KaDeWe, Café Keese, Café Kranzler. So we three girls went to Café Keese. Telephone dance. There were telephones on the tables, one could invite men to dance. We sat down at two tables and phoned each other. 'Hello, Mother, I'm your daughter, how are you?' – 'Oh, my child, how are you? What have you been eating?' – 'Meatballs, mother.' Then a German man called us. 'Dance?' We replied with what we had learned from our communist hostel warden in the German lessons: 'Remember me to my father.' The next morning the women who had found their evenings and gone out of the hossel were told by the other women: 'You are whores and go to other factory hossels, where Turkish men live, you spread the semen of these men on your bread and eat it.' So once again the women's hossel divided into the women who spread Turkish men's semen on their bread and ate it, and the women who spread margarine on their bread and ate it.

But we didn't know any Turkish men yet. We knew only our communist hostel warden. Soon, however, some women got to know quite a different side of Turkish men. The women came from the night shift, the men stood at the bus stop at night and struck the most beautiful woman in the face. It was dark, none of the women saw the men properly, they only heard their voices: 'Whores, what are you doing here in the night?' After that the communist hostel warden went to the bus stop every night and met the women who were coming from the night shift.

Then a man came into the hossel after all. One night outside the hossel door we found a man lying on the ground in the snow. His trouser buttons were undone, and he wasn't wearing any underpants. He had peed himself. Upstairs the whole women's hossel was asleep, and we three girls tried to help the man to his feet. He did stand up, but went to the middle of the road and sat down in the snow again. We thought the cars would run him over. So we brought the man into the hossel lounge, laid him on a couch and went to sleep. In the morning the man was still lying on the couch, asleep, smiling in his sleep, and a stiff penis stuck out of his trousers when the women switched on the light. 'The three girls are rabid,' said the women to one another, 'we will go to factory boss Herschering.' The Dove, the wife of our communist hostel warden, was supposed to translate their sentences for Schering. The communist hostel warden listened to them, then he spoke to the women who wanted to go to Herschering.

For the first time he began his sentences not with 'Sugar' or 'Sugars', but said: 'Children'. This word silenced the women. The communist hostel warden gathered us all in the hossel lounge, addressed some women now as 'Children', others as 'Sugar' or 'Sugars' and redistributed the women in the rooms. Now the children lived with children, sugars with sugars, donkeys with donkeys, whores with whores.

After that things were quiet in our women's hossel, so quiet that one could hear the snow falling. The hossel lounge was empty, the big clock on the wall ticked and waited. The snow covered the big dustbin in the courtyard and the sign: 'Children are forbidden to play in the courtyard'. On the first evenings no woman left her room. In all the rooms they talked about the women in the other rooms. The children in their rooms mimicked the sugars and donkeys and whores in front of the other children, the sugars and donkeys and whores in their rooms mimicked the children. All the women mimicked the expressions, the gestures and the dialects of the others, they made fun of the way they walked, the way they ate, and so at some point the women began to look like one another again. Their faces and bodies and mouths absorbed the faces and bodies and dialects of the others, became accustomed to them. Sugars now lived inside children. Children lived in whores and donkeys, and they came together again. In the bus they sat mixed up together again, in the hossel kitchen they passed pots and pans from hand to hand, without asking themselves whether these hands belonged to the sugars or donkeys or children or whores. Now everyone got to know the half-chicken at Wienerwald and the pea soup in the Aschinger restaurant.

When all the others went to Wienerwald and to Aschinger, we three girls and a couple of other women went with our communist hostel warden and his Dove to the Turkish Workers' Association in an apartment converted from a shop opposite our hossel, between the horse meatballs snack bar and the Hebbel Theatre. There for the first time in Berlin we met Turkish men. We didn't see them, we heard them. They stood there as if in a dream. The room was full of smoke. A man's voice said: 'Friends, let us open the door, no eye can see an eye here.' One man opened the door, outside the snow was whirling in the wind, and the street glittered. When the smoke went out with the wind the snow whirled outside the open door and looked like a fluttering net curtain. The men had already begun to smile when we had come in and no eye could see an eye because of the smoke. They had kept their smiles on their lips until the wind had carried the smoke on to the street. So at first they couldn't speak, they shook their heads and looked at us, until their smiles rose to their eyes and their eyes smiled at us. Then they could talk. The men took their cigarettes from their right hand in their left and shook our hands. One hand still smelt of cold cigar smoke. A student, his cigar, which had gone out, still in his mouth, said: 'My name is Yagmur (Rain).' As a joke one of the girls from the women's hossel said: 'And my name is Camur (Mud).' The girl and the young student immediately fell in love and smoked a cigarette together. In the Turkish Workers' Association everyone smoked as in an old French film, everyone had a cigarette in his hand. Big part, small part – it didn't matter, smoking made life and waiting photogenic. The men had got on to the buses in Turkey, then on to trains, then on to the aeroplanes and had come to Berlin. Now they stood here at the bottom of a ladder, whose top disappeared in the sky. They climbed this ladder and thought: just a little bit, then we'll come down again. After that they wanted to get on to trains and buses again and return to the places they had come from. The men talked like the women in our hossel: 'After a year, you won't see me here again.' They talked about this year, for which they had come to Berlin, as if it didn't belong to their life, smoked, drank tea and walked through the city together as if they were in a jungle – without fathers walking in front of them. The factory hooters, the opening and shutting bus doors, the lights suddenly switched on above sweet sleep, the lather in the mirrors, razor-blade voices, hair falling into washbasins, tiled stoves, colder in the morning even than the walls of the rooms, the electric light switches, the nervous light of the bakeries, the dirty snow between the wheels of the bus, sleeping people on trains, not a bird in the sky, no telegraph poles, only lonely, wrecked phone booths. If the men had walked along the streets alone, they would perhaps have been wafted off the ground and their heads would have struck the walls of the buildings. That's why these men always walked together. The snow covered their moustaches. Three moustaches covered in snow make more headway against the snow than one moustache covered in snow. So each man, when he was with others, found his father, his grandfather, and it was good to be walking beside a father or beside grandfather feet, when one was on a path whose end one couldn't see. The men walked together along the Berlin streets and spoke their language loudly, it looked as if they were walking along behind their words, which they spoke loudly, as if their loud language cleared the way for them. When they crossed a street, they didn't cross it in order to get to another street, but because their loud words went in front of them. So they walked behind their words and to the people who didn't understand these words it looked as if they were walking through another country with their donkeys or chickens. The men walked behind their words until they reached the Turkish Workers' Association, there they smoked and drank tea. They didn't say: 'I'm going,' instead one stood up and said: 'We're going.' When one poured tea into a glass, he said: 'We're drinking tea.' When a newspaper lay on the table, one said: 'We're going to read the newspaper.' Each 'I' sewed itself on to the next 'I' and made a 'We'. Only the cloth of their trousers or their knitted cardigans told their 'I' stories, or the colour of their skin, the wrinkles on their neck, only their different dialects showed that they had been born of different mothers. When they didn't speak and simply stood in the room, it looked as if they were standing around a horse, their hands on the horse, on which they warmed themselves together. When a car skidded in the snow on the street outside or braked loudly, they said: 'We'll go and take a look.' They looked and then they came back with wet shoes, jackets and hair, took off their jackets at the same time and turned the spoons in the tea glasses at the same time. One said: 'Drink another mouthful of tea.' The other said: 'We'll drink another mouthful of tea.' Then he drank from his glass. Rain, who was the only student in the Turkish Workers' Association, said to one of them: 'You are a worker, a worker has no homeland. Where there is work, there is his homeland, the great Turkish poet Nazim Hikmet said that. He was in prison for thirteen years.' The worker to whom Rain had said these sentences repeated Rain's sentences and said: 'What you say is right, brother, we are workers. Workers have no homeland.' When one was ill and sat at the table with his temperature, he didn't say 'I am ill', the others said about him: 'He is ill.'

At the Turkish Workers' Association only Rain and our communist hostel warden said 'I'. They went to the cinema together, then they came to the Turkish Workers' Association, and Rain said: 'I have seen a film, shall I tell you the story, the film is called *The Silence*, the director is called Ingmar Bergman.' Then they both told the story of the film. They began together, but at some point each of the two said: 'No, it wasn't like that, let me tell how I saw it.' They constantly interrupted one another, one stole the film from the other, and so we always saw two different films playing before our eyes. Only at the end, when they were finished with the story of the film, did they say together: 'Bergman wants to show us that Europe has eaten shit.' And as they did so they laughed and looked into our eyes. They both smoked cigars. When one spoke, the other stretched his head up and blew a couple of rings in the air, and we, the three girls at the table, tried to get our wedding fingers inside these rings and hold on to them.

Rain went to the doctor with workers when they were sick, looked for flats or placed notices in the newspapers for them. He had a friend, a peasant, who had now become a worker. He wore a cheap pair of spectacles and was called Hamza. He, too, looked as if he was walking around Berlin with his donkey. He had left his wife in his village in Turkey, and said to us: 'Sisters, capitalist hammers have shattered me.' He smoked so much that once, instead of putting his cigarette in the ashtray, he put it in his shirt pocket. He said to Rain: 'Brother, my heart is burning.'

Hamza was looking for a German woman for Berlin and so Rain put a notice in the paper for him: 'Looking for language teacher, to learn German.' The German teacher came to Hamza's room, she taught him, and during the lesson Hamza sighed all the time, so that the woman would understand what he wanted. The teacher asked: 'Hamza, is something wrong?' Hamza replied: 'Homesickness.' The teacher came and went. Rain and Hamza thought a bit more. They bought a bra, and Hamza stuck one half of the bra under his pillow, the other hung down the side of the bed. He thought if the German language teacher saw the bra she would realise that he was a man, and she would make love with him. But just before the teacher came into the room, Hamza quickly hid all of the bra under the pillow. Another time he and Rain bought women's perfume and poured it out in the room. But just before the German teacher arrived, he opened the window and let in air. He didn't learn any German. The teacher went.

Rain placed another notice for Hamza: 'I am a married man, I make love to my wife every night, then she falls asleep, but I need more. I am looking for a married woman who is in just the same situation as me. Discretion assured'. Hamza got an answer, the letter said: 'Shut your mouth, the next time we'll report you to the inspector.' Stuck next to that was the photo of a famous TV detective. Shaking, Hamza came to the Turkish Workers' Association and said to Rain: 'Police, they're going to hand us over to the police.' Rain placed a third notice for Hamza: 'Dancing teacher'. Hamza took tango lessons with her, 1, 2, 3, 4, 5, 6. Then he came to the Workers' Association and repeated what happened in the tango lessons: 'She puts her hand on my shoulder, one, two. I put my arm around her, three. She puts her leg between my legs, four. I put my legs between her legs, five. My hands slide from her back to her backside, six. She slaps my face.'

Rain and Hamza went on looking for women teachers, but didn't
find any more. Hamza began to cook. He cooked beans and lamb
for us three girls. He had a thick moustache and was wearing a
headscarf. When he cooks, he said, he copies his grandmother, so
that there were two people in the room. In a woman's voice he sang
a Turkish song about a garden, in which flowers have bloomed. A
man says to his beloved she should not be late but come to him
quickly. She should not become another man's lover. She should
rather hang herself. Another man will make her beautiful life hell.

Hamza translated the song into the German he had learned from
his teacher:

> In garden
> flowers open
> and so on
> tell my darling
> don't stand
> quick, come now
> my love not
> married bad man
> even kill her
> have bad man
> nice life
> not at all.

We ate the beans and lamb, he didn't eat himself, smoked and
blew the smoke in our faces.
  'Eat, my roses, eat, in this world and the next you are my sisters.'
Then he wept. His tears dropped on to the lamb on his plate. His
wife had had a letter written to him. She told that one day she
had stood under the cherry tree in the village and eaten cherries.
Then Hamza's uncle had come and had begun to eat cherries from
the same branch with her. In Berlin Hamza thought of only one
thing: who was the first to stand under the cherry tree? Her or

his uncle? Who had gone to whom? His wife to his uncle, who had been standing under the cherry tree first, or his uncle to his wife, who had perhaps been standing under the cherry tree first. Hamza talked, we three girls ate, he didn't eat, and the fat of his lamb, which had gone cold, turned hard. This white, hard fat reminded me how far from Turkey we were. If Hamza had stayed in his village, perhaps he, too, would have gone to this cherry tree and would have eaten the cherries from the same branch with his wife and uncle. Now he only had this letter. He said to us: 'The letter will kill me yet.'

We three girls continued going to our Workers' Association. When we came out of the Association, the audience was also coming out of the Hebbel Theatre. Outside the Hebbel Theatre people parted, opened their umbrellas because of the snow, outside the Turkish Workers' Association we lit our last cigarettes, snow in our mouths. The cigarettes wet in our hands, we parted, and sometimes people slipped in the snow outside the Hebbel Theatre and outside our Workers' Association and then walked more slowly than the others. There were big clouds of breath amidst the snowflakes.

In some Turkish workers we three girls found our mothers again. They cooked for us. When these men spoke, the voices of their mothers came out of their mouths. I loved these mothers and we could see these mothers or their grandmothers in the bodies of the men. It was nice to see the body of a man in which many women lived. I learned their different dialects and practised them as I assembled radio valves or walked down the long corridors of the hossel, just as I practised the sentences from the German headlines: WHAT A STORM, ITCHY SKIN? DDT CURES IT, ROMY SCHNEIDER'S SON IS CALLED DAVID-CHRISTOPHER, PIG FLIGHTS TO BERLIN HAVE STARTED, THERE WAS GRUNTING IN MID-AIR.

One of these workers was called Şükrü. He, too, looked as if he were walking around Berlin with his donkey. In Turkey Şükrü was a peasant, and there in his village he really had a donkey. With this donkey he went from village to village, sold cloth for women's clothes and married six women in different villages. No wife knew about the others. When he came back from one of his wives he brought the next wife fresh eggs as a present, which he had collected from the hens of the previous wife. When the six wives slowly realised where the eggs were coming from, Şükrü went to Berlin. From time to time he sent his wives some money and asked: 'What is the donkey doing now without me?' Şükrü drove baggage trolleys at Berlin Zoo station and loved an English girl, who went to the station for heroin. He said: 'If you could see her – she's four inches taller than me.' Once, he told us, he had gone for a walk with her. In a department store she had seen a red jacket costing 750 marks – almost double Şükrü's monthly wage. Şükrü went to see the store director with Rain and wanted to bargain with him. Afterwards he said to us: 'I'll go there again, the store director knows me now, he's called Werner, I'll beat the price down.' We three girls said: 'Şükrü, watch out, the women want to eat your money.' Şükrü laughed: 'Let me tell you something, the women who don't eat money, I don't love them.' When he had come to Berlin, Şükrü had lived in a men's hostel. The men in this hostel divided into those who let their money be eaten by women and those who didn't let their money be eaten by women. Now Şükrü lived in a flat that had been a shop on Karl Marx Strasse. Beads of water ran down the walls of the room. Şükrü laughed and said: 'My weeping walls.' The toilet was outside on the stairs, he said: 'You won't believe me, but with my own eyes I've seen my shit freeze in a couple of minutes with the cold.'

When he had moved into this flat, he had sworn not to think about women any more. But it didn't work, he was always thinking about women, so he looked for a religious Turkish man, to help him. The religious man came to his flat on Karl Marx Strasse, prayed for Şükrü, blew his breath in Şükrü's face and gave him holy texts, which he was to put under his bed. But Şükrü went on thinking about women. So one day he took the texts away from under the bed, the paper had turned yellow. Şükrü was afraid to throw the paper into the rubbish bin or flush it away in the toilet with water. He got on to an underground train and quietly placed the holy texts on the seat. Then he stood up without looking back and let the texts travel on in the underground train.

When the door of the Association room opened and someone came in, Şükrü always said: 'What's he supposed to do, the lonely man!' Şükrü wanted to learn German and go to the trade union school. 'When I'm a trade unionist, I'll also demand pensions for the donkeys, so that the donkeys can lie down sometimes, too. My donkey's got more brains in his head than I have, he stayed where he was.'

After we three girls started going to the Turkish Workers' Association, the other women in our women's hostel asked us: 'You eat the men's money, don't they kiss you?' They didn't kiss us, but soon a man did kiss us, a Turkish man who had been studying engineering for fourteen years. Next to the Workers' Association there was a pub, we three girls sat at a table with him. He kissed one of us and said to her: 'Now order me a beer.' The beer came, he drained the glass, then said sentences in French to us:

*Je suis belle, ô mortels! comme un rêve de pierre,*
*Et mon sein, où chacun s'est meurtri tour à tour,*
*Est fait pour inspirer au poète un amour.*

'Do you know Baudelaire? You don't! Order me another beer.' He went on drinking and wanted to know what our communist hostel warden told us, what he did. He noted our answers on the wet beer mats and said:

*Que diras-tu, mon coeur...*
*A la très-belle, à la très-bonne, à la très-chère.*

Our communist hostel warden said the man was from the secret police. Rain said: 'He loves men, he's a queer.' We had never seen a secret policeman or a queer before. He kissed very badly. His lips were sticky with beer, as if with glue; when he kissed, his mouth didn't open. On his mouth we practised all the film kisses we had seen in the cinema, and for a beer he offered us his closed mouth. But if a worker said to him: 'Yesterday I said to the German…', he opened his mouth and said: 'A German won't listen to you. The German listens to Nietzsche.' We thought Nietzsche was the German prime minister. We told the women in the hossel that he had kissed us. 'You'll end up communists,' they said to us. 'You'll end up losing your maidenhead, that is your diamond, you will lose your diamonds.' During the night I dreamed that I was standing in heaven, the clouds beneath me were like a big, smooth, white blanket. I parted the clouds and saw below me, on a steep green meadow, my parents and people who were already dead. They waited there until I came down, then I walked with them on this steep meadow. When I woke up, Rezzan and Gül, the two other girls, said that they had also seen their mothers in a dream. We smoked a cigarette together in the dark hossel corridor and told each other our dreams. As she was listening, Rezzan stubbed out our cigarettes on her left hand and cried out: 'Mother!' We cried out with her: 'Mother,' 'Little Mother.' Gül said: 'If we go there again, may our eyes go blind, may our eyes go blind.'

We never went to the Workers' Association again.

Sometimes I still looked from the hossel window over to the lit-up Workers' Association. The door opened, the workers went in, the cigarette smoke poured out on to the street, the door closed. With every man who went in and came out new cigarette smoke came out of the door. I, too, smoked at the hossel window and blew the smoke in the direction of the workers' cigarette smoke. We three girls started going to our offended station again. We took our diamonds for a walk and stamped loudly outside the telephone booth, so that our parents could hear us in Istanbul. We walked around on the plot of land of the offended station, as if we had our fathers' breath at our backs. Even Rezzan, who didn't have a father any more, felt the fathers' breath at her back. We wept there like donkeys who could cry out with their whole body, and cried: 'Mother, my little mother, my little mother,' then we looked in each other's faces and wept even louder. Sometimes we stumbled over the old railway tracks, which were overgrown with grass. No one could hear us apart from this broken offended station. Sometimes we stood still and looked at the street as if it were starting to rain. There were still lights in the windows of our women's hossel, we walked towards our women's hossel, without looking at the lights of our Workers' Association.

We walked on along the Berlin streets, our fathers' breath at our backs. I often turned round, to see whether my father was behind me. When we stood in the dark in front of a brightly lit house, we heard the fork, knife and plate noises of the people who were just eating supper. We held our breath, the fork and plate noises grew louder and went through my body like a knife.

When we stood among the other women in front of the pots in the kitchen, in the steam of the boiling potatoes, we three girls looked like three chicks who had just broken their eggshells to come into the world.

We went to the zoo and visited the monkeys there. Each of us had a monkey, Rezzan had a monkey, Gül had a monkey, I had a monkey, a family. They scratched each other's itchy faces, looked for fleas in the hair of the other monkeys and laughed without being afraid that anyone could see their gums. In order to test their love of us, we quickly ran around to the other side of the cage. Then they turned their faces towards us and looked in our eyes.

In the factory, the lens in my right eye, I now pushed my tongue behind my upper lip and looked like my monkey. Knocking-off time was called monkey-time, the weekend was called monkey-end. After work we went to the zoo, later, in the dark, to our offended station.

Then a new Turkish girl arrived at the hossel, Engel – Angel. Angel was very small; when Angel walked beside us, we saw the holes in the Berlin streets for the first time, because we always had to look down at Angel. Cigarette ends lay on the street, and we kicked them ahead of us with our shoes. Angel had a soft voice and spoke very slowly. So we also began to speak more slowly. I saw my slowed-down arm and hand movements as if in a slow-motion film, my feet rose slowly, came down on the street again, the snow fell slowly, our hair floated slowly, the cigarette ends moved slowly in front of our feet, the dry grass between the disused tracks of the offended station moved slowly. Only in the factory did the slowness disappear, although Angel was working in front of me. I saw only her back, she had swivelled her chair higher, so that she could work at the green iron table. In the hossel, I immediately began to move more slowly because of Angel. I walked behind Angel and felt that even my breathing slowed down. Even the clock in the hossel lounge ticked more slowly and made the evening long. The evening sat down slowly on the chairs against the walls. When I sat down on the slow evenings and wrote a letter to my mother, the words appeared slowly on the piece of paper. I could see whether they were bright, whether they had mouths, could sing, could weep, could laugh, whether they talked to one another, whether they took a deep breath or a short one, whether they smelled good – and whether they came out when they reached my mother and could walk over her hand, over her arms like little animals.

With Angel I visited Martha. Martha was a German radio valve worker and as small as Angel. She had invited Angel home and lived on an allotment. She had a parrot, which was always saying 'you you'. Martha had a big head, blonde curls, as if cemented to her head, and a big bosom, so big that in the factory she could easily put the radio valves on her breasts as on a table and inspect them. Martha went 'hm hm', that meant, sit down. I sat down. Martha and Angel together cut the cake, which Martha had baked.

We went 'himm mm mm', and if we couldn't think of any thing else, 'mm mm hm hm'. When the parrot said 'you you', we laughed and also said 'you you'. Then Martha embraced us, and we walked through many allotment gardens back to the road; the trees were covered in snow, someone had forgotten a spade, it was frozen to the wall of a house.

Our communist hostel warden had a good friend called Ataman. When we got off the bus, he held his hand out for us, so that we didn't slip on the snow; we giggled, but didn't take his hand. Then Ataman laughed and said: 'Otherwise you'll lose your diamonds, won't you? Diamonds, diamonds, girls, hand over your diamonds!'
    Whenever we saw Ataman, he laughed and sang: 'Diamonds, diamonds, when are you going to hand over your diamonds?' He also called out: 'Diamonds have to be spent like small change.' Once, when we were walking to the bus stop together, Ataman suddenly started running and shouted: 'Quick, girls, the bus is coming.' We ran after him, but no bus came. 'I only wanted to see if your breasts bounce.' When he took off his cap, a smell came out from underneath like that of a new-born calf. The snow was cold, our teeth chattered, but the smell from Ataman's head promised us warm rooms, arrival in a warm house entrance. We followed the smell of his head. He had a pair of glasses that made his eyes three times larger than they were. A couple of eyelashes were stuck to the lenses, which he never cleaned, perhaps because he didn't want to lose what he had so far seen in his life through these glasses. His face was the same colour as the Berlin streets. Angel more and more often followed the smell of Ataman's head, and I followed Angel. So the three of us walked together, soon they were kissing. When they kissed, I laughed, then they laughed with me and kissed again.

The Berlin streets had many gaps, here stood a house, then came a hole, in which only the night lived, then again a house, out of which a tree had grown. When we wandered around in the Berlin holes at night, our life disappeared. Then Angel, Ataman and I walked close together like three sheep. If we had spoken, perhaps the night, which stood in these holes like a big razor blade, would have cut our bodies to pieces. Not until we stood at an intersection and the light was red or green did our life return to us again. We then crossed the street, without turning round to the holes. One night, on which a storm pushed the night before it, the night pushed us and an old man against the wall of a building. The man tried to hold on to the bullet and shrapnel holes in the wall. He hadn't buttoned up his coat, the coat flew behind him like a wing and fluttered flapflap, a camel-hair coat. The man went from one tree to the next, embraced the trees and his coat went on flapping and pushed him on to the next tree. Ataman said: 'Old man, poor man.' After the last tree the old man fell down in the street. He sat there in the snow, we lifted him up and buttoned his coat buttons. He wore glasses that made his eyes very small and there was ice on the glasses. We walked with him to his flat, and he invited us in. A big bed, a carpet, an easy chair. He sat down in this easy chair. Angel, Ataman and I sat down in a row on the bed. Between our feet and his feet stood a bottle of schnapps. Outside in the storm a nylon tarpaulin fluttered, which the workers on a building site hadn't secured properly. Tired sponge fingers lay on a plate on the table, which stood between the bed and the apartment door. Perhaps every time he put on his coat the old man took a sponge finger from the plate and ate it on the stairs. Ataman and the old man frequently bent down to the carpet, to the bottle of schnapps, and talked to one another in German. Angel couldn't see Ataman any more, because he bent down to the bottle again and again and looked at the old man, who sat in his greasy armchair opposite the three of us. So Angel, too, began to bend down to the bottle. Ataman looked at her: 'You're too young for that,' said Ataman. The old man asked Ataman how many lovers we had, Ataman translated the sentence for us. 'None,' we said. 'Every little girl,' said the old man, 'has a lover.' He repeated the sentence a couple of times, as if his head stuck to this sentence like a magnet. When he spoke these sentences, his body made movements as if he felt very cold. But he was still wearing his coat, and the ice on his glasses, which made his eyes three times smaller than they were, slowly melted. Soon he closed his eyes completely, but went on talking loudly with closed eyes. 'Yes, yes,' he said, 'yes, yes' and 'well, yes'. If he had fallen asleep on the greasy armchair, we might have gone away and would have put out the light. But at short intervals he said 'yes yes' and 'well, yes', and the light stayed on, and these words kept us on the bed, on which we were sitting in a row. Because we couldn't go away, Ataman and Angel started kissing each other. They kissed each other for such a long time that they slowly fell on to the bed. First I saw their feet still beside mine on the yellow carpet, then their feet pulled off their shoes. The two pairs of shoes remained on the yellow carpet next to my feet, feet and legs disappeared on to the bed, and they made love very quietly behind my back. Ataman's jacket covered the bedside lamp, and the old man knelt down in front of my legs. I was wearing nylon stockings. He began to kiss my stockings at the knee and cried out at the same time, as if someone were cutting him with a blunt knife. My knees shook so much that the old man licked the air, crying out, then there was silence. He took off his glasses, cleaned then with the quilt, put them on again. Then he sat down in his armchair. After a couple of minutes he said: 'I'm fed up with this symmetry.' The old man stood up, took the clock which stood exactly in the middle on top of a linen cupboard, moved it a little to the left and sat down in the easy chair again. The clock ticked loudly, Ataman and Angel made love behind me without a sound, the clock ticked, later on the bells of a church struck dong dong dong. The clock said three minutes past three, but the church was only striking three. The old man was cross with his clock, because it wasn't keeping perfect time. He opened the window and threw the clock into the street. Now no clock ticked any more, only the curtains in front of the open window flapped, and the snow came into the room with the storm. Angel and Ataman began to shiver a bit. I stood up and immediately my legs gave way. I gripped the greasy chair arm and stood up again. The arm of the greasy easy chair was very old, with time the cloth had worn very thin. Probably the old man always sat in the easy chair and looked at his bed, and when he lay in bed, he looked at the easy chair. When he went out of the apartment door, he left the bed and the easy chair behind him, when he came in and turned the light switch, he saw the easy chair and the bed standing there. Ataman and Angel put on their clothes and closed the window. As he brought us to the door, the old man picked up one of the tired sponge fingers, which were lying on the table, ate it and closed the door behind us. In the street we saw his clock lying in the snow.

When she got dressed Angel had quickly put her underpants into her coat pocket. When we bent down to the clock and held it to our ears, to hear whether it was still ticking, blood dripped from Angel's legs on to the Berlin snow. The clock was still ticking. 'Now the diamond's gone,' said Ataman, took the clock and put it in his jacket pocket. In the snow and wind we walked back to our women's hossel. Angel and Ataman went on kissing one another in the night, and the clock ticked in Ataman's jacket pocket tick tack tick tack.

After Angel had lost her diamond, the Dove, the wife of our communist hostel warden, helped her find a flat for ninety marks in Kreuzberg. Angel wanted me to move in with her. With two suitcases we went to the Kreuzberg flat. Her suitcase was large and she was small. As she walked through the snow her right foot left deeper prints in the snow than her left.

In the flat two light bulbs came on, which had belonged to the dead old woman who had lived here. Forty watts. We sat down in the kitchen. There was a coal kitchen range, which was not lit. We needed coal. On the range stood a pan, in which old fat and old tea were sticking. Presumably the dead woman had made tea in the greasy pan. We sat in our coats in front of the range, as if it could warm us. Ataman had given Angel the clock that the old man had thrown out of the window. The clock ticked in the suitcase, which we hadn't opened yet, and water dripped into the sink tip tip tip. In some places the electric wiring was exposed, and many insects had died on the light bulbs. Their dirty light provided hardly any brightness for us, but only weakly illuminated the insect death. Every cigarette we smoked that night showed us that we had made a mistake. We had run away from the herd and now we wept for the herd. Ataman wasn't there either, the smell of whose head would at least have been able to warm us. As we sat there, even the kitchen walls were surprised that we were sitting there. One of the 40 watt light bulbs flickered, went on and off. This was Berlin. This Berlin had not existed for us yet. We had our hossel, and the hossel was not Berlin. Berlin began only when we left the hossel, just as one goes to the cinema, sees a film and comes back on the bus and tells the others the story of the film while taking one's clothes off. Now we were in this film, but the image had frozen, had come to a stop. No one knocked, no one stood up and opened the door. We lay on the beds in our clothes and coats, wept in the darkness and before the dew fell we went back with our not yet opened suitcases to our women's hossel. The clock went on ticking in the suitcase and with the gleaming snow showed us the way to our offended station. When we arrived in the hossel, the women were already awake. The corridor smelt of women's sleep and boiling eggs. We stood outside the bathroom doors and heard the sound of the water splashing on the women's bodies. We opened the door and saw the lather on the stone floor and on the women's faces. The soap slipped out of one woman's hand, I picked the soap up and gave it back to her, she had shut her eyes, soap was running from her hair over her eyes. I smelled my hand, it smelled of the soap, and when we waited at the bus stop again with all the other women and came closer together because of the cold, all the women smelt of the soap. In the bus Angel and I still sat with the fear that we were still sitting in the Kreuzberg flat with the dead insects. I surreptitiously sniffed at the hair of the women sitting in front of me, and at my hand, on which the soap smell still lived. In the factory some sounds scared me for the first time, as if they were the extension of the room's voices. Drawing out the cigarettes from the cigarette machine, the one-mark coins dropping in, the sound of a broken radio valve, when it's thrown into the bin, the tink tink of the time clock. I forgot the sounds for a little when the Greek women workers again shouted 'Frau Missel, comere', because they couldn't say 'sch'.

At night in the hossel I dreamed. Small holes opened in the ceiling and in the walls of the room. I was lying on the floor, and out of the holes in the wall and the ceiling poked little snakes, the other half of their bodies remained in the ceiling and in the walls. A big snake was in my body and its head in my mouth. A voice said to me: Don't pull the snake out of your throat, otherwise it'll bite you. I woke up and cried out. The two sisters who always wore pale blue dressing gowns of electrically charged material moved in bed under their blankets and muttered incomprehensible words. Above me Rezzan woke up. The neon sign of the Hebbel Theatre went on and off. Rezzan went with me to the bathroom. I rubbed my gums with my toothbrush to stay awake. Rezzan didn't sleep either, her head hung down from her bed to mine, and she told me a story by Chekhov, 'The Lady with the Little Dog'. The lady went walking along a seafront with her little dog, and a man, Dmitry – his wife called him Dimitry – saw the lady with the little dog. She was blonde. He also saw her with the little dog in a park; no one knew her name, so she was called 'the lady with the little dog'. Dmitry wanted to get to know her. He was married and had children. Because he had married very young, his wife was too old for him now. He often went to other women, but always spoke badly of women. When other people talked to him about women, he said: 'A lesser species.' But he couldn't live two days without the lesser species. When he sat with men, he yawned, it was so boring. With women, he knew what he could talk to them about, and it was easier for him to be silent with women than with men. One evening in a restaurant in the park he sat down beside the table of this unknown lady with the little dog. People had talked about her. She was married, but a stranger here and alone with her dog. Dmitry racked his brains, how could he start talking to the lady with the little dog? Then Rezzan fell silent. 'And then, what happened then?' Rezzan said: 'I'll go on reading, tomorrow evening I'll tell you how he did it.' I forgot the snakes and the old woman's greasy pan with the crumbs of tea and thought only about how he had started to talk to the lady with the little dog.

We went to the factory. That morning the headline in the newspaper display case was THEY'RE SHOOTING AGAIN. 'They're shooting again', 'They're shooting again' – I practised my sentences on the bus, and in the evening in the hossel I noticed that the other women were practising something, too. One practised how to find her way back from the city centre. She often went into the department stores there and one evening had lost her way, because in the Berlin winter darkness fell very quickly. At first she had cried, then, to calm down, she said to herself: 'It's a good thing that no man is waiting for me at home.' But then she cried even more. Then she heard the bells of a half-church, and because she knew this half-church, she followed the voice of the bells, found the half-church, from there she could find the bus stop again, which took her to the hossel. She called this half-church broken church, one half had been bombed in the war. The half-church helped her to find her way again every time. When she told us about crying in the darkness and how she had lost her way, she always talked about a husband she didn't have: 'It's a good thing, I said to myself, that no man is waiting for me at home.' Another woman practised walking backwards on an escalator. She also said: 'It's a good thing that I don't have a husband, if he could see me like this, he would pull out my hair.' Every story ended with a husband. One woman said: 'I've burned the meat again, it's turned to charcoal. But it doesn't matter, I don't have a husband who shouts at me because of it.' Overcooked macaroni, too much salt in the food, too many pounds on the body, uncombed hair, a torn bra under her clothes – everything always ended with: 'I have, may Allah be thanked, no man who can see it.' When a glass or plate fell and broke, a woman said: 'It's a good thing that the men can't see it.' When a woman turned up the record player too loud in the hossel lounge, when a loud male voice sang: 'Seven bridges you will cross', and the woman put this song on again and again, as if she wanted to get drunk on this song, the other women said: 'Unfortunately there's no man to make her shut up.' Another woman practised on the vacuum cleaner, the other women called her the Hoover girl. She said: 'Allah is my witness, I hear every sound, every little bit of dirt that goes in, goes tink tink, I hear this sound very well.' The women said: 'Hoover girl, do you have a man whom you can show how clean you are?'

One group of women said: 'It's a good thing we don't have a husband...' the others said: 'Unfortunately we don't have a husband...' But each sentence, whether it began with 'good' or 'unfortunately', always gave birth to a man, a husband. The word 'husband' was like a big piece of chewing gum, which they chewed together. When this piece of chewing gum had lost its taste because of all the chewing and ended up under their tongues and between their teeth, they pulled it out with their fingers and drew long threads in the air. When I walked past the tables in the hossel lounge I tried to cover my breasts a little with my hands and to avoid making the wooden floor beneath my feet creak too loudly, so that their chewing gum didn't stick to my hair or to my pullover. Every single bit of noise helped them make the chewing gum bigger. 'Girl, just you go on and make your bosom bounce. If a husband saw that.' The women who chewed the men in their mouths fell silent only when a woman blew a bubble out of this chewing gum and let it burst in the air. PAP.

A beautiful woman told that she had got into a car on the street, had sat down in the back, the man sat in front. She could speak English, and the man said to her he would give her 100 marks, if she would sit in his car for an hour. She asked him in English: 'What must I do?' He explained it to her, and she said: 'I can not good English.' She told the story to the women using many English sentences. 'He said: "Can you sit down one hour in my car", I said: "What must I do in this one hour?"' When she repeated the sentences in English, the women nodded and didn't understand them. They nodded and no woman said anything behind this girl's back because of the 100 marks. Because she spoke such good English, no one asked her why she had got into the car. She was the girl who could speak good English. The women asked her what pills they should take for headaches, whether they should take aspirin or Saridon or Optalidon. She read the women stories from English women's magazines: How can I seduce my boss? Or: How can I make my husband believe that I've been cooking for him all day? For example, like this: The woman goes out with her friends all day or to the cinema, but shortly before her husband gets back, she heats up the pan, puts in oil that has a strong smell, and fries garlic in it. The whole house smells of garlic, and the man comes in and smiles. She also read out: If a husband is looking for a secretary under twenty-five, his wife should not say: 'I know what you're looking for'. She should rather get together with the secretary and make it clear: She is the woman in the marriage and the secretary is the woman at work. The wife who managed to think like that was smart, because as a woman one had to know that the man is a helpless creature, even though he is the crown of creation.

Her hands in her pockets, Rezzan sat in the hossel lounge and went on reading Chekhov's 'The Lady with the Little Dog', she turned the pages of the book with her tongue or her chin. No one said to her: 'If a husband could see that.' Rezzan told me that the man had started talking to the lady with the little dog in the park restaurant by saying: 'Can I give your dog a bone?' The woman had nodded, and he asked her: 'Have you been in Yalta long?' – 'About five days.' And the man said: 'This is already my second week.' Then they both said nothing for a while. It was very pleasant to imagine two people who didn't say anything. But perhaps they, too, were practising something by not saying anything. Just as the women practised how to seduce their husband in the evening with garlic or how one earns a hundred marks in an hour, how wives make friends with their husband's secretaries and the husband has to practise being a helpless creature, so that he keeps the crown of creation on his head.

While the women in the hossel lounge talked about men who weren't there, our communist hostel warden also talked in his room about a man who wasn't there. After Angel had lost her diamond, she didn't sit in the six-bed room anymore, but often in the room of our communist hostel warden, because Ataman, too, was almost always there. Ataman loved our communist hostel warden, and he loved Ataman. When they sat in the hossel warden room, they looked very like one another, and when they smoked, they both stubbed out their cigarettes against the wall or against the door frame. In the room they talked about a man. Darkness fell very quickly in Berlin, and they didn't put on any light. Angel sat there on the bed and went on leafing through a book she held in her hand. And the two men went on talking in the dark about this man, as if switching on the light would take this man away from them. The man's name was Brecht. They said Brecht, Brecht, Brecht, Brecht, and when they said the name Brecht, at the letters 'cht', a little bit of spittle sprayed out between their teeth, which were not close together. Like our communist hostel warden Ataman had also worked at a theatre in Turkey and had written two plays. He, too, loved Brecht, went to the other Berlin, to the Berliner Ensemble, with our hostel warden, and knew Brecht's wife Helene Weigel. To Helene Weigel they said Helli. When the Dove, the wife of our communist hostel warden, heard the name Helli, her cheeks reddened, her mouth remained a little open, and she touched the big mole above her mouth with her finger each time and stroked it. Our hostel warden often said: 'My Dove, I shall make Helli out of you.' He wanted to write a play, in which the Dove would play the lead. He and Ataman learned Brecht by heart and always spoke the same lines together:

*Baal grew up within the whiteness of the womb*
*With the sky already large and pale and calm*
*Naked, young, endlessly marvellous*
*As Baal loved it when he came to us.*

When we three girls came into the hostel warden room, Ataman interrupted the Brecht poem and said in the same tone of voice: 'When will you give up your diamonds?' Then the poem continued:

*Lots of space, says Baal, inside this woman's womb...*

*Powerful limbs are needed, and experience too*
*Swollen bellies may discourage you.*
*Naked, young, endlessly marvellous...*

When our communist hostel warden and Ataman went out, they didn't put on coats, even in winter. It was snowing outside, they turned up their jacket collars. Their hands in their pockets, they walked, saying Brecht Brecht, behind their Brecht words, as if these words warmed them up. Their breath steamed in the cold air and went before them. When they crossed a street, they didn't wait for green, but kept on following their breath until they came to a pub. Before they went in, Ataman always said the same sentence: '*What hempen homespuns have we swaggering here.*' And when they came out in the night again, he always said: '*Before I have combed my hair I never go out in the moonlight,*' and kissed Angel.

Once our communist hostel warden took a couple of pieces of paper out of a drawer in the hossel warden room. He had cut them carefully out of a book. He and Ataman looked at the photos and giggled. The Dove wanted to look, too, but they hid them from her, as if they were porn pictures. Our communist hostel warden drew the Dove towards him, set her on his knees, kissed her, but even as he was kissing held the photos up in the air behind the Dove's back. They weren't pictures of naked women, but three childhood photos of Brecht. In one he was wearing a girl's white dress, he held a stick in his hand, with which he was taking a wooden horse for a walk.

Angel had given up her diamond, we three girls not yet, and all four of us loved the back of our communist hostel warden and of Ataman. When they went out, the four of us, food still in our mouths, came out of our rooms and asked, just as we had once asked our parents: 'Can we come, too?' – 'Come on,' they said, and so we followed their backs. Their backs were our Berlin street map. They always went to the same pub. We didn't look at the names of the underground stations, we looked at their backs, we got on, changed lines, and I knew all the seams of their jackets, the dandruff on their shoulders, their hair. I saw that at night they had lain on the right or the left half of their heads. In the pub, however, their backs got lost, there the beer gleamed, and people's eyes gleamed when they had a beer in their hand. When their glasses were empty, the lights in their eyes went out. The fat landlord saw that and immediately asked: 'Another beer, another beer?' As often as the word beer was said, the word communist was said just as often. If someone poured some beer from his full beer glass into the empty glass of his friend, then he was a communist. And if someone didn't pour some of his beer into the empty glass of another, then he was an anti-communist or a capitalist. After these words they always laughed. Communists and capitalists laughed at the same table. And at the same time our communist hostel warden read the newspaper and said: 'The truth is in here, but it depends how you read it.' Then he laughed. One day a Franz-Josef Strauss, party boss of the Christian Social Union, went into a restaurant, the 'Tiroler-Stuben' in Munich, there men in short trousers were playing music, the band was called Schrammel Trio, and Strauss asked these musicians in short trousers to play a march for him. The march was 'The Badenweiler March' and was supposed to have been Hitler's favourite march. We didn't know who Franz-Josef Strauss was, but laughed, because the moustache of our communist hossel warden went up and down so comically when he was telling a story. Sometimes he laughed so much, that his spittle rained down on the magazine. The magazine was called DER SPIEGEL. This magazine smelled of cigarettes, because many people who read it in the pub smoked. In one photo elderly men with glasses or without glasses sat behind one another, as in a courtroom, their hands in their lap. To the left of them stood young soldiers in uniforms and with rifles. Above it were the words: 'With helmet and rifle'. The elderly men with glasses or without glasses were old soldiers, the others with helmets and rifles and without glasses were new soldiers. They were celebrating their military decorations in a church. A colonel, he was called Schott, had said: 'The Standard Service Regulation Manual states that an honour guard must always present itself in helmets and with rifles.' But in this Regulation Manual there was no rule about how one is supposed to present oneself in a church – with helmet and rifle or without helmet and rifle. So a general who had also read the manual said: 'From now on the soldiers should no longer bear a rifle or wear a helmet in church.' A Defence Ministry spokesman said: 'This decision is surely an unfortunate decision.'

I had not yet seen any German officers or soldiers in Berlin. The only uniforms I had seen were white or grey overalls in the factory. On the picture in DER SPIEGEL Ataman drew helmets on the heads of the old soldiers who sat in the church without helmets, put very small moustaches under their nose and said Hitler had been a wicked genius, because he had chosen a mask with a moustache and a couple of strands of hair on its forehead, which any person could easily have copied. A child, a woman, it didn't make any difference. Ataman said: 'It's not so easy to look like Napoleon, it only works with Hitler. If everyone can look like him so quickly, that means that everyone has a little bit of this guy, so one always has to watch out that one doesn't become Hitler.' Then Ataman made himself look like Hitler. He spat in his hand, with his spit he stuck a couple of strands of hair to his forehead, took Angel's hair in his hand, held it in front of his nose as a moustache and laughed. Our communist hostel warden said: 'Ataman, this Hitler mask theory isn't yours, but Godard's. Sell your own sentences to the girls.' Then he himself sold us newspaper sentences. He read a sentence again and first of all laughed so long that we all wanted to know what it was about. 'Konrad Adenauer is ninety the day after tomorrow' and 'How much should schnapps cost' and 'A German cabinet minister has said, if every German worked an hour longer a week, Germany doesn't need any guest workers'. At our table the men were interested in the last sentence, and at another table four young German men were interested in the four girls. Of the four of us Angel always looked at Ataman's mouth, Rezzan looked at the mouth of our communist hostel warden, who laughed and read and spat at the newspaper. The third girl, Gül, looked at Rezzan's face and from her face followed what was happening, I was the only one to look over to the four young men. 'Istanbul, Istanbul?' they asked across the tables. 'Istanbul, Istanbul,' I said. After ten minutes they threw their words across to our table again. 'Istanbul, Istanbul?' – 'Istanbul, Istanbul,' I said. When the four young men said 'Istanbul, Istanbul' for the third time, Ataman shouted to them across the tables: 'Danger virgin.' Then he said to me: 'Istanbul, Mistanbul, diamond becomes miamond.' When I went to the toilet, I went past their table, and when I came back a chair was empty. They looked at me and laughed, I laughed, too, and sat down on the empty chair. Each one took a photo out of his jacket pocket and showed it to me. All four photos were the same. They were sitting one behind the other on a bicycle that had four saddles and on which they had cycled from one city to the next. Two of them were building workers, the other two students. All four shook my hand; the hands of the building workers were like a piece of wood, in which there were nails. 'Communist,' they said, as they shook my hand. The two students said, 'Capitalist.' I liked a capitalist hand. They asked me: 'Communist?' I said: 'Telefunken.' So I sat there at the table, my left hand in a capitalist hand, and my right in a communist hand.

And I liked the boy with the capitalist hand. He was thin. The fat boy, who had the communist hand, wrote down the address of the women's hossel on Stresemannstrasse. When they had my address, they let go of my hand. In the night I walked behind the back of our communist hostel warden again and of Rezzan and Gül all the way to our hossel. Angel stayed with Ataman. The snowflakes became smaller and wetter. Then the snow disappeared and it began to rain. The old snow on the roofs came down with the rain and made our shoes wet. At night we three girls washed our stockings and hung them up in a row in the bathroom. The next day, even before our stockings had dried, a woman came up and said to me: 'There's a man looking for you.' It was the fat boy with the communist hand, he stood in the middle of the women in the hossel lounge, and everyone who had been talking about nothing but men for days suddenly had nothing to say and was rigid, as if someone had turned them to stone. I pulled on my still-half-wet stockings and went out with him, so that the women could move again. We walked, it rained. He was very fat, I was very thin, we had no language to talk in. He didn't get on any bus, didn't take any underground train, he walked and walked and I walked with him. There weren't many people to be seen. It was a Saturday, sometimes there was someone with an umbrella walking on the street, and for a while we followed this umbrella. If this person went into a house, we crossed to the other side of the street and kept on walking there. Sometimes there was a flash of lightning, which briefly lit up the lonely streets. The rain had beaten the snow, now the rain beat on the wet streets and the walls of the buildings. The bullet and shrapnel holes in the walls held the rain for a moment and then sprayed it out again. We walked silently across a cemetery. There were more people to be seen here than on the streets. There were many dead in Berlin. The rain kept people in the houses, but the dead brought them out again. They stood in front of the dead in the cemetery, just as they stood at the cheese counter in the Hertie department store or at the bus stop. Tired flowers and little rakes lay on the dead earth. The people didn't look at us, but worked as if a foreman were watching their work. The rain didn't stop, but now the fat boy with the communist hand came to a halt. We had arrived at the pub. Outside it was already dark, inside the landlord was drawing beer. The fat boy put ten pfennigs in the nut machine, took out a handful of nuts and put them in my wet hand. The other three boys were already sitting at the table. I put the nuts on the table and sat down. I was wet, now the nuts were wet, too. The fat boy wanted to take my hand, but the thin boy with the capitalist hand took both my hands and blew his warm breath into them. When he left, he still had my hand in his hand, so I left with him.

He lived on the fifth floor of a house right against the Wall. If one looked down from the window, one saw the East Berlin police walking backwards and forwards under powerful searchlights. The boy threw little stones at them, which he had collected in a pail. Whenever he had thrown one, he immediately stepped back into the room. The East Berlin policemen swore from below, and he swore at them through the open window. The dogs below barked and I shivered. All night the thin boy threw stones at the East Berlin police, and it rained and rained. I sat on the bed in my half-wet clothes, and between the barking of the dogs and the swearing I fell asleep sitting. When I woke up the rain was falling just as it had in the night. The window was shut and the thin boy had fallen asleep in the bathtub in water that had gone cold. When I woke him up, he gave me a quick kiss, I took it. It was a tired kiss. He came down to the street with me. The only thing we saw was the rain. A floury light shone from some windows, and I thought, nothing but these weak light bulbs lives in the houses, no one looks out of the window, no shadow falls on the walls of the rooms, no child makes his shoes dirty in the rainwater. The boy got on to a bus with me, which went to a district with villas, and I saw the lake for the first time. The ducks came out of the water and splashed on the shore with their feet. We went into a villa, the other three boys were already sitting on a bed in one room, watching TV. It was dark in the room, only the television provided some light. I sat down on the bed too, it was the only piece of furniture in the room on which one could sit. There was a Charlie Chaplin film on TV, I knew it from Turkey and said my first word in a day: 'Sharlo, Sharlo'. That was what Charlie Chaplin was called in Turkey. While I laughed at Sharlo, one of the boys quickly pushed my pullover up my back and stubbed out his burning cigarette. I screamed and turned round to see which hand had done it. But the four young men sat there, their hands on their legs, and went on watching TV. I remained sitting and couldn't move any more, couldn't stand up and leave the room. The four young men sat there, as if the four bodies had only one head and one face, and this common face hid from me who had stubbed out the cigarette on my back. Then the door opened and a woman came in. She switched on the light, stood by the door and looked at the boys for so long that the four lowered their heads. I stood up, walked past the woman, she smelled of eau de cologne. She didn't look at me, she went on looking at the four men, and I could leave the room.

When I got back to the women's hossel, I went to the bathroom and immediately looked at my back in the mirror. A brown wound. Rezzan's and Gül's stockings were still hanging on the clothes line, I washed my stockings and hung them up next to theirs. Rezzan and Gül weren't in the hostel, but Rezzan's Chekhov book was lying on her bed. It was still raining, and now our Stresemannstrasse looked different to how it looked in the snow. The snow had made the city a little more merciful, I had got used to the snow. It fell softly, so softly that the time, when one was writing a letter or sewing on a button, also became softer. The holes of the button, the thread and the needle, the pencil in a hand moving across a white sheet of paper, always promised silence when it was snowing outside. The steam of boiling water or of the hot water that splashed on a body in the bathroom formed a bond with the snow. One saw the snow, one saw the objects, pans, pots, soap, the tables, the quilts, the shoes, a book on the bed. The snow said that we are born with it and will live only with it. We will rinse the pans in the room, it will be snowing outside, we will pull back the quilts, it will be snowing outside, we will sleep, and it will be snowing outside, and when we wake up, it will be the first thing we see. We will see it from the bus, from the factory window, the snow will fall into the black canals, make the heads of the ducks white. We could leave our footprints in it. When we worked in the factory and produced radio valves, our footprints remained in it in front of the hostel. The snow could embrace one and create spaces in which silence could expand. Now it was gone. I thought, perhaps I only dreamed, that I have a cigarette burn on my back, because the snow is gone. I went to the bathroom again, looked at my back once more, the brown wound was still there, and water was dripping from my stockings which I had just washed. Rezzan's and Gül's stockings had been hanging there for two days. I didn't want to stay in the room alone. The linoleum floor was cold, and the rain showed me how dark the corridors were. The clock on the wall was grey, the tables had thin legs, the rain struck the dustbin in the courtyard and didn't cover it up like the snow did. I sat down in the bathroom next to Rezzan's and Gül's stockings and waited.

Rezzan came back with our communist hostel warden, with the Dove, Angel, Gül and Ataman. 'Sugar, where were you?' asked our communist hostel warden. I didn't know where I had been. 'In Berlin,' I said. Ataman's head was bleeding. They all went into the bathroom and let water run on to Ataman's head. The blood flowed into the washbasin with the water and Ataman said: 'We wanted to fold up the American stars.' The German students had wanted to demonstrate against the Vietnam War at the university, but the head of the university had said: 'The fire brigade doesn't permit it.' Then the students went to a building in the city centre, on which the American flag with the stars was hanging. The students shouted, 'Yanks out of Vietnam.' Some of the students wanted to lower the American flag to half-mast, the police had truncheons and struck their heads. Ataman, too, had been struck. He said: 'I wanted to fold up the American stars on the flag, but when the truncheon struck my head, I really saw the stars.'

The next day the headline in the newspaper display case was: 'Revolt of the Neurotics'. I remembered this sentence easily, because Turkish also had the word neurotic. *Nevrotik*. In the factory toilet the women workers went on smoking against the tiled walls, and when they drew on their cigarettes, they now often said the word 'hooligans'. I also heard the word when I stood in the bread shop. As always the bread passed from the hand of the old woman into the hand of a customer, but the word 'hooligans' also went backwards and forwards in their mouths. Our communist hostel warden said: 'The police have arrested seventy-four students.' The room of our communist hostel warden was even more full of cigarette smoke than on other evenings. He smoked his cigarettes down to the filter and talked and talked to Ataman. When the night was tired, the Dove stood behind her husband, briefly massaged his shoulder and said like a bird chik chik chik, to invite him to bed. The communist hostel warden said to her, without turning his head: 'Sleep, my Dove, sleep,' and then went on talking to Ataman. Angel and the Dove lay on the bed at the back in their clothes, watched their talking men and so fell asleep. In the morning when Angel and the Dove got on to the bus to the factory with us, they always got on in their sleep-crumpled clothes.

One Saturday morning our communist hostel warden called out in the hossel corridor: 'Sugars.' A couple of sugars looked out of their rooms. 'Come with me.' We three girls and a couple of other sugars walked behind his back to the Turkish Students' Association in the city centre. That Saturday the students were going to elect a new chairman, our communist hostel warden knew a student and wanted him to be elected. He said to us: 'Sugars, open your eyes and watch exactly what happens.' We three girls opened our eyes and saw the friend of our communist hostel warden, who was to be elected, and his opponent, who was called 'Mobil Oil', because his father did business with Mobil Oil in Istanbul. Mobil Oil, who looked like the young Onassis, had two friends. All three were very good looking, they opened their eyes and immediately talked to the three of us. The students here also smoked as in an old French film – like the workers in the Turkish Workers' Association. They carried chairs around, placed them next to one another and, cigarettes in their mouths, talked to each other. Our communist hostel warden sat down on a chair, he kept the chairs beside him free for us. But we went on talking to Mobil Oil and his two friends. They sat down in such a way that a chair remained free next to each of them. We three girls sat down on these empty chairs, and so we looked like three couples in the cinema. A student who wanted Mobil Oil to be elected chairman stood up and made a speech. He said: 'The Turkish students must look on the Berlin student movement like a tourist who has a good camera. We must photograph everything, but must not be in the photo ourselves. All of it is too soon for the Turks. Even the Rector of Berlin University said in DER SPIEGEL: "I wouldn't have let myself be elected Rector, if I had foreseen all that's happened. One would have to be a masochist, no, no, no." And we also say no, no, no.' Our communist hostel warden asked him: 'Why no?' The student replied: 'We don't want our leaders to be Marx or Mao, Khrushchev or Castro, Trotsky or Tito. We have Atatürk and the Bolshevists can leave the room.' Our communist hostel warden said to the students: 'When the Turks fought against the Sultan, they often called themselves Bolshevists, because the Russian Bolshevists supported the Turkish liberation war with weapons and gold. Perhaps your grandfather also said that he's a Bolshevist, why are you afraid of this word?' The student went red in the face, so red that I thought the colour would never leave his face. He shouted three times:

'We are Turks, we are Turks, we are Turks.'

Our communist hostel warden shouted: 'Provincial clowns.' After an hour the provincial clowns had won. Our communist hostel warden disappeared and left us with Mobil Oil and his two friends. Mobil Oil had won. I didn't know who Marx, Mao,

Khrushchev, Castro and Trotsky were. Of these names I knew only Atatürk and I knew what Mobil Oil was: petrol stations. In Istanbul there were many petrol stations with this name. Mobil Oil and his two friends had a car. They drove through Berlin with us and constantly sounded the horn. Then they went to a dance place with us, the Big Apple. Rezzan and Mobil Oil danced. Rezzan was very beautiful, Gül was very beautiful, and the second boy, Salim, was also very good looking. We often forgot the third boy. He was small, sat there, smiled at his wine glass and held the wine glass as if it were his best friend. Salim smiled at Gül and me, and so all three of us didn't dance. We just stood there, and the third boy went home. The two remaining boys then brought us three girls to the hossel. Because it was raining so heavily, we sat in their car for a long time outside the women's hossel. In our hossel all the lights were out, the only light came from the room of our communist hostel warden. I saw his shadow going backwards and forwards in the little room, but his shadow didn't fall on the street, because there was no snow lying there any more. Once we had pressed the light switch in the entrance, we three girls went up the stairs as if each one of us were quite alone. Mobil Oil and Salim had separated us. When we opened the hossel door, our communist warden was standing behind the door and said: 'What are you doing here?' Then he turned round, went back to his room and for the first time closed the door behind him. Without speaking the three of us washed our stockings and hung them on the clothes line, no longer next to one another, but in different places. The next day, when we sat on the bus to the factory, we three girls had our summer clothes on under our coats. We froze, our knees froze, and in the factory each of us worked as if Mobil Oil and Salim were constantly watching us. When the three of us smoked against the tiled walls in the factory toilet, we didn't look at each other's faces any more, each smoked by herself and looked at herself in the mirror.

The phone booth next to our offended station, in front of which we had talked quietly or loudly before, so that our parents in Turkey could or couldn't hear us, was now only the telephone box, from which we called Eichkamp student hall of residence. Mobil Oil and Salim lived in this hall of residence. When we stood by the telephone booth, I always looked towards the room of our hossel warden and felt tired. When we called them, they often said 'yes' and gave us addresses where we could meet them this evening. There were always other friends there, they sat with them at the table or stood with them at the bar. Once I was wearing a shiny blouse. But when Salim first danced with me and then with another girl, I was ashamed of the shininess of my blouse. After that I sat alone at the bar and had too much time to look at this blouse. My legs hung down from the bar stool and dangled in mid-air, with nothing to rest on. I wanted to go, but remained sitting on the stool as if stuck to it and watched the movements of the barman. When I returned to the hossel that night, I went to the refuse bin in the courtyard, lifted up the lid, took off my shiny blouse and threw it in the bin.

It had been easy to part from the workers and the Workers' Association, but it was not easy to part from the students. The workers had wrinkles around their eyes, their mouth and chin, which were constantly in motion and spread across the face. Their faces were like different masks, one could love these masks, laugh about them, cry and leave them again. They themselves could make fun of their masks. The students, however, had no wrinkles, they stood there as if a second person were constantly inspecting their face. Because they were inspecting themselves, we inspected ourselves, too. When they looked us in the face, that meant: I want to tell you something, but I'll tell you the next time. So we each put the other off until the next time, blew hot and cold at the same time.

Chekhov had disappeared between me and Rezzan, when we lay one above the other at night in the hossel beds. Rezzan did go on reading Chekhov in the light of the Hebbel Theatre sign flashing on and off, but then she only talked down from above about Mobil Oil. She didn't say much about him, she said only what Mobil Oil had said to her: 'He said... he said...' She talked like our communist hostel warden or Ataman, when they talked about Brecht, 'Brecht would have said...' So every night Mobil Oil's sentences came into the women's hossel. Rezzan's language changed. She said words like realistic, unrealistic, masochistic or: That's something that can be discussed. But then she didn't discuss it. The sentences that Mobil Oil had given her always remained unsolved riddles. And then at night in the light of the Hebbel Theatre neon sign flashing on and off she tried to solve these riddles. Once Rezzan called Mobil Oil from our telephone box; at some point Mobil Oil had a pee and said: 'I'm just having a pee.' On the phone Rezzan heard the sounds of Mobil Oil having a pee, while another three people were waiting outside. She gestured from the telephone booth – the conversation was very important.

Mobil Oil and Salim had made the night their day, there they lived. I asked Gül why she loved Salim. She said: 'I don't know, he smells so clean.' We said we would stay here for one year, they said they would stay here for five years. When they talked so easily about these five years, I immediately thought of death – that death could hear what they were saying and kill them. When they talked about their fathers, mothers, uncles, brothers, nephews, nieces, cousins, sisters, they talked without being afraid that death could also touch them. They said: 'My brother wants to come here, too, in six years' time and study in Berlin.' It sounded as if the families of students did not die.

They knew Berlin very well and said: 'Now we're driving to the Café Old Vienna, now we're driving to the Old Eden, now we're driving to the Wannsee Lake.' Once we had followed the backs of our communist hostel warden and Ataman, now we followed Mobil Oil and Salim's car. 'Where did we park?' – 'Let's get into the car.' – 'We don't want to get our shoes wet.' With Salim and Mobil Oil our shoes always remained dry. They took money out of their pockets and spent it as in an American film. In an American film, when a man left a bar, he always left paper money on the bar, and didn't wait for the change. They also left money lying as if it were theatre money. Mobil Oil and Salim told us how it was even possible to phone America from telephone boxes without any money. In a mould in the freezer compartment of the refrigerator they made one mark coins out of ice, put them in the payphone and made their phone call. Later the one-mark coins made of ice melted and no one from the German Post Office could understand why the machines were so wet.

Sometimes we drove to the Wannsee Lake. The car was parked on the sand, and we sang old Turkish songs. That's where I noticed that they had very beautiful voices. One had to close one's eyes when one sang, because the songs told of difficult love and longing. When everyone had their eyes closed, that was a beautiful moment. We sang about the love of other people who were already long dead, and tried to feel it. The rain also rained on the Wannsee and mingled with our voices. Sometimes we got out of the car and ran across the sand in the rain, until we were all wet.

When we three girls came back to our hossel, the first women were already walking along the corridor in their nightshirts. They said: 'You have cut yourselves off from your mothers and fathers. Your fathers and mothers should tie you to them with ropes. You will lose your diamonds. The bones of your dead will be in pain because of you.' It was hard for me to forget the pains of the dead, because it was always raining in Berlin. Next to the bones of the dead, I always saw the rain that rained on these bones, and some nights stayed in the women's hossel. Rezzan and Gül went into the night with Mobil Oil and Salim, drank coffee in the Old Vienna early in the morning and came straight to the factory from there. Sometimes Salim and Mobil Oil had two cars and raced them at dawn in the empty streets, once Gül came to the factory bleeding from her head. The car had turned over twice, she climbed out of the upside-down car, was bleeding from the head and got on the bus to the factory.

Rezzan and Gül moved out of the women's hossel. They rented an apartment in a villa close to the student hall of residence in which Salim and Mobil Oil lived. The rent was 400 marks, their monthly wage was 380 marks. When they came into the flat and pressed a button, the curtains went to the side, and in front of the window there was a green forest. There they waited for Mobil Oil and Salim, who didn't come. The money didn't last long enough for them to wait for the two men. So they rented a thirty-square-foot apartment, a tiny room, in which there was nothing but a small bed. Rezzan and Gül always came to the factory in crumpled clothes, because at night they fell asleep in their clothes on this narrow bed. Then Rezzan went to the student residence once again and looked for Mobil Oil, but he wasn't there. She met a small Turkish student, who was also waiting for him and who talked to Rezzan. They waited and waited, and then they bought curry wurst and ketchup at a stand, got on a bus and went to the thirty-square-foot apartment. There they ate the curry wurst sitting on the bed and put the paper plates on the floor. At some point they started kissing and embracing each other. They took off their clothes, the bed was old and wobbled, and at some point the bed collapsed on to the curry wurst and the ketchup. The ketchup was smeared on their arms, their faces and their legs. Very frightened, Rezzan phoned our communist hostel warden: 'Help, I'm bleeding to death!' The communist hostel warden immediately alerted the fire brigade and himself ran to Rezzan's flat. The firemen laughed: 'That's not blood, that's curry wurst with ketchup.' Rezzan didn't believe them, however, and was afraid that her diamond was gone. She came along to the hossel, because there was no mirror in the thirty-foot-square apartment, and immediately ran to the bathroom, sat on the stone floor, spread her legs and looked in the mirror, to see whether her diamond was still there.

Out in the courtyard it went on raining on to the dustbins. Rezzan's bed above me had already been empty for a long time. In the night I now heard only the sounds made by the sisters' two pale blue dressing gowns of electrified material. The two sisters cooked their meals, put them on the table, and when they ate they began to cry. Sometimes I went alone to our offended station, and when I walked past our telephone booth, I wanted to call Rezzan and Gül, but they didn't have a telephone. Once I visited them in their thirty-foot-square apartment on Potsdamer Strasse. There were whores standing on the street below. It was raining and they stood in the doorways. If a whore had a too-big bosom, her bosom stuck out a bit and the rain fell between her breasts. The older whores, even sixty- and seventy-year-old women, wore hats and too much lipstick. Mobil Oil and Salim didn't come to this flat either, and Rezzan and Gül often looked out of the window. The street was nice, snack bars, whores, lights. Braking car tyres splashed rain on the whores' miniskirts. Sometimes a whore had a little dog. These dogs, too, were wet from the rain, constantly shook their heads and bodies and with the rainwater made the whores' legs wet. Rezzan and Gül in turn made the whores wet from their window. They poured a glass of water over the whores and then quickly withdrew into the small room. Then they sat on the bed, laughed and after half an hour again poured a glass of water over a whore and over her dog. The whores swore, their dogs barked. A bus was just driving away from a bus stop. Then a man came up, waited for the next bus, while a whore came out of the hotel with her client. Then she crossed the street and waited there for a new client. The night buses came every twenty minutes, and I often saw that the whore had found a new client just when the bus came and the man, who had been waiting for it, got on. The bus drove up, the rainwater at the edge of the road splashed up, and the whore crossed the wet street towards the hotel with the new customer. Often the men wore glasses, and the whores talked to them as if they were showing someone who had asked them for an address the way.

In the radio valve factory I had learned a new phrase. Piecework. People no longer said, I'm coming from the factory, they said, I'm coming from piecework. 'Piecework does my hands, my arms in, piecework cuts off my wings, the piecework went well, piecework is no good.' Since piecework started, women could no longer go to the toilet. Often hair fell out and lay on their table, but they went on working on the radio valves with the hair around them. Sometimes they said: 'This piecework will kill me.' Because of piecework, the women in the factory divided into two groups, the women who managed the piecework, and those who didn't manage it. Ataman saw the women who came from piecework and quoted Brecht:

Brush down that coat
Brush it twice over
When you've finished brushing it
You're left with just a clean rag.

It was raining on Stresemannstrasse. People went into the Hebbel Theatre with their umbrellas and left with umbrellas. The taxis stopped, the umbrellas closed, the women lifted their long dresses a little and got in. The rain still struck the street. I missed Rezzan's voice at night. I smoked in bed and threw the stubs under my bed. I often went to the toilet, sat down on the toilet seat lid and looked out of the little toilet window. The hossel building was U-shaped. When I sat on the toilet I sometimes saw on the other side of the courtyard but still in the same building a woman sitting on the toilet. During the night the wall clock in the hossel lounge ticked, and it rained and rained. Only our communist hostel warden and Ataman were awake and at night they went across the corridor to the toilet together, but only one of them peed. Ataman walked behind our communist warden and went on talking to him through the half-open toilet door, while he peed. One night I walked behind them; outside the toilet door Ataman once again listened to our hostel warden, they talked, and I stood behind Ataman and listened to them. All the women were sleeping, everything was quiet in the hossel. When they went back, I followed Ataman and sat down with them. In the room the Dove and Angel were already sleeping. The two men went on talking, but what they were talking about I didn't understand. But I remained sitting with them like a lonely person, looking for foreign stations on his radio at night. Towards morning, as I went away, I said to our communist hostel warden: 'Can I become a communist, too?' – 'Yes, Sugar,' he said, and gave me a book to read. The book was in Turkish, Engels' *Ailenin Asıllari* (The Origin of the Family, Private Property and the State). He said, 'Marx is too difficult for you, but perhaps you can read Engels, he's my favourite.' When I leafed through the book by Engels, I saw lots of tobacco crumbs between the pages. I tried to leave the tobacco crumbs in the book, as if they belonged to the book. The word family was easy to understand, but not the sentences as a whole. I also understood the word life, but not reproduction of the immediate essentials of life. I understood the words food, foodstuffs, clothing, work, home, but not production and reproduction. I always tried to use my father as an example. He worked, procured food, foodstuffs, clothing, home and had a family. But then I was stuck. Kinship bonds – the phrase was just as strange to me in Turkish as the German headlines I always practised: HUNT FOR AXEMAN. BEGGAR KING POLDI BEGS HIS LAST. A DOZEN CORPSES. NO SHINE WITHOUT ELBOW GREASE. I understood the section in Engels about group marriage. On the island of Sakhalin a man was married to all the wives of his brother and all the sisters of his wife. But therefore these women were also simultaneously married to many men. A child did not call only his real father 'father', but also all his father's brothers. All the wives of these brothers and the sisters of his mother he called mother. The children of all these fathers and mothers he called his brothers and sisters, and they ate fish and game, and they heated water by dropping glowing stones into the water, they were at the stage of civilisation called savagery. Descent was reckoned not from the father but from the mother. Only mothers were valid. The mother of the child was known, but not who the father was. It reminded me of Turkish funerals. When a person dies, he is carried in a coffin to the cemetery, then he's taken out of the coffin, four men grip the sheet in which the dead man is lying and lay the dead man in the grave. The imam from the mosque calls out his name with the name of his mother: 'Osman, the son of Leyla.' The name of the father of the dead man is not called out. If the father of the dead man is also standing by the open grave, he is not offended. The word 'fashionable' in the book by Friedrich Engels was also easy to understand. Engels said: 'Lately it has become fashionable to deny the existence of this initial stage in human sexual life. Humanity must be spared this "shame".' The birds only lived as a couple, because the female sat on her eggs and incubated them and needed help, and so the male was faithful to her. But men were not descended from birds. Engels said that the tapeworm deserved the palm for faithfulness, 'which has a complete set of male and female organs in each of its 50–200 proglottides or sections, and it spends its whole life copulating in all its sections with itself'. Women who had lots of husbands reminded me of the Hollywood stars Zsa Zsa Gabor, Liz Taylor and of Turkish peasant women. Their husbands went to the big city to work, worked there as porters or as construction workers, slept on the building site, died young or died in the war and their wives were given to their brothers as wife. So the Turkish women from the villages also had many husbands.

When I didn't understand something I often read the price given on the back – so many lira. The word lira reassured me, because it was easy to understand. Then I opened the book again. In the factory I sometimes went up to Angel, who had already read a lot because of Ataman, and asked her what production meant. She turned to me, the lens in her right eye, and said: 'I don't know, it's what we do here.' We made radio valves. I looked at her right eye enlarged behind the lens. She had very beautiful eyes, and at that moment I believed I had understood what the word production meant. But when I went back to my chair, I forgot it again. Then came the word reproduction. I asked the Dove what reproduction meant. She frowned, one furrow became two furrows, then she had three furrows. She said: 'Reproduction means to produce again. For example, a piece of period furniture from the eighteenth century is reproduced.' She looked at me with the three furrows on her forehead, until I nodded, then the furrows disappeared from her forehead again.

I also loved the translations of the title of Engels's book. I liked Italian very much: *L'origine della Famiglia, della proprietà privata e dello stato.* Romanian was: *Originà Familiei proprietátii, private si a Statului.* Danish was: *Familjens, Privatejendommens og statens Oprindelse.* On the book were the words Pocket Book. A book that fits in a jacket pocket, a coat pocket. It was nice to think that a book was made to fit in a pocket. When one held it in one's hand at night, one's shoulder didn't hurt. The book smelt of cigarettes, like the magazine DER SPIEGEL in the pub. Between the pages there were not only tobacco crumbs, there were also eyelashes, hairs, flakes of dandruff; the book had creases like the clothes of the Dove and Angel on the nights when they slept in their clothes in the hostel warden's room. The book also had coffee-cup stains. Some lines were marked in pencil, and there were many eraser crumbs between the pages. My first book, a Turkish alphabet book, had also had many creases, because there was so much one had to learn by heart. One poem went:

*The crow, the crow, the crow said cawk,*
*climbs on a branch and then says look,*
*I've climbed on the branch and had a look –*
*says the crow.*

I gave Friedrich Engels' book back to our communist hostel warden. 'Put it there, Sugar,' he said, and gave me a cigarette. We smoked the cigarette together and listened to the rain. When I left, he gave me a new book, Maxim Gorky's *The Mother.* The word mother. I hadn't said the word for a long time. I got on the bus in the morning, and sometimes half asleep I showed the bus driver Gorky's book instead of the bus ticket. He then looked me in the eye until I showed him the bus ticket.

At night I read *The Mother*, just as Rezzan read *The Picture of Dorian Gray* or Chekhov's 'The Lady with the Little Dog' – in the light of the Hebbel Theatre neon sign going on and off. Sometimes I wept for this mother. But then the sign went out, and I lost the place where I was reading. Then I stopped crying, in order to find the place when the neon sign came on again. When the neon sign went off again, I listened to the rain for a little while. The rain didn't stop, it rained and rained. I thought, when the rain stops, I'll go back to my mother. Yet I had a one-year contract with the factory. If one listened to the street, one also heard other sounds, but I heard only the rain. I thought, that is the only sound that keeps me here. I wrote a letter to my mother: 'My doe-eyed mother, I love you, it's raining, I love you, it's raining on my love. One day this rain will stop, and I will see you.' Then I waited for a letter from her. But my mother had never written letters. When she wanted to talk to her father, she took a bus or a train and travelled for three days to reach him. I waited and waited for her letter. When the sisters who wore pale blue dressing gowns of electrified material came into the room, I looked at their hands, then in their eyes. But they were only carrying plastic bags or the steaming pot. Often I asked our communist hostel warden whether he had a letter for me. He said: 'No, Sugar, I haven't written to you yet.' Then I walked around our offended station again, between the broken railway tracks where grass was growing. I thought, if I don't wait for the letter, or act as if I'm not waiting for it, just go for a walk, it will come. The letter should not know that I was waiting for it, then it would come. But no letter came. When other women in the hossel got letters, I looked at them and thought, perhaps there's some news for me in them. When the women's faces became excited and the veins in their neck throbbed, I thought, now they're reading a bit of news for me, but don't want to tell me. When, during piecework in the factory, women threw the broken valves into the rubbish bins too violently, I thought, this sound is the news, which they don't want to reveal to me. I didn't manage the piecework . The forewoman, Frau Missel, gave me a simpler job on the night shift. I drew wires on a machine and collected them on a metal sheet.

On the night shift there was a foreman and a woman worker who were in love. While they were placing the drawn wire on the metal sheet, which was above the green iron machine, they briefly looked up, looked at each other and laughed. The night outside was dark, and it was raining, but inside under the strip lights this woman and this man looked at each other and laughed. They never did it for long, because their heads had to look at the wires again, but their laughter remained on their faces while they went on working. When they looked at each other again, the laughter from before was still there. Because they loved one another, they also loved me. Hannes and Katharina. After they had briefly looked at one another, they also looked over to me and laughed. Because the laughter of the pair never disappeared from their faces, my laughter also remained in my face all night. After the night shift Hannes and Katharina went to a Berlin corner pub and had a beer and a schnapps. They laughed when they saw me at the time-clock and took me with them. I walked behind their laughter and drank beer and schnapps with them. I didn't speak any German, but they hardly spoke either. They drank, left their arms and hands on the table beside their glasses and laughed silently at one another. Only when the landlord put the chairs on the tables, did they take their arms from the table, take out their little purses and place coins next to each other on the table, as if they had no paper money. The leather of their little purses had stretched because of all the small change, and in places the leather had become paper thin. I walked behind their laughter for a couple of months and forgot the letter I was waiting for, and the rain. My face laughed during the night shift and in my sleep. The sisters in their pale blue dressing gowns of electrified material worked on the morning shift. When they got up I was just falling asleep. Later they said to me: 'Girl, you laugh in your sleep, you sleep like an angel.'

One day the laughter of Katharina and Hannes stopped. They

continued working in their places on the night shift, but they didn't look at each other any more. It was as if the stove in a room had gone out, and to keep warm they walked backwards and forwards in their jackets and matted pullovers. Because they didn't look at each other any more, they didn't look at me any more either.

The factory hall was very large and high, the people who worked there looked as if they had been cut out of a small photo and stuck into a much larger photo. The high room amplified the noise of the machines or the falling metal sheets, and because of the loud echoes the people looked even smaller. Each person stood alone in front of his big machine. One heard the loud noises in the hall and the rain outside, but not the people. They practised being silent and looked straight ahead. If the wires in a machine had been drawn crooked, a foreman sometimes came and talked quietly to the worker, whose body at that moment also looked like a wire that is being stretched between two handles. On the last working day of the week each worker greased his machine with a cloth and left the factory with a little bit of grease between his fingers. Drops of rainwater stuck to the greasy fingers, it looked like a piece of butter sweating.

During work I often went to a cigarette machine, which was on the stairs one floor up. One had to press the automatic light button, then quickly run up the steps, already holding the money in one's hand, put it in the machine, pull the handle, take out the packet, push back the empty drawer and quickly run down the stairs again. At the last step the automatic light went out again. Once, after I had drawn out a packet of Stuyvesant, I tried to take out a second packet, without putting in money again. While I was pulling out the next packet by force with my fingers, the automatic light went out. My white nylon work coat shone in the dark. The packet was torn and squashed in several places. I put the damaged cigarette packet in my bra between my breasts and went down the stairs in the dark. My heart beat during the whole of the night shift, and the damaged Stuyvesant packet rustled between my breasts. When I got the night bus to the hossel, out of fear I showed the bus driver the Stuyvesant packet instead of my ticket. The driver laughed and said something I didn't understand. A woman translated it for me: 'Thanks, but I don't smoke.' That night I went to the offended station, pulled the damaged Stuyvesant packet out of my bra and threw the cigarettes on the ground; the rain immediately made them soggy.

One day the sun came out. People immediately took off their clothes and gathered in undershirts in the weak rays of the sun. When the sun shone on the left side of the street, they all went to the left side. People had a new face, as if they had all suddenly put on the same masks. Their mouths stretched, they pushed their noses towards the sun. Many elderly women came on to the street with their dogs and looked as if they had come out of a cupboard that had been shut for a long time. Men and women ate ice cream and kissed one another with mouths smeared with ice cream, then they ate some more ice. An old man in short trousers walked under the trees as if he had just climbed out of an open grave. When the sun went down, he would return to the grave. People came out of the dark gateways, immediately looked up at the sun, as if they wanted to apologise for being late. In their short shirtsleeves their arms looked as if they were just taking a pair of white bones for a walk. When the sun shone on the middle of the road, the pedestrians followed it there, the cars sounded their horns, the drivers in the cars behind the panes of glass moved their mouths, in which the swear words could be seen. Everyone wanted to catch the sun, hold on to it, put it under their coats, lock it into their apartments. Some shop owners sat on chairs in front of their shops, went into the dark shop with their customers, came out, saw their chair standing in the shade again, pushed the chair to the weak sun, sat down again and looked at the buses driving past. The people sitting in the dark buses looked at the shop owners, as if the latter had just taken the sun, and behind the panes of glass turned their heads away from them. In the weak sun Berlin was an offended city. Everyone looked at everyone else and thought, my neighbour is doing better than me. Then the rain came back and removed people's mask of joy. Rain suited the city better. People went to the Hertie department store, stood at the cheese counters and the sausage counters, everything was lit by strip lights. They stood there without masks, the slicing machine worked, four slices, five slices. The greaseproof paper was shiny, the grease was shiny under the strip lights, the scales moved, the needle came to a stop, and the ballpoint of the sales assistant wrote the price in large figures on the paper.

I returned to the hostel with two hundred grams of salami and wet shoes and in front of the hostel I saw two suitcases. A taxi was waiting. The labels were coming away from the suitcases because of the rain. Then our communist hostel warden and his wife, the Dove, came out, Ataman carried a third suitcase and Angel a typewriter. The taxi driver was smoking and threw his cigarette on to the street and the rain had already made it soggy in mid-air. I asked them: 'Where to?' Our communist hostel warden said: 'I am a spirit of no common rate. The summer still doth tend upon my state.' He kissed my forehead and said: 'Titania, we are returning to Turkey. A theatre wants me to direct.' As he got into the taxi with the Dove, he quoted Shakespeare again:

*A calendar, a calendar! Look in the almanac – find out moonshine, find out moonshine!*

'Let me tell you something, Titania: if you want to be a good actress, sleep with men, it doesn't matter with whom, sleeping is important. It's good for art.'

*And I will purge thy mortal grossness so*
*That thou shalt like an airy spirit go.*

They drove away in the taxi. He wound down the window and waved to Ataman, Angel and me. At that moment a flash of lightning briefly coloured his hand an electric blue. On a piece of paper Ataman wrote down his telephone number, but it quickly blurred in the rain. Then he wrote it on my arm: 'He's right, you must sleep with men, free yourself of your diamond, if you want to be a good actress. Only art is important, not the diamond.'

The bus came, splashed rain on our clothes, and Ataman and Angel drove off. I held my left elbow in my right hand and carried my arm, which had Ataman and Angel's telephone number on it, carefully up the hostel stairs, took off my wet clothes and looked in the mirror. They were all gone. Rezzan, Gül, our communist hostel warden, the Dove, Ataman, Angel. I saw only myself in the mirror, alone and with the telephone number of Ataman and Angel on my left arm. Outside the rain still beat on the refuse bin and in the light of a flash of lightning I briefly saw the words: 'Children are forbidden to play in the courtyard'.

When it started to snow again my contract with the radio factory had run out, we all got a roast Christmas goose from the factory. I bought tickets and travelled with the German goose from Berlin to Istanbul. While I waited for the train, I practised my last German sentences from the newspapers:

SECRET DEVICES ON BOARD
BABY DIED TWICE
FORDS ARE MORE EXPENSIVE TOO.

The Berlin–Istanbul ticket consisted of four different little tickets, and once the inspector had punched a hole in one of these tickets, I thought the first of these tickets was used up and threw it out of the train window. After that I said to the three Turkish men in my compartment: 'Throw the tickets away, we've already covered the stretch for these tickets.' The three of them also threw their tickets out of the window. Later another inspector came, and all four of us had to pay for our tickets again. One of the men had a big moustache. He said to me: 'Girl, give me your tickets, your hands won't stay still, you'll throw them out of the window again.' The journey lasted three days and three nights, there was no restaurant car, the toilets were blocked, it was cold.

We sat in the compartment in our coats and for three days ate German goose. Two of the men were miners. One said: 'Oh, this coal with vitamins.' The other said: 'I had promised myself, when I return to Turkey, I'll take a sackful of coal as a souvenir. The German coal has vitamins, no dust, it doesn't make you ill. The Turkish coal makes you ill, there they drill underground without water, and the coal raises dust like flour in the mill. In Germany there are machines that drill ninety feet into the rock. I've left my hair in Germany, what can I do, a year is over, Allah be thanked.' The third man worked in a coffin factory in Berlin, he often went to the whores on Potsdamer Strasse. The whores had asked him: 'Do you want to sleep with me?' He had said no and written in his notebook: 'Today I said NO to three women.' I sat there with greasy hands and listened to them. The man with the moustache often shook his head, laughed and said: 'Girl, when you arrive your mother should wash you with Arabian soap.' The men slept sitting next to one another and let me sleep on the other wooden bench. While they slept, I looked at their faces. In their sleep the heads of the two men without moustaches had fallen on to the shoulders of the man with the moustache. The bones of the German goose lay on a sheet of newspaper on the floor; when the train rattled or braked suddenly, the bones slid backwards and forwards on the newspaper and made a rustling sound. When the men woke up, they asked the man with the big moustache: 'Where are we?' He then replied: 'We're among the Bulgarians.' When the train reached Istanbul, I wanted to stand up, but my legs gave way with tiredness.

# We Stood Day and Night in the Light

Outside in the railway station the seagulls and pigeons flew between the people who were putting down their suitcases on the station floor and embracing one other. Sometimes the birds settled so long on the suitcases it was as if they had arrived after a long journey. Only when the people picked up their suitcases again did the birds fly off. My mother and my father took me between them and held me tight. My father said: 'My lion daughter, have you come back?' My mother said: 'My daughter, do you recognise us again?' Their hair was electrified with excitement, which then also electrified my hair. So we walked, our hair twisted together, down the streets. I was amazed how many men there were in Istanbul. I pushed the air in front of me, my movements seemed so slow to me, everyone's movements. The donkeys' feet slipped on the small cobblestones, the donkeys cried with their whole bodies. The carriers bore heavy packages on their backs and sweated, their faces almost kissed the ground. Donkeys, carriers, cars, ships, seagulls, people, everything was moving, but it all seemed much slower than the movements in Berlin. One could smell shitting horses, the sea, and the dirt on the streets splashed on to the women's stockings, and everyone's shoes looked dirty and old, even the shoes of the rich men. With the street dirt still on our shoes, we boarded the ferry. Sometimes it rocked to the left, sometimes to the right, so sometimes I fell on my mother's shoulder, then on my father's shoulder, and so fell asleep. In the evening when the street lights came on, I asked: 'Mother, has Istanbul become darker?' – 'No, my daughter, Istanbul always had this light, your eyes have got used to German light.'

My father had a Pontiac car. 'You are longing for Istanbul,' he said, 'I shall take you for a little drive!' He sometimes gave lifts to people who were waiting for the bus. I sat beside my father, and he said to a woman sitting in the back: 'This is my daughter, she has just come from Germany, she has seen Europe.' The woman replied: 'To have seen Europe is a fine thing. One can tell from a person's face that she has seen Europe. The Europeans are progressive, we are dragging our feet and always taking one step forward and two steps back.' Then the woman asked my father whether I had learned German there. My father asked me: 'My daughter, have you learned German?' I replied: 'No, I haven't learned German.' My father looked into the rear-view mirror and said to the woman whom he saw there: 'No, she hasn't learned any German.' The woman went on talking in the mirror to my father: 'But that's not right – to see Germany and not to speak the language! She must learn the language.' My father said to me: 'My daughter, do you want to learn the language, listen to what the lady says, you must learn the language.' – 'Yes, Father, I would like to learn.'

In Istanbul everything was in the same place as before, the mosques, the ships, the men who worked on the ships, the men who made tea, the greengrocer opposite our apartment. Even an old car that had broken down stood in exactly the same place as I had seen it a year before. Grass was growing out of the door. The sea was still the same colour, and as before the ships sailed backwards and forwards between Asia and Europe. I thought, I can leave again, everything will stay in the same place and wait for me. The same light bulb, which a year before had already flickered and constantly gone on and off, still hung in the entrance to our house. When I come back, I thought, it will still be flickering and going on and off, I can leave. I wanted to learn German, and then rid myself of my diamond in order to become a good actress. Here I would have to come home every evening and look in my parents' eyes. Not in Germany.

My father gave me three thousand marks and sent me to the Goethe Institute in a small town on Lake Constance. My first sentences were 'Excuse me, can I say something', 'Excuse me, what's the time' and 'Excuse me, may I have another potato'. Only at the weekends did I not excuse myself. At the weekends I hitchhiked towards Switzerland with the Italian girl who was learning German with me. Often French soldiers stopped, and once again we had no language, because the soldiers spoke only French. I had learned some German but went on excusing myself with every sentence.

When the course was finished, I went to the railway station. I could return to Istanbul, but had not yet rid myself of my diamond. I called Ataman in Berlin: 'Ataman, I can speak German.' – 'Do you still have your diamond? Come to Berlin, there's a lot happening here. Angel would like you to come to Berlin, too.' To the ticket clerk I said: 'Excuse me, may I have a ticket to Berlin?' On the train a Turkish woman said: 'I'm working at Siemens, Siemens is taking on women workers.' In the station at Berlin I heard people's voices and realised that now I also understood their sentences. 'Excuse me, what's the time?' – 'Almost nine.' I called Ataman and Angel from the station. A voice told me: 'They're in Erlangen, at the theatre festival, they won't be back for another six days.'

I left the station, walked past the Wienerwald chicken restaurant and the broken church to Aschinger and ate a pea soup standing up. Through the window I saw the Turkish woman whom I had met on the train. She was waiting at the bus stop. My plate was empty, I got on the bus behind the Turkish woman, got off again with her and was once again standing in front of a women workers' hostel. Somewhere behind the hostel I saw factory towers. The woman said to me: 'That's Siemens.' The next day I had a job at Siemens and was living in the new women workers' hostel, it had six floors and was beside a main road. On the first Saturday all the women watched a Turkish film in the lounge. When the film was over a German Siemens manageress asked the girls what the film had been about. The girls didn't understand her, but I said: 'Excuse me, may I tell you the story of the film? The girl and the boy were in love, but the bad mother separated them. The girl goes to the big city, and there she becomes a singer in a nightclub. Because of a broken heart the boy goes blind, walks past this nightclub one day, hears her voice, and his eyes can see again, but the girl has a bad boss.' The Siemens manageress, her name was Gerda, said: 'Listen, how do you speak such good German, come and see me in the factory tomorrow.' The next day she patted me on the back. 'You are the new interpreter in the Siemens' women workers' hostel.' The hostel warden was Greek, Madame Gutsio. All the Turkish women called her: Madame Gusa. Four years earlier her hair had turned white in three nights, because her boyfriend had died in his car of a heart attack when he saw a truck coming towards him. At that time Gutsio had a child inside her, which after the birth she had left with her mother in Greece, because she was a communist and had to flee to Germany. In the evening she was always phoning Greece, because her sister and brother-in-law were also communists and she was afraid that the Greek military junta would send both of them to prison. Then she came to my room and said: 'I've been talking to my sister and my brother-in-law.' Her eyelashes blinked a couple of times and she waited at the door until my eyelashes blinked too. Then she said: 'Now I'm going to my Kafka and Camus.' I loved Madame Gutsio very much, she had given me a book by Kafka in German, in which there was a big photo of Kafka. I read the book, and again and again I looked at Kafka's face, and imagined a good-looking, slim man with black hair, who tap-danced. In the evening, when we switched off the office light, Madame Gutsio always said to me:

'Sugar doll, let us go to our Kafkas.' She went to her Kafka, I went to my Kafka. The interpreters' room looked like a convent cell – a narrow bed, a table, a chair, a standard lamp, a little cupboard on the wall. Outside on the main road the cars raced past, only if no car happened to be passing did I hear Madame Gutsio in the room next door turning a page in Kafka's book.

The hostel had six floors, the Turkish women lived on the fourth, fifth and sixth floors, the first, second and third floor were empty. When the cars drove past on the main road, the windows on the first three floors rattled much more loudly than on the fourth, fifth and sixth floors. The factory management announced that Turkish married couples would soon move into these empty floors. The couples arrived by plane, I brought them to the factory, translated a description of the work they were going to do, and took them to the factory doctor. While I translated, the foreman stood on my right and the couples stood on my left. When I spoke German, I again began my sentences with 'Excuse me'. To the right I said to the foreman: 'Excuse me...' When I translated into Turkish to my left, the words 'Excuse me' were missing. The workers said, 'Tell the foreman, I want to know exactly...' I translated it to the right to the foreman. 'Excuse me, but the worker says, you should excuse him, but he wants to know exactly...' When I translated at the doctor's and a sheet of paper fell from the doctor's hands, I said: 'Oh, excuse me.' – 'Not at all, not at all,' said the doctor. He then bent down to pick up the sheet of paper, I bent down too, and my head banged into his head. Again I said: 'Oh, excuse me.' When I pulled the door towards me on which there was the word 'Push' and the door didn't open, I said to the porter: 'Oh, excuse me.'

Once I was sitting in the hostel office, one hand under my chin, it was dark in the office and Madame Gutsio came in. She switched on the light and I said: 'Oh, excuse me.' Gutsio's hand remained on the switch, and she said: 'Why are you excusing yourself?' – 'Yes, that's right, excuse me,' I said.

'Why are you excusing yourself, sugar doll?'

'Yes, that's right, excuse me.'

'But don't excuse yourself.'

'OK, excuse me.'

Gutsio sat down in front of me and said: 'Please excuse me, but why are you excusing yourself so much?'

'Excuse me, I won't excuse myself any more.'

Gutsio said: 'Excuse me, sugar doll, but you're still excusing yourself.'

'Yes, excuse me, I really won't excuse myself any more.'

'Don't excuse yourself, that's it.'

'Good, I won't excuse myself, excuse me.'

Gutsio shook her head and said: 'Sugar doll, sugar doll, I don't like you always excusing yourself.'

The new workers, who didn't speak any German yet, also soon learned from me the words 'excuse me' and said 'susme'. They sat at their machines, the foreman walked backwards and forwards between them, and when they wanted to ask the foreman something, they called out loudly 'susme', as if that was the foreman's name. Soon all the workers called the foreman 'susme'. The foreman sat in a room whose walls were made of glass. The workers knocked on the glass and called 'susme'. Behind the glass the foreman read the word 'susme' from their lips, stood up and went with them to their machines, and suddenly I didn't excuse myself any more.

One German word felt too harsh for me: must. So I translated 'You must do this and that' for the workers as 'You will do this and that'. But when the foreman asked me: 'Have you told them they must only pull the lever gently?', I answered him in German: 'Yes, I have told them that they must only pull the lever gently.' I could separate the Turkish language from the word 'must', but not the German.

The married couples were now living on the first three floors and on the three floors above them were the single women. Some husbands from the first three floors pressed the button in the lift to the fourth, fifth and sixth floors, where there were always women who after work were walking half naked along the corridors to the kitchen or the bathroom. The men stepped out of the lift and the women screamed: 'Aaaa.' The men also screamed 'Aaa', smiled and went down in the lift to their wives again. Although the single women had already been living in this hostel for more than a year, the married couples immediately started worrying about the honour of the women on the fourth, fifth and sixth floors. In their opinion some of the single women had taken off their Turkish honour in Berlin like a dress, and the men in particular wanted to put this dress on them again. Once all the husbands ran out of their rooms and down to the street, like crazy men who had just been freed from their chains, because they had seen one of the women from the upper storeys. She had got out of a car and had given the driver her hand or her cheek or perhaps even her mouth. I heard the men's feet on the stairs and ran out ahead of them. The girl was just opening the garden gate, and I stood in front of her. The men came, twenty-five or thirty men, I spread my arms and said to them: 'You can crush me first, then the girl.' They stopped where they were, the girl behind me trembled, and because her hand was still on the garden gate, the iron gate trembled too.

Then I pushed the men up to the hostel lounge. Madame Gutsio gave me a two-litre bottle of red wine. I opened it, drank a mouthful, all the men looked at me. I drank another mouthful, gave the bottle to the man next to me and said: 'Drink, brother, drink.' The bottle of wine now went from one man's mouth to the next. When the bottle came back to me, it was empty. I said: 'Friends, soon you will also find bars and perhaps even one day kiss German women. Will it be nice if then forty women come rushing at you, to beat you up?' The men listened to what I said, and suddenly they laughed and went back to their wives.

Life on the married floors wasn't easy. All the rooms were next to one another. At night when someone switched on the automatic light in the corridor, the light came in under the doors. So the corridor light was constantly going on and off

on the floors of their rooms, outside on the main road the cars
drove past, and when they had made love at night and the next
morning had to wash themselves from head to foot because of
the Koran, everyone could see who was going to work with wet
hair. In Turkey the men had been boxers or teachers, shoemakers,
workers, unemployed, peasants, bus drivers or tailors. If they
had remained in Turkey, they would perhaps never have come
together on one street, would never have seen each other.
Chance had gathered them here, and now they went, snow on
their moustaches, water dripping from their hair, to Siemens.
The single women also went to the factory at the same time and
noticed which husbands and wives went to the Siemens factory
with wet hair. So the single women took an interest in the wet
hair of the husbands, who lived on the first three floors and were
not their husbands, and the husbands took an interest in the
honour of the single women who lived on the upper floors of the
Siemens hostel and were not their wives. In the factory, however,
these thoughts ceased. The people from all six floors took off
their coats, hung them on top of each other, and the snow on the
coat shoulders melted from one coat on to the others.

When a man was angry, he came to me and said: 'Miss
Interpreter, shall I give up all my strength for this piecework,
or shall I give up all my strength in order to live under one roof
with these people?' or 'Miss Interpreter, I've just come from
doing piecework, I already don't know whether I'm coming or
going, they've got the radio on so loud, how am I going to come
to rest again with this volume?' I didn't have to translate only
between Germans and Turks, but also between Turks and Turks.
Every day I had to carry out an inspection in the kitchen, to see
whether the pots had been washed and were in their places. One
woman exclaimed: 'Tell her over there, she should wash up the
pot.' I went to the woman: 'Please do wash the pot.' – 'Tell her,
she should first of all clean the bath, then I'll wash the pot.' I
went back to the first woman and said: 'Clean the bath, then she'll
wash the pot.' Once they had sent me backwards and forwards

a couple of times as postman, I cleaned the bath and the pot myself. Accidents were also liable to happen in the corridors on the lower floors. If someone slammed a door, the others woke up, if a window banged because of the wind, they woke up. If someone spoke loudly in the corridor at night, the doors opened immediately. Men in pyjamas stood in the doorway, their wives in nightshirts behind them. The ones who had spoken too loudly and had woken them up were no longer there. Then the men shouted in the corridor: 'We don't even get any peace when we're sleeping, what kind of people are you?' When they had shut their doors again, other doors on to the corridor opened, in the doorways stood other men and women, who had just been woken by the men complaining about being woken up. They, too, shouted in the empty corridor and woke others in turn, who then woke me up in their pyjamas. 'Miss Interpreter, you tell them, we want to sleep.' I went up in the lift with them and woke yet others with the lift. When we got out, they went to their rooms again, and I remained alone in the corridor and saw nothing but a cockroach scuttling across the wall.

Sometimes a man even came to me who didn't want to talk to anyone: 'Tell them, I'm not talking to anyone any more, I'm finished with all of them, tell them that, I don't have anything more to say to them.' Sometimes a wife looked out of the window at her husband, who was just leaving. She called after him, he should button up his jacket. Then she shouted to me: 'Miss Interpreter, tell him, he should button up his jacket, otherwise he'll catch cold.' Now he buttoned up his jacket and crossed the main road to the bus stop. A husband took his hat off, greeted me and said: 'Miss Interpreter, can you tell my wife, if she keeps on the way she's doing now, I'm going back to Turkey.' No one went back to Turkey, and I bore the sentences from one to the other. Later, when I read Shakespeare plays, I saw that there the messengers often get killed.

The married couples who lived downstairs and who were always together appeared threatening to the single women. When a single woman met a married couple in front of the lift, she didn't get in with them, but walked up the stairs. Because the married couples on the lower floors only went out together, soon the single women on the upper floors only went out in twos. Soon every woman had a best friend and just as on the first three floors there was always lovemaking, so on the upper floors there was a constant talking about love. 'No one can love like I can,' said one. 'When I love, I love him more than my life,' said the other. They talked and talked, and the water collected on the kitchen floor and made their feet wet.

Accidents were often liable to happen in the lift between the six floors. Once a man's voice called from the lift: 'Miss Interpreter! Help!' The lift had stopped between ground floor and first floor. I shouted into the lift: 'What's wrong? Is the lift broken?' Then a woman's voice called out: 'The guy deliberately pressed the button for our sixth floor. I'm not letting him out of here until his wife comes.' Then the man again: 'Miss Interpreter, what's she saying, tell me, what's she saying?' – 'She says you deliberately pressed the button to the women's floors.' – 'If I did that, may my eyes go blind.' – 'What's he saying, what?' she shouted. 'He says if he has done something like that, his eyes should go blind.' She cursed him in the lift: 'If you've lied, may you eat pork.' Then she let the lift move again, he got out on one of the married-couple floors, and she went up to the women's floors.

Once a woman saw a married man, who often deliberately pressed the lift button to the women's floors, get into the lift at the bottom. At the top, the woman pressed the button for the sixth floor, took off her dressing gown, opened the lift door and briefly showed herself to the man naked. Then she let him go down again and exclaimed: 'Now the guy can burst a blood vessel.' The married man said to me: 'Tell her I'll pull the liver out of her body.' The walls of the lift now got sentences: 'Anyone who presses the wrong button here is a donkey.'

When one stood on the street opposite the hostel, all one saw were the cars racing past and the six lit-up floors of the hostel. The house stood there isolated; a long way behind one could see the factory building. If we had screamed in the middle of the night, no neighbour would have heard us. Cars didn't stop here, only ambulances sometimes. Often women or men came to my door if they had to go to hospital at night. Stomach, a finger that was sore, a high temperature, a throbbing tooth. I then went with them to the hospital. There we stood in the light. The sick stood in this light like lambs and practised the foreign names of their illness, in order to say it to the others later. The doctor had a round mirror on his head, exactly in the middle of his forehead.

Once one of the single women had a high temperature and pains. First women came from their floor to me and said: 'She's been crying for days, can you tell us why she's crying?' Then she came to see me herself. She was standing perhaps eighteen inches away from me, but even I could feel her heat. I went with her to the hospital. The doctor said: 'Tell her I don't understand what she's got.' – 'I'm homesick,' she said and wept. The doctor gave her drugs for flu. We went back to the hostel in the ambulance, then I took her up to her room. When I went down in the lift, the lift was still warm from her fever. The next evening she called me to her: 'Come, I'll show you something.' She didn't have a temperature any more, but an ice-cold body. She showed me a three-month-old embryo, which she had wrapped in newspaper. For weeks she had been trying to abort the child. When I left, she said to me: 'Don't tell anyone, my beauty.'

After a few months Madame Gutsio wanted to travel to Yugoslavia, to meet her mother and her child from Greece there. Because of the military coup Gutsio couldn't go to Greece. A Greek friend, Yorgi, stood in for her. Yorgi brought his cat. The cat always sat on his lap or walked on the table between the telephone and the documents. To me Yorgi said: 'Turcala Turcala,' to his cat: 'Sit down and take a look at the beautiful Turcala.' Yorgi had a beautiful nose. When he lowered his head, it cast a long shadow because of the light of the table lamp. I wanted to stroke this shadow, but instead stroked his cat and sent him my love that way

– just like in a Hollywood film: Gary Cooper sits on his horse and the beautiful woman strokes the head of the horse and sends him her love that way. With my left hand I picked up the telephone receiver, with the right I stroked his cat, suddenly I realised that Yorgi was also stroking his cat and the shadow over his nose was trembling a little. The cat became a little restless, then, at the same moment, we took a cigarette out of the cigarette packet and our fingers touched briefly. When the telephone rang, our hands met above the telephone. Sometimes we switched the light off together when we left the office. During the night I heard Yorgi turning the pages of a book in Madame Gutsio's room, and I also turned the pages of my book loudly and coughed. Then he, too, coughed in the next room, his cat began to miaow. I felt hot, I poured cold water over my nightshirt and lay down in bed in the wet nightshirt. I had once heard that's what sailors do. It was no good. I opened the window, sat on the windowsill, my legs dangling. Suddenly Yorgi's cat jumped on to my legs, and I saw that Yorgi, too, was sitting by the window in his pyjamas. I asked Yorgi: 'Shall we go for a little drive?' We jumped out of the window into the garden and drove in our nightshirt and pyjamas to the lake. It was dark and we heard our footsteps on the sand as if we were strangers. The lake lay there, as if it agreed with us coming. A searchlight from East Berlin combed the dark night. Yorgi didn't speak, he smoked and put his cigarette in my mouth. When the cigarette was finished, Yorgi suddenly said the same thing as Ataman: 'You still have your diamond, don't you?' I laughed and said: 'Yes, I still have my diamond, but I want to save myself from it.' – 'Give it to me,' said Yorgi. I didn't know how one gave away one's diamond, but Yorgi took his handkerchief out of his pyjama pocket and laid it on the sand by the lake. I sat down on the handkerchief, and Yorgi kissed me, all the time shaking his head and saying: 'Turcala Turcala.' The East Berlin searchlight lit up Yorgi's forehead and nose. Yorgi lay on top of me, and when he grasped my breasts or legs, he spoke Greek sentences in the direction of the lake, between which he always said: 'Turcala Turcala.' The lake didn't move, it was listening. I looked at the lake, and waited for a star to fall from the sky; at that moment I, too, would lose my diamond. Then Yorgi said: 'You're still a child,' first shook the sand out of my nightshirt, then out of his pyjamas, and picked up his handkerchief, folded it and drove back with me to the Siemens hostel. In the car we both laughed, in the hostel we hung the wet nightshirt and the pyjamas next to each other on the clothes line and went to sleep separately.

The next morning he called Madame Gutsio and told her in German that he had kissed me by the lake. On the telephone Madame Gutsio laughed so loudly that I heard her voice. 'Aah, Yorgi, can't you see the girl is still a child.' Then Yorgi said a sentence in Greek. Madame Gutsio told me loudly in the receiver what Yorgi had said: 'Yorgi says she also kisses like a child.'

Later, while he was working, Yorgi took the handkerchief that he had put down on the sand for me out of his pocket, and a few grains of sand fell on the table. He cleaned his glasses with the handkerchief and so couldn't see that I was looking at these grains of sand. I gathered up the grains, and Yorgi said: 'Let me do that.' He took them out of my hand and put them in the ashtray.

In the evening, like Madame Gutsio, he phoned Greece, because his sisters and brothers were in military prisons. Then he came to my door, said: 'I've phoned Greece,' blinked like Madame Gutsio, and waited for me to blink, too. The light went out in the corridor. Only the cars driving past on the main road cast light on our faces. 'Yorgi, should I be ashamed that I couldn't save myself from my diamond?' – 'No, you will only save yourself when you want to.' – 'Good night, Yorgi.' – 'Goodnight, my little Turcala.'

I wanted to give up my diamond at last. I thought, before I return to Istanbul I must save myself from this diamond in Berlin. Angel had given up her diamond, Gutsio didn't have a diamond any more, up on the sixth floor the girl with the dead embryo didn't have a diamond either. And all of them put on and took off their coats just as I did and could open doors. Open letters. Smoke a cigarette. Switch off a light. They still liked the taste of macaroni. They could also look at a film at the cinema without a diamond. I lay in bed and swore by the headlights of the passing cars on the wall that I would save myself from my diamond. But I didn't know how and wanted to ask Gutsio when she came back. But she didn't come back again. I heard from Yorgi that she had gone to Greece. Yorgi said: 'She'll end up in prison one day, but she wanted to fight there, instead of phoning Greece from here.' After that Yorgi left too. The Siemens managers said: 'Tomorrow we'll send you a new hostel warden, a Turkish one.' In the night I walked up and down the six corridors, and again saw cockroaches scuttling along the walls. When I switched on the automatic light, they disappeared under the doors of the workers' rooms. I sat down in my room and waited for Gutsio to turn a page in Kafka's book next door again or for Yorgi to cough. I said a few words in Greek out loud to myself: *'Bre pedakimu sagapo.'* No page was turned next door, no one coughed. Only the cars raced past outside on the main road. I opened the door to Gutsio's room; in the ashtray on the table there were still a couple of Yorgi's cigarette stubs, and on the floor there was a little plate with water, which Yorgi's cat had half drunk. I phoned Gutsio in Greece. 'Sugar doll,' she said, 'how are you? I miss you.' – 'I don't want to stay here any more. Yorgi's gone. The cat's gone.' – 'You should go, too. Have you seen Paris? Go to Paris. I've got a friend there. Write down the address. Then go to drama school. And I shall come to see you on the stage. You're my Cassandra. *Yasu pedakimu yasu.'*

# The Sudden Rain Came Down Like Thousands of Bright Needles

I bought a plane ticket from Berlin to Hanover, from Hanover I took the train to Paris. When people got on, I told them which compartments were empty. I was once again the interpreter at Siemens, who picked people up and brought them to their rooms. Men came in, I said to them: 'Do sit down, I'll put your suitcases on the rack.' If it was raining outside, I translated: 'It's raining', 'The rain has stopped' or: 'Now we're in Liège'. When the man with the coffee trolley came past, I walked along the train corridor in front of him and said to people: 'The coffee man's coming.' When the lid of the train ashtray snapped shut, I said: 'The ashtray lid has shut.' I asked the ticket inspector how many hours it was before we reached Paris. Then I told people: 'Another three hours to Paris.'

In Paris I had to get to the Cité Universitaire station by Métro; first I got lost and looked for the German language on the Paris streets. When I heard German-speaking people, I asked them the way. A German man took me to Cité Universitaire on the Métro. The Métro was full of people and so our faces came very close. I had never stood so close to a German before. He asked me: 'Can you speak English' – 'No, I cannot, little bit. I can say only: "The maid washed the dishes and can I put my head on your shoulder". After I had handed out all my English words, I asked why he wanted to talk to me in English. He said: 'In Paris I'm ashamed of the German language, it's the language of Goebbels and Hitler.' I said: 'I love Kafka.' On the Métro I noticed that when he spoke to French people the young German man was always excusing himself, just as I did in German. *'Pardon, madame, pardon, monsieur'.* With a lot of *'pardon, madame, pardon, monsieur'* we found the Greek student *maison* in the Cité Universitaire in which Gutsio's friend lived. It was already well after nightfall. The janitor said to the young man I should take a seat, he would look for Gutsio's friend, because there was a big party going on in the house and all the students were dancing. The German boy said 'goodbye' and left. I was very tired. The janitor couldn't find Gutsio's friend, because he had gone to Marseilles. Another Greek boy came and told me in English: 'He went to Marseilles, conference contra militaire junta Greek.' The janitor's wife invited me into her room, I lay down on a couch and fell asleep. The next day the janitor took me to another *maison*, where Turkish students lived. I knocked on a door, the Turkish student was still in his pyjamas. He pulled his trousers over them, poured tea into a tumbler and gave it to me. I sat down on a chair beside his desk and told him that I had come from Berlin, Madame Gutsio had given me the address of her Greek friend, who had, however, gone to Marseilles for a political meeting against the Greek military coup. The Turkish student said: 'We will take care of you, miss,' put two spoonfuls of sugar in my tea glass, stirred it for a long time with a spoon and, as the sugar dissolved in the tea glass, all the time looked into my eyes, as if he could read something in them. 'Wait here,' he said, and went out. The chair had very short legs and very high armrests. When I placed my arms on them, I looked like someone sitting in a wheelchair. A clock ticked in the room and from time to time two students or a single student walked past the window. I saw only their heads, the heads looked almost identical. No doubt every one of them had a ticking clock in his little room and the same curtains, the same tables and chairs, in which one looked as if one were sitting in a wheelchair. The room was a bit like a hospital room, but the patient, who had perhaps been living there for two years, was allowed to wash his own clothes. The student had put his shirt, his underpants and socks in the one basin, in which they lay entwined in yellowish water. The floor was freshly polished; my shoes had rubber soles which stuck a little to the polished floor. Then the student came back with two other Turkish students. They all shook my hand and sat down next to one another on the bed. They waited and didn't say anything. Except the bed creaked somewhat. My chair creaked too. I bent down to the polished floor to my holdall and saw the shadows of the three students on the polished floor. The shadows looked as if their heads were close together and they were whispering. Startled, I sat up, but I had been mistaken. Each sat there isolated from the others with a sleepy expression on his face. The zip on my bag was half open, I drew it shut and was about to stand up. At that moment a man wearing glasses came into the room. He smiled and sat down on the empty chair beside the desk, a normal chair, so that he was sitting a little higher than I was. He put on the desk lamp. It was a sunny day, but he put on the light. 'It's a quarter to eleven,' he said, as he pressed the top of his ballpoint down. I stared at this ballpoint for a while, and thought how skilfully he was handling the ballpoint, how little noise he was making. He asked me what the Turkish students in Berlin were doing, what the atmosphere was like. I said 'cool', but he meant the political atmosphere – whether some of the students were communists. I said: 'Yes.' He wanted to know the names of the communists and pressed the top of his ballpoint again. But I replied: 'I can't ever remember names.' He wrote something down. Then a chubby, older Turkish man came into the room. He, too, sat down, switched off the desk lamp, gave me a cigarette, showed me postcards of the Eiffel Tower and the Champs Elysées and told me when they had been built. When he showed me the Eiffel Tower photographs, he breathed heavily, as if he were just climbing the Eiffel Tower stairs, and in between he asked me again for the names of the Turkish communists in Berlin. The others all had their teacups at their mouths, as the chubby Turk asked me for the names, and suddenly the cups remained at their mouths. I told the older Turk what I had already told the other with the glasses. He waited a little, then he took his postcards from the table, straightened them like playing cards and put them in his pocketbook. At that the others put their teacups, which had still been at their mouths without them having drunk anything, on the saucers and stood up. The older Turk took me to a hotel, where a couple of other Turkish students were also living.

During the night there was a knock at the door, a good-looking Turkish man came in and sat on my bed, the room was very small. He said: 'We are both far from our country, we are both Turks, we could console one another.' I did not know why the Turks should console the Turks in Paris, laughed and pulled the blanket over my face. He kissed me through the blanket and also asked me how many Turks in Berlin were communists, what were their names, what did they say. I said: 'I'm a communist myself.' Then he was suddenly naked and hot. I liked it very much, that he had such a hot body. I said: 'I still have my diamond.' He didn't understand. I said: 'I'm a virgin, but want to free myself of it.' The Paris hotel bed was small and had a hollow in the middle. The Turkish student with the hot body wanted to free me of my diamond, but he constantly observed his body as he kissed my mouth or my breast. He tensed his arm muscles and his chest as if he were a statue on a plinth and observed how well he was doing everything. I, too, began to observe him, and with all the observing that was going on my diamond stayed with me. When he left towards morning, he said: 'You don't even know what you've missed, I could have made a woman of you, in the capital, Ankara, I was the lover of a famous opera singer.' Then he left. His heat remained in the bed, and I liked this quiet fire, I embraced this heat and fell asleep. In the morning, when I left the room, the older Turk was suddenly standing in the hotel lobby. He had been waiting for me, quickly brushed the croissant crumbs from his jacket and wanted to show me Montmartre. As we walked up the steps of a Montmartre street, he asked me again which Turks in Berlin were communists. He again breathed very heavily, at some point I began breathing like him, then we were standing at the bottom of a very steep, long stairway, which he had difficulty climbing. I ran ahead, ran down another street, found the Métro and went to the Cité Universitaire.

In the Cité Universitaire garden I looked for the cafeteria. Suddenly someone whistled behind me, I was wearing black net stockings. I didn't turn round, from Istanbul I was used to men whistling. Nevertheless I wiggled my bum a little because of the whistles. I walked between the shadows of the trees, as if I didn't want to disturb these shadows. The earth showed me the shadows of my legs, they were very thin, very long, then another leg shadow was walking beside mine, I only looked at the ground. Then the other leg shadow walked through my legs. We walked and walked. The cafeteria had a swing door, there our shadows disappeared. As I stood in front of the cafeteria woman with my empty tray and pointed at what I wanted to eat, another tray bumped into mine and the water in the glass on my tray trembled a little. The boy wore glasses, his arm touched mine, but he too only looked at the food, which the cafeteria woman was just putting on his plate. I sat down at a free table and soon I saw another tray there beside mine. I saw only his hands, which cut the meat on the plate at the same time as my hands or put the mashed potato on the spoon. Then I left my spoon lying beside the mashed potato, he did the same. Then I took the glass of water and drank, and he, too, took his glass of water and spoke – the glass of water in front of his mouth – to me, as if he was speaking to his glass. 'Pardon,' I said, 'I cannot speak French.' He swallowed a mouthful of water, then he said: 'Can you speak English?' I swallowed a mouthful of water and said: 'No, little bit.' He too swallowed a mouthful and said: 'I cannot speak English too, little bit.' Simultaneously we put our glasses on the cafeteria trays. Both glasses were only half empty, and the water in both glasses trembled a little. His jacket arm touched my pullover arm. My mohair pullover left hairs on his jacket arm. Behind us the canteen ladies counted the small change on the plates. The lights were on, it was very loud in the canteen. Nobody noticed when someone left. I didn't notice either, when I left. It was as if a second self were walking beside me. The sudden rain came down like thousands of bright needles, and the water needles went on playing with one another on the ground. The rain went through my black net stocking holes and soon made my shoes wet from the inside. The self beside me walked beside the boy, who had thrown his raincoat over his shoulders like a matador. He took this raincoat and held it over his head and over the head of the self walking beside me. They walked and walked, and the rain made loud noises on the material of the coat as if it were a tent. Then they went into a student hostel, they were lucky, the janitor was just making a phone call with his back to the window. They ran up the stairs and went into a room, me with them. The big room had a staircase, at the top there was another room. I sat down on the staircase and looked at the girl, who was supposed to be me, and at the boy. The boy said: 'I am from Spain.' The girl said: 'I am Turkish.' The boy went over to his books, took a book of poetry and read a poem in French.

He said: 'Nazim Hikmet, great socialist poet Turk.' I had only heard the name. Then the boy put on a record by Yves Montand and said: 'Yves Montand sings a poem of Nazim Hikmet, you know?' – 'No, I don't know,' said the girl. He took the arm of the record player and put the needle on a particular song. Yves Montand sang: '*Tu es comme un scorpion frère. Tu es comme un scorpion frère.*' The boy sat down beside the girl on the stairs. He spoke French and sang with Yves Montand: '*Tu es comme un scorpion frère.*' The girl didn't understand any French, but when the word *frère* came, she repeated it. The boy laughed and said: '*Frère* like brother.' I asked: 'Have you brother?' – 'Yes, five brother, and my father is great mathematic professor in Spain.' The girl repeated the word 'Mathematic'. 'Yes, mathematic,' said the boy. Suddenly

Yves Montand wasn't singing any more. I got frightened. I said to myself, what will the girl do now, the music is over, will she have to stand up, will she have to go? The boy stood up, however, and put on another record, Ravel's 'Bolero'. The girl took off her wet shoes, pushed her fingers through the holes of her net stockings and put her warm hands on her wet feet. She listened to the music, but not with her ears, with her eyes and her mouth, and the boy, too, looked at her face, as if he was hearing Ravel's 'Bolero' from her face. I looked at the room. Opposite the staircase next to the record player there was a desk, on which there were books and a couple of framed photographs. In one the boy danced with a girl, and in the other this girl with curly hair looked into my eyes. Outside the rain had stopped, the powerful sun grew into the room and broke into more beams against the silver frames of the pictures, in the room the rain from before still dripped from the boy's raincoat. When Ravel's 'Bolero' was finished, the sun in the room had dried the raincoat and the girl's net stockings a bit. Suddenly the two of them went up the stairs. At the top, at the end of the staircase, stood a bed. I remained standing further down the stairs, and saw my pullover, my skirt, the net stockings, the suspender, bra and the underpants slowly slide down the handrail from the top, to be left hanging on top of one another at the end of the rail. The sun fell through the holes of the net stockings hanging on the banister, and in the sun the mohair hair of my pullover rose very slowly in the room. The mohair tickled in my nose. Then the boy's trousers and shirt slid down from the top and covered my clothes on the handrail. The sun now fell straight on to the metal of the boy's belt and remained hanging in the air as a long beam. I tried to take this sunbeam in my hand, then I went upstairs and took a look at the bed. The boy and the girl had disappeared under the blanket. The blanket was moving, and I didn't know where the girl was, on top, below, beside the boy, on the right or the left. They remained under the blanket for so long that I laid my head on the bed and waited. Suddenly the boy's hand was in my hair, he divided my hair on the pillow and said:

'You are a child.' When he said 'child', he made a slight movement of his head towards my legs. 'Yes, yes,' I said, 'I am a child.' Both had thick lips from all the kissing, the blood flowed quickly under their lips and showed three different colours. I looked at their mouths, and they threw off the blankets. The boy had put down his glasses beside the bed and had to concentrate on looking, that way his eyes looked very beautiful. The girl drew him to her again, but I found an English word in my head, which I had long ago forgotten, the word came suddenly, like a smell from a chest that had been shut for too long: 'Wait'. I prompted the girl 'Wait.' She said 'Wait,' the boy waited, she waited. They both waited naked on top of one another, the sun warmed the back and the stomach of the boy and it warmed the stomach of the girl. Her breasts didn't listen to her eyes. The eyes waited, but the nipples didn't wait. I looked at the girl's breasts, and the girl looked into the boy's eyes. The girl's eyes enlarged the boy's eyes for so long, until he became a single eye. The sun gave its last breath and slowly withdrew from their bodies. So, in the shade, they stood up, they got dressed at the same time. When they walked past the photographs on the desk, I asked the boy: 'Who is this girl?' – 'She's my wife, she's in England this time,' he said. The girl buttoned up her jacket. They drove in a car, and the girl looked at Paris behind the boy's profile. There is the Eiffel Tower lit up, it disappeared so quickly, then she saw the boy's profile again. The people outside walked slowly home, their long loaves in their hands. The boy and the girl sat down at a table in a restaurant. The long bread, which the French carried in their hand or under their arm, lay cut in slices on the table. The boy broke the bread into small pieces, as if they were two birds, and from time to time put a piece in her mouth, then he told her about a Spanish poet, Lorca. The military had killed him when he was a young man, but he had written many poems. The boy recited a poem by Lorca: 'Hei Luna, Luna, Lunada'. Luna means moon. He translated: Gypsies took the moon, cut it up and made earrings of it. The restaurant was small and had a sloping floor. An old woman brought the food, then she went on rinsing plates behind the bar; the restaurant was called 'Chez Marie'. The door was opening and closing all the time, new people were constantly coming in, at the tables everyone bit loudly into the baguettes, they crackled so loudly that the conversations couldn't be heard because of it. Everyone sat there and ate snails. It wasn't easy to eat snails. As a child I had once seen my parents collecting snails in the wood, they were still sticking to the wet leaves or to the earth and were leaving behind their slime. They collected them and put them in a pot with a lot of water overnight. The snails were supposed to lose consciousness and release their slime. My parents put this pot with the snails in the bathroom, but forgot to weigh down the lid with a stone. The next morning we woke up surrounded by many snails. Together they had raised the pot lid, had crawled out of the pot and were now sticking to the walls and the floor in all the rooms. My mother said she couldn't eat snails any more, because they had now become our guests. We collected all the snails and brought them back to the wood wrapped in soft cloths. The girl wanted to tell the boy this story in English, but there weren't enough words, so she went on eating. They said nothing and ate and laughed. All the objects the waitress placed on the table made a small noise, but these noises didn't pull them away from one another. The objects came and went, he took a bottle, poured out water or wine, but there was no risk to the two of them. They registered the colour of the wine or water, but these colours or noises did not distract the couple from one another. All objects served the couple, the couple didn't serve the objects.

When they left, the boy took his white raincoat from the hook and again threw it over his shoulders like a matador. So they walked to the car, the Eiffel Tower twinkled in the car window. But the girl didn't turn round. Then the boy realised that the coat he had taken from the hook in the restaurant was not his. His coat was lying on the back seat. He looked at the strange coat and said: 'It is okay' and put it on top of his white raincoat on the back seat. So they drove to the Cité Universitaire with two raincoats. When they got out of the car, it was raining again, and again the rain in the headlights looked like thousands of bright needles. The boy took his coat and again covered his head and the girl's head with it, again there was the noise, as if rain were falling on a tent. The rain was good, warm hearted. It was good to enter a room with wet stockings, hair and shoes. Fresh air came out of the sleeves of the jackets. Because of the wet and cold clothes they naturally got undressed. So they came close to one another like lambs. The boy put on a record again, a choir of Spanish men sang love songs. Outside it rained, and the rain struck the window, but inside men sang, and the girl listened more to them than to the rain. The boy knelt down, and while all the men called out for love, he sang along with them: 'Que bella rosa' and embraced the girl's legs. I listened to the songs, it sounded as if some didn't have any teeth in their mouth any more. It was good to hear the voices of the men, of those who still had teeth in their mouth, and of those who no longer had teeth in their mouth, and all of them talked about love, 'Que bella rosa, rosa, rosa'. It was nice to put one's hand in the hair of a man, who was on his knees and singing along. I felt that the girl was in good men's hands and voices. I closed my eyes and the last thing I heard amid the singing men's voices was the voice of the boy. He said to the girl: 'You are a crazy horse.' When he had brought her to his room the first time, she had been child, now she was a crazy horse. The boy reminded me of a picture in which a boy, in short trousers and barefoot, stood in front of a dog and held the hand of another boy above the big dog, they were talking to one another and were so serious against a big sky. That's how the girl and the boy lay in bed. The boy followed the girl's movements with tremendous concentration, that way they both looked like a single body. It kept on raining, and each time rain struck the window another piece of furniture disappeared. Then all the objects in the room disappeared. The bed, too, in which the boy and the girl were lying, disappeared. The girl and the boy slowly flew up in the room, on the floor I saw only the girl's and boy's clothes and shoes mixed up together. The boy and the girl breathed deeply and took hold of one another in mid-air. Their breathing was so strong that now their clothes, too, floated into the air. Here one of the boy's shoes, there the girl's skirt. My net stockings also floated slowly through the room, became entangled with the boy's shoelaces and floated together. Suddenly I saw two women standing next to one another in the air. One was my mother, the other the boy's mother. I thought, good, that you gave birth to us, and clapped my hands. The boy's mother blew me a kiss in mid-air, and my mother looked at the boy as if she, too, loved him very much. I floated towards my mother, but the boy held me tight, ran his hands through my hair and divided it in the air, to the right, to the left. He had very beautiful hair, I held my hands in his hair and felt the beard growing in the night against my cheeks and my chin. The beard from his cheeks and above his mouth grew into my cheeks, so that our faces stuck together. Small fires lit up above our bodies. Sometimes beads of sweat fell from the neck, the forehead or the breast of the boy on to my body. These beads of sweat extinguished a flame, then the flame lit up again. Outside it went on raining, and in the room now a fire, now drops of water dripped from our bodies. *lovely*

I woke up. The wind and the rain blew open a window, and the window knocked over the things on the desk. The picture of the boy's wife fell over, paper flew through the room, and the pages of a newspaper opened. I saw the girl and the boy in the bed. The boy, too, was woken by the banging window; half asleep, he went downstairs and shut the window. I put the photo of his wife back in its place. He went to the refrigerator, took out a gin bottle and a whisky bottle, poured something from both bottles into a glass, went up to the bed again, sat on the edge, looked at the girl lying in the bed, and then looked at the floor, where their clothes lay tossed together. He took the girl's vest, it was a man's vest, laid it across his naked knee, looked at it and emptied the glass very quickly, then he looked helplessly into the air. Now his hands looked for his spectacles beside the bed. He found them, put them on and, as if he had regained his hands because of the spectacles, took hold of the girl, put on her clothes, put on his own clothes and tied the laces of the girl's shoes and his own shoes. I glanced at the bed, it was still warm from their bodies, but I saw no spots of blood. I quickly followed the girl and sat down behind her in the car, I wanted to tell her, free yourself from your diamond, do it with the boy. But I didn't manage to, because the boy drove with his left hand and with his right drew the girl towards him and put his arm around her. She sang a Turkish song in his ear:

> When I went to Üsküdar, it had begun to rain.
> Oh, the starched shirt suits my love so well.
> I belong to him, he belongs to me.
> What is there left for strangers' mouths to say.

The boy drove through Paris for a long time, until he could sing along. So the girl didn't see much of Paris, because she was constantly singing the song in his ears, she only saw his profile, his eyelashes, his unshaven cheeks, his lips, saw them enlarged – and she didn't see Paris. Then I saw the horses. The boy said: 'Crazy horse, here are the horses.' The horses ran, the people held the betting slips in their hands. I saw the hoofs of the horses, the open mouths of the people. The people moved to the rhythm of the horses they had backed. The boy and the girl had no betting slips in their hands, so they loved all the horses. At the end the people went home. Everything was empty now, only the betting slips lay on the grass. The boy and the girl sat down in the empty stadium, the betting slips moved between their feet with the evening wind. They said nothing for a long time, their English was only *a little bit*. He took off his glasses, cleaned them and looked at the girl without his glasses, his eyes again looked very beautiful. He said: 'Crazy horse.' The girl laughed. He looked into these laughing eyes for a long time. 'You know guillotine?' asked the boy. 'Yes,' said the girl, 'I know guillotine from film.' They drove to Versailles, the guillotine was not to be seen, but many mirrors and a polished floor and lots of people following tourist guides. The

pair were unable to stand alone in front of the mirrors in which
Marie Antoinette had looked at herself every day.

But then the people, who had walked from one room to the
next in Versailles as if sewn together, were in the garden and there
they also followed their tourist guides as if sewn together. The
garden was laid out geometrically, in it the people, too, looked
like geometric signs. The boy and the girl stayed by the window
and looked at the people walking past below. As they walked back
through the now empty rooms and again passed by a mirror, the
boy went down on his knees in front of the mirror and kissed the
girl's knees. His head remained leaning against the girl's knees
for quite a while, so that the girl could look at this picture in the
mirror alone. There she saw a whole girl and half a man, who was
kneeling in front of her. The half-man said in the mirror: 'Mon
amour.' Then he said: 'What is *mon amour* in Turkish?' She said to
the mirror: 'Sevgilim.' 'Sevgilim, Sevgilim, Sevgilim,' said the half-man.
I looked at the girl. She held her hands in his hair and thought
about him and looked towards the end of the room, where a door
was open; she kept her hands in the boy's hair, but suddenly she
saw the same boy go out through this door. She left the mirror
and followed the second boy. For a moment I still saw the first
boy on his knees in the mirror, then he, too, left the place in front
of the mirror, in the mirror there remained only the empty room
with a window. The girl walked behind the second boy, the first
boy walked behind the girl, I walked behind all of them.

Outside stood the first boy's car and it took us all. I sat in the
back, and the second boy sat beside me. No one said anything.
The darkness came and swallowed us all, the car moved as if it
had something heavy to carry, slowly. So the light of the street
lamps or of the many light bulbs, which hung above the wet
fish in the fishmongers', stayed in the car for longer. When these
street lamps shone into the car for a while, the girl looked in
the rear-view mirror, to see whether the second boy was still
sitting there. She saw him sitting there and took a deep breath.
Then the lights disappeared, she sat in the darkness, afraid that

he wouldn't be there any more. The first boy in front noticed that the girl was somewhere else. From the girl's body he heard voices, as if a child were crying. The girl smoked a cigarette and blew the smoke towards the back seat. The first boy saw the smoke in the rear-view mirror and wound the window down a little. The night voices came in through the open window. Parked cars, moving cars, quietly opening café doors. The lights in the houses looked so safe, as if no one inside would ever die. It was impossible to see how the people inside walked, sat, there was no one to be seen standing at the window with a glass of water in his hand. The houses rebuffed the life outside. But one was curious to get inside them. The whole city was a big museum, only the cafés were as lively as brothels. The city flowed backwards beside the car, the bridges came, the water flowed below. The second boy, who sat beside me, looked out of the window into the water. The four of us got out of the car at the Cité Universitaire. The girl again walked behind the second boy. The janitor of the student hostel wasn't there, the curtains of his window were drawn. The first boy was about to press the automatic light switch in the corridor. I said to him: 'I must go to Berlin tomorrow morning. My fly ticket finished tomorrow.' Immediately he began to tremble so badly that he missed the light switch. So we went upstairs in the dark. He opened the door in the dark, the four of us entered the room. Then he put on the lights everywhere and nevertheless went from one switch to the next like a blind man. The girl sat on the stairs, and the second boy sat in front of her. The first boy still looked like a blind man, knelt with closed eyes in front of the steps on which the girl was sitting and recited a poem.

> Mon enfant, ma soeur,
> Songe à la douceur
> D'aller là-bas vivre ensemble!
> Aimer à loisir,
> Aimer et mourir

*Au pays qui te ressemble!*
*Les soleils mouillés*
*De ces ciels brouillés*
*Pour mon esprit ont les charmes*
*Si mystérieux*
*De tes traîtres yeux,*
*Brillant à travers leurs larmes.*


*Là, tout n'est qu'ordre et beauté,*
*Luxe, calme et volupté.*


After that the first boy remained kneeling in front of the girl. The girl began to cry and between her tears went on looking at the shoulder of the second boy. I scratched both my cheeks, they itched and stung. All four of us went to bed, the lights stayed on, I went on scratching at both my cheeks. The girl embraced the second boy, the first boy said: 'I have cold' and pulled on his pyjama jacket, and as he was buttoning up the jacket, I whispered to the girl, 'This is the last night. Sleep with him,' and undid the pyjama buttons of the first boy again. He had a temperature, so that even the buttons were hot. 'You are sick,' I said. 'Yes, I am,' he said, 'this is a *Love Story*.' I turned the girl to him, placed her arms and hands on him, but the girl was holding the second boy in her right arm, so the second boy turned over to the first boy with her and the three of them embraced. She could hardly see the first boy any more, the second boy was always coming between them, and she embraced him more than the first boy. The first boy pulled a blanket over the girl, she couldn't be seen any more. He said: 'You are already in Berlin, you are already lost in the black forest. I cannot find you.' Then he embraced the girl with the blanket. The blanket was soon wet because of his temperature, I kept on scratching my cheeks, they stung and itched. My wet hair stuck to my cheeks and hurt them. The boy fell asleep in a fever. The girl under the blanket listened to his breathing, embraced the second boy and wept. The blanket, the bed, everything was wet. I stood up, went down the stairs, all the boy's things stood in their places, table, chairs, shoes, everything cast shadows on the floor or against the walls, as if they had grown out of their shadows. I sat down on a chair, and soon the chair, too, was wet. My body stuck to it. Opposite the chair stood the desk, on it were the photographs of his wife. I stood up, took one of the photos, kissed both her cheeks, switched off the lights, went to the wet bed and waited there for the heavens to come crashing down. The boy sometimes cried out in his fever in his sleep, and I scratched my itchy, stinging cheeks. In the morning the boy had got up, his fever fogged up the lenses of his glasses, he cleaned them with his shirt. The girl had got dressed, stood downstairs with the second boy and was zipping up her bag. The first boy said, 'Wait.' He sat down at his desk, asked the girl what her name was, took an English–Spanish dictionary, looked in it from time to time and wrote something on a sheet of paper, it was a poem and began 'Sevgilim – mon amour'. Underneath the poem was the boy's name, Jordi. 'Your name is Jordi?' asked the girl. Then everything happened very quickly, the four of us were sitting in the car again and no one said anything. Only the first boy stopped the car from time to time and cleaned his glasses, which had steamed up again because of his fever. Then the girl got on the train to Hanover with the second boy. I got on as well and stood behind her at the train window. She had pushed down the window and was looking out at Jordi. Jordi's glasses were steamed up, but he didn't clean them any more, but constantly said the girl's name and 'Sevgilim, Sevgilim'. The train slowly drew out, and I no longer saw Jordi's eyes behind the foggy glasses. So he ran after the train without eyes, and then he was gone. The girl closed the window and sat down in the compartment beside the second boy. Opposite her sat a German woman and a German man, to whom she showed Jordi's poem. As they both read the poem, they smiled, they liked the poem. They translated it into German for the girl, she wrote down their sentences. In English Jordi had written:

Sevgilim
I like Turkish mare,
and your black helmet,
Trotting in Marmara Sea.
I see in this occidental Megalopois,
a joyful poppy,
disturbing all the circulation planning.
This little alcove is broken
and it is impossible to come back
and it is impossible to come on.
To dawn it is a thing of yesterday,
and only a carnation in the night
under the same moon,
in Istanbul, in Barcelona,
remain for tomorrow.
The beginning and the end,
Sevgilim end, Sevgilim beginning.
Your wind, my wind,
in our passionate sky,
only in our.

The German couple who had translated the poem into German
smiled. The woman's eyes glistened, the man had a couple of beads
of sweat on his forehead. They had laboured for love.

# The Free-Range Chickens
# and the Limping Socialist

*I*n Hanover I went with the girl and the second boy to
the airport, but because it was Easter didn't get a seat. I
went to the Travellers' Aid at the railway station, a nun
showed me to a bed with a straw mattress and a stiff blanket in
a dark room. When I sat down on the bed, I noticed that the
girl and the second boy had gone away, I only had Jordi's poem
in my jacket pocket. I went out of the Travellers' Aid on to the
station concourse and wanted to pull a packet of cigarettes out
of a machine. In the station a man was lying on the ground, he
had covered himself with a few old sheets of newspaper. I bent
down and read: SO DON'T SHOOT IN THE HEAD. The magazine
*Pardon* reported that in many big German factories armed works
security units were already being set up. During his research into
the companies *Pardon* journalist Günter Wallraff had introduced
himself as a representative of a fictitious Civil Defence Committee
of a federal ministry. The man who had covered himself with
sheets of newspaper had puked, his eyes were shut, and spittle
was dribbling out of his mouth and slowly collecting on the puke.
I went back to the Travellers' Aid, the nun opened the door to
me and immediately turned round again, the soles of her shoes
were quiet. The nuns were silent, didn't talk to each other nor to
themselves and looked as if they were made only of bones. I sat

down on the straw mattress and wanted to think about Jordi, but in the room it was impossible even to think of hunger or cigarettes. One could only sit there like a stone, everything was like stone, the straw bed, the stiff blanket, oneself. I tried to move the toes of my left foot, they too were made of stone. Through a swing door I came into a naked neon-lit room with a big, long table, a couple of chairs of grey wood. When someone left this room to go to the toilet, the iron doors slammed shut before one could close them behind one, the noise threw iron echoes across the room. The floor was of worn stone, all the people sitting here were either walking with sticks or crutches or were sitting in a wheelchair. When they walked or wheeled themselves around, their crutches or wheels also echoed on the stone floor. When someone with crutches walked towards the toilet, the others followed him with their glances step by step. Echo by echo their eyes went with this man, as far as the toilet, then came the iron-door echo, and they abandoned him for a few moments. Then the toilet flush made loud noises, and they waited for him to come out of the toilet again, and accompanied him at his crutch tempo to his place at the table. Everything moved slowly, only the nuns flitted quickly backwards and forwards. They brought thin hospital tea and grey pieces of bread spread with thin fat. They didn't look at the people, they knew the table and the trays they were carrying.

A woman in a wheelchair was wearing glasses, which always slid down her nose, her son sat beside her and each time pushed the glasses back to their place again.

'What will we cook tomorrow, Mama,' he said, 'when we're at home?' She didn't reply. Then the woman wheeled her chair towards the washbasin, to wash her hands. Her son took off his jacket, laid it across his legs and took a sweet out of the jacket pocket. Then he looked at the sweet so sadly, so sadly; he, too, was wearing glasses, which made his eyes three times larger, so that his sadness also looked three times larger. Very slowly he unwrapped the sweet, put it in his mouth, and then he didn't know what to do with the wrapper, a blue piece of paper. The tea glass didn't have a saucer on which to place the paper. So first he laid the sweet wrapper on the table and ironed it flat. Once he had ironed it flat, he listened to the sounds of water from the washbasin, where his mother was washing her hands. I wanted to think of Jordi, but only looked at the blue sweet wrapper. Now his mother slowly wheeled herself back, the rubber wheels slowed down on the stone, and the boy folded the sweet wrapper until it was very small. The woman said: 'Jürgen, shall we go to sleep?' – 'Yes, Mama,' he said, left the folded sweet paper on the table, and they went out through the swing door. I remained alone in the big room and thought, now I can think about Jordi – how his leg shadow walked between my leg shadows, how the rain came down as thousands of bright needles, how he held his coat over our heads and the rain made sounds on it as on a tent. Then the swing door opened again, and a nun came with a tray and collected all the tea glasses. I took the sweet wrapper away before she discovered it. The neon light was so bright that I kept on looking at the cracks in the wooden table and in the stone floor and counted the holes. Then I, too, began to iron the sweet wrapper flat on the table. I ironed it and ironed it, it was not possible to think about Jordi.

The swing door opened again, and a young man in a black suit came in, he said 'Good evening' and sat down at the table opposite me. 'My name's Olaf,' he said. He hadn't got a seat on the plane either. He saw the sweet wrapper, put his cigarette packet down beside it and said: 'My father is a pastor, but I'm not religious.' He smoked, also gave me a cigarette each time, blew smoke in my face and talked. 'Oh,' he said, 'how I enjoy smoking.' Then: 'You know, you won't believe it, but... You know, my grandfather was in the Foreign Legion. His brothers had to buy him out with their study allowances, that's why they were mad at him. He came back, married, and you won't believe it, he ordered his wife not to smoke in the house. She only smoked in the shed. You won't believe it, but he died, and she still only smokes in the shed. You won't believe it, but my father is a pastor and has a doctorate. He got married three times, he always has to screw. He also wanted to write novels, but instead he had to write his life story for his psychiatrist. The psychiatrist had to give this life story to the private health insurance, so that the treatment was paid for. So he had a career with the private health insurance company as a happy fucker. As a pastor he wasn't allowed to marry a fourth time, otherwise he would have lost his pension and would not have been allowed to be a pastor any more. His third wife had cancer, her teeth fell out. You won't believe it, but during the cancer operation on his third wife he sat beside her for four hours and held her hand so that she didn't die. But even if she had died, he wouldn't have been allowed to marry a fourth time. Now he's retired and is working as a taxi driver. You won't believe it, but he told me he had a woman fare, who wanted to go to a male brothel, she wanted to be screwed by a man. So my father said to her, I can do that for you too, madame, I'll simply leave the clock running. Once, as pastor, he had to help a ninety-two-year-old blind woman across the road. He gave her his arm, and you won't believe it, but she said to him: "Young man, don't hold on to me so tightly, otherwise I can't help you across the road."'

Then Olaf asked me: 'Have you slept with someone yet?' Before I could say something, he again blew his cigarette smoke in my face and said: 'I've slept with two fourteen-year-old sisters, one night with the blonde one, the next night with the black-haired one. I hope later on they'll be as beautiful as you. But I don't sleep with girls any more. Imagine two sheets of paper, which you stick together. Try to take them apart, one sheet gets torn, because parts of it remains sticking to the other. It's the same with man and woman. Men have a cock, women a hole. You can take the cock out, but the woman is still left sticking to the man nevertheless.' A nun came through the swing door, looked crossly at the cigarettes in our hands and withdrew. Olaf stood up and said: 'Thank you for listening to me. You won't believe it, but now I have to go to sleep.' And he, too, disappeared through the swing door.

The next morning I flew to Berlin with two marks in my pocket and looked in Kafka's book for the telephone number of

Ataman's friend Bodo. A girl's voice said on the telephone: 'Bodo's at the university. I know, you're Ataman's friend, Bodo told me. Do you know your way around Berlin?' – 'At Zoo Station I know Aschinger's pea soup restaurant.' – 'Wait there, we'll pick you up. I'm Heidi.' Heidi had buck teeth, she giggled when she saw me. Bodo had big blue eyes and his head was a little too big for his body. He blinked a couple of times and said: 'I've already got somewhere for you to stay, in the flat of an old lady, quite far out, but the underground goes right to the door. What do you want to do in Berlin?' – 'I have to earn money, then I'd like to go to drama school.' – 'Today and tomorrow you can sleep at my grandfather's, he's an old Social Democrat and half blind.' Bodo said: 'I'm in the Socialist Students' Association, the SDS. You know, I'm German, but I find the Germans creepy. Every German looks at his neighbour and thinks he's better off than I am.'

Bodo's grandfather had only one room and was already in bed. Bodo said to him: 'Grandfather, here's a Turkish sultaness.' Bodo's grandfather had a very thick moustache. The room was dark. He twirled his moustache and said: 'Am but a poor shoemaker, my lamp it burns so low.' Bodo laughed and said: 'That's not by him. It's by a German writer, Büchner. He recited it when he was six.' Bodo and Heidi pulled out the settee, to make a bed for me. Bodo said: 'I live downstairs, tomorrow we'll look for a job for you. Till tomorrow.' I remained with the old, half-blind grandfather and lay down in bed. Some time later the old man asked me in the dark: 'Are you really a Turkish sultaness?' – 'No, no, I'm a socialist.' The old man said: 'Back then I wrapped my sandwiches in the *Workers' Paper* and during the break secretly read it under my sandwiches. Everyone had to give the Hitler salute, I did it with my right hand, but I kept the left hand in my pocket and made a fist. Give me your hand.' I got up, went over to the old man and gave him my hand. He held it for a couple of minutes in his, then he let go, and held the hand in which he had been holding my hand to his nose and so went to sleep. That night in the room of the old, half-blind man I was able to think of Jordi for the first time. All the moments we had together passed in front of my eyes, and I knew at that moment that in my whole life he would remain my great love. I told myself, you wanted to free yourself of your diamond, why didn't you leave it with him in Paris? Because I was angry with myself, I saw Jordi alone in front of me. I followed his movements – how he looked for his glasses, how he had thrown his coat over his shoulders, how he sat at the table and wrote a poem. I took myself out of the remembered pictures and enlarged only the pictures of him. Towards morning I was still lying awake in bed, no one could take him away from me. Then I fell asleep. In the morning Bodo came, brought fresh rolls, his half-blind grandfather spread jam on the roll for me. 'Eat, Turkish sultaness, eat,' he said. Bodo opened the newspaper and looked for a job for me. Then he said: 'Hotel Berlin is looking for chambermaids,' and drove me to Hotel Berlin. I could already start there the next day as a chambermaid. Then he said: 'Now we'll go to the Café Steinplatz, the Café Steinplatz is the heart of the student movement. Everyone meets there. There's a cinema there, it shows all the best films. Do you know the film-makers Eisenstein, Godard, Alexander Kluge?' – 'No, I've never been to a cinema in Berlin.' Bodo said: 'Films are the only common language of the world.' We got to the Café Steinplatz. *La Chinoise* by Godard was running in the cinema. We drank coffee, and Bodo told me about the student movement. He blinked at almost every sentence, as if each blink was a comma or a full stop in one of his sentences. He said: 'We students boo, whistle, provoke, we oppose professors who can't see anything beyond their subject and we're against reaction in the German education system. We condemn the grand coalition in Bonn, the war in Vietnam and the dictatorship in Athens. When we have sit-ins, the rector, Hans-Joachim Lieber, says that has fascist features. The Germans have always tried to cut off their left side. When a woman journalist asked this Hans-Joachim Lieber whether he would have stood for election as rector if he had foreseen the student attacks, he replied: "One would have to be a masochist, no, no, no." Yet he's a sadist. He cancelled our matriculation ceremony. But we collected money for the Vietcong in Berlin and demonstrated in the streets against US intervention in Vietnam. We simply went on to the street. Last Wednesday the German president, Heinrich Lübke, came to the Free University, for a 125th anniversary commemoration of the decoration Pour le mérite. We were there to whistle and boo him and shouted: "Give money for the Vietcong." Lübke was accompanied by Ernst Lämmer of the CDU, who tapped his head and shouted: "You're all drunk." But just look at the SPD. Already weeks ago when we were demonstrating on Kurfürstendamm, Herbert Wehner asked the local politician with him, in front of all of us: "Tell me, is the whole of Berlin a zoo?" The students who live in hostels in Dahlem don't even have a student bar, there are only posh villas for the traditional CDU voters out there. Prize-winning poodles are allowed to shit everywhere there, but what do you think would happen if a student were to pee against a tree? The Berlin CDU boss, Franz Amrehn, said about the student movement: "Result of mental softening of the bones." The SPD says almost exactly the same word for word. The office of the SDS, the Socialist Students' Association, is in a half-ruined building on Kurfürstendamm. Two floors down, there's a coffin store, on the door it says: "Funerals of every kind". Two floors up there's the SDS, and they have a sign: "Rebellion is justified". Have you heard of Dutschke? Do you know he's a non-smoker? In the East he was a member of a church youth group, he came to the West three days before the Wall was built. He has an American wife, a theology student, her name's Gretchen. Dutschke says: "The commune is a new form of freedom, and the long-term aim is to turn the whole of Berlin into communes." Since then two groups have set about putting Dutschke's theory into practice. One group wants to work in such a way that thanks to them gradually the whole of society can be radically changed. The second group is the "Horror Commune". They are looking for a new form of freedom, that is, the dissolution of all private relations, including sexual relations. The "Horror Commune" once distributed leaflets which had not been approved by the association, and the SDS expelled the leader of the commune. You know, there are two kinds of students, about one group the papers say: "university variant of beatniks", the other group doesn't have Beatle haircuts, is neatly dressed, washed, but they know all the theories of society from Marx to Marcuse, they go swimming, running in the woods. But one set of clothes or another set of clothes, it's six and half a dozen, we want to get rid of authoritarianism in the university and in society and practise democracy. The whole of the Springer press says about us "matriculated, manipulated mob" and links our movement to the East Berlin communist boss Ulbricht.'

While Bodo was telling me about the students, he had drunk eight cups of coffee. He smoked with his left hand, and raised the coffee cup to his mouth with his right hand, and at the points where he talked about the police or about politicians, he didn't stub out his cigarette in the ashtray, but in his coffee cup. Then I heard a quiet hiss, and an unpleasant smell spread, of wet cigarette ends gone soggy in coffee, and this smell stayed in my mind as the smell of the German police and politicians.

In the evening I went to the cinema and saw Godard's film *La Chinoise*. At one point a young man and a young woman sat at a table, on the wall behind them was a poster of Mao. They read political books, made notes and the radio was on. They were lovers, from time to time the boy looked up at the girl, the girl didn't look at him, but concentrated on her work. He looked at her again a couple of times, became restless and said: 'I don't understand, how can you read and listen to the radio at the same time?' She looked at him and said: 'You know, I don't love you.' He became sad, afraid, and said: 'But why, what's the reason?' The girl replied: 'You see, the radio's on, and at the same time you can be sad and afraid.' When the Godard film was over, the students immediately went into the café again and talked about the film. The café looked as if it was everyone's shared kitchen. Everyone could sit down at every table and join in the conversation, without having known someone before. Someone said: 'Don't you think, too, that the film deals with the changes in people who want to change something?' – 'No, they're bourgeois, this girl and the boy, and the way they express themselves is ridiculous. She's sitting in her parents' big apartment and is playing at Marxism-Leninism for two months. But it's her parents' apartment.' – 'I mean, her attitude is anti-bourgeois.' – 'I think her behaviour is bourgeois. Godard is bourgeois too.' In the past, in Istanbul, with my parents, I had seen films like *The Three Musketeers* or films with Liz Taylor, Marilyn Monroe, Clark Gable. Things were said like: 'It's a beautiful film. The end is tragic. Liz Taylor is wonderful'. Or: 'Clark drew too much Clark again'. To draw Clark meant that Clark Gable had pulled too many tragic expressions with his eyebrows. With these old films it was easy to copy the characters. When she was angry at her lover, Liz Taylor poured a glass of water over his jacket. Or she left the apartment and wrote on the mirror in lipstick: 'I'm not for sale'. She always did something theatrical, which was easy to copy. But the characters in the Godard film were not easy to copy, they spoke a new language, which one had to learn first. About Liz Taylor we said: beautiful or fat, that was enough. Beautiful or fat one could imagine. But with the Godard characters one said bourgeois or anti-bourgeois. It was difficult to imagine what bourgeois or anti-bourgeois is.

I started work as a chambermaid in the Hotel Berlin. I made the beds and cleaned the rooms and hotel stairs. Some days as I was working I heard the voices of the demonstrating students outside: 'Killers out of Vietnam, Ho-Ho-Ho-Chi-Minh'. In between these slogans there was sometimes the sound of police sirens, then I heard thousands of people whistling. After work I went to the Café Steinplatz. On the main street, Kurfürstendamm, there were bits of pudding, blancmange, lying on the ground everywhere. The students had demonstrated against the American vice-president, Hubert Humphrey, and tried to throw blancmange at him, the police had arrested many demonstrators for 'Attempts to harm the life and health of US Vice-President Humphrey with blancmange'. During the day the students demonstrated on the streets, in the evening, on the radio or TV, the spokesmen of the Berlin Senate talked about the day, and one said: 'The more cramped the chicken yard – the more wildly the chickens flap about.' To the Berlin Senate the students were chickens. Berlin a henhouse. The politicians were henhouse owners, and the police plucked the chickens' feathers. So during the day the chickens went on to the streets, and in the evening, their feathers half plucked by the police, they drank cocoa, weak beer, coffee in Café Steinplatz. The chickens smoked, the chickens went to the cinema and talked about the films of Godard, Eisenstein and Kluge. Sometimes, among the chickens on the Berlin streets, there was a famous chicken, e.g. Günter Grass, who walked with the other chickens and had a sign around his neck: 'Will Swap Bible for Basic Law'. If university professors were on the side of the chickens, the henhouse owner senate dismissed them, and the henhouse owner senate issued a four-step emergency programme against the free-range chickens:

+ uncompromising application of disciplinary measures against ringleaders and ban on unauthorised chickens in the university;
+ thereafter state-sanctioned action by the university against political chicken groups;
+ after that authority granted to state institutions to issue directives to the chicken university administration;
+ ultimately suspension of the chicken university constitution and appointment of a state commissioner.

The chicken rector ordered that 305 marks monthly be deducted from the grants of five young chicken leaders, including Häussermann, a twenty-three-year-old chicken, and Dutschke. In the chicken lecture theatres one often heard enemies of the chickens say: 'It's crazy here.' The chickens were all supposed to be the secret chickens of the East Berlin leader Ulbricht. Because he wasn't allowed to keep any free-range chickens there, he had raised chickens in West Berlin. But the chickens went on running free, voted at the Free University, and the left-wing chickens won. The rector was sent a leaflet by the Chicken Commune: 'No one wants to take your post as rector of the Walt Disney University away from you.' There were many chickens to be seen on the Berlin streets, all very young chickens, there were hardly any old chickens to be seen.

I lived in the room in the old lady's flat that Bodo had found for me. At night, when I came into the flat, her dog barked; I went to work early in the morning, so that I almost never saw the old lady and her dog, I only knew the voice of her dog. After my work as a chambermaid I went to the chickens, smoked cigarettes with them, drank coffee, beer and went to the cinema. And soon I also got to know Turkish chickens, who walked with the German chickens on the streets and spoke the same chicken language. Every evening the Turkish students went to a Greek bar, in which there sat Greek chickens, whose feathers had been plucked by the Greek military junta, or who were afraid of having their feathers plucked by the Greek military junta. Turkish and Greek chickens danced syrtaki together, drank ouzo, talked together against the Greek military junta, and many Greek chickens, who couldn't go to Greece, went to Turkey on holiday out of homesickness. Turkish and Greek chickens exchanged addresses in Greece and Turkey. Sometimes a chicken that had been really plucked by the army arrived from Greece, and all the other Turkish, Greek, German chickens, who still had their feathers, gathered around it and had enormous respect for this plucked chicken. At that time the students were demonstrating against the Greek military junta, they marched and marched and the next day the newspapers wrote: 'We expect rotten eggs.' Everyone was preoccupied with Greece. Once I was sitting in the Café Steinplatz with the students, and a sculptress came up to me and said: 'Excuse me, I'm a sculptress. You have a very good head, a classic Greek profile. Would you be willing to sit as a model for me and my friend at the art academy?' So after work I sometimes went to the art academy and the two sculptors modelled my head as a classic Greek bust. In the travel agencies there were cheap flights to Greece or cheap hotels, and in the department store one could buy dustbins in the shape of classical columns, but the students refused to support the Greek military junta through tourism. When the students organised a demonstration, old people on the street sometimes talked to them. Once I heard an old man say to a girl: 'But at least Hitler built the autobahn.' Others said they should all go and live on the other side of the Wall in East Berlin. The students listened to these sentences from the non-students with heroic charm. Sometimes the students tried to talk to their enemies, but the students' language was different from that of the older people. It was about words. All the students had big ears, because they heard every word and, like surgeons, immediately dissected them. There were constant post-mortems on the words used, then there were post-mortem reports, which in turn required post-mortems. The Turkish political students also liked to dissect words. When they dissected words, it looked as if they were holding a medical textbook in their right hand and a scalpel in their left. They stood in a circle around the words and read in German how to dissect, then translated it into Turkish and tried it out. They looked like very inexperienced word surgeons, who were just learning to dissect. There were many wrong cuts. Behaviour was also dissected. Once I walked to Café Steinplatz with a Turkish woman student and had my arm in her arm. She said to me: 'Take your arm away, otherwise they'll think we're lesbian.' Earlier in Istanbul I had always walked arm in arm with women, but no one had thought about lesbians because of it. There men, too, walked around arm in arm.

The German students had Dutschke as student leader, soon the Turkish students in Berlin had their own leader. In Café Steinplatz the Turkish students said, this evening there's a meeting at the Turkish Students' Club with the new man from Turkey, he's a communist. After work I went to the Turkish Students' Club; first there was a beauty contest between a couple of Turkish girls. The winner got a floral wreath round her neck. Then the man who had come from Turkey spoke. He announced that the Socialist Workers' Party in Turkey had sent him to Berlin, he had come to set up a Socialist Association with us. Who else wanted to?

The windows of the club room were open, it was a very beautiful evening, there was a lime tree outside the window, there was a strong smell of lime-tree blossom. Eleven students raised their hands. I saw these eleven hands, behind them the lime tree. It looked as if the hands and arms had grown out of the lime tree. Someone counted and said: 'Eleven. Let us be a round dozen.' The word dozen reminded me of our coloured crayons in the art lesson. There were always twelve crayons in a packet, my father gave me a dozen coloured crayons and said: 'Take them, my daughter, these are your crayons, a dozen. Now you can draw beautifully.' I loved the twelve crayons; when one was missing, the other eleven looked sad. In front of me a very slim girl had raised her hand. While they waited for a twelfth hand, the eleven hands remained in the air for a long time. The girl in front of me had a small hand, it trembled in the air. I saw that and raised my hand. 'Now we're okay,' said a voice. Then a photographer came and photographed us. On this photo we were laughing. In the evening the twelve of us went to East Berlin, bought records of Brecht songs and wanted to go dancing in East Berlin and celebrate the new association. The dance place was very full, and we didn't get in. We returned to West Berlin, went to our Greek bar and danced syrtaki with the Greek students there. The socialist man, who had been sent from Turkey to Berlin to set up the association, had one short leg and limped, a limping socialist.

Since coming back from Paris, I thought more and more about freeing myself of my diamond. I said to myself, in Paris you fell in love with Jordi, but didn't leave your diamond with him. One day, when I saw the limping Turkish socialist outside Café Steinplatz, he was just crossing the road, limping, I said to myself, sleep with the limping socialist, he limps, he's a socialist, he'll leave you in peace afterwards, he's a socialist, he won't be afraid that you want to force him into marriage. I thought, I should be able to manage it in Berlin, I wouldn't have the courage to do it in Istanbul. He came into the café, sat down at the table I was sitting at, we drank tea, he asked me what my father's job was. But I felt too ashamed to tell the limping socialist that my father was a building contractor and therefore a capitalist. So I said: 'He's a retired teacher.' In the Steinplatz Cinema they were showing *Alexander Nevsky*, a film by the Russian director Eisenstein. The limping socialist asked me: 'Are you going in, too?'

I sat in the cinema and all I was thinking about was how I could manage to free myself of my diamond this evening. The copy of the film was old, it tore a couple of times, and in the cinema the lights briefly came on, until the film had been stuck together again. The soundtrack was scratchy, too, but I wasn't listening to the film anyway, only to the threatening sentences in my head: You tart, if you don't free yourself of your diamond tonight, you'll never save yourself, then you'll marry as a virgin and sell yourself to a man as a virgin. I made plans in my head, how I could get the limping socialist to free me from my diamond tonight. The film was over, the lights went up, the students slowly went outside and lit cigarettes. The limping socialist was waiting at the cinema doors and asked me whether he could invite me for a cup of tea. Then he went with me to another café, Café Kranzler; during the day elderly German women and widows sat there, not any political students. We sat down, I looked into his face and thought, the poor man, he doesn't know anything about my plan. There was a big clock in the café, which I looked at frequently, because I hoped to miss the last underground. But even before the last underground had gone, he asked me: 'I've got a bottle of raki from Turkey at home, do you want to drink some raki with me?' So we walked towards his flat. He limped and was slow, I walked slowly beside him. This evening I'm going to free myself of the diamond. Poor man, he doesn't know anything about it. We sat at the table in his flat, drank raki, and I didn't know how to start. He asked me what my ideal would be. I said: 'I want to be an actress.' – 'Have you already been on the stage?' – 'Yes, already when I was twelve. In one play I had the part of an elderly English woman, and I wore my mother's dress.' He suddenly stood up and said: 'What a pity, to have to play an old woman, when you were such a young girl.' He kissed my cheeks, as if he felt sorry for me. I laughed, and he said: 'Poor young girl,' and kissed my mouth. I was sitting in an easy chair, he pulled me up, stood in front of me and had to stretch his short foot, so that he was standing up straight. He kissed me for a long time, his foot remained stretched for just as long and then suddenly gave way. 'You've made me dizzy.' With his hands on my waist he limped with me towards the bed. I laughed and felt that my laughter was seducing him. Because of the laughter no wrong word came out of my mouth, I went on laughing as he undressed me and himself. Then he slept with me immediately. It hurt a lot, I trembled and said to him: 'I'm still a virgin, be a little patient.' He sat up in bed and said: 'I don't sleep with virgins. I thought you were an experienced woman.' – 'Tonight is my last chance,' I said, 'tomorrow I won't be so brave any more.' – 'No,' he said, 'virgins sleep with a man, and then force him to marry her.' In Turkish newspapers there were often news items like that: 'He took her gold away from her, now he has to go to the registry office.' I said: 'I don't want to marry, I want to free myself of my maidenhead.' – 'No,' he said, 'we'll sleep here as brother and sister until morning,' and placed a pillow between us. The pillow reminded me of adultery stories in Turkey. A man sleeps with his lover in a hotel room, his wife follows him, goes to the hotel with the police, the police open the room door, the photographers come in, but the husband had placed a pillow between himself and his lover. So in court he could say to the judge: 'But, Your Honour, there was a pillow between us.' Whether a pillow really was so important to the law, I didn't know, perhaps the newspapers made it all up. The limping socialist, however, couldn't leave the pillow between us for long, he pulled it away, I went on trembling, he was very excited and slept with me again and again. Afterwards he got up each time, limped to the washbasin and washed himself. I was to wash myself, too, and put a small piece of soap in my vagina. 'The soap kills the sperm,' he said. In the morning I got up, to go to work, and didn't see any blood in the bed. 'I slept with you six times, you weren't a virgin.' I went to work at Hotel Berlin on the early morning bus, it was still early and at the hotel I washed myself for a long time under a shower. Because of the hot water the shower room was thick with fog. I looked at my hands, legs, breasts in the fog, and there in the fog I understood that I had already left my diamond with Jordi in Paris, I had already been a woman since Paris, without knowing it. As a child I had often read stories about maidenheads in a very old book, which my mother had hidden from me. The book had a cover of old leather, on which a man and a woman were embracing among the stars. There the loss of the maidenhead was described as a tragedy, in an old-fashioned language which I often found difficult to understand. I remained under the shower for a long time and in the fog I said: 'Jordi.' While I was working I suddenly noticed that I felt embarrassed in front of men. Before they hadn't been there at all, now they were there. I now noticed many details about them – whether they were well shaven, for how many days they hadn't shaved, what their hands looked like. Now when I made the beds in the hotel rooms I looked at their suits or shoes in the wardrobes. I had been standing behind a mountain, I had run to the top, and behind the mountain there were men. I had cleared my way to them. In a fairy tale a boy entered a room that it was forbidden to open, saw a very beautiful girl there and was overcome by sleep because of her beauty. The next evening, before he entered the room again, he cut his little finger, so that it hurt, he wouldn't fall asleep again and could pursue her beauty. I, too, had cut my finger, so as not to sleep any more and to be able to pursue the beauty of men.

So after that I went to work and in the evening to the Café Steinplatz and the political students. The limping socialist was waiting in front of the café, took my arm, got on a bus with me and said: 'Let's go.' We arrived at his flat, he showed me a toothbrush and said: 'Look, I've bought it for you.' We slept with one another again, and again he said to me: 'You must use soap, so there are no children. I would like to sleep with you again in a couple of years.' – 'Why?' – 'In a couple of years you will be a very good woman, now you are still a child-woman. But you'll learn very fast.' He wrote down the telephone number of my parents in Istanbul, to call me there again after two years.

In our Socialist Association the Turkish students had heard that I had slept with the limping socialist. At this time I spent the night with a couple from the association, in the morning the girl went to work and the boy came to my bed and said: 'Let's sleep together.' – 'No, what will your girlfriend say, she's my friend, too, no.' – 'She won't be angry, she'll understand, she's a socialist.' We didn't sleep together, but talked in our pyjamas about what was right: to be angry or not to be angry, if a boyfriend or girlfriend sleeps with someone else. The room was tired, it smelled of cold cigarette smoke and sleepy bodies. I had said no, but the no was much harder to insist on than a yes. If one said yes, one had to work, but if one had said no, one had to work, too. I asked him: 'What would you do if she sleeps with someone else?'

'She won't do it.'

'No, you can't know that.'

'Yes, I do know.'

'No, you can't know that.'

'Yes, with her I know, but with you I don't.'

'Yes?'

'No, you laugh seductively. The other boys in the association talk about it too.'

'Yes?'

'No, no,' he said, and laughed.

He walked away, opened the window, fresh air came in, I got dressed. He asked: 'You're going, yeah?' – 'Yes, I'm going.'

That same day the limping socialist came to me at the hotel. I was just washing the stairs, a pail of water stood on the step. Once I had washed one step, I went down one step backwards with the pail, always stooping. Suddenly I saw a limping leg coming downstairs. 'I've been looking for you, you have to help me.' – 'What's happened?' We stood on the stairs, the pail of water between us, he smoked and threw the cigarette ends into the pail. The night before he had taken home another Turkish girl from the café. She had asked him to whom the second toothbrush belonged. She already knew that he had slept with me, and he admitted that he had bought a toothbrush for me and put it beside his in the tumbler. Then he had tried to sleep with her, too; now the girl wanted to go to the Turkish consulate and inform against him, because he wanted to sleep with her. 'Please, talk to her, you are a girl with consciousness, she mustn't do it.' In the evening I met the girl, we drank tea, and she said: 'I'm not going to report him, but he made me angry. You know what he said? "I'll buy a toothbrush for you as well."' I laughed, and now she laughed, too. He came limping up to our table. 'She doesn't want a toothbrush,' I giggled. She stood up and as she went spilled the rest of her tea on to the jacket of the limping Turkish socialist who liked to buy toothbrushes. She did it like Liz Taylor, not like the women from the Godard films. He sat there like a half-empty bottle of water that had been open for days.

I met other men, Turkish students, who were studying in Germany. Meanwhile I had been sacked from the hotel where I had been working because I had washed the stairs with too little water and they hadn't been properly clean. But there were lots of jobs in Berlin and I got a half-day job in a student hotel. In the afternoon I attended a theatre school and got an ID card as a drama student. I loved this ID card very much, on the photo I was laughing.

The teacher, Frau Kirschoff, had been an actress. She said: 'Now I want you all to go out and enter as moonshine or as wind.' One could be the Turkish crescent moon or a full moon and make a career for oneself as the moon. I looked at my passport. Profession 'Worker'. I went to the Turkish consulate and wanted to have 'Moonshine' or 'Clown' entered instead. 'If you're Moonshine, the German police will shoot you to the moon,' said the officials. One of the men stood in the middle of the room: 'I'm the world, Moonshine. Please revolve around me.' When I went out on to the street again downstairs, I could still hear their laughter through the open window.

All the women students stood in front of a mirror and did ballet exercises, we bent our arms over our raised, outstretched legs and smiled at ourselves in the mirror, for two hours. Through the window we looked into a garden. The light grew towards the bar, and it looked as if this light kept our legs in the air. We did exercises – Who can look longest into someone else's eyes? Who arouses the strongest emotions in the other? What do two emotions do with one another? Who fills the whole room with emotions? I was so happy I did cartwheels in the streets. In the evening I went to the theatres and sat down so loudly in the gallery or in the balcony that many in the audience looked at me, as if the play were going to start with me. In the darkness I pouted and watched the play with exaggeratedly sad or interested eyes. Then I went to the late-night cinema with the other women students. When the lights went down in the cinema, one of us asked: 'What would happen now, if I were to throw my Coke bottle to the front?' We looked at every film star with the thought: how would we have played the part in her place? We killed ourselves laughing in a film about Liz Taylor, because she was as fat as a pregnant woman, and an actress could never be pregnant. *Foreshadowing?*

*↓ yp.*

One day I was suddenly pregnant and <u>didn't know by whom</u>. In the student hotel I jumped down from the tall cupboards and tables, in order to get rid of the child, but it didn't go away. At the theatre school I did gymnastic exercises for hours, but that didn't make the child go away either. I didn't know what to do and went to the cinema often in order to forget the child. One day a film of Peter Brook's theatre production of Peter Weiss's <u>Marat/Sade</u> was showing. The French revolutionary Jean-Paul Marat is murdered in his bath by Charlotte Corday, and when I came out of the cinema, the Berlin streets were full of police and people. 'Benno Ohnesorg is dead, shot by the police.' The police had shot a chicken, but a human being was lying there. The next day there was a photo of the dead student. A thin man, he lay beside the exhaust pipe of a Volkswagen. A woman was bent over him, she was wearing earrings and an evening coat. Perhaps she wanted to go to the opera or the theatre with him after the demonstration. She was holding Benno's head up a little, perhaps she wanted to lift his head out of the blood. The Shah of Persia had been in Berlin that day, and Benno had taken part in the demonstration, policemen had shot him in the head. The city didn't sleep for days.

It was at this time that a letter came from my father; he wrote: 'My daughter, your mother is ill. Come back quickly to Istanbul.' I was immediately afraid that my mother could die and wanted to go back to Istanbul. It was summer; two students from the Turkish Students' Club said: 'If you want, come with us, we want to drive through Czechoslovakia, Hungary and Bulgaria to smell socialist air.'

As we drove south from Berlin, the Shah of Persia was also travelling through the country by train and visiting various German cities. We spent the night in a farmhouse in Bavaria and went to a pub, the television was showing police helicopters in the sky above the railway station at which his train was arriving. A senior surgeon was in readiness to carry out emergency operations. Before the Shah's train arrived, empty trains were shunted on to the tracks on either side to shield the main line. The Shah was wearing patent-leather shoes, everywhere he set down these shoes there was an emergency alert. Sixty parked cars were towed away around Munich's main railway station, their owners were supposed to pay. The airspace above him was barred to air traffic to a height of six thousand feet. Divers looked for explosive devices on steamers on the River Main. A locomotive preceded his train, in order to trigger charges. He sat in a palace in Bonn, the orchestra played Bach, and the police radios bleeped throughout the music. The policemen wore tails. After the news there was a documentary, which showed how, if one has an artificial hand, one can cut the fingernails of the other hand. At that time there were many men in Germany with prosthetic hands, the artificial hands were in black leather gloves.

From Bavaria we drove to Hungary. I hoped the bumpy roads would help me to lose the child. I went to the toilet again and again and looked at my underwear. In a café in Hungary I saw a couple of drops of blood in my underwear, but I wasn't sure whether the child had gone away so easily.

We reached Budapest; it was as if we had arrived in another time. The light of the street lamps was weak, our eyes had got used to the bright Berlin light. But the weak lights were beautiful. We stood by the water on the Buda side of the Danube, the door of a bar opened, a young girl and a boy came out and sad gypsy music, then the door shut again. The girl and the boy were laughing. Everything was very quiet in Budapest, only their laughter was to be heard. We loved all opening and closing doors, the broken stones of the pavements, the flowing Danube. We shouted, 'Socialism' and breathed the air in deeply a couple of times. We slept in the car, in the morning the sun shone, and it was hard to find a café. At the side of the road a woman sold us warm milk and sweet bread, once again socialism made us happy. Then we drove through Yugoslavia for a long time, we also loved Yugoslavia. We wound down the windows, smelled the air and were happy because of the socialist clouds. On the main roads we met Turkish workers from Germany. One told us that his car had been making funny noises, and he had been driving slowly because of it. Despite that the Yugoslav police had come and said: 'You've been overtaking.' – 'No, I didn't overtake,' he had said. 'You overtook, and the car behind you had to brake.' – 'It was obvious, the policeman wanted to eat money. I said to him: "Look, I was a policeman in Turkey, just as you are here. I ate money and they threw me out of the police force. Look, that's why I became a navvy in Germany, in a strange country. But take these ten marks, you can get yourself a meal for that." But he took my passport and said: "If you give me thirty marks, you can have your passport back." Then he simply drove off, and I drove after him through the whole town. The bastard. Wherever he drove, I drove after him. When my petrol tank was almost empty, he stopped at a petrol station. I gave him the thirty marks, in order to get my passport back, and filled up for another twenty marks.' We didn't believe his story; we thought, in socialism there weren't any people who eat money, that only happened in Turkey.

# Part 2

# The Bridge of the Golden Horn

# The Long Table at the 'Captain' Restaurant

We arrived in Istanbul, where many people ate money. The students drove me to my parents. In front of the house a man came driving toward us in a Pontiac. Out of the car window he said: 'Welcome, my daughter, don't you know your father any more? Have you forgotten us in Germany?' He thanked the two students and said: 'Let us drink a tiredness tea.' We followed him up to the third floor, a woman opened the door and cried out: 'My daughter!', kissed me and looked at me again and again, as if she couldn't believe that I had come back. I hadn't recognised my mother. 'I could only fetch you back to Istanbul with a lie, you were in Germany too long, it's too dangerous for a young girl to live alone in a foreign country for so long.' I sat on the couch with the two students as if I were in a strange house. The room was full of sun, but I didn't recognise the sun again either. A bird in a cage began to sing. The woman who was supposed to be my mother said: 'Look, Memish the bird has recognised you, he's singing for you.'

I had forgotten the bird, too. The two students wanted to drive on, but remained sitting until Memish the bird had finished singing. Then they stood up as if a concert were over, gave me their left hand on leaving, and my parents their right hand, and said in

German: 'Be on your guard with the capitalists.' From the balcony, I saw them turn right and disappear in a tunnel of chestnuts; the sun still twinkled on the metal of their Berlin number plate. The last bit of Berlin.

I went to my holdall, the zip stuck, in it were two Berlin blouses, two jackets, a skirt, a dress, a pair of boots, two pairs of shoes, two records of Kurt Weill and Bertolt Brecht and Jordi's poem. I took out one of the blouses. It was made of thin, white material with yellow flowers. I had been wearing it the day Benno Ohnesorg was killed. The blouse still had coffee stains from Café Steinplatz and smelt of the cigarettes and cigars of the left-wing German students. The clothes were crumpled after the long journey. I laid them across the settee and looked at the many creases: there were three days and nights between Istanbul and Berlin. The woman who was supposed to be my mother said: 'My child, why are you sitting there as if all your ships have sunk? Say something. Say a sentence in German.' In Berlin, when discussions went round in circles and the starting point couldn't be found, someone would ask a question that I had often heard there: 'Which came first: the chicken or the egg?' I said this sentence in German. 'What does it mean in Turkish?' asked my mother. I translated. My mother said: 'We have a similar sentence. The cockerel crawled out of the egg and thought the shell wasn't beautiful enough for him. Perhaps you don't think we're good enough for you either, because you've seen Europe.' My father said: 'Your mother wanted to be a European, too. She's had her hair dyed blonde.'

Apart from my mother's blonde hair everything in the apartment was as it had been. When I had gone to Germany two years before, the light bulb in the entrance hall of the building had flickered. It still flickered. The old radio was still there, too. My father talked to it, as if he were talking to a person. 'Speak up, otherwise I'll hit you.' Or he said: 'Now it doesn't feel like it again.' The refrigerator in the kitchen made the same loud noises. The neighbour with her cats still sat in the same chair under our balcony. She wore a kimono, and as before, looking down from above, I saw her huge breasts. As before, the women neighbours walked loudly down the stairs in their high heels. In their apartments the doors slammed as always because of the open windows. Only I had come back to Istanbul with things which I now had to hide from my parents. First of all I hid Jordi's poem in one of my boots and stuffed some newspaper on top of it as well. My father sometimes put his trousers under the mattresses, so that they kept their creases. I found one of his pairs of trousers under my mattress and immediately became nervous: 'Don't put your trousers under my bed!' My mother wanted to wash my blouses together with my father's shirts. 'No, I'll wash my blouses separately,' I said. 'You're bringing a new fashion home, did you learn it in Europe?' she asked.

My parents sat in their easy chairs, read newspapers, and from time to time exchanged pages. The strong sun shone on the open newspaper pages. When they held the open newspapers in front of their faces, I became a little calmer. When they lowered their newspapers, I went to the toilet to see whether my period had started. I pulled the plug, the water splashed, and my mother called from outside: 'What is it, my daughter, are you ill, do you have diarrhoea?' – 'No,' I shouted angrily, and showed her my teeth in the toilet mirror. Perhaps my period will come, I thought, if I wash and iron all my clothes that I brought from Berlin and hang them in the wardrobe. Then I will be my parents' girl again. I washed and ironed everything and hung it in the familiar places in the wardrobe. Then I went to the toilet again. No blood. My mother showed me photos and letters that I had sent from Berlin two years before. In one of these photos I was eating soup with five girls, the girls from the women's hostel. In the second photo I was standing laughing between our communist hostel warden and his wife. To me it was as if the two photos had been taken thirty years before – when I was still a virgin. Now I had new photos in my bag. In one I could be seen on the day we had founded the Socialist Association in Berlin with the limping socialist. Our twelve left fists were high in the air, as if we were all holding on to the leather straps in a tramcar rocking from side to side. My mother said: 'After you had gone away, for me the time was like a long night. You had hidden yourself in this night. I could no longer find you. Sometimes I kissed the door of the room where you used to sleep, and said: "My Allah, protect her there from bad things."' She began to cry. 'For two years I've kept control of my feelings, but now the tears are coming.' My father said: 'Don't cry, don't cry. Look, she's there, she has come back just the same as when she left.' – 'Yes, I know. Even when a pear falls from the tree, it doesn't fall far from its tree. I'm sure that over there she didn't allow any blots on our family honour.' I went to the toilet again. When I came out again, Aunt Topus was also sitting in the lounge, my mother had got to know the lonely woman on a ship many years ago and adopted her. Aunt Topus said: 'The chicken that walks around a lot returns home with lots of shit under its feet. What have you brought back from Alamania under your feet?' My mother said: 'She has learned German. A language is like a person, two languages are like two people.' My father said: 'She flew to Alamania as a nightingale and there she became a parrot, she has learned German. Now she is a Turkish nightingale and at the same time a German parrot.' Everyone sat in the lounge and drank tea and looked at me, the nightingale, which was now also a German parrot. Because of the slowness of these three people in the lounge, I suddenly felt afraid, that I was running out of time to do anything about my pregnancy. As a child, when there were too many people in a room, I had immediately run out on to the street and had played there until evening. I went across to our neighbours, an officer's family with three daughters. All three girls were at home, they, too, were dyed blonde like my mother. As they were drinking tea they pushed up their nose with their left index finger. They thought that if one pressed long enough one got a snub nose like Liz Taylor or Kim Novak. The fashion of snub noses and blonde hair had started in Istanbul after I had gone to Berlin. The famous pop singer Ajda Pekkan had had an operation on her nose and her hair dyed blonde, she had become the idol of many Istanbul women. She looks like a European, said the three girls, and studied me, to see what I had too much of. I should have the bones of my feet operated on, and my eyebrows were too thick. There, too, I went to the toilet a couple of times, to see whether my period had started at last. The three girls said: 'You were in Europe a long time. You can be considered a European, but it's impossible with your thick eyebrows like those of a peasant woman.' They immediately took me to a neighbour, a dressmaker and widow, who dyed the hair of all of them blonde and plucked their eyebrows. She also plucked out half of my eyebrows and asked me what I had done for two years in Germany. I thought about whether I should perhaps tell her that I was pregnant. She didn't have any children, perhaps she knew what could be done. I said: 'I'm...' – but before I said 'pregnant', I looked at her table, to see what kind of newspaper she read, whether it was a left-wing one. She read *Hürriyet*, a Turkish tabloid, and instead of 'pregnant' I said: 'I've become a socialist.' She went on plucking my eyebrows and said: 'I hope you get better soon. In this world all kinds of things can fall on a person's head!' Here, too, I went to the toilet a couple of times. No blood. Then I looked at myself in the mirror and sighed. The three girls and the dressmaker drank tea outside and talked about what women had to do in order to get a slim waist. At night the girls had to sleep for months with a very tightly laced girdle, and one day one would wake up with a slim waist and find a man. When one had found a husband one could get fat again with him. One even had to make a husband fatter intentionally, so that the other women didn't think he was good looking. One of the girls said: 'Oh, I'm getting my period,' and knocked on the toilet door. When she quickly ran past me, I simply wanted to be her and no one else, and when she had come out of the toilet again, I kept looking at her face and at her stomach, I simply wanted to be her and no one else. She bit into a sponge finger, little crumbs fell on to her skirt, and I brushed my skirt, as if the crumbs had fallen on it. 'I'm bleeding so heavily,' she said.

When I went up to my parents' apartment, I saw, one floor below them, the cat of the old woman who always sat in the same place on the balcony in her kimono. The cat was miaowing and scratching at the door to her apartment. The old woman opened the door, saw me and said: 'Come in.' I wanted to pick up the cat, but it scratched my hand. The old woman said: 'The cat's afraid, it's pregnant.'

The old woman in the kimono lived with her sister, whom my mother called 'the dead madame'. The two women were eighty years old, Turkish Greeks. The woman in the kimono had never married, but when dancing became fashionable under Atatürk had, as a young girl, once danced with Atatürk, and he had told her: 'You are a butterfly, Mademoiselle.' That's why my mother called her 'mademoiselle Butterfly'. Her sister, 'the dead madame', had been lying in bed for almost ten years. One day, when her husband died, she had stopped eating and drinking. On the woman's kitchen table my mother had found a piece of paper on which was written: 'My God, help me, my husband died today'. She had been struck by melancholy, she stopped getting out of bed, she lived there like a dead woman. A cleaner fed her soup and gave her medicine. The dead madame swallowed and spat and sang children's songs in Greek to the cleaning woman. For ten years Mademoiselle Butterfly had been doing everything to keep her sister alive, she didn't have anyone else. I went to the bed of the dead madame, the cleaning woman was just turning her from left to right, so that the flesh didn't get any sores from all the lying. The cleaning woman said: 'I have back pains, because I'm always having to lift Madame up and lay her down on her other side.' Mademoiselle Butterfly said to her: 'You don't have back pains from work, but because you've had twenty abortions. I'm telling you once again, you must go to the doctor and get him to prescribe these new anti-baby pills for you, otherwise you'll die.' I didn't dare ask the cleaning woman, but so there were abortions in Istanbul. I liked the women in this apartment, there were tragedies here, and now I, too, had my tragedy. Above the bed of the dead madame hung an icon, on which Mother Mary held Jesus in her arms. As a child I had thought, if I should ever be pregnant without a husband, I can say that I became pregnant like Mother Mary, because Allah so wished it. In the women's hostel in Berlin our communist hostel warden had said: 'Mother Mary was the most intelligent whore in the world. She lied so well that the whole world still believes her today.'

There was a library in the apartment of the two sisters, and there I saw several thick, leather-bound books by Karl Marx and Friedrich Engels in French. The books had belonged to the husband of the dead madame. The names Karl Marx and Engels. All my friends in Berlin had books by them. And I would not have hidden my pregnancy from these people who read Karl Marx and Engels. Suddenly the books of the dead husband of the dead madame took away my fear, and I ran and hopped up the stairs and sang in German a part of Nanna's song by Brecht, which I had learned by heart in Berlin:

> *Thank the Lord the whole thing's quickly over*
> *All the loving and the sorrow my dear.*
> *Where are the teardrops you wept last evening?*
> *Where are the snows of yesteryear?*

When night fell, my mother covered the cage of the bird Memish with a cloth. It was very warm. I got up and went into the kitchen, where the refrigerator was humming loudly. Then I went to the toilet again, which hissed, and I thought, if my period were to come, then I wouldn't hear all these noises any more. Aunt Topus was snoring in the room, mosquitoes were buzzing around her face. To kill a mosquito I struck Aunt Topus on the cheek. The old woman woke up: 'Why are you hitting me?' Then I sat down on the balcony. Sometimes a couple of chestnuts fell from the chestnut trees on to the street. A couple of fishing boats with little lights were moving on the sea. I talked aloud to myself in

German: 'You must do something. You can go to Germany as a worker again.' But in order to go to Germany, one had to have a medical check-up. They would have seen from the urine sample that I was pregnant, pregnant women weren't allowed to go to Germany. Apart from that I didn't want to be a worker any more. I wanted to be an actress; everything that was difficult in life was easier in the theatre. Death, hate, love, being pregnant. One could put a cushion under one's dress and act pregnant, then take the cushion away again and the next evening put it under one's dress again. One could kill oneself for love, but stand up again, wipe away the stage blood, smoke a cigarette.

When the bird Memish began to sing the next morning, I went for a walk under the chestnut trees, up and down, as in a prison yard, and thought about how I could flee this prison. At the end of the chestnut-tree tunnel, there was a newspaper kiosk. I sought strength from the left-wing paper CUMHURIYET (Republic). The big news stories that day were: 'The American soldiers who refused to take part in the Vietnam war flew first to Japan, then to Russia, then they arrived in Stockholm'. – 'Heart surgeon Dr Barnard carried out his second heart transplant. The dentist, in whom Dr Barnard transplanted a woman's heart, came to after the operation and his first sentences were: Say hello to my wife'. Now every morning I walked under the chestnut trees to the newspaper kiosk and stood in front of CUMHURIYET: 'In Hue American soldiers injured and arrested a Vietnamese. It was claimed he was spying for the communist Vietcong'. – 'The miners in the coal mines on the Turkish Black Sea coast demonstrated and went on strike. There were clashes between workers and police and two workers were killed. The progressive trade union has protested against these murders, and in Istanbul the students have left their universities and taken to the streets'. – 'Thousands of street sweepers have begun a protest. They will walk 470 miles from Anatolia to Istanbul. The Socialist Youth is showing its solidarity with the workers and demonstrating'. Written on their placards in the photographs were the words: 'The flowing blood of workers will choke fascism. If you hit us, we will grow stronger. Turkish youth will make a revolution'.

The striking workers and demonstrating students were somewhere close to me in Istanbul, and I was only walking between my parents' apartment, the newspaper kiosk and the chestnut-tree tunnel. I felt as if were a coiled spring in a box. If the lid of the box were to be lifted, the spring would jump out. In CUMHURIYET there was a photo of a man without hands, a peasant. When he had been ploughing his field with a machine, he had seen a tortoise under the machine and wanted to save it from the machine's blades. He saved the tortoise, but the blades of the machine cut off both his hands. I, too, loved tortoises, and that reminded me of a boy, a friend, with whom I had often thrown chestnuts into the air above the sea. This boy had a tortoise. At night he sat on the balcony, stuck a burning candle on the back of the tortoise, which was walking across the table, and read a book. The mosquitoes burned up in the candle flame with a hiss. Sometimes he talked to me from his balcony. The tortoise walked slowly backwards and forwards across the table, the burning candle on its back, and the boy changed his place with the movement of the tortoise. I often asked him from our balcony: 'How is your tortoise? What are you reading?' – 'Poems.' And just as he had thrown chestnuts into the air with me, he sometimes threw a sentence from a poem across to me.

Perhaps he could help me. I went home and looked at the balcony on which the boy used to sit with his tortoise. His father was just cutting up a big watermelon and then ate the big melon alone for hours. My mother told me that the boy's parents had got divorced and he had moved away with his mother. 'I've heard that he suddenly fell ill. They say he's schizophrenic now. He's left university, where he was studying law.' I got the boy's address from his father, he lived on the European side of Istanbul. Between the two parts was the Sea of Marmara, big ships sailed from one side to the other. The next day when the bird Memish began to sing

I went to the harbour and sailed over to the European side. It was dangerous to jump on to the ship. The sea was often rough, the ship moved from side to side, drew away from the quay wall and then smacked against the wall again. There were stories of accidents, people had fallen into the water and been crushed by the ship. So parents constantly repeated to their children: 'Don't jump on to the ship before the gangway has been set down.' But when I was younger I had jumped anyway, and just at that moment men's hands had often pinched my thigh from behind. Then I couldn't turn round and shout 'Donkey!' because the ship was rocking too much. Now I jumped again and just as in the past a hand from behind pinched my thigh. On the ship people drank tea from little glasses, I heard the sounds of small change in the apron pockets of the tea sellers walking around, looked at the girls and knew that they, too, had been pinched. So the girls sat crossly on the ship, and when they got off on the European side, they tried to stand in front of women or the older men.

I walked towards the Bridge of the Golden Horn, which links the two European parts of Istanbul. As before the men in the streets scratched themselves between the legs. The many ships beside the bridge gleamed in the sun. The long shadows of the people walking across the Bridge of the Golden Horn fell on to the ships from both sides of the bridge and walked along their white bodies. Sometimes the shadow of a street dog or a donkey also fell there, black on white. After the last ship the shadows of people and animals fell on to the sea and kept walking there. Across these shadows flew the seagulls with their white wings, their shadows also fell on the water, and their cries mingled with the ships' sirens and the cries of the street sellers. As I walked across the bridge, it seemed to me as if I had to push the air ahead of me with my hands. Everything moved very slowly, as in an overexposed, old slow-motion film. Small children and old men carried water canisters left over from Ottoman times on their backs and sold the water to passers-by. They shouted: 'Waateerr' into the sky, and people looked as if they were holding on tight to these 'waateerr' voices, so as not to faint because of the heat.

At the end of the Bridge of the Golden Horn there was a big mosque, there blind men sat in the sun, and pigeons sat on their heads and legs, because the blind men were selling grain. When people walked along there, the pigeons suddenly flew up, came down again and went on pecking the blind men's grain. Two blind men walked arm in arm and smiled, they were wearing shoes with high heels from the fifties like Elvis Presley. Another blind man turned from left to right and said: 'Muslims, help me, give me an arm.' A well-dressed man helped him. Holding on to his arm the blind man walked calmly towards the Bridge of the Golden Horn, and the pigeons flew up in front of him again.

I walked up the steep streets and found the house of the schizophrenic boy, a wooden house, whose door was open. The house smelt of basil, which grew in flowerpots in front of the windows. I entered a very large room, the floor was covered in carpets, and many chairs stood against the walls in the dim light. Under one of the chairs I saw the tortoise. The schizophrenic boy was kneeling and praying in front of the holy turban and coat of his grandfather, who had been a famous religious leader. I left him praying there and went from room to room. A relative was living in almost every room; in one room a woman was sitting in a wheelchair and said: 'I am his aunt.' There were old women, young women, lonely men, married men. Four cats were sitting in one room and looking out of the window. Down in the alley a young boy walked past with eight loaves in his arms, two old women went along the wall of the house with two cows. The schizophrenic boy had stopped praying. 'How did you land here?' – 'I wanted to see you and your tortoise.' He put the tortoise on his hand, stood directly opposite me, stroked the shell of the tortoise and its feet and said to me: 'You have become a beautiful girl in Germany.' We sat down in the room of his holy grandfather. An oil lamp on the wall shone on the holy turban and coat, the tortoise walked slowly across the carpet. The boy was silent. We sat there for two hours. I wanted to tell him that I was pregnant and didn't know what to do. But before I began, the boy suddenly said: 'We're being watched. The building workers are watching us. Let's leave the room.' He was terribly afraid. I embraced him, and we went into another room. This room, too, was dark, the heavy curtains were drawn. He lay down on the bed, looked at the ceiling of the room and said quietly: 'The building workers come through the walls.' I sat beside him on the bed and looked, not at the walls, but at his face. I passed my hand in front of his eyes, he didn't see it, he saw men with hammers in their hands coming through the walls. I wanted to save him. When I was young I had sometimes gone to see 3-D films with my parents. When I cried out and hugged my mother out of fear of the Red Indian arrows, she took the special glasses away from my face. I thought I could simply take these glasses away from the schizophrenic boy, kissed him, and we slept with one another. Then he didn't look at the walls any more, because now he was looking at me. Afterwards he lit two cigarettes, gave me one and opened the curtains. We sat on the bed, smoked and looked out of the window on to the alley. Again the two old women came past with their cows, and a couple of children pulled an old gramophone, underneath which four wheels had been added on, behind them like a cart. The schizophrenic boy said: 'You know, that used to be our gramophone. My grandfather had just died. All the people in the rooms of this house came out and cried: "Your grandfather is dead." I was seven years old, I cried uninterruptedly and wanted my grandfather back. People brought me thin chocolate, so that I would stop crying. In one bar of chocolate I found a prize ticket and with it I won this gramophone. The Nestlé factory gave away two records with it as well, "His Master's Voice", with a picture in the middle of the label, on which a dog was looking into the gramophone horn. One was soon broken. When I went to play in the street, I took the gramophone out with me. All the neighbours came to our house to hear the record. But often there was a power cut, so we turned the record on the gramophone by hand. One person after another turned the record with his right forefinger, so fast that the picture of the dog on the record couldn't be seen any more. Then the gramophone broke, the whole alley was fed up constantly having to turn the record with their fingers. For years the broken gramophone was left like that in a room, now the children have put the gramophone on four wheels and made a car out of it.'

As he told me this gramophone story, he didn't see any walls opening up any more. I thought I had made this miracle.

The schizophrenic boy absolutely wanted to introduce me to his best friend, who also lived in the house. We walked over the creaking wooden floors of the long corridors, in one room canaries were flying around. The friend of the schizophrenic boy was called Hüseyin, a small man with a thin moustache, who looked like the son of a sultan. The schizophrenic boy told me Hüseyin was the son of a whirling dervish. The men in his Mevlevi order spun round for hours and through spinning round wanted to go into a trance, so that in this state of ecstasy they could mediate between God and earth.

When Hüseyin heard that I had been in Germany, he asked me whether I had read Heinrich Böll. I didn't know Böll. He gave me a book in German and said: 'Here, it's my favourite book. You must read it.' They made tea, I opened the book, and Hüseyin said: 'It's a story after the Second World War in Germany.' The name of the book by Böll was *And Never Said a Word*. I said: 'I'm pregnant.' – 'Are you sure?' they both asked. – 'Wait another couple of days, perhaps your period is late because of the long journey. Otherwise we have to find a solution.' Hüseyin said: 'I have a girlfriend who knows a doctor. She had to go to him once herself.'

I took the boat back to my parents on the Asian side, to wait for another couple of days.

The next day, just before the bird Memish had begun to sing, the mother of the schizophrenic boy suddenly called on us and explained to my parents that her son wanted to marry me. My mother said: 'I don't know what to say now. I thought they were just friends from balcony to balcony.' The boy's mother said: 'I thought so, too, but he says he's loved her for years, ever since the time the two of them were still throwing chestnuts into the sea. But please consider it carefully, he's ill. But we hope that he will become healthy.' The mother of the schizophrenic boy had not come alone. Beside her sat a man, a relative, my parents knew this man, he was the chairman of a party, his picture was in the newspaper every day. Perhaps that was why my parents didn't dare say no. When the two of them had gone, my parents said to me: 'We love this boy. But don't do it, one only does something like that if one wants to sacrifice oneself. It could end up making you ill.'

The mother of the boy said to me: 'His doctor would like to talk to you.' – 'I think,' said the doctor, 'you don't know what schizophrenia is. If you leave him, he'll become even more ill. Consider it very carefully.' Afterwards I walked down a street with the boy's mother and looked at her profile. She was a beautiful woman, still young, but she walked very slowly, as if she were carrying her boy with her on her back. I said to her: 'I want to marry him.' She called on us with her son, we drank lemonade. The next day the boy visited me with his friend, the dervish-son Hüseyin, and the three of us went to the cemetery, where the boy's holy grandfather was buried. The cemetery was on a hill by the sea. Between the crooked gravestones we saw the Bosporus. The ferries sailed past, girls sat on the deck, and I thought, they've all been pinched on the thigh. While the schizophrenic boy was praying in front of the gravestone of his grandfather and didn't see us, Hüseyin gave me a book. 'Read this novel. It's about a French woman in the eighteenth century who sacrifices herself for a man. You are like that woman. Come to the harbour on the European side in four days and give the book back to me.' After four days I took the ship back to the European side. Hüseyin asked me: 'Did you like the book?' – 'Yes, but I am not that woman.' – 'Perhaps you want to be her,' said Hüseyin. 'Hüseyin, I don't think I want to marry, I only wanted to save him.' – 'You won't manage it,' said Hüseyin, 'my friend is very ill. After two days you'll leave, then you're the guilty one.' These words struck me like a smack in the face. I worked my fingers and heard the cracking sounds. When I had worked all my fingers three times, Hüseyin asked me: 'What did you want to do before this marriage business started?' – 'Actress.' – 'Save the actress.'

A ship docked, many people jumped down and walked towards a sunny street. 'Think about it very carefully,' said Hüseyin. The ship waited. I took it back to the Asian side, many men and women on the ship were reading newspapers. In CUMHURIYET there was a photo: 'Red Rudi Dutschke'. The news was: 'Thousands of students clashed with police on the streets of West Berlin'.

Berlin had been like a street to me. As a child I had stayed in the street until midnight, in Berlin I had found my street again. From Berlin I had returned to my parents' house, but now it was like a hotel, I wanted to go back on to the street again. On the ship the men took the newspapers down from their faces and looked at me. Every evening a shipful of people would come to see me on stage as an actress. The men would fall in love with me. I suddenly realised that I was very curious about what these men who would fall in love with me would look like. I wanted to die onstage like Molière, in the middle of the set. I saw myself onstage, other actors carried me in their arms, I bled from my mouth, died and left behind no children who had to weep after my death. The ship was just in the middle between Asian and European Istanbul. The actress came out of my body, she pushed a man and a child in front of her and threw them from the ship into the Sea of Marmara. Then she came back and entered me again. When the ship reached the Asian side, I knew that I never ever wanted to get married. I could hardly wait to get home. Before I got on the bus, I called my mother. 'I don't want to marry, I want to go to drama school.'

'You can speak German, why do you want to get married? When you want to marry one day, there are so many men.' I noticed that I found it easier to talk to my mother on the telephone than at home. The telephone was in the street, and the street gave me courage, but at home I shut myself into my room for a whole day, until Hüseyin had told the schizophrenic boy that I couldn't marry him.

Hüseyin introduced me to his friends, they called themselves Surrealists – a couple of young men who were studying art, and a girl. Hüseyin said: 'Let me now introduce to you a wonderful actress of tomorrow.' One of the boys exclaimed: 'Welcome, Medea!' They met in the homes of their parents, wrapped their mothers' sheets around their naked bodies like the Romans, sat in a circle in a room and asked each other questions they had learned from a book about the French and Spanish surrealist movement. 'We want to live poetically, that's why the needs suppressed by civilisation must be liberated.' When one boy asked a question, his neighbour sitting beside him had to reply immediately. The girl stood behind the young men and watched them the way women stand and watch behind men playing poker in a casino. One boy asked: 'What do you think of the man masturbating in front of the woman and the woman masturbating in front of the man?' The other said immediately: 'I think it's very good.'

Another asked: 'What do you think of male exhibitionism?'

'It leaves me cold.'

'I agree. It is of social significance only.'

'What do you think about brothels?'

'They're a fact. They're not very good, but they're better than nothing.'

'I have the lowest possible opinion of them.'

'In circumstances where I find the woman attractive.'

'What importance do you attach to speech during the sexual act?'

'A great importance in a negative sense. Certain phrases can entirely prevent me from making love.'

'Certain words can intensify pleasure.'

'To what extent and how often can a man and a woman making love reach orgasm simultaneously?'

'Very rarely.'

'This simultaneity we are discussing, is it desirable?'

'Very.'

'What do you think of homosexuality?'

'I accept it but have no interest in it.'

'If two men love each other, I have no moral objections.'

'And two women?'

'I imagine that one woman plays the part of the man and the other that of the woman – sixty-nine.'

'I have never interviewed a lesbian.'

'What do you think of onanism?'

'Onanism can only be a compensation.'

'I don't believe onanism has anything to do with compensation or consolation. Onanism is as absolutely legitimate in itself as homosexuality.'

'They have nothing in common.'

'There cannot be onanism without images of women.'

'How about animals?'

'You're joking!'

'What distinction do you make between images of women in a proper sexual act and in onanism?'

'The distinction between dream and waking imagination.'

'That answer couldn't be any vaguer. One difference is that with onanism one chooses what one sees, one is indeed very particular about it, whereas in the proper sex act one does not have a choice.'

'That's right.'

The girl, who stood and listened to the boys, interrupted them sometimes and corrected their sentences. She knew the sentences by heart, because she had translated them from French into Turkish. She was studying in Paris and said to me: 'The sentences are from the French Surrealists Breton, Tanguy, Péret, Prévert, Man Ray in 1928.' The boys gave me sheets as well, I wrapped them around my body, they took my photograph from the front and in profile and said: 'Welcome to surrealism.' I immediately had to relate a dream. The girl said: 'They want you to enchant them

with your dream pictures and to open a door in their imagination.'
I related a dream I had had in Berlin. I had stood in the sky above
a cloud. The cloud had been like a big blanket. I bent down and
opened it and down below on earth saw my mother and father
standing on a steep meadow.

The girl, who was studying in Paris, said: 'Politically the
Surrealist Movement made common cause with the Communist
Party in France in 1928, but preserved its internal freedom, which
is why one day the Party distanced itself from the Surrealists.' The
girl had a very dark, deep voice, which sounded as if a handful of
sand were constantly being rubbed against a piece of silk cloth.
She loved her voice and enjoyed listening to herself. She said:
'A brain is like the body of a ballet dancer, only if she practises
a lot can she dance well. The good ballerinas first practise with
heavy costumes, in order to be able to dance lightly later on. They
hang lead from their trouser legs and practise and practise. The
rule is to first practise dancing with heavy costumes. Our brain
must take the work of a ballerina as an example. All the concepts
that are very hard to learn must be learned and learned, in order
to awaken the passive life of our intelligence.' I listened to these
difficult sentences with big eyes. That is the lead on my skirt,
as with a ballerina who is starting her exercises, I thought. She
had awoken the passive life of her own intelligence, and now she
wanted to awaken mine. I liked the girl's deep voice very much.
She said: 'The surrealist language consists of dialogues. Several
ideas stand in opposition to one another. The words, the dream
pictures, present themselves to the listener as a springboard for
the mind. They don't want to analyse, they want to be intoxicated
by pictures as if intoxicated by opium. In the depths of our mind
there are strange forces. That's why all spontaneous writing,
storytelling, responding, asking is important. The Surrealists were
against the ideals of family, fatherland, religion, producing children.
These were threats, because one had to play a subordinate role,
and that set limits to the imagination, enslaved the imagination.
Freedom, love, poetry, art, those were the flames which expanded

personality and imagination.' The girl would have gone on talking, but the mother of the boy in whose home we had met opened the door, saw us all wrapped in her sheets. 'Children, I know you're playing, but couldn't you leave my bedlinen alone?' Her son tried to push the door, behind which she was standing, shut. She called from behind the door: 'My son, am I supposed to be constantly washing the sheets. Look, the electricity is off again, who knows when it will be back on. There's other washing waiting in the washing machine.' Her son shouted: 'Mother, we haven't dirtied the sheets, we'll fold them up again, too.' As Hüseyin and the girl with the dark voice folded the sheets together and stood opposite one another as they did so, Hüseyin said to her: 'Our friend needs a doctor, she's pregnant.' The girl tugged at the sheet and folded it once with Hüseyin: 'I know a doctor. I'll call him today. Of course he'll do it illegally, he's very good.' As they folded the sheet once again, Hüseyin said: 'She doesn't have any money.' They folded the sheet once again, and the girl gave Hüseyin the folded-up sheet, turned round to her bag, took out six hundred lira, gave it to me and said: 'Give that to the doctor. And don't be afraid. It's like cutting your fingernail.' When I took the ship back home there were many newspaper sellers standing in a line at the harbour, holding the newspapers up in their left hand and shouting: 'Che Guevara has been killed.' The dead Che Guevara lay on a wooden frame, around him stood three soldiers, three young men, a policeman. None of them wore a tie, and the dead Che Guevara seemed to be looking at the camera. Many people collected in front of the newspaper sellers, bought the newspapers, and because they didn't believe it was true, constantly looked at the newspaper of the person standing next to them, in case something different was written there. They forgot to board the ship. The ship hooted and sailed off with only a few people.

Two days later Hüseyin took me to the doctor. He carried out the illegal operation with his nurse in his lunch break and said to Hüseyin: 'She should eat meat with lots of salt today.' When I walked across the Bridge of the Golden Horn with Hüseyin, I couldn't tell whether it was the bridge swaying or me. Hüseyin brought me to the harbour and said: 'In two days I'll be waiting for you here at nine o'clock. I'll take you to the drama school. The best theatre people in Turkey teach there.' On the ship people again sat with open newspapers in front of their faces. I read the news: 'America sends another 10,000 soldiers to Vietnam', 'Heart surgeon Dr Barnard carried out his third heart transplant'. I went to the ship's toilet. Next to the toilet, two of the ship's crew were sitting at a table, one was reading a news item from *Cumhuriyet* to his friend, who couldn't read. He read the words like a child in his first year at school. I could still hear his voice in the toilet.

'The mem-ber of par-lia-ment of the Tur-kish Wor-kers' Par-ty Cetin Altan was beat-en up in par-lia-ment by right-wing mem-bers. One of the right-wing MPs shout-ed at Cetin Altan: "You are a com-mu-nist, your bro-ther is prob-ably a com-mu-nist too." Çetin Altan's head was bleed-ing. He said: "We are not com-mu-nists, not So-viets, we are so-cial-ists."' When I came home, I said to my mother: 'My period's just come.' She gave me two aspirin, I threw them in the washbasin and looked at myself in the mirror.

Two days later, before the bird Memish had begun to sing, I went over to the European side. Hüseyin was waiting at the harbour and smoking. The director of the drama school was Memet, a famous actor and director. He had studied at the Actors' Studio in America, Marlon Brando had been his teacher. I loved Marlon Brando. Memet sat opposite me at a table, said nothing for four, five minutes and looked me in the eye. Then, almost angrily, he asked me: 'Why do you want to be an actress?'

'I want to live poetically. I want to awaken the passive life of my intelligence.'

'Other reasons?'

'I love films. Because in one and a half hours one sees a story without holes. It's very beautiful to sit a dark room and to cry and to laugh. In the theatre I'd like to waken the emotions of the audience.'

Memet gave me a book, *Hamlet* by Shakespeare, and said: 'Please read.' As I was reading, he stood up, walked behind me and covered my eyes with his hands. 'Tell me quickly what I'm wearing. What colour is my shirt? And my hair? Is it combed to the left, to the right or combed back? Am I wearing a watch? And tell me what's lying on the table!' With my eyes closed I told him what I had seen. 'Imitate your mother or your father.' I imitated the way my father smoked. Memet said: 'The first condition of becoming an actress is the ability to imitate. Father and mother are easy to imitate, because one knows them. But one must be able to imitate anyone, and that's only possible if one learns to observe and to observe the essentials. Come on Monday at nine for the first class and read three plays by then.'

Down in the street I took Hüseyin on my back and carried him down the steep street. While he was on my back Hüseyin talked: 'Did you know that the first actresses in Istanbul were Armenian? Later there were also a couple of Turkish women who went on stage. The newspapers wrote about them: the women without underpants are on stage again. The chief of police came to the theatre and said to the actresses: "Don't perform without underpants. Put on your underpants." Sometimes they were taken to police headquarters, where they were asked: "Are you putting on your underpants?" The actresses said: "Yes, we're putting them on." Then they were released again.' Hüseyin got down from my back and said: 'Now you're one of the women without underpants.'

Our teacher Memet kept us in school from nine o'clock in the morning until midnight. He started lessons with two hours of gymnastics and said: 'Negro-neutral-front'. When he said negro, one had to stick out one's bum like a negro. Neutral meant drawing it back to its usual place. And front meant pushing it forward. I immediately found a friend, she spoke five languages and absolutely wanted to know what orgasm was. She told me that she had done our gymnastic exercise negro-neutral-front in bed with her husband and still couldn't get an orgasm. When Memet kept us too long at school some evenings, I slept at her apartment. She and her husband had a very large bed, and because they didn't make love often, I slept in the same bed with them, and we read the parts in the plays together. Once I was supposed to watch how they made love, to see who was to blame for her not getting an orgasm. They started to kiss each other, I giggled, they began to laugh, too, and couldn't go on. Sometimes during a lesson she wrote a little note and secretly gave it to me to read. It said: 'I have been married for six hundred and sixty days and still haven't had an orgasm. Is that not lost time?' Our teacher Memet also talked about lost time. Once he arrived in class with three dolls. He told us he was the Greek demigod Saturn – 'Saturn was the father of Zeus – Saturn ate his sons, only Zeus was able to escape.' Memet pretended to eat these three dolls and said: 'Saturn ate his children because he wanted to eat time, children were time.' Memet said that we, too, ate our time with empty thoughts, we didn't read. We shouldn't eat time, but fill it. 'Which of you knows Jean-Paul Sartre? Do you know his books? Sartre didn't eat time, that's why he's ahead of the times.' Every weekend Memet gave us a questionnaire to take home. The questions were: What have I done this week to expand my consciousness? Which book have I read? In order to be able to give answers, I read the play *Woyzeck*, which I loved very much. In the book there was a picture of Büchner, a boy who reminded me of a bird and looked me in the eye. I was ashamed in front of Büchner, because at twenty he had written such beautiful plays and had died so young and at the same age we ate our time. I didn't want to sleep any more, because when one was asleep one ate time. At night I read until four or five in the morning, my mother came into my room, switched off the light and said: 'Electricity is expensive.' I answered her in the dark with a line from *Hamlet*: 'To die, to sleep; To sleep: perchance….'. In these nights, when I remained awake until morning, I saw that the light was on in many other houses. Sometimes the light went off and after two minutes came on again. Perhaps mothers were switching off the light there, too, and their children, who were reading, put it on again. I would have liked to know what they were reading. The nights were hot, and my books were spotted with blood, because I killed mosquitoes with them. I thought, perhaps the books of the others, who read a long time at night, are also spotted with mosquito blood.

Memet, too, once brought a book to school that was spotted with blood, *The Legend of Prometheus*. The name Prometheus meant: he who already saw everything beforehand. Prometheus lived on Olympus with the other Greek gods, he stole fire and gave it to mankind. But fire belonged to the gods alone. That's why Zeus was angry with Prometheus, chained him on a mountain top and sent an eagle there during the day. The eagle ate Prometheus's liver, but in the night the liver regenerated itself, the next day the eagle came back and ate the liver again. In class Memet lay down on the floor like the chained Prometheus. When the eagle came and ate his liver, Memet screamed for several minutes and then said to us: 'Like Prometheus you must steal fire from the gods and bring it to mankind! Which of you knows about Turkey's petrol problems? Do you know that we're not allowed to make use of our natural resources, so that America can sell us its natural resources at a high price? Even if the snake doesn't bite you, it bites the others, who are weaker. And what will you do? Applaud the snake? Or mingle with those who have been bitten and like Prometheus bring them fire?' Memet also loved Kleist's *Michael Kohlhaas*. He said: 'Michael rebelled against the powerful because of a horse. That's exactly it! One can burn a blanket because of a flea. These are the great characters, who went beyond their limits. You must go beyond your limits! You must draw all the emotions out of your body, until you have got to know them. Then your limits will fall away. Theatre is a laboratory, in which the emotions are studied under a microscope. But first you have to draw them out of your body.' At the last sentence Memet put his hand on his genitals, then raised his hand again very slowly, as if he were pulling his internal organs out of his body, screaming as he did so.

Another teacher had studied in Germany and like the communist hostel warden in Berlin loved the epic theatre and Bertolt Brecht. He said: 'You mustn't act with the emotions, but must act with your head, you must draw on science and analyse the relations between people sociologically. You can't get everything from your bodies. You shouldn't listen to what's inside you, but look at, observe your surroundings. With screaming and roaring you don't display the world, but only yourselves. But the drama only comes into existence between the stage and the auditorium and not just on the stage.' With him we had to research and portray the characters sociologically. In that way the audience could learn something about themselves and their view of the world and have a positive or negative attitude to the play and its characters. They could start struggling with one another or even hit one another. Some of the audience would perhaps leave the theatre. 'The head of a good actor must work like a trapeze artist or a tightrope walker, between death and life at every second.'

We students called our two teachers Body Man and Head Man. With one we left our bodies at the classroom door and went into the lesson only with our heads, with the other we left our heads at the classroom door and went into the class as bodies. I came home, lay down on the carpet, threw my body from side to side, screamed and practised fetching emotions out of my body. Old Aunt Topus saw that and said: 'Your father should have you put in the madhouse.' Or as head I sat down at the table opposite my mother and said to her: 'What have you done this week to expand your consciousness?' My mother asked me what consciousness was supposed to mean. Because I couldn't answer properly, I asked her, like the students in Berlin: 'Mother, which came first, the chicken or the egg?' My mother laughed and said: 'You are the egg that came out of my bottom, and you think the hen you came out of is no longer good enough. Don't make me cross, or I'll piss on the word consciousness. You fill your stomach thanks to your father's money and want to sell me fashionable new words. Sell your words in the theatre.' I answered my mother as Hamlet: 'There is something rotten in the state of Denmark.'

Once during a lesson Memet handed round photos and said: 'Photographs constantly influence our idea of the appearance of things. If one looks at something, one doesn't simply look at it, but is also influenced by what photographs have already conveyed to one beforehand. You have to walk into a picture and decode what you think is its reality. And onstage you have to represent the emotion this photo has conveyed to you, with a voice and with the body.' He gave me a photo. A dead man lay on the ground, his mouth open, he was as thin as a skeleton, naked, his cheekbones, his knees and shoulder blades stuck out of the body as if he were lying in a desert and the body was slowly drying up. But on the photo there were trees nearby. I went on to the stage, looked at the photo for two minutes, screamed and threw myself from side to side, pulled at my hair and really did vomit on to the stage. After this improvisation our teacher, Memet, embraced me. I breathed in deeply at his chest and groaned. Memet said he couldn't do any more teaching today. 'The dead man in the photo is a Jew, and the place is a concentration camp.' It made me almost crazy, that there were trees close to this dead man. During classes I was constantly scratching my legs, until they bled.

When I sat on the ship between Europe and Asia and read other people's newspapers, I now always looked at the newspaper photographs and tried to observe the emotions these photos conveyed to me. In one photo a man held a big knife to the throat of his child. The child was holding a toy in his hand, the man was unshaven, and from his shirt one could see that he had been sweating heavily, he was standing among dusty stones and wooden beams. The police had torn down his illegally built slum home. In order to prevent the police knocking anything more down, he was threatening to cut his little son's throat, if they continued. The child's pyjama top was also stained with sweat. In the newspapers there were often photos of Demirel, the ruling party leader, who, for example, was standing beside the American president, Johnson, they weren't sweating. But the shirt of the American soldier, who in another photo was walking alone through the thick jungle in Vietnam with his sub-machine gun, was soaked through at the chest, like the shirt of the poor man in the slum quarter of Istanbul. Or the photo of a Vietcong fighter who had just been shot in the head: this man's hands had been tied behind his back, and his shirt too was sweaty. There were often photos of mining accidents on the Black Sea coast. The families of the dead carried sixty coffins under the hot sun, and the shirts of the men who were carrying the coffins were also stained with sweat. The hair of the wives of the dead miners stuck to their cheeks or foreheads. Very often there were pictures of Palestinians and Jews, they stood on the streets, bodies lay in front of them, and the shirts and hair of the Jews and Palestinians were sweaty. In one photo a Jewish man was wearing a pair of glasses, but the glasses had slid down because he was sweating. He was in the street looking at the body parts of his son, which had been shattered by bombs. I had already seen sweating in a big way as a child. My school class had been taken to a factory. There was a large fire, the workers placed large pieces of iron from the fire in water and sweated. We children began to sweat too, and emerged from the factory with wet school smocks and hair. I had stolen a small piece of iron, took it home with me, and when I was doing my homework I often held it in my hand, it was very heavy. The porters bore heavy loads on their backs and sweated. When I got on the bus, I sometimes saw a free seat, on which there were traces of sweat. A dwarf once stood next to me on the bus. He looked up at me from below and sweated. We were standing by the door of the bus. The door opened at every stop, our shadows fell on the street, and his shadow, too, remained small next to mine. Perhaps that's why the dwarf moved closer to me at every stop, so at some point his shadow fell exactly across mine, and there was a single large shadow. When he hid his shadow in mine at the following bus stops as well, I too began to sweat. Once I saw a water-seller under the Bridge of the Golden Horn, he was just wiping his sweat with a cloth, fell over and was dead. The beads of sweat still fell on to the ground from his dead face. In the newspapers there were headlines about striking workers: 'The employer wants to buy the sweat of his workers cheap'.

Onstage I tried to improvise the sweating figures, and wanted to show the drama of a character. But it was hard to sweat properly onstage, so I took a glass of water and poured it over my hair before I went onstage, or I daubed little drops of vaseline on my forehead and stuck some hair on top.

Once I played a woman worker who was killed by police bullets. As she was dying, she was supposed to bleed from her mouth. In my mouth I had a small plastic sachet with fake blood, bit the sachet, which was supposed to burst, but it didn't. I bit again and again, and that made me and the others laugh. But then we asked ourselves: People are really dying, and we're laughing, what are we doing here? We thought, we're parasites and are living on the blood of others, who really bled or sweated. Those students who were left-wing asked: Theatre for art's sake or theatre for the people? How could one go down to the people with theatre? So they played workers, who were either heroes or poor, good people. Our Brecht teacher said: 'You're not playing the workers, but an opinion about them, and you're only shouting to arouse pity and pain.' In the newspaper I saw a working-class woman whose husband had been killed by the police. She was pressing a corner of her headscarf to her mouth, perhaps so as not to cry out. I also saw a scarf coming away from the head of a woman in Palestine, who was standing in front of the body of her child who had been killed, or the hat of a Jew which was just falling off, as he bent down to a dying child in the street. But screaming and shouting was a big fashion at the drama school. The whole school screamed and shouted. The street sweepers from Anatolia were walking 470 miles to Istanbul because of their low wages, and at drama school we shouted while acting the part of one of these street sweepers. We shouted like the popular press: 'Cry of a worker's child', 'The unheard cry of a poor man', 'A starving people cries out'. Our teacher, who loved Brecht, said: 'You mustn't shout, but research the story. Because you don't research the story, the things that happen in the world fall on top of you like a nightmare and you don't represent the reality of these people, but your feelings in the face of this nightmare, and out of that you create a new nightmare. Which of you knows a worker? No one. Or people in a war? You portray shouting statues, but the analysis of society is missing. Stop all the shouting, you'll make yourselves ill. Shouting is your mask. Take off the mask and read history books about the Ottoman Empire.' But we went on shouting and screaming, the shouting went right into our bedrooms, even there we didn't take off this mask. I slept with a couple of boys from the drama school. They lived in basement apartments with other young people; either there were three or four birds flying around in the flat and shitting on everything, or lots of empty wine bottles fell out of the cupboard when one opened it. We slept with one another, and the birds flying around the flats sometimes shat on our naked bodies and our hair, it was nice to kiss in beds full of bird shit, but the orgasm absolutely had to be a cry. I hadn't had an orgasm yet, but acted it with various cries. The boys, too, thought they absolutely had to shout out when they came, otherwise coming didn't count. I practised the best way for me to shout, so that it didn't sound fake. Sometimes we got a fit of coughing, we coughed and coughed, and at that very moment spatch spatch the birds shat on our backs, forehead or legs as well. The next morning the boy said to me: 'I think it was very nice for you, you cried out so nicely. Let's meet again, it was very nice with you.' So we arranged to meet, in order to practise shouting again.

One of our teachers, who did speech and articulation with us, interrupted the class when down in the street a street seller came past shouting. Every one of the street sellers of Istanbul had their own way of shouting. They were very poor men, who in order to sell water or sesame rings or fruit walked along the streets for seventeen hours a day and shouted.

Waateerrr.

Seesssaameerinnngs.

Goood baanaaanaas.

Late in the evening I often saw street sellers, pushing their wooden barrows or pulling them on the steep lanes of Istanbul. Their barrows were still half full of wares. Where did they take their wares when they slept in their one-room homes with their whole families? Did they put the aubergines or cucumbers or bananas beside their beds, so as to sell them the next day? Did the room smell all night not only of sleeping, tired people, but also of bananas and apples? It was forbidden to sell on the street. There was a special police force, which was supposed to catch the street sellers. I also often saw vendors suddenly making off with their barrows on the steep streets. The apples fell off the barrows and rolled down the steep streets. Or the wooden barrow toppled on its side and again aubergines or artichokes rolled down the steep streets. Then the street seller remained standing beside his toppled cart and looked at the faces of the people walking past and wanted to pick up their sympathy, before he went to pick up his apples. Their cries, which they used to reach people, sounded like composed music, their various calls flowed into each other, and our teacher who did speech and articulation with us said: 'If I had the opportunity, ladies and gentlemen, I would let some street sellers sing as opera singers at the opera.' We should walk around Istanbul and listen to all these voices, so that we learned the oratorio of Istanbul. All these men had been peasants and had come to Istanbul with their rolled-up beds. I often saw them on the Bridge of the Golden Horn. The low bridge across the sea wobbled under their feet, and they walked with their rolled-up beds on top of their heads as if they were walking across a desert which no one could see the end, and as if they were dreaming of arriving at a watering place. The peasants said: 'The streets of Istanbul are paved with gold,' and they travelled six or seven days by truck from their villages to Istanbul, to find work there. There was a joke about the golden streets of Istanbul: A poor peasant arrived in Istanbul and immediately tripped over a lump of gold, as big as a brick. He lifted up the piece of gold and threw it into the sea, because he believed all the streets were paved with gold, so why should he hold on to the first bit? Our teacher who taught us speech and articulation said: 'Let the street sellers shout, their cry is artistic, it is their pain, which has developed into a music. Instead of shouting, you should look at silent films and practise saying nothing for a while. You will see that it is hard, but who told you that it was easy to be a good artist. In the Brecht film *Kuhle Wampe* an unemployed man commits suicide. He jumps out of the window. But before he jumps, he takes off his watch and carefully puts it on the table. Then he jumps and dies. How would you play the scene? He is still able to think of taking off his watch, so that his family can sell the watch and feed themselves for a little while from that. And the moment when he puts down his watch tells the viewers something more precise about the character and about unemployment. It's with such precision that you can catch the emotions of the audience and at the same time force it to think about the social circumstances of the unemployed. You must go and look at good films and observe the camera movements in the films. How does the camera move from a close-up to a detail?'

There were silent films in only one cinema, in the Cinematheque. Hüseyin said: 'The Cinematheque is the centre of the left-wing intellectuals. And the left-wing trade unions reserve twenty tickets for every film and send twenty street sweepers or steel workers to the Cinematheque. They watch the film and then recount it to their workmates. The French film-maker Jean-Luc Godard has said: "The first thing to be exchanged between countries is films."' The films shown in the Istanbul Cinematheque were Soviet revolutionary films, e.g. *Battleship Potemkin* by Eisenstein. I had already seen this film in Berlin with German leftists, now I saw it for the second time with Turkish leftists. Hüseyin said: 'It's good that we came here today. Today a Russian-speaker will translate the film live. A famous Turkish communist who lived in exile in Russia for years.' The man was short, held the microphone in his hand and translated the Russian subtitles into Turkish. When it rained in the film, he said: 'Now it's raining, ladies and gentlemen.' When a couple kissed, he said: 'Now they're kissing each other, ladies and gentlemen.' The whole cinema burst into laughter, and he said into the microphone: 'Oh.' The left-wing sailors were rebelling against the Tsarist regime. I paid attention to the movement of the camera all the time and quietly repeated what I saw: I see an old woman, a bullet strikes her glasses, the camera closes up to the glasses, I see the broken glass. Then I see a ship. On the ship there are dissatisfied sailors. The camera travels close to the meat that is going to be cooked for the sailors. In the meat I see many worms, the meat is rotten.

The next day I tried to act onstage what I had seen in the close-ups of details. I bought two pairs of glasses, I broke the lenses of one pair, then acted that I was being struck in the face, surreptitiously exchanged my glasses for the broken ones, turned back to face the students and my teacher Memet. They saw the cracked lenses of the glasses, and they liked this detail. It was as if a camera were showing them the detail in close-up. Even our teacher Memet thought this technically prepared number very good. I saw a film that was called *Weeping*. In one scene a girl said to the male lead: 'You play violin and I'll play piano.' She began to play the piano, on the piano there was a violin case. The man took out the violin, but before he put the violin to his shoulder to play, the music had already begun, because image and sound had been poorly synchronised. At the end of the film the girl got TB, and before she died she wanted once more to play a piano and violin duet. But even before the lead actor opened the violin case, a member of the audience shouted at the screen: 'Don't bother, brother. The violin will play by itself.'

After that in class I played a violin player onstage, and another student started playing even before I had opened the case, that made the other students laugh.

I had found my secret acting school: movies. But I didn't just go to the Cinematheque for the films. In a normal cinema, when the lights came up after the film, people left slowly, buttoning up their jackets. But in the Cinematheque all the people looked at one another and greeted one another. They stood outside the cinema in large groups and talked about the film and again and again someone who was just coming out of the cinema joined the group. Everyone knew everyone else, or one quickly got to know other people, as at a mosque.

The Cinematheque in Istanbul was a centre for the left, like the Steinplatz Cinema in Berlin. But in Berlin I had seen only students. Here in Istanbul I also saw many workers or older men and women. We saw Russian films about the childhood of Maxim Gorki or about Tolstoy; Tolstoy gave away his estates to the poor Russian peasants. In the films about the Russian Revolution many people died from the bullets of the Tsarist soldiers, and when we came out of the Cinematheque, the people who gathered in the street outside the cinema looked as if they had come to a funeral. The stories of the Revolution in the films took place on the Russian streets, and we, the audience then stood in the street outside the cinema for a long time, as if the Istanbul streets were the extension of the streets of the Revolution from the Russian films. Then we slowly set off in groups, as if we were bearing these dead to their graves, and looked at those walking in front of us and who were bearing the same dead to their graves with us. We wanted to stay in the street for a long time. The intellectuals first of all talked about the dead, but then they began to talk about the camerawork or the lighting of the film. As they were doing so they got into the same buses or taxis, went on talking in them and, still talking, they arrived at the 'Captain' restaurant, and when the waiters pushed the tables together for them, they went on talking about the film as they were standing. And in order to extend the revolutionary streets even further and to remain in the street for even longer, I also always went with them. The street sweepers, however, who had been sent to the Cinematheque by their left-wing trade unions, never came to the 'Captain' restaurant with us. I often heard them say outside the cinema: 'Quick, let's go, it's dark now,' and they hurried away. When the workers and the intellectuals left at different speeds, it was as if there were two different nights. One night belonged to the workers to sleep in, and the other belonged to the intellectuals to keep on talking.

The waiters in the restaurant immediately brought raki to the table. The restaurant was right by the sea next to the harbour. When a ship sailed past close to the houses, the captain of the ship greeted the people who were eating supper in their houses, reading the newspaper in their pyjamas or, like us, sitting in the restaurant. We raised our raki glasses to him and some women threw apples on to the ship. We sat at a long table in the restaurant. The old men had white beards and sat at the head of the table. There were very few girls or women, and if I sat down somewhere at the table to greet someone, I was reminded of the whores in a bar. The whores in Istanbul were called consumatrists, they went from table to table, at which only men were sitting, to get the latter to pay for an expensive drink. So, before I sat down somewhere at the table, I said: 'I have come as a consumatrist.' The men laughed; to them I was a girl with consciousness. The word consciousness was an important word. And I loved sitting among these bearded or clean-shaven intellectuals as the only girl. It was like playing the lead, and the men were my audience. But when I went home alone at night, I sailed on the last ship, the 'ship of drunks', because at that time only the men who had got drunk on the European side of Istanbul were on the ship. 'Now they think I'm a whore.' I walked as if I had swallowed a long stick, and raised one eyebrow, so that my face looked serious. But it was an effort constantly to be playing 'I am not a whore'. 'Where are you coming from, my pretty, so late at night?' Good, just let them think I'm a whore, I thought suddenly. Whores had also had mothers as I had. And a girl who was really poor could find her feet again in a couple of days in the whores' world. Just two days of hunger, two days without a roof and no two people who could help her, that was enough. Then a girl would knock on the door of a whorehouse. I had been pregnant, but other people had helped me. A poor girl in my place would have entered the whores' world. That I now knew people like Hüseyin, the Surrealists, the Cinematheque intellectuals or the drama students was my good fortune. Many other girls who didn't find any help had to go to work as whores. Of all the women I saw on the street, suddenly only the whores interested me. They sat under bright neon lights in the late-night restaurants that were still open and gave me courage.

In the 'Captain' restaurant a couple of intellectuals related what had happened to them the night before. They had gone to a brothel, but the brothel was already shut. They had knocked on the window: 'Open up, we'll pay.' The whores shouted: 'Go home, we've finished work for the night.' – 'We'll pay!' One of the whores leaned out of the window and hit the head of one of the intellectuals with her high-heeled shoe and shouted: 'You want to pay? Now you've paid!' Then everyone drank a raki to the whores. The raki loosened the tied tongues and one of the men with the white beards started talking about the erotic book *Bahname*. The seven-hundred-year-old book was in an Istanbul library, but only a few professors were allowed to borrow it. One of the authors of this book was called Nasreddin, actually the father of astronomy. He wrote about a sultan's son, who slept with the most beautiful women in the world, but one day he lost his potency. The doctors tried everything, but he no longer felt any desire. The astronomer Nasreddin was summoned to the seraglio, and the sultan wanted Nasreddin to write a book, so that his son would feel desire again. Nasreddin's thirteenth recipe for lust was: First take a baby bird, but it must not have any feathers yet, and place it next to a beehive. The bees should sting it. Throttle the baby bird and place the bloody body in a pot, add oil of basil, cook it, then crush the cooked baby bird, pour it into a bottle and seal the opening of the bottle with a candle. Leave the bottle in the sun for three days. Pour some oil from the bottle on to a piece of cloth, rub it between toes and fingers and then make love. The white-bearded professor did not know whether the recipe had been any help, but immediately related other recipes. 'To turn wives who were no longer virgins back into virgins: Boil 5 grams goat's beard, 16 grams grape juice and vinegar. Seat the woman next to the boiling pot, let her breathe in the steam seven times, pour the boiled goat's beard, vinegar and grape juice on to a piece of cloth and rub the woman's organ with it.' The waiters also listened to the recipes and brought one raki after another, so that the stories continued. Another old man at the end of the table began: 'In the *Bahname* there is advice on how men and women should smell and kiss one another, and how many times one should make love at which age. Those who were still in puberty should make love every second day, between twenty and thirty twice a day, once a night. Between thirty and forty three times a day. When one's seventy, twice a day. When one's eighty, two or three times a year, but if one feels a great deal of desire, four times a year.' There was advice as to how one could tell whether women felt desire. Lack of desire could be discerned from women's eyebrows, the length of their fingers, hair colour, heels, ankles and wrists, nostrils, navels, neck, ears and their laughter. On the size of female and male organs: the male organs were divided into three groups. First group: twelve finger breadths long. Second group: eight finger breadths long. Third group: six finger breadths long. The book recommends that the big women's organs meet with twelve-finger-breadth men's organs, middling women's organs with eight-finger-breadth men's organs, and tight women's organs with six-finger-breadth men's organs. The intellectual who had been hit on the head by a whore the previous night also knew the book: 'The first Ottoman whores appeared in 1565. They first of all worked in the laundries, to which single men brought their laundry to be washed. Then these laundries were forbidden. After that they worked in the yogurt and cream shops, until the Ottoman police discovered that men were not only eating cream in the cream shops, and the cream shops were also forbidden. Legal prostitution took place in the slave bazaars. There a man rented a female slave, kept her for a couple of days and then took her back to the slave bazaar and said: 'She's got a fault.' There were also male prostitutes: in 1577 a man sought out nine boys from various quarters of Istanbul. He had them grow their hair long, dressed them in women's clothes and sent them to the wealthy Ottoman houses as sellers of bedlinen or as fortune-tellers. That's how the married, rich women got their lovers. But one day the police found out about it, and many rich men divorced their wives, because they weren't sure whether these men with long hair had come into their houses as well. So in 1577 there were suddenly many divorced women in Istanbul.

We sat for many hours in the 'Captain' restaurant, because the stories never stopped. The owner of the 'Captain' never said that he had to close now, he didn't even show us that he was waiting, instead he sent us chopped-up fruit on a plate and in a dark corner raised his raki glass to us. Istanbul Greeks also came to the 'Captain'. And at the end of the night they smashed plates on the floor for sheer enjoyment, the waiters swept the broken pieces into the sea, and in the moonshine they gleamed in the water. One of the intellectuals related that, after nationalist Turks had destroyed the shops, Orthodox churches and cemeteries of the Istanbul Greeks on a September night in 1955, many Istanbul Greeks had gone to Athens because they were afraid. Before they left Istanbul one family, who lived on an Istanbul island, threw all their old records into the sea, and the beautiful old Greek songs on the records floated for days in the Sea of Marmara. As the intellectual related that, the waves dashed against the 'Captain' restaurant and made us all wet. The night was warm and soon dried us. We sat there in the arms of the sea and of the warm night, and the world dwindled to this restaurant; it was as if I had been born there with all these old and young men and would die there at the end of the night, and meanwhile we would listen to many stories. Perhaps I myself will tell one and then close my eyes, and the sea will rock our dead in its arms and we will float in the Sea of Marmara like the beautiful old Greek records, and everyone who sees us will know that a couple of beautiful songs come from each of the dead.

At night, if I came home late, my father was sometimes still sitting in front of the radio, he was looking for music, hit the old radio a couple of times, so that the voice came out of it, and said

to me: 'My daughter, you have become a man. You have brought
a new fashion from Germany. You come home in the middle of
the night.' He also said: 'My daughter, you are spinning in space
like the world, I hope you won't get lost in the sky.' During the
day I went to the drama school on the European side, then to the
Cinematheque, then to the 'Captain' restaurant, and then I came
back to the Asian side of Istanbul to my parents' house as if to a
hotel. I slept in Asia and when the bird Memish began to sing in
the morning sailed to Europe again.

# The Cigarette is the Most Important Prop of a Socialist

At that time, in 1967, there was no bridge yet between Asia and Europe. The sea separated the two sides, and when I had the water between my parents and myself, I felt free. In a fairy tale a young man threw a mirror behind him, he was being chased by giants who wanted to eat him, but the mirror turned into an ocean and the giants remained on the other shore. I could also lie and say: 'Father, I missed the last ship, I slept at the house of a woman teacher.' The Asian and the European side in Istanbul were two different countries. It was said that one of our drama teachers had used these two sides of Istanbul to become famous. As a young man he had supposedly gone to Russia and had worked there as an assistant to the famous Russian theatre director Stanislavsky. Then he had come back and worked as a theatre director in Istanbul; there were many who said he was the best man of the theatre in the whole country, he was our Stanislavsky. His enemies, however, said that on the European side of Istanbul he had told all his friends, 'Goodbye, I'm travelling to Russia, to Stanislavsky,' but had then gone only to the Asian side of Istanbul. The trip took twenty minutes. There he had hidden in a house for six months, read all of Stanislavsky's books, learned them by heart, and after six months he had come out of his hiding place on the Asian side of Istanbul again and returned

to the European side on the ferry. I didn't know whether it was
true, perhaps it was a pack of lies made up against this teacher
because he was very famous. There was a saying: 'Anyone whose
tree bears many apples will be stoned.' I loved this teacher very
much. He was over ninety years old; in his class we had to invent
a story very quickly, go on to the stage and ourselves play all the
characters in our story. Sometimes he fell asleep during the class.
Memet said: 'He does it deliberately, because you don't surprise
him on the stage with your talent. He represents your future
audience.' When acting in the theatre the actors had to wake up
the members of the audience who had paid for their seats and had
eaten beforehand and now wanted to sleep in the theatre. In his
class I once played a woman who was going for a walk with her
child. I also played the child. The teacher said: 'My child, nothing
can separate you from the theatre, only a child. Children, did you
see how tender she was to her child?' In the part of the mother I
imitated my mother and then noticed how tender my mother was
to me. So it was at the theatre that I discovered my mother.❧

The ninety-year-old teacher also gave fat female students diet
recipes: 'My child, every morning before breakfast, you must
squeeze a lemon and drink the juice, then you can eat what you
want.' When we did something funny onstage, he laughed, and he
laughed so much he slapped the female student sitting beside him
on the thigh. After that I, too, once slapped an intellectual from
the 'Captain' restaurant on the thigh – as always at the end of
the night the intellectuals had risen from the long table together
and gone out as if stuck to one another. A cartoonist who with
his cartoons stood on the side of the left-wing movement drove
me to the harbour in his car. He said: 'The men in the "Captain"
restaurant always stand up from the table together, so that no
one can talk behind the back of another.' I laughed at that and
slapped his thigh with my left hand. 'Did I hurt you?' he asked.
'What kind of leg have you got?' – 'A wooden leg, I stand in the
left-wing movement. "Let me die in my bed with the moon that I
know." That's a poem by the Spanish poet Lorca, who was killed

by Franco's fascist Guardia Civil.' There was also a moon over Istanbul, and it was large. I said to Wooden Leg: 'A whole poem by Lorca, please.' Lorca, that was my love in Paris, Jordi. I thought, now Jordi is looking at the same moon as I am.

*So I took her to the river*
*thinking she was a virgin,*
*but it seems she had a husband.*
*It was the night of Saint Iago,*
*and it almost was a duty.*
*The lamps went out,*
*the crickets lit up.*
*By the last street corners*
*I touched her sleeping breasts,*
*and they suddenly had opened*
*like the hyacinth petals.*
*The starch*
*of her slip crackled*
*in my ears like silk fragments*
*ripped apart by ten daggers.*
*The tree crowns*
*free of silver light are larger,*
*and a horizon, of dogs, howls*
*far away from the river.*

*Past the hawthorns,*
*the reeds, and the brambles,*
*below her dome of hair*
*I made a hollow in the sand.*
*I took off my tie.*
*She took off a garment.*
*I my belt with my revolver.*
*She four bodices.*
*Creamy tuberoses*
*or shells are not as smooth as*

*This was the first Lorca poem I ever read, years ago*

*her skin was, or, in the moonlight,*
*crystals shining brilliantly.*

At this point the cartoonist Wooden Leg reached the harbour, where I had to get out. I said to him: 'Keep on driving, I want to hear the poem to the end.'

*Her thighs slipped from me*
*like fish that are startled,*
*one half full of fire,*
*one half full of coldness.*
*That night I galloped*
*on the best of roadways,*
*on a mare of nacre*
*without stirrups, without bridle.*
*As a man I cannot tell you*
*the things she said to me.*
*The light of understanding*
*has made me most discreet.*
*Smeared with sand and kisses,*
*I took her from the river.*
*The blades of the lilies*
*were fighting with the air.*

*I behaved as what I am,*
*as a true gypsy.*
*I gave her a sewing basket,*
*big, with straw-coloured satin.*
*I did not want to love her,*
*for though she had a husband,*
*she said she was a virgin*
*when I took her to the river.*

When the poem by Lorca was finished, we arrived at Wooden Leg's house. He said to me: 'Quiet, I live with my mother.' He took off his wooden leg, we slept with each other, and he told funny stories in bed; again I laughed, but didn't slap his thigh, but the mattress, and this time he laughed at that. Towards morning he said: 'Now my mother will get up for the morning prayer, let's go.' He put his leg on again and showed me a white, empty liqueur bottle. In one place there was a speck of blood. 'There's a glass factory in Istanbul where workers blow the glass. Many of the glass-blowers have TB, and one of them coughed and spat blood, just as he was blowing this liqueur bottle.' Wooden Leg drove over the Bridge of the Golden Horn to the harbour, but suddenly he stopped, because the bridge was being raised, so that the big Russian ships could pass through. We remained sitting in the car on one side of the bridge, the big ships sailed by very close to us on their way to Arabia and hooted loudly. Wooden Leg cried out:

> At times one sees the tiny form
> flitting across his eyes.
> Sailor and all, he forgets
> oranges and bars.
> He gazes at the water.

As the bridge slowly came down again, Wooden Leg took a book by Lorca out of the glove compartment. 'For you.' On the ship I read one of the poems in the book. Lorca wrote about two nuns. They sat in a meadow under the hot sun and embroidered the colours of nature on pieces of cloth. There were photos in the book; I saw a little house, from which the fascist Guardia Civil had perhaps fetched Lorca to kill him. He had written in his poem: 'Let me die in my bed with the moon that I know.' The house, the nuns, embroidering the colours of nature on their cloth, perhaps Lorca had seen these nuns from the window of this house, from which one day he had also seen the Guardia Civil coming. I imagined that moment, Lorca in the house, the Guardia Civil comes to fetch him. Sun outside, the wind stirs the grass, and the fascists left footprints in the grass. The grass died under their boots, and perhaps the green of the grass and the dampness coloured the tips of the fascist boots green. Lorca is alone in the dark house. One of the Guardia Civil kicked the door with his boots, perhaps green traces of grass were left on the door. At that moment what was Lorca doing in the house? His minutes seemed so long to me. The time inside the house was different from the time of those coming to fetch him. I imagined saving Lorca. I entered the house before the Guardia Civil. I am disguised as a nun and bring him a nun's clothes. He has to shave quickly, disguise himself as a nun, and we go out of the house together into the countryside, sit down on the grass and embroider our cloth with the colours we see in nature. All the dead gave one the feeling that one had come too late. I began to read books about the Spanish Civil War, Hemingway's *For Whom the Bell Tolls*. In it there was a scene in which the anti-fascist hero slept with the anti-fascist heroine – at that moment the earth moved, but not because of an earthquake or because of explosions, but because of their love. For me the hero was my first love in Paris, the Spaniard Jordi. Why is Franco still in power? I often thought; I felt powerless because he was still alive and Jordi and many others had to live under his rule. It was in those days that a postcard arrived from Jordi in Barcelona. On the card I saw a beautiful square full of cafés, chairs and pigeons. Jordi wrote to me that he was raising his glass to my beautiful eyes and sent me greetings. I looked at the card for a long time and was astonished that under the fascist Franco there was such a beautiful square in Spain, that in the cafés there were chairs and that pigeons were walking in front of these chairs and Jordi could raise and drink a glass of wine to my beautiful eyes. I was astonished that in Spain a left-winger like Jordi could legally go to the post office, buy a stamp and send a card to another country. That's also why I read the card in secret, so that in Spain he wouldn't have any problems with the police. On a card I wrote two lines by Lorca – 'Green, as I love you, greenly./Green the wind, and green the branches' – and threw it into the sea with Jordi's address. The sea would take it to him. Jordi's card made me so happy that I got electric shocks when

I touched an object. I walked across the Bridge of the Golden Horn, at that moment it was raining, and I thought: 'Jordi, out of the sky, which we sometimes gave our love to bear, love is raining on the shirts of the poor men on the Golden Bridge.'

Poverty ran through the streets like an infectious disease. I looked on the poor as on plague victims and could do nothing for them. If I saw a half-man in a wheelchair, I tried to avoid eye contact with him from the front, but my eyes followed him for a long time from behind. It was only the blind that I looked at from the front. To look into the eyes of the poor was very hard. I looked over my left shoulder so often, to see poverty from behind, that my left shoulder hurt. On the steep streets there were many book vendors. They laid their books on the ground, and the wind leafed through them, books about the Russian and the French Revolutions or about resistance fighters who had been beheaded five hundred years ago by the Ottomans, books by Nazim Hikmet, books about the Spanish Civil War. All killed, strangled, beheaded people, who had not died in their beds, rose up in those years. Poverty ran in the streets, and the people who in their lives had wanted to do something about it and had been killed as a result now lay in the streets as books. One only had to bend down to them, buy them, and hence many of those who had been killed entered homes, gathered on the bookshelves next to the pillows and lived in the houses. The people who shut and opened their eyes with these books went out into the streets again in the morning as Lorca, Sacco and Vanzetti, Robespierre, Danton, Nazim Hikmet, Pir Sultan Abdal, Rosa Luxemburg. At home I opened the refrigerator, and if there was meat or fruit there, I said to my mother: 'Are you not ashamed to be buying so much meat, when so many people are starving?' My mother said: 'If we starve, then there are a couple more people starving. If you don't want to, don't eat.' I ate, but I glanced angrily around me. Sometimes I tried to puke up a chop, but I didn't manage it. My father said to me: 'My daughter, you probably caught a head cold in Germany.' I slammed the door, went out into the street, where I bought another book about one of the killed. Tolstoy had distributed his land to the poor peasants. I had a jacket, which I lent to two boys at the drama school who didn't have much money, I gave it to one for a week, then to the other for a week. That created a legend: I was very generous, like a real left-winger. I started stealing books, particularly in expensive bookshops; there, between luxury editions of atlases of the world or the encyclopedias, I saw books of the killed and stole them. So I collected five copies of the same Nazim Hikmet book in the bookcase at home. I also stole money from my father and with it again bought books about those who had been killed. When I had so many books that I couldn't read them all, these unread books began to make me feel guilty. I constantly rearranged them and wiped dust from the shelves; that reassured me, but not for long. The intellectuals of the 'Captain' restaurant also reassured me; they had read a great deal and told many stories out of books, it seemed to me that I was sitting at the table with living books. The men asked each other: 'What do you think about that?' No one asked me what I thought about a subject; to them I played the part of the audience, they played with one another, and I watched them. I enjoyed being the audience. Wooden Leg said: 'Someone who speaks can make themselves guilty.' Perhaps they were protecting me from that. In between their conversations they wanted me to sing old songs from the days of the Ottomans. They applauded with closed eyes, and sometimes they sang along.

One day a new intellectual was sitting with them, he looked like an owl, he had the gaze of the leader of a religious sect in India. I loved owls very much, and he looked familiar to me. I said to the intellectual sitting beside me: 'I know that face.' – 'You know his father from the newspapers. In the fifties he was a famous minister of the Americanised party.' He sat there like the ghost of his father, with the same owl face, and was a member of the new left-wing Turkish Workers' Party, which at the last election had immediately won fifteen seats in Parliament. Usually the intellectuals had wanted to drink raki, eat slowly and tell long stories from the Ottoman times. This evening, however, they forgot the raki in their glasses and the food on their plates. They all looked at the man who looked like an owl, and if one spoke a sentence, then another went into the sentence like a big pair of scissors, cut the sentence through the middle and completed the sentence himself. Then this sentence was cut up by another pair of scissors. Suddenly twenty big pairs of scissors were sitting at the table, turning to left and right.

One pair of scissors said: 'The potential of the Turkish working class...'

Another pair of scissors said: 'What working class? The Ottomans didn't even create an aristocracy...'

Another pair of scissors said: 'Because the people in the seraglio were allowed to have a career, they had to...'

Another pair of scissors said: '...leave their families and only serve...'

Another pair of scissors said: '...the Sultan.'

Another pair of scissors: 'It's impossible to talk of a Turkish national bourgeoisie, because...'

Another pair of scissors said: '...the Turkish bourgeoisie only assembles things, it doesn't make them, it's dependent on America and they deposit...'

Another pair of scissors said: '...their money in Switzerland.'

Another pair of scissors said: 'Conditions in Turkey are still...'

Another pair of scissors said: '...feudal.'

Another pair of scissors said: 'No, industrialisation is happening very fast, and if the objective conditions are right, the consciousness of the working class can...'

Another pair of scissors said: '...bring the Party to power. But only if they learn to have a consciousness about imperialism...'

Another pair of scissors said: '...because Turkey is still an American colony like Africa and...'

Another pair of scissors said: '...Latin America. First one has to go to the people and bring it...'

Another pair of scissors said: '...consciousness and not forget that we are a...'

Another pair of scissors said: '...nation of peasants. What about the role...'

Another pair of scissors said: '...of the peasants?'

Another pair of scissors said: 'Wrong. Feudalism only exists in eastern Turkey...'

Another pair of scissors said: '...among the Kurds and...'

Another pair of scissors said: '...the rest of the peasants are bound to the capitalist...'

Another pair of scissors said: '...bazaar.'

Another pair of scissors said: 'The legal struggle against capitalism with Leninism...'

I listened to the sentences of the twenty pairs of scissors as the only girl and stuck the words next to one another for myself: consciousness, going to the people, imperialism, dependent bourgeoisie, feudalism, Latin America, Africa, Swiss bank, Kurds, feudal peasantry, potential of the Turkish working class, national bourgeoisie, Leninism, objective and subjective conditions. While I was sticking the words together, the intellectuals went on talking, went on forgetting to eat and drink, scratched their hair, and I saw dandruff raining from their hair on to the table.

Suddenly the intellectual who looked like an owl asked all the way down the table: 'And what do you think about the subject?' I was sitting exactly opposite him at the other end of the table. All heads now turned as if in slow motion to look at me. The nightmare of an actress is that she forgets her lines. Now I was in this nightmare. I didn't know my lines and had to go onstage. I was sweating, and my hair was sticking to my cheeks. One of the white-bearded intellectuals picked up his glass of raki and said: 'Let's not forget the raki.' And everyone said 'Şerefe' – cheers – picked up their raki glasses, and the intellectual with the white beard said to me: 'Sing a beautiful song.' I sang: 'Oh why, my love, why. I have loved you, that's my fault.' The intellectual who looked like an owl looked at me for a long time as I was singing. He reminded me of the newspapers of my childhood. I heard him say to someone: 'I, as a true Bolshevist...', he had very beautiful eyes. When everyone had got up from the table and was walking towards the door, I bent down under the table, as if I had to lace up my shoes. Under the table I saw him coming in my direction. I saw only his legs, which stood still for a moment. He was the last to leave and walked very slowly towards the door, we arrived there together and each wanted to let the other go first, but with all our politeness we bumped into each other, and we laughed. The other intellectuals saw our laughter and left us alone. I said: 'Take me with you.'

His house looked down on the sea from a hill. We stood at the bottom of the stairs and switched on the light. He pushed up my blouse, the blouse with the yellow flowers, which I had been wearing the day the student, Benno Ohnesorg, was killed, when the Shah visited Berlin. The man who looked like an owl said: 'What a nice blouse.' He grasped my breasts and said: 'What beautiful breasts you have.' As we kissed, I heard the sounds of sand under our shoes. With sand under our shoes we went into the flat, and there, above the bed and a couple of chairs, the big moon was waiting for us. We sat in the moonlight, smoked a cigarette together and lay down on the moon, which was lying on the bed. In the moonlight I had my first orgasm with this owl. He brought a big plate of cherries, put them on the table, and now the cherries, too, were in the moonlight. We sat on two chairs, I saw his hands and mine taking cherries from the plate, putting the stones on another plate and taking another cherry, with each cherry we ate the moonlight along with it. He covered me up in bed and said: 'Go to sleep, I'm going downstairs.' And he went out in the moonlight. Again I heard the sounds of sand under his shoes. What was he doing when he left the room? I fell asleep with the moon and woke up with the sun. The man who looked like an owl was sitting on the bed, this time with the sun in his hair, and he said: 'You sleep very beautifully, very peacefully, like a child.' I was the child, he was the owl.

After that I met the owl often; once he bought every flower from a night-time flower seller, and in his room, where the moon lived, he spread them all over me. I had an orgasm again, then he left again in the moonlight, to go downstairs, and only the smell of the flowers remained in the room. In the morning I was about to make the bed, he came in and said: 'Leave it. You know, I was married and went to London with my wife. She only made our bed before we went to bed. She fell in love with an English postman and married him.' The story suited the room: the moon, the flowers, the owl who was an intellectual, had a famous father and who was a Bolshevist – and his wealthy wife, who no doubt was also an intellectual, had fallen in love with an English postman.

Once he went downstairs before I had an orgasm. I had bought a contraceptive cream at the chemist's. He had to help me with it, but then I had too much cream in my body, we couldn't go on. We didn't sleep with one another and sat in bed in the moonlight. For the first time the moonlight bothered me. He asked me: 'What is your father's profession?' Again I was ashamed of my father's profession. 'Building contractor.' He asked: 'What's his name?' There were well-known building contractors, but my father was not well known. He had originally been a stonemason, and in the 1950s, when the party in which the father of the man who looked like an owl was a minister came to power and opened the door to American capital and there was a lot of building in Turkey with the American money, my father had become a building contractor. Now, in the 1960s, there were big construction companies, and building contractors like my father got less and less work. I didn't know what I was ashamed of – that my father was a building contractor, a capitalist, or that he wasn't a famous building contractor. Owl asked: 'Did you take your school-leaving certificate?' I lied and said, 'Yes.' Then he asked: 'Where? At which grammar school?' – 'Ankara.' Ankara was the capital and many ministers with an academic background lived there. Owl covered me up again and went downstairs in the moonlight once more. The flowers he had bought a couple of days before had withered in the room. I had a date with the man who looked like an owl the next evening. But our teacher, Memet, kept us at school very late. So I got to the bar where we had arranged to meet a couple of hours late. He had left, I took a taxi and it was the middle of the night by the time I reached his house. I stood at his door and heard his voice and the voice of a woman. I couldn't go back, because the taxi was waiting below and I didn't have any money. I had to knock, he paid the taxi, took me up to the top floor and accompanied the woman, whom I hadn't seen, to the taxi by which I had come. He came upstairs to me and said: 'Sleep here tonight, I have to work. I'll call you in the next few days.' Downstairs I heard only the noises he was making. He drew a chair or table across the stone floor, I heard sounds of paper, books he was leafing through. So upstairs I, too, leafed through his books. Marx, Lenin, Trotsky, Lunacharsky. The moon was no longer there, the withered flowers were also gone. The room with its many books was like a big reproach. No school-leaving certificate. I fell asleep as a blind donkey. The next morning he didn't come up. I heard the door snap shut and the sounds of sand under his shoes. He didn't call me. I bought a book by Lenin, but again felt like a blind donkey. I was also ashamed because I had gone by taxi to see him. Perhaps that's why I went to the Workers' Party and became a member.

The fifteen deputies of the Party often wore bandages on their noses, mouths and cheeks, because the right-wing deputies beat them up in Parliament. At a Party conference the young members like me stood at the doors of a large building and pinned paper Party badges to the jackets of members as they came in. As I pinned the Party badges to their lapels my hands felt how different the jacket materials were. Many members wore jackets that were too large or too small, perhaps they had borrowed the jackets from someone else for the day. The parliamentary deputies with the bandages on their faces also came, all the members turned their heads towards them and clapped, the ash from the cigarettes in their hands fell on to the floor or on to their trousers. When new delegates stopped in front of me at the door, so that I could pin the Party badge to them, they left their lit cigarettes in their mouths and looked me in the eye. They went into the hall and I remained standing at the doors with the other young members. We smoked, too, without saying anything, and laughed and again and again lit the next cigarette. I had small change in the pocket of my skirt, I frequently dropped it, and wanted the young, good-looking men who were standing around everywhere to see my legs. When someone at the Party conference went onstage and spoke into the microphone, the others listened to him as if they were watching an act on the trapeze. Their emotions went up with him: Will he make it? Will he not make it? While they were listening they looked like a single body, like a crowd in a football stadium, which stands up together, says Ah or Boo or applauds together. When listeners walked through the hall, while at the same time at the front someone was speaking into the microphone, that confused me, because it looked as if the body was breaking up. I went to the toilet and looked at my face in the mirror, suddenly it was hard to be alone in front of a mirror. I then walked very quickly down the long corridor back to the hall, as if I quickly had to find my body again. Like a child that had lost its street. Like the Cinematheque and the 'Captain' restaurant, the Party to me was like an extension of the street. Many streets came together here, and all those who met here were street children who, without knowing each other's names, immediately followed a cat or a crazy man and could pull the cat by the tail. Here the cat was America, American imperialism and its collaborators, the Turkish Justice Party, which was in power, and its boss, Demirel. There was a pyramid, in which the workers and socialists were right at the bottom and the rich were at the top. This pyramid was to be turned upside down, turned round. There was a slogan: 'The feet will one day be the head'. We were the feet, and when there were enough feet the pyramid could be turned upside down. Many feet still had a false consciousness, which could, however, be turned into a proper consciousness; the means to that had to be democratic and legal – to go to the people and bring them the proper consciousness. And the proper consciousness of the masses would bring the Party of Workers to power through elections. Bringing consciousness meant being able to speak, so that the others listened to one: 'America is a paper tiger', 'Land for the peasants, work for the workers, books for the students', 'We will make many Vietnams'. At the Party conference I often heard: 'Now listen to me.' – 'Friends, let's listen to him now.' – 'We are the ear of the Party.' At left-wing demonstrations the police cut the cables of the microphones, but the left-wingers had brought generators with them and shouted: 'Friends, comrades, they want to turn off our voice, but we will turn our voice up.' In the left-wing movement there were many generator stories: for example, in many villages there was no electricity. The left-wingers put the generator for the loudspeakers on the back of a donkey, the first speaker began, but the donkey ran away with the generator and the left-wingers and the peasants ran after the donkey and laughed. At the Party Conference some members were radios, some radio listeners. The radios and the radio listeners stood in small or large groups and smoked. The radios had dandruff on their collars. There were many who used their hands as ashtrays, one in the group held his open hand in the middle of the group and made it into an ashtray for all. Often their various voices resulted in an echo, as if five thousand radios were switched on simultaneously. I thought, if the roof of this building were to fly up because of the many voices, the radios and the radio listeners would fly after it, go on smoking and laughing up in the air, and the people who were sitting in their houses and offices would go to the window and look at the sky and see all the flying, smoking, laughing radios and radio listeners and much ash and dandruff would rain down from the sky.

There was a Workers' Party House in every Istanbul district, a large room in which chairs stood in rows as in a cinema. One man made tea, and all the members smoked. Each had to stand up and say something about the day's topic. The chair creaked, and the one who had stood up smoked as he was standing, his smoke stood higher than the smoke of those sitting. I always sat down right at the back, and before it was my turn to speak, I quickly went to the toilet, also smoked in front of the mirror there and heard the questions: Is Turkey sufficiently industrialised, so that the working class can put a workers' party in power? Or is Turkey still feudal or a colony? Are objective conditions already sufficiently ripe to allow a democratic transition from capitalism to socialism? Or is it first of all necessary to fight feudalism and to enlist all the progressive forces in the country, officers, intellectuals and civilians, for that? Which is the head? The workers or the peasants, the bourgeois intelligentsia or the officers? I had no idea what feudalism was. I stood in front of words like feudalism, imperialism, base of a society, superstructure of a society, as before a very deep well. I sought help from the dead. All the books I had to read! Rosa Luxemburg had read and written so much. But I still had time to become like her. I was only nineteen. And one sentence which I heard very often at Party meetings was a great relief: 'We can discuss that'. With that sentence discussion was put off to the next day. Not today, but tomorrow. The sentence was a good escape route. Either one discussed, or one said: 'We can discuss that.'

I met Owl again at a Party meeting and afterwards went with him and others to a restaurant. Suddenly Owl asked me, as he had done the first time: 'What do you think about that?' I said: 'We can discuss it.' When the restaurant wanted to close, Owl invited us all to his house. I went along too, and we sat in the room in which I had slept in the moonlight. Owl and all the other men went downstairs and let me sleep upstairs. From the bed I saw the balcony door, a snail was sticking to the pane, perhaps it had lost its way, had crawled higher and higher up the pane of glass and had finally died, but its body had remained sticking to the glass. I went to the balcony and looked down at the balcony of the lower floor. All the men were standing there in a group in their dark suits, smoking and looking at the sea. They stood there motionless, as in a dark black-and-white photo; my eyes no longer looked for Owl.

The next morning I looked down from the balcony again, and the men were again standing in a group and smoking. The sun shone, and they smoked in very different ways, very slowly, very fast. The cigarette was the most important prop of a socialist. When I smoked at home, I forgot my lit cigarette in the ashtray, went into the kitchen, where I lit another cigarette, came back, saw the other cigarette in the ashtray and smoked both cigarettes. When I came home from a Party meeting, old Aunt Topus said to me: 'How you stink. Air your clothes.' I saw jackets and trousers hung up to air on many balconies, and I thought, we're multiplying, socialist trousers are being aired on every balcony. I thought all left-wingers smoked. At night when I crossed to the Asian side on the last ship and saw young men with cigarettes in their hands, I thought they were left-wing. Then I smoked a cigarette as well, so that they understood that I, too, was left-wing. Many porters who were walking across the Bridge of the Golden Horn were smoking. They had saddles on their backs like donkeys, and on them they bore stacks of paper, cloth, oil canisters. Their heads and backs were bent almost parallel to the ground. Sweat dripped from their faces, and they spat the burning cigarette ends on to the street.

In old photos from 1872 the first hat-makers smoked or in 1885 the first workers' leader, a porter who had been arrested. The first striking dock workers in 1872 smoked. In 1927 fifteen dock workers were killed in Istanbul; their friends stood around the dead men smoking.

I was pleased when Memet, our acting teacher, lit a cigarette in the corridor as soon as the class was over. If a cobbler smoked, I brought him my old shoes, sat down on a chair, and while he had the nails in his mouth and was just hammering one of them into my shoe, I tried to explain to him why he should vote for the Workers' Party. I said: 'We are being crushed by America. If you smash your hand with the hammer, you don't even have insurance. Capitalism is the hammer, its nail is Demirel, we are the shoes.' The cobbler couldn't speak, because he had the nails in his mouth. His lit cigarette lay beside him on a tin can. If a fruit seller smoked, I also went to his shop. I bought two apples, then I wanted to start talking about the Party, but it was difficult to find a beginning when I was standing up. The fruit seller asked me: 'What else, sister? Do you want anything else? If you want anything else, I'll give it to you.'

Another young fruit seller had a cigarette stuck behind his left ear. I said: 'Do the apples go rotten very quickly?' – 'Yes,' he said. 'Just as the apples go rotten, so do people also grow older,' I said, 'do you have old-age insurance? America exploits us. America grows fatter and fatter, we grow thinner and thinner. The fruit seller had red cheeks, now they turned even redder. 'Are you a teacher?' I saw that he had got an erection, and I quickly ran out of the shop. He called out: 'Goodbye, my teacher.'

In the 'Captain' restaurant an intellectual told me that a beautiful, wealthy woman had invited them all to her apartment. Fourteen men. They went there, sat in a beautiful salon, she played the piano, then she stood up and said: 'Now all of you get undressed. I'll go and get undressed too and then come back.' The intellectuals laughed, took off their clothes, sat there and waited. The woman came back into the room, but she wasn't undressed. She sat down on the piano stool and looked at the fourteen naked intellectuals. Then she gave each of them a cigarette and lit it for them.

Sometimes Aunt Topus wanted a cigarette from me, she said: 'Give me some money for my shroud.' Sometimes a male friend came home with me from school or from the Party. Late at night we sat in the kitchen, made tea and talked. My father called from his bed: 'What's wrong, my daughter, why aren't you sleeping?' – 'Nothing, Father,' I called, 'I'm only smoking a cigarette with a friend.' My father went on sleeping, the word cigarette set his mind at rest. We smoked our cigarettes, and my friend told me that the Marxists thought an uncle was the right father for a child and not the real father, because an uncle was not so authoritarian with a child. So a child would grow up more free. Or the friend asked: 'As a Marxist, what should one say to a child if one day it asks: "Father, is there a God?"' If God gave a child warmth, was it right to take this warmth away? What did one give the child instead, if one took that away? We smoked and couldn't find an answer.

One night I went home on the last ship from the European side to the Asian side. I shared a taxi with a friend who was also a drama student. The driver threw his glowing stub out of the window, drove off and immediately lit a new one. My friend got out first and paid only for his journey. 'German habits, eh?' said the driver. In Turkey men paid for women. I said: 'He hasn't got enough money. Why should he pay for me? I feel sorry for men, they always have to pay, and that's why they die earlier than women.' The driver lit the next cigarette, drove me to my street and stopped. When I had paid he said: 'I've seen that you are a modern girl. May I talk to you a bit?' It was pitch dark, only a street dog ran quickly past the car. I was a little afraid. 'No, my father will be angry.' But the driver gave me a cigarette and a light. He drove towards the sea, the wheels rolled over the sand. In the headlights I saw the sand thrown up. He switched off the engine and the lights, opened the glove compartment, took out a revolver and held it in his right hand. The cigarette glowed in his left hand. 'Look, sister, Allah has sent you to me, otherwise I would have killed myself with this gun. I wanted to talk to you because you are a modern person. I understood that when you didn't let your friend pay your fare.' He gave me the next cigarette and talked: 'My wife has the school-leaving certificate, I don't. And my wife's family says: "Our daughter is worth more than you. You are a donkey."' He wept and smoked. I said nothing, listened to his weeping and always blew my cigarette smoke into the car after he had exhaled his smoke. Then he wound down the window and said: 'It's daybreak, sister. I'll take you home.' When I had told my father the story, he said: 'My daughter, are you a fool? What if he had killed you with the gun?' – 'We only smoked a cigarette,' I said. After that my father stayed awake for a couple of nights and waited for me. When I came home, he heaved a deep sigh and said: 'Come, my daughter, let's smoke one.'

At the drama school, too, the cigarette was the most important prop. When we rehearsed short scenes from plays, the students often acted the parts with a cigarette in their hand. Hamlet was a smoker, Othello was a smoker, Ophelia smoked, Medea was a smoker. But onstage smoking looked boring. It looked as if we didn't know what to do with our hands, so we stuck our hands in our pockets or we smoked. Our teacher Memet sent us on to the stage, each of us simply had to stand there for five minutes and tell something, without smoking or sticking our hands in our pockets.

# The Coffin of the Dead Student Floated for Days in the Sea of Marmara

O ne day I came home from drama school, and Bodo and Heidi, my two friends from Berlin, were sitting in my parents' apartment. My mother spoke to them with her hands and movements of the head and constantly said the German word '*gut*'. My father spoke very calmly in Turkish. Bodo and Heidi didn't understand a word, but sat there, listened to my father and smiled. My father and my mother gave Bodo and Heidi their own bedroom and went walking by the sea all night. They could also have slept in the lounge, but they said it was so romantic that my friends from Germany had come to Turkey, it reminded them of their youth, and so they walked along the seashore all night. Bodo and Heidi liked that. Bodo constantly said: 'Incredible, incredible,' and Heidi: 'How beautiful it is, how beautiful.' Bodo and Heidi had come for the International Left-wing Student Festival at the Technical University in Istanbul. The next day they went to the meeting. An orchestra was playing, the left-wing students from Europe and Turkey began to dance with one another. The famous Turkish student leader Deniz – his name meant The Sea – went up to the orchestra and kicked and wrecked the drums. The music stopped, everyone looked at him. Deniz shouted in English: 'There's war in the Middle East, there's war in Vietnam, but here you're dancing to American music. Death to American imperialism, long live the revolutionary struggle of the peoples of the world.'

So Bodo and Heidi came back early. Bodo drank raki in the kitchen with my father, my father kissed him and said: 'Oh my soul, look what beautiful blue eyes he has,' and kissed his eyes. My mother said: 'Leave the children in peace, they don't understand your language.' But my father just kept on: 'You are the honey flowing down from Allah's trees.' I translated that and giggled. Then my father said: 'Let us go to the sea.' The sea was five minutes away from the apartment. My father lay down on the sand, the sea came, the waves beat against the shore, withdrew and came again. There were so many stars, since returning from Berlin I hadn't thought about the stars any more. I had forgotten them, but they had always been there. Now I saw them again with my friends from Germany and was happy, just as if I had stuck the stars to the sky for them. My father passed us a bottle of raki and said: 'Oh, oh.' Bodo said: 'The Turk feels at ease by the sea, the German in the forest. The writer Elias Canetti said: "The German feels at ease in the forest, because the upright trees remind the German of an army." But because they had lived so long in the forests, they had become mistrustful. They saw danger behind every tree, in the deep, dark forests there were shadows everywhere. Only when the Germans had chopped down their forests and made paths did they notice that there were other people in the world as well and other lands. The English, Spanish and Dutch had colonies very early, because they were sea people. They had stood on the seashore and seen very early on that the world is big.' Then Bodo fell silent and looked at the stars. My father was already sleeping on the sand, and Heidi said: 'Karl Marx said the Germans were latecomers in colonising the world, that's why the German divides up the world in his head, like you do, Bodo.' Then Heidi laughed, Bodo took a handful of sand and let the sand trickle on to Heidi's naked legs.

The next day Bodo and Heidi found a little dog on the Istanbul streets and gave it the name of an Ottoman sultan, 'Murat'. And because they wanted to take the little dog with them to Berlin, they bought valerian, so that it wouldn't bark at the border. When they had arrived back in Berlin, they called me, brought the little Turkish dog to the phone, and he barked.

The telephone, that was something new. When the telephone rang, my mother picked up the receiver like an actress. She had seen Liz Taylor making telephone calls in her films and copied her. The telephone had an authority. When the telephone rang and someone from the Party was calling me – 'Come immediately, famous communists, who were in prison for years, are coming tonight' – or from the drama school – 'Come to the Goethe Institute this evening, Heinar Kipphardt is there' – I said to my mother: 'I have to go.' – 'Why, it's late, where do you want to go?' – 'I have to go, they've called me.' – 'Oh, I see, don't be late.'

At drama school, students talked about the Kipphardt visit for many days. A man from Europe. What he said was like sentences cast in concrete. A Turk who had studied in Europe got the top seat at a table, and everyone hung on his lips. If a couple of people were discussing something at a table and a European was present, one said to the other: 'Man, even the European believes me, so how can you dare not believe me, you blockhead.' Europe was a club with which we smashed each other's heads. 'We are too much *à la turc*,' said the Turks, and didn't know that even this expression came from Europe. 'Don't be so *à la turc*,' 'Don't behave *à la turc*'. European aspirin cured heart disease. With European cloth one could tell from a distance of forty yards that it was good. European shoes never wore out. European dogs had all studied at European dog schools. European women were natural blondes. European cars didn't cause any accidents. A painter who was studying in Paris was asked by his friend, who lived in Istanbul, to buy a nylon sex-doll. The painter brought it to his friend in Istanbul and said: 'For you. But I will sleep with it first. Then I'll give it to you.' The friend looked at the sex organ of the nylon doll and shouted: 'You bastard, you have slept with it already! The seams are open. Its organ should still be sewed up.'

Then I, too, met a man who had studied in Europe. I was sitting in the 'Captain' restaurant with four young actors and feeding a cat under the table with fish. The other four also began to feed and stroke, then there was a power cut, and we saw only the gleaming eyes of the cat in the darkness. One of the actors began:

> *The night spurs*
> *its dark flanks*
> *with silver stars*

In this darkness a ship sailed by very close to the 'Captain' restaurant, the tables wobbled and a couple of glasses fell over. At the railing someone lit a cigarette, and in the flame of the matchstick I saw his face, he had a head like Lenin. The four actors had seen him too. 'Here he comes!' The four talked about him until the ship had docked at the quay. He came from an old middle-class family and his father had sent him to study architecture in Europe. But instead he had studied film in Italy with Fellini and Pasolini and had come back as a Marxist. His family didn't want to have anything to do with him any more and didn't give him any money for his film projects. The four said in chorus: 'A great intellectual, an important artist, a fantastic mind!' He was called Kerim. Kerim Kerim Kerim.

The power came on again, and the lights, and suddenly Kerim was standing at our table. He had a hand of velvet. All four stood up and offered him their chair. He sat down opposite me, and later, when the waiters brought his fish, and he put half of the fish on my plate, the four took their leave. I didn't eat and only laughed. 'Don't move in that silk dress,' said Kerim, and later, when he undressed me in bed:

> *A light flashes up in the breast*
> *Of the rippling stream, is reflected.*

'Don't hide your breasts,' he said, when I stood in front of him, 'run openly before me, spray perfume, display your nakedness like a beautiful dress.'

A picture of Pasolini hung in his room. When he got out of bed and left the room, he looked over his right shoulder at this picture every time; when he came back, he looked over his left shoulder at the picture. Kerim said: 'The Chinese girls who have achieved greater consciousness with the Mao revolution have also become more conscious in love. Good sex depends on revolutionary consciousness.' While Kerim rubbed a ripe peach against my naked right breast and then ate it, I thought about a little Chinese girl and her consciousness. I didn't talk much to Kerim, because I didn't know how conscious my sentences were. He said: 'The Italian actress Anna Magnani only dresses in black. She is a very good, conscious actress.' I immediately began to dress in black as well, and wanted to be Anna Magnani and the Chinese girl for him. Anna Magnani was easier, black clothes every day, but to be a conscious Chinese girl with conscious sex was difficult. We stayed in one room for three days and made love. Sometimes he left the house for a little while, bought a lot of fruit, came and emptied it out of the bag over me. I took a peach, smelt it and wanted to become more conscious, but was unable to think of anything else, except having sex with him. My body got to know new feelings and didn't forget them again, and began to be addicted to them. When we got up and went out, I felt as if our flesh had been woven together and was now being separated from head to toe with a big knife. Then Kerim walked beside me in the fog of Istanbul, and I thought, he's already left me. He's going to leave me. What will I do when he leaves me? I wanted to go to Red China. In the newspaper I saw Brigitte Bardot in a Mao suit. BRIGITTE BARDOT WORE A MAO SUIT. I tried to find such a Mao jacket.

After a week, after I had become so addicted, Kerim suddenly had to start military service in another town, and I began to buy newspapers and magazines and to read during the lessons at drama school, in order to become as conscious as the Chinese girl. I sat at the very back, it was snowing outside, and through the window of the drowsy classroom we heard the cars sounding their horns outside. The taxi drivers were striking against the new tax law, and the students were marching through the snow and shouting: 'The university professors only love money. We have come to make the Revolution.' The next day it went on snowing, and in class I read what had happened yesterday. The students who had been demonstrating yesterday had gone to the rector of the university and demanded that the university should at last say yes to their reform requests. The rector said: 'Friends, as your older friend, I beg you to remain calm, as university students don't make so much noise.' The students shouted: 'This isn't noise, this is the voice of youth. Resign! We are the Atatürk Youth.' The rector said: 'And what am I? I was the Atatürk Youth before you. I heard Atatürk's speeches from his own mouth.' The students said: 'Don't make the same mistake as the professors in France and Italy. We want revolution at the university. The university must not collaborate with the American government. Resign!' Deniz, the famous student leader, smashed the rector's glass desktop to pieces with a stick. The students occupied the law faculty, sang, the next day they brought a big photograph of Atatürk with them and hung it on the wall behind the rector's desk. On it they wrote: 'This is a present from the Defence Committee which has occupied the university.' The rector asked: 'Why are you hanging Atatürk's picture on the wall? I already have a bronze Atatürk bust and a photograph on my desk. By working calmly we will achieve a good outcome for your reform requests.' So ended the occupation of the university. The students went back to their classes, the big picture of Atatürk remained on the rector's office wall. After school I immediately went towards the university and in the snow in front of the university I saw the footprints of the demonstrating students. Kerim wrote beautiful letters to me from his military service, he wrote poems and in a letter sent me a winter flower from the mountains. I went on reading the newspapers every day during the drama classes. It went on snowing. The fascist group the Grey Wolves marched through the streets, I heard their voices through the window, as I read newspapers. They shouted: 'Turkey will be a graveyard for communists.' It was reported in the newspaper that the mayor of Istanbul had banned the miniskirt, and the religious groups said: 'The milk of a cow is better than the milk of an unbelieving woman. If one is looking for a mother, one must look for a woman who is a believer. Long live our army! Our goal is Islam.'

Another news item was: 'The Americans have now stopped bombing North Vietnam. The American president is going to Honolulu for peace talks'.

It was also snowing in Istanbul when I read this news: 'Martin Luther King has been murdered'. His wife wept at his coffin. When I walked down the street after school with the newspaper, I looked at the page with the picture of the weeping woman. The snow soon made the newspaper wet, it came apart, and black printer's ink dripped from the picture of the dead Martin Luther King on to the white snow. In those days buildings burned in Washington and Chicago, and black American soldiers came to blows with white American soldiers in Japan. The American army occupied Chicago and there was a curfew in Washington. In those days an Istanbul taxi driver drove around with a sheet on his taxi on which was written: 'No to NATO'. Children ran behind his taxi, shouting: 'No to NATO', and the taxi driver was sacked. Then he wore the sheet like a dress and walked through the streets with it: 'No to NATO'. Three hundred and sixty thousand teachers, trade unionists and students demonstrated against religious fanatics and imperialism. The spokeswoman of a religious party said: 'Husbands may hit their wives, but not in the face.'

Kerim went on sending me letters and winter flowers from the mountains, and it began to rain in Istanbul. With the rain the hippies came to Istanbul and lived in the streets, in their cars or in the park. They dried their washing on lines that they had hung between trees. With the first rain the following was printed in the newspaper: 'The novel *Hope* by the French Minister of Culture, André Malraux, has been banned and confiscated because of its communist bias'. In those days of rain the fascist students, the Grey Wolves, blocked the way of the socialist women students of the teachers' training college and forcibly grabbed their breasts and between their legs. 'Death to the communists!' At drama school we heard through the window that outside sticks were striking heads, and when we went home we saw bloodstains on the walls and in the house entrances sheltered from the rain. The next day we heard the leftists marching past the windows and singing into the microphones:

> *How can it be, how can it be?*
> *That brother kills brother, how can it be.*
> *Damned dictators!*
> *This world will not remain yours.*

The police cut the cables to the students' microphones, and we no longer heard their voices. In the newspaper it said: 'Burt Lancaster has said: "We Americans shouldn't be in Vietnam today"'. The Soviet Union sent thousands of troops to the Romanian border: Moscow, Budapest and East Berlin formed a united front against the wave of liberalisation. In Rome policemen beat up students. In Paris there were a thousand injured students and police. In Paris there's a bread shortage. The people of Paris are hoarding bread as in wartime. De Gaulle plans to come to Turkey. The Turkish government has had a bed made for de Gaulle's height. While the Turkish bed-makers made a bed for de Gaulle's height, the Paris students and the striking French workers made barricades. The workers occupied hundreds of factories. The French began to take their money out of the banks. In Turkey the fascist group the Grey Wolves beat up a minister of the Workers' Party. And Demirel, the prime minister of the Americanised ruling party, said: 'The Social Democrats are cannibals'. In Lyons and Paris there were 22 dead, 477 injured. De Gaulle said: 'I want to rebuild the universities'. In the newspapers there were photos of burned-out cars with Paris and Lyons number plates and of the burnt bodies of dogs in front of the barricades. The girls of Paris in their miniskirts kicked the policemen, which made their miniskirts ruck up even higher. In northern Spain, in Asturias, miners went on strike and died from the bullets of the fascist Guardia Civil of General Franco.

When I read this news item, I went to the window, put my head out in the rain and thought that perhaps my Spanish love, Jordi, had been killed in Asturias with the miners. I sat down again, the raindrops from my hair dripped on to the newspaper, right on to the photo of the French dog corpses. Outside the drama school the striking workers and students were marching in the rain. The left-wing students shouted: 'We want a uni for the people. You want puppet students. We want cheap books.' The Grey Wolves beat the heads of the workers and the left-wing students, and the police threw tear gas. When we came out of the drama school, the air smelt of tear gas, and the heavy rain fell on the sticks the Grey Wolves had dropped. The rain didn't stop. I bought a newspaper and arrived in the school with a wet newspaper. As I read, the wet letters dyed my knees and legs and my light-coloured miniskirt. In the newspaper Paris was burning. The police had occupied the Sorbonne. In Istanbul and Ankara the left-wing students had occupied the universities and were sleeping in the corridors. The chairs from the university classrooms were piled up behind the university doors in order to block them, and the boss of the Americanised ruling party, Demirel, blamed the Social Democrats and the Workers' Party for the barricaded universities. I came out of the school and walked towards the Technical University. In front of the university many knives, sticks and broken chair legs were lying in the street, and the corridor windows were foggy from cigarette smoke. The unintelligible voices of the left-wing students echoed in the corridors. Suddenly crowds of people ran across the road in the heavy rain, I thought the police were chasing them, but the Italian film star Gina Lollobrigida had come to Istanbul, was being driven in a car and was waving. The heavy rain beat against the car windows and turned Gina's face into a watery outline. The car was decorated with flowers, because of the rain the flower petals fell on to the streets and remained lying among the sticks and knives, the cars drove over them. Around the Atatürk statue in the city centre lay thousands of soggy flowers and banners of all parties, which were now complaining to Atatürk. The slogans on the banners were: 'Death to the communists!' Or: 'Turkey will not be another Vietnam!', 'God will protect the Turks!' Some letters had run because of the heavy rain, and the flower petals and the demonstrators' placards floated down the steep streets of Istanbul towards the sea in the heavy rain. The evening newspaper sellers shouted in the rain: 'Robert Kennedy shot!' Robert Kennedy lay dead. His sister-in-law Jacqueline Kennedy wept; at that moment a bright flash of lightning lit up the dead Robert Kennedy. I was on the ship going from Europe to Asia. On the ship two men were talking about Robert and John F. Kennedy. One said: 'John F. Kennedy was very brave. Because of his many trips to Palm Beach his face was always suntanned. A dumb reporter asked whether that wasn't a symptom of a liver problem. At that, Kennedy, who was usually very reserved with journalists, showed him the part of his body which wasn't tanned by the sun.' Lightning flashed in the sky again and for a second bathed all the evening newspapers open in people's hands in a blue light, in which I saw several weeping Jacqueline Kennedys and several dead Robert Kennedys. Then everything was dark again. Only the rain beat against the windows, and I heard the newspapers rustle as the pages were turned.

Then the rain stopped, and the sun and the summer came. Kerim sent me summer flowers in his letters from the mountains, where he was doing his military service as an officer of the reserves. The pages on which he wrote about his love were bleached by the sun. Perhaps he had sat for hours in the strong sun, as he tried to find words for his love. I walked through the streets, his letter in my hand, the sun warmed the envelope, I put it in the pocket of my miniskirt, and there the envelope warmed my thigh. Everywhere glaziers were repairing the broken windows.

Now workers occupied factories, students sent flowers from the occupied universities to the occupied factories, and the police again smashed the windows of occupied buildings. Workers' and students' blood still accumulated on some walls in Istanbul, the sun dried it and turned it white. In the drama school we heard twenty-one cannon shots and at each cannon shot the classroom windows shook. The evening paper wrote: 'The American 6th Fleet in Istanbul waters. The government welcomed the 6th Fleet with a 21-gun salute'. The next morning in the city centre many Istanbul shoes walked over ink marks. The night before in the city centre left-wing students had thrown ink, paint and crackers at the white uniform jackets of the American sailors. At the harbour the students had hauled down the Turkish flag. 'We don't believe that Turkey is a free country, that's why we've hauled down the flag.' The police raised the flag again and during the night the windows of some American buildings were broken. At about four in the morning the police stormed the student hostels and arrested all students who had paint or ink marks on their hands. One student, Vedat Demircioğlu, fell into the street from the student hostel window and was seriously injured. The next day, from the ferry, I saw American sailors of the 6th Fleet swimming in the sea in their uniforms. The students had beaten them up and thrown them into the Sea of Marmara. In the evening paper I saw Deniz, the left-wing student leader, on the shoulders of the other students. The students shouted: 'We want blood for blood,' they wanted revenge for their friend Vedat Demircioğlu. Vedat was in a coma for a couple of days, then he died. On the day of his death the student leader, Deniz, lay in the university corridor for two hours with his face to the floor. When he stood up the stone floor of the corridor was wet with his tears.

The students marched through the streets with a symbolic coffin – the police had spirited away the corpse – now the police also demanded the symbolic coffin. The students ran across the Bridge of the Golden Horn with the coffin, the stones of the police flew over their heads, they jumped on a ship and occupied it. Police who tried to board the ship fell into the water and swam in the water with their helmets on their heads, the students sounded the ship's siren for hours. Thousands of people gathered on the Bridge of the Golden Horn. Their shadows fell into the sea and mingled with the shadow of the ship and the shadows of the students carrying the coffin on their heads. The students shouted the first lines of a poem by Nazim Hikmet in chorus: 'My boy, take a good look at the stars.'

Then they sang again:

*How can it be, how can it be?*
*That brother kills brother, how can it be?*
*Damned dictators!*
*This world will not remain yours.*

Then the moon came, and the ship sailed in the moonlight with the coffin, and the students went on singing: 'How can it be, how can it be?', then they lowered the symbolic coffin into the Sea of Marmara, in which it floated for days. The next day the students printed big photos of the dead Vedat, carrying them as they marched and threw stones at the police. Then the stones of the police flew against the photos of the dead Vedat and tore them to pieces.

Bleeding, the students ran to the Atatürk statue in the city centre and shouted: 'You murderers.' The government sent soldiers to help the police. The students went on throwing stones at the police, but not at the soldiers, and shouted: 'People and army – in solidarity hand in hand. Long live Atatürk. Atatürk is coming.' The rifles and the helmets of police and soldiers twinkled together in the strong sun. The students stood around the Atatürk statue and sang the Turkish hymn, and the police and the soldiers stood ready. Then the students sang the Internationale, and the police began to use their batons. After that the Fascist Grey Wolves came with sticks and shouted: 'Armenian Jewish sons of whores, Turkey will remain Turkish. Turks tremble and find your way back to Turkishness.' The police threw tear gas at the students in front of the Atatürk statue, everyone cried and coughed, weeping voices shouted: 'Revolution or death.'

[While the left-wing students left their real blood in front of the Atatürk statue, in the drama school we rehearsed another scene from Weiss's *Marat/Sade* with fake stage blood, then we washed ourselves and left the school with the lines we had memorised. My text as Charlotte Corday was:

> *What kind of town is this*
> *The sun can hardly pierce the haze*
> *not a haze made out of rain and fog*
> *but steaming thick and hot*
> *like the mist in a slaughterhouse*
> *Why are they howling*
> *What are they dragging through the streets*
> *They carry stakes but what's impaled on those stakes*
> *Why do they hop what are they dancing for*

The next day, as the crickets were chirping and the leaves were hanging tiredly from the trees, a photo of Deniz, the student leader, appeared in the newspapers. He had been arrested by the police shortly after taking his criminal law examination. He and many others were in prison for fifty-eight days, and every day after that there were photos in the papers of unshaven students. The government didn't let the famous leftists from Europe who had been invited to a peace festival come to Istanbul, their planes turned back. Now the Grey Wolves marched and at the Atatürk statue vowed a war against communism. 'Army and people hand in hand in solidarity.' People now told each other stories about Deniz. As a child he was said to have stood at a refuse dump and given away his little bit of money to the refuse workers. He and his friends called each other 'Goat Beards' or 'Tortoise Faces'. 'Goat Beards' were the followers of the Vietnamese communist leader Ho Chi Minh, 'Tortoise Faces' followed Che Guevara and Fidel Castro.

Before his arrest Deniz had gone to the peasants in Anatolia with other Tortoise Faces and had campaigned for land reform there, and now perhaps many pairs of scissors cut his photos out of the newspapers, and many hands hung his photo on the walls of rooms. Then one day Deniz had suddenly disappeared from the newspaper. Now the news was: 'They're going to the moon on Apollo 7'. I tore the moon picture out of the newspaper and put it in my notebook, as if I wanted to hide the moon from the astronauts. Under the photo of the moon was a picture of a Turkish village that had been taken from a helicopter: 'They're going to the moon, and we're still living in the darkness of the Middle Ages.' On the Turkish–Iranian–Iraqi border masses of snow had broken loose in the high mountains, and the meltwater had destroyed the tracks between villages and the roads to Hakkǎri. The peasants could no longer reach the town, their fields were flooded and they were starving in their villages. The government dropped food and medicines from helicopters, but the newspapers reported that it landed in the hands of officials. When I read this news, I put the newspaper on my knees out of helplessness and beside me I saw another drama school student, Haydar, who had read the same piece of news. He was the youngest student in the drama school and was from Cappadocia. Haydar said: 'If they're going to the moon, then we can go to the Iranian border and write a report about the starving peasants.' I immediately said yes and thought about the peasants, but also about Kerim. I could take photos on the trip, surprise him with them later and read many books on the long journey. Rosa Luxemburg, too, had certainly read books on the train between Berlin and Warsaw and from time to time looked at the rain beating against the train window, and outside maybe the deer and the rabbits had hopped past in the meadows. At drama school Haydar asked another student whether he wanted to come too. He was the fattest student in the class, and the two of them sometimes took off Laurel and Hardy. We went to the newspaper of the Workers' Party and said: 'We want to write a report at the Iranian–Turkish border.' The newspaper director gave us journalists' cards. 'If you need help, go to the Workers' Party in the towns.' When I told my parents that I was going to Anatolia, my mother asked: 'Aren't you afraid?' – 'No, the peasants are starving, I want to do something for them.' – 'My daughter, I ask you once again, are you not afraid, as a girl, to set out on this journey? It's over a thousand miles.' – 'No, the peasants are starving. I can't eat another chop here.' – 'You were already dangerous as a child,' said my mother. 'I put the hot soup pot down on the floor to cool, and you sat down on the hot soup.' My father said: 'My daughter, you have lost your brain compass. Where are you running to? To hell. And you'll have us burn along with you.' Aunt Topus said: 'This girl must have lost her head. A doctor should give her an injection. Girl, put your brain together.' My father said: 'If you were a man, but you're a girl.' At the school theatre I tried on a male wig and a moustache. Haydar said: 'What are you doing? I thought we were going to write a report. If the way there is dangerous, then it's also dangerous for a man.' So at least I put on a long, large shirt belonging to my father, so that men would leave me in peace. My father said: 'To make you learn something is harder than getting a camel to jump.' He gave me three hundred lira for the journey. At the pharmacy I bought a medicine to treat snake bites. With the three hundred lira we bought three bus tickets to Cappadocia, Haydar's father was a doctor there. We hoped he would give us money to continue the journey. I bought two books, *Capital* by Marx, *State and Revolution* by Lenin.

# We Could Feed the Moon with the Corn

The bus to Cappadocia was full of peasants, returning to their villages without any money in their pockets. Many of them had been taken in by an Istanbul con man, who had sold them the clock next to the Atatürk statue. The con man had taken up position in front of this municipal clock, and one of his accomplices came past, looked at the clock, set his watch accordingly, and gave the con man money. Then a second man came along, also set his watch by the municipal clock and also paid. The peasants, who were looking for work there, asked the con man why the men were giving him money. 'The clock belongs to me. And all the people who set their watch by my clock must give me money for that. I've already earned quite a lot of money with it, if you like, I'll sell you the clock.' The peasants bought the municipal clock from him and now wanted to collect money from people who happened to set their watches in front of the municipal clock, but they fetched the police.

Just before we departed the next con man got on the bus. He showed a bail of cloth for making trousers and wanted one hundred lira for twenty yards of cloth. A peasant bought, the con man got out, the bus drove off, and the twenty yards of cloth were only three yards of cloth. The duped peasant wrapped the three yards of cloth around his legs, and wanted to go on believing that it was twenty yards. I said to him: 'America exploits us, and its slaves in this rotten society also exploit you. It's all because of our rotten economy.' I repeated these sentences a couple of times, until one of the peasants said to me: 'My sister, America is going to the moon. America doesn't have any time to bother about us.' The peasants had sheep with them on the bus, which were constantly bleating, 'America – baaa – exploits – baaa – us – baaa, baaa, baaa.' I stopped talking and opened Lenin's book *State and Revolution*. The bus office had sold me the ticket for the seat immediately behind the bus driver, and the driver looked through the mirror at my legs. I gave up reading the Lenin book and placed the book open on my knees. The bus driver adjusted the mirror and now looked at my face. I held the Lenin book in front of my face, but didn't understand a single word I read, because I was constantly keeping an eye on the bus driver; the Lenin book went up and down with the bus mirror, until night fell. The moon travelled with us during the night, all the peasants looked up at the moon through the right-hand windows of the bus and thought about Apollo 7 and the Americans.

When we arrived at Haydar's house in Cappadocia, his mother exclaimed: 'The children have come! Have you heard more about the journey to the moon in Istanbul than we have here in the middle of Anatolia?' I said to Haydar's mother: 'The moon is our moon too. But the Americans didn't ask us whether we wanted them to go there. They come into our seas too and don't ask us.' Haydar's mother said: 'The moon belongs only to Allah.' His father asked us why on earth we wanted to go to the Iranian–Iraqi border. 'We want to study people for drama school,' we lied. We were afraid that otherwise he wouldn't give us any money. Haydar's garden was full of cherry trees. Each of us climbed a cherry tree, we sat there for a long time, ate cherries, talked from one tree to the other about American imperialism, threw the cherry stones on to a big stone in the garden and shouted: 'Long live the deliverance of the oppressed peoples.'

In the evening Haydar's father invited us to eat in the officers' mess. As a provincial doctor he was friendly with the senior officers. We sat at a long table in the moonlight, and almost the only person to speak was the highest-ranking officer. When he spoke, no one ate, but if he paused, the forks and knives clattered. The senior officer asked Haydar's father: 'What are your son and his friends doing here?' – 'They are artists and want to study people and characters of our country.' Now the senior officer turned to us: 'We hope that young modern people like you will bring us the milieu of modern countries and of America. Atatürk has left this country to its youth. We expect that you will take this country to the moon.' The three of us didn't say a word, only our three chairs creaked simultaneously. The others looked at the moon and saw us, youth, there already. Before we went home, the wife of the most senior officer suggested that the next morning the women go to the Turkish bath together. 'We want to see what the body of an Istanbul girl who has seen Europe looks like.' At home, Haydar's father brought out an old gramophone, put on a tango record and danced with me. His two daughters lay on the sofas and watched us. Haydar went up to his room with the fat boy and the next day didn't speak to me for a while. 'Haydar, why aren't you speaking to me?' He walked backwards and forwards under the cherry trees and said: 'The peasants are starving and we're wasting our time here with tango dancing.' – 'We don't have any money to travel farther. Why don't you talk to your father, he has to give us some money.' But he didn't dare talk to his father. So we went on climbing the cherry trees, ate the cherries and threw the cherry stones on to the big stone. I always took my Marx and Lenin books with me to the garden, but left them lying under the tree. Sometimes ripe cherries fell from the tree and dyed the Marx pages red with their juice.

Haydar's father drove us to the famous volcanic landscape of Cappadocia. The Italian film director Pasolini was just then shooting his film *Medea* there with the Greek opera singer Maria Callas. I very much wanted to see and talk to him and then write to Kerim.

We stood in the landscape in front of the caves, and after a while Pasolini came out of one of the caves and stood with a couple of other men on a dusty path. I walked towards him and was going to tell him: 'I know your student Kerim.' He even looked in my direction, came slowly towards me, but walked past to a woman who was standing behind me and took her arm. It was Maria Callas in her Medea costume and her Medea wig. She had covered her face with a black cloth because of the bright sun and she walked up the dusty path with Pasolini.

In the next village many peasants, policemen and two officers were standing in the village square. A girl from the village had talked to an unknown man down by the river and her brothers had crushed her head between two stones. We stayed there until it was dark, and when the moon rose, the policemen, officers and peasants forgot the murderers and the crushed girl and looked up at the moon, as if they wanted to watch the arrival of the American spaceship Apollo 7 on the moon. The next day Haydar's father sent us to his mother in another village. 'You want to study the people of our country. Start with Haydar's grandmother.' I took *State and Revolution* in order to read it there. Haydar's grandmother was an old peasant woman. She sat me on her donkey, and Haydar and the fat boy walked behind the donkey. It was hot, the donkey flicked its tail at the flies on its body and struck my legs each time. I tried to read Lenin's book. Two peasant women came riding up behind us, and my donkey waited for the other two donkeys. As they rode past, the peasant women said: 'Oh, you've got it easy, you ride on the donkey and your husband follows you on foot. You've fed him well. When he embraces you, he surely won't let you go again.' With Lenin's book in my hand I asked the two peasant women on their donkeys: 'Do you know what an orgasm is? Orgasm is your right,' I shouted. The peasant women talked to their donkeys, to urge them on. 'Deeh, deeh,' and then to me: 'Tell us, what is this urugazum – deeh, deeh – supposed to be? – 'Do you like your men in bed? Do they play nicely with you?' The peasant women laughed: 'We peasants have only one pleasure, our pleasure in bed.

And your husband? Does he too give you a sweet taste in bed?'
We laughed, and our bodies shook on the three donkeys on the
stony village street; the donkeys' hoofs almost began to slip.

In the village community room a woman doctor had gathered
all the peasant women around her and wanted to insert the
coil in all of them as a contraceptive. The peasant women were
embarrassed and laughed. The woman doctor said: 'The world is
going to the moon and you are making as many children as the
chickens, and no chick is getting something decent to eat.' The
peasant women said: 'Let another summer pass, we have to ask our
husbands first. Peasant heads work more slowly.' Then they went to
their carpets, wove and sang: 'I weave carpets, I weave carpets. The
carpet doesn't let me go. Only by marrying an official are we saved
from the carpets.' When the evening came and the moon showed
itself, everyone went outside again and looked at the moon for a
long time which today was the colour of a mandarin orange. One
woman said: 'I saw the men. They opened the moon up and went
inside.' The children asked: 'Mother, can the moon fall on the earth,
if the men go inside?' – 'If Allah is angry, he will let the moon fall
on our heads.' Meanwhile Haydar and the fat boy had only played
dominoes with the peasants and not asked any questions about
middlemen or the way prices were kept down. Haydar said: 'Why
should I ask? The peasants know themselves what's going on. My
brain doesn't work any better then theirs.' I looked for my donkey,
but it had already gone back to Haydar's grandmother and had
eaten half of my Lenin book, *State and Revolution*. So we returned
on foot, and under the moon, which the Americans had set out
for, we loudly sang the socialist march, the Internationale. In the
night thousands of toads croaked on the village fields.

Haydar's father did then give us some money, but with that
we could go only as far as the next town. He gave us lots of
medicines for the peasants as well as old newspapers. In the
villages we were to throw the newspapers out of the bus windows,
so that the peasants, who usually didn't have any newspapers,
had something to read. In the next town we asked truck drivers

whether they would take us along for free. One driver said: 'I
never go in that direction. The route is full of Kurdish bandits.
They're all armed to the teeth.' While we waited we read the old
newspapers ourselves and took photographs of the carters, the
horses and the horse shit.

A truck took us to the next town. We stood behind the
cabin surrounded by sheep on the rickety road across Anatolia.
The sheep bleated and shat, we sang the Internationale in the
moonshine again, our voices shook because of the bumpy roads.
In the night we threw the newspapers from the truck on to the
peasants' fields. The newspaper pages were scattered by the wind.
We had kept three newspapers and put them across our chests
against the headwind; the newspapers crackled in the wind. The
sheepdogs barked and ran alongside the truck. The moonlight
shone in their open muzzles, and we saw their gleaming teeth and
the saliva at their mouths. At dawn the truck stopped outside a
slaughterhouse. First the sheep jumped from the truck, then the
three of us, our legs and shoes covered in sheep shit. Later the
driver came out of the slaughterhouse with blood on his shoes and
said to us: 'Don't ever throw newspapers from a truck again. The
children want to collect them on the village streets and get killed
under our wheels.'

The town we had come to was called Diyarbakir. The truck
driver said: 'Be careful, there are many Kurds here.' We stood
by a dusty road, next to a dried-up river; a dusty dog went past
limping, a dusty peasant held his pitchfork in his hand. He had
already been waiting a long time with his wife for a truck that
could give them a lift. His wife slept on the ground in the dust
and had covered herself with all her children. One of the children
was awake, looked on the ground for something to eat and ate
dirt from the street. The dust of the street had collected in an
old Coca-Cola bottle. Dead mosquitoes stuck to the children's
dusty hair. Now, with the morning, the flies came and settled on
their faces. The dusty peasant with the pitchfork had flies on his
face, too, but he had given up waving them away. A dusty cow

stood in the dried-up river bed, and its dry udder hung down
to the ground. From time to time birds dropped half-eaten figs
from a tree under which lay a dead dog. Many figs were sticking
to its body and were drying up there under the dusty sun along
with the dog's corpse. The dusty Kurds talked very quietly to
one another, there were hardly any trees, there was nothing but
dust and dry dirt, from which their small houses were built, half
into the ground, like caves, where people lived with flies, snakes,
mosquitoes and rats. A dusty snake crossed the dusty road and
died under the dusty wheels of a truck. Then the flies settled on
the open body of the snake. A little girl cried, her hair looked as
if it was made of old wool, her tears drew stripes on her dusty
face. I asked her: 'Why are you crying?' She didn't understand
me. The cries of the sheep in the slaughterhouse slowly went
out like the lights of evening. Then men came out of the
slaughterhouse with blood on their naked chests and on their
naked legs, crossed the dusty road with sheep's intestines in their
arms and threw them into the dried-up river bed, then, their
feet covered in dust, they went back into the slaughterhouse.
Biting each other, the hungry dogs ran to the still-warm sheep's
intestines, and soon only the blood of the intestines was drying
in the dried-up river bed. We waited and waited and didn't
know where we could get any help, to reach the starving people
on the Iranian–Iraqi border. I photographed the dead dog and
the dirty Coca-Cola bottle. We were hungry, especially the fat
boy. Haydar and I stopped talking about being hungry, because
that only made the fat boy even hungrier. We walked through
the narrow lanes like three dusty dogs. In a tailor's shop the
tailor was just ironing many trousers with a heavy, glowing iron,
American soldiers' and officers' trousers. He looked up as he was
ironing, and we looked at his ironing movements, as if we could
hold on to them. He ordered tea for us and bought us sesame
rings. Americans were stationed up in the mountains, the tailor
loved the Americans. 'Good people,' he said. 'But imperialists,'
I said. The tailor sprayed some drops of water on a pair of

trousers, the water hissed under the iron, and he asked: 'What does "imperialism" mean?' – 'They exploit us.' The tailor said: 'I fill my hungry stomach with American trousers.' – 'But you don't ask what the American trousers are doing here.' – 'Americans haven't done anything to harm me,' replied the tailor, and his iron hissed over the drops of water again. Then another man came into the tailor's shop, a young man from Ankara, who was doing his military service in Diyarbakir. He invited us to eat at the NCOs' mess. The dust of the town stopped immediately in the garden of the mess. The willow branches hung into a small stream, and the moon lay in the water. We sat under the willow, the fish made the moon in the water tremble. The soldier who had invited us to eat had brought a friend with him. They asked us whether we were left-wing. I said: 'Yes.' He said: 'That makes me happy, my sister, we are fascists. Tell me, what would you do if you came to power.' – 'Hospitals for everyone, cheap meat, cheap books, cheap homes, school for all poor children.' The fascist said: 'Good, I've listened to you. When we come to power, we're going to send all rich girls to build roads. They have to wear wooden shoes on their feet, and we'll collect ninety per cent taxes from them.' We ate and drank and laughed, and the moon went on trembling in the stream. The fascist invited Haydar and the fat boy to sleep in the barracks. He gave me money for a hotel room and sent his friend with me to find a hotel. 'Sister, double-lock your room and don't let my friend in.' I left his friend standing in the corridor and double-locked my room. There was no electricity in the room. I found my way to the bed with the help of the moonlight and fell asleep. When I woke up, I saw a spider as big as a child's hand running up the wall, and the sheet and the pillow were full of old mosquito blood. The bath smelt rottenly of old bathhouses and cockroaches were running across the stone floor. The next morning we asked a couple of truck drivers whether they could take us to the town of Hakkäri, where the peasants were starving in the villages. The trucks were loaded with stones, there was no room to stand. So we went to the tailor's shop again. The tailor, who fed his family with the American officers' trousers, told us: 'Go to the senior officer of Diyarbakir, the army has lots of trucks that go to Hakkări. Talk to him, he can send you there.' We knocked at the army building, the senior officer was a small fat man. 'We are actors from Istanbul and want to study the different people of our country. We want to get to the Iranian–Iraqi border at Hakkări.' He said: 'Bravo, children, you are the honour of our land. You are Atatürk's children. I shall send you wherever you want on our trucks.' He invited us to eat in his house, it was hot, and he drank strong raki, gave us some too. To his wife and his two beautiful daughters he said: 'Take a good look at these young people. They will bring Turkey into the milieu of modern countries. They are the light of our eyes. Europe will bite its nails in astonishment. Forward. March, children. What our country suffers, it suffers because of unmodern minds. If everything was modern, there would be neither murder nor manslaughter. For example: if I had not been a modern man, I would now be a murderer. We had married, and on our wedding night there was no blood. If I, ladies and gentlemen, had not been a modern man, I would have killed my wife. No major would be sitting opposite you now, but a murderer. Later it turned out that my wife's hymen was what science calls a star hymen.' The major's wife raised an eyebrow and said: 'Really, Necip, please don't say any more.' The major said: 'Let me continue. These children from Istanbul are very modern children.' The raised eyebrow of the major's wife remained raised, and the major said: 'Her hymen had the form of a star. My male organ went exactly through the middle of this star, and the star must have been very elastic, didn't burst, and so there was no blood.' The three of us laughed, the major got even more drunk and told us about a woman's beautiful bottom. His two daughters went into another room with me. 'Please, artist-sister, tell our father he should let us dance with the lieutenants at the officers' club. He'll listen to you.' The major had fallen asleep at the table.

We came out into the street again in the hot afternoon sun. On the big square, on which there was also an Atatürk statue, there was a demonstration by the left-wing trade union taking place. Four thousand peasants had come on foot from the villages and wanted land reform.

'Big estates must be abolished' – 'Land for the peasants, work for the workers' – 'Socialism is coming' – 'The feet will one day be the head'. Four thousand dust-covered people stood close together and listened to the trade unionists. A journalist came up to us and asked what we thought about this demonstration. Haydar said: 'We don't think anything. What do you think? You're the thinker, aren't you?' But I said: 'I believe that the liberation of the peoples is only possible through socialism.' He asked me for my name, for the address of where we were going, what we wanted to do, whether we were from the Party. I dictated it all to him. Haydar ground his teeth, but I heard only my voice, and the journalist wrote and wrote. Afterwards the fat boy said to Haydar: 'This girl will get us into terrible trouble, I'm going back to Istanbul from here. The journalist was a secret policeman.' He immediately got the bus back to Istanbul, Haydar and I stayed. But even Haydar didn't speak to me. We walked down the dusty tracks and I said: 'One can even bring consciousness to a secret policeman. He can change his part, as we do in the theatre.' Haydar went on grinding his teeth. When we went to the major, to ask whether he could send us to the town of Hakkări now, his lieutenant said to us: 'He doesn't have any time for you.' 'You see,' said Haydar, 'because of the interview you destroyed our roles, as an actress you failed. The secret policeman played his role better.'

The tailor was still ironing the trousers of the Americans stationed in the mountains and had a newspaper lying open on the table. 'The Americans are already on the moon,' he said, 'Apollo Seven has sent the first news from the moon. The astronauts said: "We're having a lot of fun." And another astronaut shouted from the moon at the director of the mission control centre: "You idiot."' We had set out at the same time as Apollo 7; they were already on the moon, and we hadn't even reached the town of Hakkǎri. The tailor said: 'Onlar Aya biz yaya.' ('They fly to the moon, we're still walking.')

The tailor then talked to a truck driver who was driving to Hakkǎri, gave us some money and then went on ironing the American officers' trousers. Now we drove to the town of Hakkǎri on the Iranian–Iraqi border on top of the load of corn on the back of the truck. The moon shone on the corn, it smelt very nice. The truck drove up steep mountain roads, higher and higher, as if we were driving to the moon; we slid backwards and forwards with the corn, our hair full of grain. We could touch the stars with our hands and feed the moon with corn. We saw shooting stars everywhere, we heard sounds as if the showers of stars were banging against the pane of glass of the truck. But it was the birds flying into the truck windscreen. And there in the corn, near to the moon, Haydar told me that he had been in love with me for a long time. I said: 'But I love another man.' – 'Kerim will make you unhappy, he's a bourgeois.' – 'No, he's a Marxist.' – 'How do you know that?' – 'Everyone says he's a Marxist.' – 'If he's read a whole book by Marx, I'll marry my mother on the spot.' I pushed Haydar deep into the corn, we tussled in it and the moon covered us. With grains of corn in my mouth I said: 'Keep your love. Perhaps we will love each other in a couple of years. Life is open.' We fell asleep on the corn and woke up with the sun next to an Atatürk statue. The town of Hakkǎri was surrounded by mountains and I was small, almost like a village. Opposite the Atatürk statue was the town hall. The mayor ordered tea for us. 'We want to go to the village of the starving peasants and study their faces for drama school,' we said. He listened to us and wasn't against it, until a fat, sweating man came in and whispered something in his ear. The mayor raised both eyebrows and listened to him with four furrows on his forehead. Then he stubbed out his cigarette for too long, looked not at us but at the ashtray and said: 'The road has become impassable and is full of bears and snakes. The bears will eat you. Come in spring. The road will be repaired by then. I'll take you there in my own car. But now I can't permit you to do it. If you die on the way, I'm responsible. On foot you would take three days to these villages.' When we stepped out of the building, six policemen in plain clothes were standing on the other side of the street. Three for Haydar, three for me. We simply stood there until a man called us into his grocery shop. He was a member of the Workers' Party, he kissed us and wept, his tears were caught on his unshaven face. 'Welcome, apples of my eye. Not even birds come here. Here we are alone with the mountains. You are heroes from a fairy tale. You have crossed Mount Ararat and have come to us. What is our Party doing in Istanbul? Are our friends well?' It was dark in his shop, we sat there, ate and drank tea, and the six secret policemen waited outside in the hot sun for us. The man shut the shop door, now we sat in the dark as if all three of us were blind, and the Party member whispered: 'The mayor belongs to the Demirel party. Now he has set his dogs on you. I will take you to the hotel, and you can eat and drink in the restaurant. Don't worry about money. But be careful. Here we, the Workers' Party, are like birds with broken wings, our word is worth as little as old money. If you need protection, seek out the Social Democratic deputy. They're afraid of him. He has a telephone and can call his party in Ankara. I don't want them to harm a hair on your head here. And return quickly to your fathers and mothers.' We stepped into the street, our six plainclothes policemen were still standing there, many cigarette ends lay on the ground in front of them. For our report, we went to look for peasants in the town who had walked here for three days from the starving villages to buy flour. We found one, he was as thin as a needle, his eyes were sunk deep in his face. On his back he carried a heavy sack of flour, he was just about to make his way back to the starving village. As we talked to him, we saw our six plainclothes policemen again behind some bushes. The peasant said: 'We ate the leaves from the trees, like animals, but now there are not even leaves left. We are dead, my daughter. No one gives us their hand. In this blind world we have seen the Day of Judgement. The children died like blossoms that the wind blows from the branches. Tell the state it should drop poison from the helicopters. We will eat it, then we'll all die. That is my wish from the state. Write that, my daughter.' Haydar left me alone with the peasant, slipped away behind the bushes with the camera in his hand and from behind photographed the six arses of the policemen, who were crouching there watching me. I heard the click of the camera and the six policemen jumped up. The peasant from the starving village couldn't stand any more, he lay down on the ground with his sack of flour, like a tortoise that had fallen on its back. 'My daughter, you see me. Write what you see, don't ask any more. I can't go on.' The ants crawled over the sack of flour and immediately turned white. Then the peasant stood up again and walked with the ants on his back towards the main road. The six plainclothes policemen followed him. Haydar came up and said: 'I hope the police haven't seen any gangster films, otherwise they'll slit open his sack of flour with a knife.'

Haydar went to the Turkish baths, I bought a newspaper and sat down in the hotel garden. In Mexico and Peru the students had clashed with the police, twenty-seven students had been killed, and their mothers wept over their bodies. In another newspaper I saw Soviet tanks that were occupying Czechoslovakia, the Czechs stood at their doors in their nightshirts and pyjamas and looked at the Russian tanks. Underneath there was a photo of Dubcek, the Czech prime minister. As I was reading this news item, I forgot to light the cigarette in my mouth. Suddenly a hand offered me a light, it was one of the six plainclothes policemen. I didn't draw on the cigarette and the match burned his finger. He laughed and sucked his fingers. Haydar came back from the baths and told me that one of the six plainclothes policemen had come naked into the baths and asked him: 'Brother, may I soap your back?' In the evening we went to the open-air cinema; the six plainclothes policemen sat in front of us and constantly turned their heads. Only when the actors in the film kissed did they look to the front. The moon cast its light over the shoulders and heads of the men and the wooden chairs in the cinema. The only two women in the cinema were

Audrey Hepburn and me. Audrey Hepburn spoke to Gregory
Peck, but one couldn't hear her voice, because the sheepdogs were
barking and the frogs were making a noise with the crickets. The
mosquitoes bit, and everyone was scratching themselves. At some
point the electricity failed, the film disappeared, and on the screen
there remained only the light of the moon. All the men stood up
and looked at me. I quietly whistled the Internationale and walked
out of the cinema to the hotel. Haydar didn't talk to me, took my
room key, double-locked my door from the outside and then went
to his room. During the night he tapped on the wall a couple of
times, as from cell to cell in a prison. I looked out of the window
for a long time, there were so many stars, the snow on the high
mountains glowed, and behind them lay Persia and Iraq. The six
plainclothes policemen stood in front of the hotel and smoked,
lonely sheepdogs passed them and barked at the moon. In the
morning the six plainclothes policemen had disappeared. A young
man, who was holding the left-wing newspaper *Cumhuriyet* in his
hand, spoke to us: 'I'll show you the countryside.' He had already
brought three donkeys with him. As he was riding on the donkey
he opened the CUMHURIYET. I saw photos of the arrested Czech
prime minister Dubcek, a little Czech girl cried in front of the
Soviet tanks. He passed us pages to read. In Istanbul the police had
rounded up the hippies and wanted to chase them out of the city.
In Iran the earth had moved, and thousands of people had died.
The young man said: 'The Iranian earthquake can reach as far as
here. When that happens, these mountains can move, one can see
it with one's eyes.' We looked from the donkeys to the mountains;
they were naked. 'Once these mountains are supposed to have been
green,' said the young man. 'Vegetables and fruit grew on them,
when the Armenians lived here. Then all the Armenians here were
slaughtered, and the mountains have become naked stone.' Haydar
asked him: 'Are you a policeman, brother?' – 'No,' he said, 'but
I have heard that the Minister of the Interior in Ankara sent a
telegram to the mayor. "Don't let these two dangerous communists
go to the villages."' Haydar said: 'We're not communists.' I said:

'But we are socialists.' The boy smiled, from his donkey he showed me in the newspaper the Soviet tanks that had occupied Prague, and said: 'Look at your people, they're in Prague.' – 'We're not Soviets.' He said: 'The Soviets are a great, heroic nation. They made a revolution, do you want to reject them?' Now I wanted to prove to him that I read Lenin, and pulled out of my bag the book *State and Revolution*, which had been partly eaten by the donkey. Because Haydar kicked the stomach of my donkey with his right foot, to give me a signal, my donkey suddenly went faster, and the young man no longer saw which book I wanted to show him.

The peasants had hung a long, thick cable from bank to bank of a river that had changed its course; hanging from it were old truck tyres, which one sat in. If the peasants wanted to go to town, this was how they had to cross the river that had changed its course. They sat in the truck tyres and pulled themselves over to the other bank with their hands. In the Workers' Party and among the left-wing students in Istanbul and Ankara the bridge was a symbol, because every year peasants died crossing the river, and the Party planned to build a proper bridge for the peasants. When we tried to sit in the tyres, I immediately fell out and injured my left arm. Haydar crossed the river, because he had done boxing and had strong arms. I sat under a tree for two hours. Newspaper pages flew one after the other into the river that had changed its course and disappeared in the constantly whirling water. When Haydar came back my arm had swollen up. The young man said: 'I'll take you to the Kurds up in the mountain village.'

Two women were just breastfeeding their children. We gave their husband the medicines that Haydar's father had entrusted to us, he placed them in the shade. We wanted to take photographs of the women, but they said no, but opened a chest and gave me a brightly coloured dress, which I was to put on. The man set me on a horse, and Haydar photographed me on the horse and wearing the dress. When we rode back on the donkeys, the women were still breastfeeding their children.

In the hospital in Hakkări a woman doctor bandaged my arm

and said: 'You've got to disappear from here. Quickly go back to your parents.'

With my bandaged arm I sat down beside some road workers in a café and asked them what they earned and whether they had a trade union that fought for their rights. They told me that they often had to wait for their wages. 'But what should we do, very honoured daughter?' they asked me. A couple of soldiers came into the café and stared, their hands on their rifles. I said to the road workers: 'You could march to Ankara, in order to get your rights.' The road workers laughed and said: 'But we only have a pair of shoes with holes in them. To get to Ankara we need many pairs of shoes.' I repeated slogans from Istanbul, and the workers laughed with me.

> Workers, peasants, youth.
> To Ankara together.
> The police on horses.
> We are on foot.
> Enough exploitation, enough.
> Even if they come with their tanks and their cannon,
> the land will be socialist.

Their rifles in their hands, the soldiers went on staring at me. The road workers said: 'Our very honoured daughter, drink another tea with us.'

Haydar had run away, it began to rain, my father's shirt and the bandage on my arm were soaked through in a couple of minutes and water collected in my shoes. Finally I found Haydar sitting on a park bench. He was sitting there as if he needed the water. 'Because you love this bourgeois man, you are not careful enough as a socialist. The bourgeois children only play at socialism,' he said. We sat for an hour in the pouring rain, when we spoke, the rain splashed into our mouths, and when we shouted, the rain splashed out of our mouths again. At some point a man wearing glasses walked past us. He was all the time wiping his glasses with his shirt and looking at us. In the evening, when I was sitting with Haydar in the hotel restaurant and drinking raki, the man who had been wiping his glasses all the time came up to our table. He was the only journalist in Hakkări. He took my hand, kissed it a couple of times and said: 'I saw you. You are like the characters in Sartre's book *Nekrasov*. He is Ivan and you are Natasha, who wanted to kill the tsar with bombs.' The journalist sat down beside us, wept and continued kissing my hand. 'I am an unimportant provincial journalist, but you are Sartre's characters.' As he went on weeping and drinking raki, our six plainclothes policemen also raised their raki glasses, we did the same. During the night the man from the Workers' Party knocked at our doors and whispered: 'A truck is driving back towards Ankara. Get away from here as fast as you can.' We got into the truck, the driver was an old man, he gave us cigarettes all the time. In the darkness we heard thousands of bird voices, and suddenly the tops of the mountains grew bright. The driver held his breath, then the sun threw itself across the mountains, went down again for a second and rose again. At that moment a couple of birds struck the windscreen and, coloured red by the sun, lay dead on the truck bonnet. The driver said: 'Some birds die for the sun.' The truck drove and drove and killed six snakes that wanted to cross the road. In the evening we arrived in the town of Van, which was beside a beautiful lake. The driver took a break at the bus station, drank tea, came back and said: 'I have to go on, but I can't take you any farther, the mayor of Hakkări has called here. I'm not allowed to drive any communists in a truck belonging to the state. I can't help you, I have children.' He gave us cigarettes and drove on towards Ankara. Haydar photographed the ground and the frogs in the dust, next to where we were sitting. First a small dog joined us, sat down beside us and also looked at the frogs, then suddenly there was a man standing in front of us who knew our names. 'I know why you're sitting here. My friend, the shopowner in Hakkări, phoned me.' He invited us to a restaurant, in front of which many women were washing their clothes in the lake. They didn't need any soap, the lake contained soda and frothed. The moon cast light on the froth, and the American astronauts were eating something on the moon, and one of them was perhaps at that moment looking for the tin opener, which was floating in space. After the meal he took us to a hotel. 'I'll pay for a room for you. You must sleep in this room together and double-lock the door. You mustn't open to anyone, do you understand me, no one! And in the morning, straight to the bus! Here's money for the bus ticket.'

When Haydar's mother in Cappadocia saw me again, she exclaimed: 'Oh, how black you are from the sun. We'll wash you white again in the bath.' Haydar took the film to the photo shop. When he went to collect the prints the next day, the photographer said to him: 'The photos were exposed to light in the darkroom, it wasn't my fault.'

Haydar's mother gave me money for the bus journey to Ankara, where Kerim was now stationed. In Ankara I got on a minibus to his barracks. The soldiers told me: 'Kerim has gone to Istanbul and isn't coming back till today.' – 'When he comes, he should look for me tonight at the Cinematheque in Ankara.'

The door of the Cinematheque was locked. A boy who was sitting in a tailor's shop opposite and sewing a jacket told me, a needle in his mouth: 'I know where the people who meet here go to eat.' He took me through many streets to a dark nightclub, where he spoke to a man who immediately sent me something to drink. I surreptitiously poured the drink, which smelt funny, on to the floor, and pretended I had fallen asleep because of it. 'She's already sleeping. Get a taxi.' I jumped up and shouted: 'You are the product of American imperialism. No to NATO, no to Vietnam! Long live the solidarity of the oppressed peoples!' I ran out of the dark club and walked aimlessly through Ankara. Then I found the Cinematheque again, the door was open now, and the tailor who had wanted to rape me was sitting in his shop again and sewing his jacket. When he saw me, he pricked his finger with the needle. I shouted: 'Friend, why did you lie to me? You should use your energy to become politically conscious. I understand you, you are exploited and so you want to exploit those even weaker than you. But your deliverance doesn't lie there. Your deliverance is the Workers' Party.' Another tailor stopped ironing and asked the boy: 'What's she saying?' – 'I think she's crazy,' said the boy.

In the Cinematheque three people were sitting together in a room. Each was holding the same CUMHURIYET in front of his face, I saw the same photo of de Gaulle three times. He had come to Istanbul and had said to the Turkish government: 'Stay in NATO.' Next to it I saw the same weeping woman from Czechoslovakia three times. Her husband was fighting the Soviet soldiers in Prague and hadn't come back. The three men folded their newspapers at the same moment and looked at me. They all had a beard like Che Guevara. As I told them about my journey, they constantly tugged at their moustaches and exclaimed: 'What a brave girl you are, unbelievable!' They all knew Kerim. On the shelves of the Cinematheque library there were film journals, in which he had written many articles about films. I was happy and hoped that when Kerim came the three men with the Che Guevara beards would tell him: 'What an unbelievably brave girl you're in love with!' We drank tea together and ate bread, tomatoes and grapes on the newspapers. In the evening a Chaplin film was being shown in the cinema. One of the Cinematheque people related that Bushmen in Africa had been shown two films – a film by Chaplin and a film about the concentration camps in Germany. The Bushmen, who knew nothing about Hitler, laughed more at the latter film than at Chaplin, because they found it funny that white men could look so starved.

When Chaplin kissed the hand of the girl he loved, someone in the dark cinema took my hand and covered it in kisses. The hand that held my hand was made of velvet. I thought a long piece of velvet cloth had wound itself around my body and was drawing me very softly out of the cinema. When Chaplin went off with the girl at the end of the film, as he twirled his stick and his oversize shoes ran on ahead of him, the velvet cloth had already drawn me out on to the street, then to a room and into a bed. The velvet cloth undressed me, I saw my clothes fall without a sound. There were no street lamps outside, but the little fireflies flew past the window. Their lights danced over my clothes. The long piece of velvet cloth fell to the floor, the firefly lights now danced over it, and it turned into a silkworm, which gave me its saliva and began to weave a house of silk. The many silk threads wound and wove round my body. I breathed, my breath too was made of silk. And with the breath I found wings and flew around the room, the fireflies dancing outside the window cast their light on my wings and made me dizzy. I fell asleep and woke up beside Kerim. In the evening he had slipped out of the barracks without permission in order to look for me at the Cinematheque. He laughed and said: 'You are the first girl I'll have to spend a couple of days in the cells for.' He had heard all about my journey from the people at the Cinematheque. He said: 'You astonished everyone.' He gave me money for the journey to Istanbul and went to the cells at the barracks. The money still had the warmth of his hand, I put on my clothes, but my body threw them away, it didn't want any clothes, it wanted to wear Kerim, who was now on his way to the barracks, like a dress. I sat on the bus to Istanbul, looked out of the window and saw myself making love with him in the meadows, steppes and lakes. Then I thought, he's sitting beside me, he's getting out with me in Istanbul. In Istanbul I saw men who looked like him from behind everywhere. I followed them for a while. One walked across the Bridge of the Golden Horn, and on the left I saw my shadow walking alone in the sea, and I turned round on the bridge and went to my mother and father.

# The Voices of the Mothers

Ever since I'd left, my mother had been taking tranquillisers and sitting in bed as in a fog. My father was again trying to get the radio to work by hitting it, and laughed when he saw me. 'Allah be thanked.' Aunt Topus came and said: 'Are you not ashamed before Allah? You have made your mother ill.' – 'Do you know how many people are dying of hunger now?' I asked Aunt Topus. 'Are you going to save the world?' – 'Yes,' I said, 'I want to save the world.' – 'If you want to save the world, why do you make your mother ill? Is she not part of this world too?' I went over to my mother, she was still crying. The moon shone through the curtains on to her pillow and her tears. 'Look, Mother, what good is your crying doing you, you must read books. They will help you.' I took a book by Dostoevsky from my bookcase and put it on her blanket. She went on crying, but picked up the book and began to read. I closed the door behind me, but remained standing at the door and heard the turning of the pages. Then I went into the lounge and said to my father: 'Father, stop playing with the radio, I'm going to work now.' My father went into the kitchen with the radio like an obedient child. I sat down at the table and wrote the piece about the starving peasants: 'Hakkări is looking for Turkey'. The next day I took it to the newspaper of the Workers' Party, which printed it immediately. At drama school the teacher who loved Brecht said: 'Your article is good, but watch out that politics doesn't draw you away from the theatre.' Politics didn't draw me away from the theatre, but my tongue divided in two. With one half I said: 'Solidarity with the oppressed peoples,' with the other half of my tongue I spoke lines by Shakespeare: 'What thou seest when thou dost wake,/Do it for thy true love take.' Kerim continued writing me love letters from the barracks, now placed autumn flowers inside and sent me brief analyses of the army: 'The NCOs in the army tend towards fascism, the young officers tend towards socialism, the army divides into two parts.' Soon the Workers' Party also divided into two factions. The first faction said: 'In Turkey there is a working class, which can legally bring the Workers' Party to power.' The second faction said: 'Turkey is a colony. First a national-democratic revolution, then socialism.' I went to the Party house. The members no longer talked to each other, but quietly in many small groups. And the members who had previously sat down wherever they liked now had definite places – first- and second-faction chairs. Sometimes the members forgot their jackets or bags when they went home. But when a jacket was left hanging on a first-faction chair, no one from the second faction shouted after the owner of the jacket.

I went on taking the ship from the Asian to the European side of Istanbul every day. The ship sailed past a big house in which two sisters lived. One was married to a deputy of the Workers' Party, · the other to a deputy of a right-wing party. Each sister had now had her half of the house repainted; one half was white, the other pink.

On the ship too people had divided into three groups. A fascist newspaper reader now sat in a row next to a fascist newspaper reader. Religious newspaper readers sat next to religious newspaper readers, left-wing newspaper readers sat in a row and read the same newspaper. No one looked at the sea, only old people or pregnant women or children. In a strong south-west wind the ship sometimes tilted to the left, sometimes to the right, and the tea glasses that stood on the tea-room counter sometimes slid to the left, sometimes to the right, and all the open newspapers, the

left-wing, fascist or religious ones, then moved with the ship to
the left, to the right. In a photo in CUMHURIYET an American
soldier held the muzzle of his sub-machine gun right up against
the temple of an old Vietcong woman. She had eight furrows on
her forehead. In the right-wing newspapers there were photos of
a shoe. In occupied Prague a Czech boy fleeing from Soviet tanks
had been killed, one of his shoes had been left lying in the road.
The ship arrived at the European side, all left-wing, right-wing
and religious newspapers were folded and went into the pockets of
the three groups. When the newspapers in people's pockets were
silent, the walls of Istanbul began to speak, left-wing, religious or
right-wing slogans.

A supporter of the first faction of the Workers' Party said to
one of the second faction: 'If you go on the way you're doing, you'll
only be able to set up socialism on the moon.' And from the moon
the astronaut sent news to the world. He said: 'The moon looks
like plaster of Paris.' Soon one couldn't see the moon in Istanbul
any more. For days a thick fog lay over the city. The ships could
no longer sail from Asia to Europe. One couldn't see the tip of
one's own nose, everything was fogged up, the buses drove slowly,
the taxis drove slowly, everything on the streets moved slowly.
Only in the lit-up rooms did people move about normally. In the
Turkish parliament the right-wing deputies attacked those from
the Workers' Party with chair legs. In the universities the fascists
or the supporters of the religious parties got into fights with the
left-wingers, in one home two brothers, one in a left-wing youth
organisation, the other in a right-wing one, hit each other with
their parents' chairs and broke the chairs and the windows. The
sound of the breaking panes of glass could be heard in the fog.
The leader of the Americanised ruling party, Demirel, said: 'This
is a phenomenon which is being masterminded from abroad.'
Suddenly there was a search for Russian spies in Istanbul, and
once a dumb man was arrested. The hippies who lived in their cars
on the streets of Istanbul were sent back to their own countries.
'The hippies set a bad example to our youth.' In order to stay

in Istanbul some hippies had their hair cut and the hippy girls went to the Turkish baths for the first time. They bought Turkish newspapers and sat in cafés for days with the same newspaper, so that the police didn't pick them up. The newspapers were also underwear for poor children. When it was cold, parents put the newspapers under their children's shirts. When one walked past a poor child one heard the rustling of newspaper.

At the newspaper kiosks the left-wing, fascist and religious newspapers hung next to one another, all in Turkish, but it was as if there were three foreign languages. On the ship everyone opened their left-wing, fascist or religious newspapers, and one didn't see any faces any more. But shortly before the ship arrived, they all folded their different newspapers, and a left-winger talked to a left-winger who sat beside him and had read the same newspaper. A fascist talked to the fascist who sat beside him, and so they all practised the newly learned words with one another. If two people were reading different newspapers at a bus stop, the newspaper readers who were in the minority didn't get on the bus. So often people travelled on the buses who read the same newspaper. Sometimes the fascists bought the left-wing newspapers and threw them from the ship into the sea. Sometimes two political groups fought each other with rolled-up newspapers.

On a Sunday in February 1969 the left-wingers assembled at the Atatürk statue in the city centre for a legal demonstration. All had newspapers in their hands and pockets. Protesting against them were fifteen thousand people who had come by bus to Istanbul from many towns. In the end two left-wing demonstrators lay dead, bleeding on their newspapers. The left-wingers fled, their left-wing newspapers fell on to the streets. 'Bloody Sunday'. When in the newspapers that was followed by the headlines 'Bloody Wednesday' or 'Bloody Monday', many left-wing students left the Workers' Party, founded Dev Genç (Revolutionary Youth) and armed themselves: 'We can only achieve the independence of our people through armed struggle.' They dressed up like the famous fighters of the world: Trotsky glasses, Mao jackets, Lenin jackets,

Stalin jackets, Che Guevara beard, and their language divided into new languages. There were new, left-wing periodicals, I bought all these periodicals and sat in the toilet for a long time to learn these new languages.

Some nights I sat until morning with a poet, a friend of Kerim. The house on the hill in which he lived shook when the Russian ships sailed past on the Bosporus below. Then the poet shouted, 'The Russians are coming' and laughed.

Sometimes I slept at his house. When he saw me sitting in the cold room, wrapped in the blanket, surrounded by my Leninist-Maoist-Trotskyist newspapers, he laughed and said: 'Are they all your men? Lenin was a drunken vodka drinker and drunk he rode a bike in Switzerland, where he lived in exile. And drunk he mounted Rosa Luxemburg.'

When Kerim, half bald like Lenin, was staying with his friend in Istanbul and was writing at the table, I didn't dare go into the room. And when he slept and I heard his breath, I often asked myself whether he was dead like Lenin or not. Then I wrote something about him in my notebook, as if I were writing about Lenin. The poet read these sentences and said: 'You take men too seriously. You think if he's sitting at the table in the room he's thinking something important. But maybe he's thinking that his trousers are dirty and that he has to take them to his mother. Or he's thinking about a good cheese.' At night young poets tapped on his window, came in with snow on their shoes and read out their poems. When they recited their poems, even the cold in the room seemed like a poem. One of the young poets who visited at night said to me: 'You believe too much in the written word. Stalin was a murderer, because he believed in the written word, because he was a student of theology. Stop believing in the texts. Try to be a good actress. All poetic sentences are sketches of a future reality. Poetry never forces you to kill.' What I had understood from the books was: the revolution comes in a single night, and then paradise. Until then the way there is hell. The poet said: 'That's when hell really begins.' Then he laughed. I laughed with him and noticed that I laughed with him, but never with Kerim. I took Kerim too seriously, no matter what he did, whether he read, ate or scratched himself.

One morning, when all the little fishing boats on the Sea of Marmara were on strike and the dolphins were turning somersaults between the fishing boats, I took the train to Ankara because I had finished drama school and a theatre there, the Ankara Ensemble, had offered me a part. The head of the Ankara Ensemble was our communist hostel warden from Berlin, who had meanwhile become a well-known writer and Brecht director in Turkey. 'Welcome, Sugar,' he exclaimed with his wife, the Dove, as he had once done in Berlin. He was directing his own play about a girl who can only save herself in capitalism by becoming a whore and a madam. I was afraid of portraying the whores wrongly onstage, and asked the policeman standing at the door of the brothel in Ankara whether I could talk to the whores, because I had to play the part of a whore in the theatre. 'I want to learn from the whores, how the part of a whore has to be played.' The policeman laughed and said: 'Please go to the Vice Section, they have to send three of my colleagues with you, who will protect you here.' The head of the police Vice Section said: 'I've heard about this play.' He allocated me three policemen, who accompanied me; I went into every brothel and spoke to the whores. The old whores sat by a stove, the young ones talked to me. It was cold, so many whores wore short woollen socks and woollen waistcoats. Each whore had two beds, one was her own bed, the bed of a princess, large, with a beautiful bedspread, the other was her workplace. All the whores wanted to help me. 'Tell me, my sister, what do you want to learn?' – 'Teach me how you ask a man for money.' The whores showed me their diaries, they all said: 'My life is a novel.' The madam stood outside, the men came out, paid her, she rolled up the banknotes like a cigarette and stuck them under her gold bracelets.

In my part as a whore, I put on short white socks, like the real whores, and I rolled up the banknotes men gave me and stuck them under my bracelet. The men in the auditorium laughed, the women didn't. Many whores from the Ankara brothel came to the first night, watched the political play about whores and clapped. Next to them sat famous Turkish communists who had taken part in the Spanish Civil War. One of them had been so badly injured by Franco's Guardia Civil that he had only half a chin. At the first-night party I sat with the whores and with him and said that I had a Spanish boyfriend; the whores immediately wanted to hear his name. 'Jordi,' I said. All the whores, one after the other, repeated his name, 'Jordi,' 'Jordi,' 'Jordi,' and the man with half a chin said: 'Franco will never die.' The whores asked: 'Who is Franco?' The man with half a chin said: 'The enemy of Jordi.' The whores cursed and prayed that this Franco who was the enemy of Jordi would soon die and go to hell as a damned son of a whore.

After the first-night party the whores and the man with half a chin wanted to accompany me home, suddenly there was a power failure on the street and in all the houses. The whores lit matches and brought me to the flat with burning matches. The flat belonged to a blind student, who was just washing the dishes with a blind friend. One washed up, the other dried, and both were talking in the dark about Marx and Engels, without knowing that everyone else was standing in the dark too. The man with half a chin immediately joined in the conversation in the dark, and the whores asked me whether their language was a language for the blind. They started to talk to one another in their whores' language, Marx's, Engels' and whores' language in the dark, we laughed, and the man with half a chin related that in 1960 a Spanish priest had sold Spanish peasants a place in heaven. Thousands of square metres or five square metres, whatever, and the peasants bought the place in heaven in which they wanted to live after their death. In the dark, the whores decided to buy sixty square metres of heaven. One exclaimed that true life took place in bed, that space would be enough in heaven. No one knew how many square metres that was, but one of the Marxist blind men said: 'Let us measure it, sister.' He took her hand and walked quite confidently into the next room, while the whore walked in the darkness as if she were blind.

Every evening other whores, socialists, workers came to the performances, and in the interval they smoked their cigarettes together.

When a state of emergency was declared in Istanbul because of a general strike by two hundred thousand workers, and a night-time curfew was implemented, many students came to Ankara from Istanbul. In the evening people waited in the queue outside the theatre, sometimes a member of the audience jumped out of the queue in fright, he had seen a weapon under the jacket of the student in front of him or behind him. Students were seen with a book: *Urban Guerrilla*. During the night street lights in Ankara were smashed by bullets. The next morning I walked on broken glass to the theatre, and suddenly I saw a man, hands behind his back, walking slowly through the nervous crowd – the former Czech prime minister, Dubcek, whom the Russians had sent into exile in Ankara. He always walked up the same street. In the Anatolian towns the police had killed left-wing students; their mothers came to Ankara and marched with the demonstrators to the Atatürk mausoleum, in order to complain to Atatürk. The mothers were veiled, one could see only their eyes. When they wept for their dead sons in the Atatürk Mausoleum, their tears made the black material of their veils wet. Some also came to our theatre and saw Brecht's *The Mother*. At the end of the play the veiled mothers raised their fists in the air out of their veils.

A friend told me that his youth organisation had given him a packet of illegal leaflets, which he was secretly to hand over to someone in the university toilets. He had taken the bus to the university, found the prearranged toilet cubicle, stood on the toilet seat of the next cubicle and handed the packet over. At that moment he recognised the other's hands, it was his own brother. Both flushed the toilets and left the cubicles without talking to one another, got on the same bus and went with the packet to their shared flat.

While we went on a tour of forty towns in Turkey with our whores' play, some left-wing students founded the THKO, the People's Liberation Army of Turkey. They wanted to start the armed struggle and thought they could learn it from the Latin American guerrillas or in Vietnam, but Vietnam was far away. So they decided to go to Fatah, the Palestinian liberation movement, in Lebanon. In a guerrilla camp they did gymnastics, learned to assemble weapons and soon saw that Palestine had a different geography from Turkey. The sixteen students returned to Turkey, wanted to bury their weapons somewhere in southern Anatolia and then return to their universities. But the police arrested them. Students came from every town and visited them in prison. In court the accused said: 'Fatah is an Arab nationalist organisation, which is fighting to regain their territory occupied by Israel, we only wanted to help them.' The court could not decide whether Palestine's Fatah was a nationalist or a communist organisation. It wrote to the Foreign Ministry and put the question: 'Is Fatah nationalist or communist?' The Turkish Foreign Ministry replied: 'Fatah is an Arab nationalist organisation.' So the court released the students. But while they were still in prison, the opium farmers went on strike, because America wanted to forbid the planting of opium in Turkey. The striking peasants visited the students in prison, and the students thought they would be able to organise the peasants for the popular struggle of the THKO, the People's Liberation Army of Turkey. Deniz, the student leader, had just been released from another prison and joined the THKO. A couple of young military academy students said: 'It's too early for the guerrilla struggle, soon the Turkish army will form a left-wing military junta.' The THKO students said: 'The Turkish army is in NATO. We want to go into the mountains and begin the guerrilla struggle, the progressive officers and soldiers of the Turkish army can join our people's liberation struggle.'

A famous singer composed the song 'Mountains, Mountains'. The man with half a chin debated with Deniz. 'Climb up the mountain. They will destroy you and the mountain.' Deniz and the THKO students bought maps of Turkey and motorcycles like Che Guevara. On 1 January 1971 Deniz robbed a bank with two friends and disappeared. Deniz's father declared: 'My son is not a thief.' In those days many students said to their parents: 'Forget me' and disappeared. The police threw students out of the windows of the universities, some died, the government ordered police and army to occupy the university, then the universities were shut down completely. The police looked for the guerrillas in bookshops, beat the booksellers with the heavy books and arrested motorcyclists. Meetings and demonstrations were banned, and the Cinematheque and our theatre closed down as communists dens. The police carried the Russian films to police headquarters. Our theatre was just performing the whores' play in Istanbul, the police came in the evening, waited till the performance was over, then arrested the actors in their costumes and make-up and our theatre director. The theatre was shut down, the theatre management was supposed to have given the Liberation Army money. The street sweepers in Istanbul went on strike, and rats ran over the mountains of rubbish in the streets. The police searched Turkish ships arriving from abroad for weapons. The peasants occupied the estates of the big landowners and the peasant women lay down on the ground to block the soldiers' way. The electrical engineers went on strike and wanted to cut off power to the whole of Istanbul. The deaf and dumb organised a conference and demanded that the government give them work. The police held a conference, and demanded that anyone who had hit a policeman should be hung. Customers who bought fruit at the fruiterer, and found the price too high, shouted that the fruiterer should be hung. That way order could be established.

With six friends, who like him wanted to make revolutionary films, Kerim rented a flat opposite the English consulate. Downstairs

Istanbul Greeks worked as tailors, I heard sewing-machine sounds from below all the time, prostitutes lived upstairs and brought men home at night, I heard their beds creaking until morning. After we had put tables and beds in the flat, so that we could live there together, one night the friends came into the room in which Kerim and I slept and said: 'From now on we share everything. We want to sleep with her too.' Then they laughed and ran out again. No one had any money. On the street below there were many bars. If we needed some alcohol, we opened the window, and the smell of raki rose to our nostrils. One of the friends tapped the power cable, so that we could have free electric heating in every room. Then he put pieces of dry bread on the windowsill as bait and caught eight pigeons in a cage, which he made into a soup. As in the Chinese Cultural Revolution I smashed my two Beethoven records, the boys tore up their childhood photos. I always wore the same pair of trousers and the same pullover. It bothered me that I still owned two blouses. Even the bed I slept in bothered me. I dreamed of living in a tent. If by chance I looked into the windows of shoe or clothes shops, I saw myself in the shop window glass and was ashamed. I stopped only in front of bookshops. I went to my parents, stole food and brought it back to our film commune. During the day the boys went out into the streets and with an eight-millimetre camera filmed people they thought were being exploited. Then they developed the film in a darkroom, hung it on a clothes line in the big room and dried it with my hairdryer. The sewing machines of the Turkish Greeks worked below, the whores' beds worked above, and the hairdryer worked in the film commune. We got Eisenstein films from the Russian consulate and watched them in the film commune; from France young French communists came to our commune and gave us film stock. During the day they went to the Turkish bazaar, pinched things, and in the evening they talked to Kerim about the French film-makers Truffaut and Godard. I was constantly thinking about how I could find money, so that Kerim could make a film like Eisenstein or Godard. I also thought about working as a whore, and I once went upstairs to ask how much they earned. I earned more in the theatre. One of the whores said: 'Let your man pay for you.' – 'He doesn't work, because he's a theorist.' Our poet friend visited us and said: 'Don't take men so seriously, have fun in bed. It's good for art.' I became pregnant again, but we said: 'No child for this rotten society,' and I had the child aborted. Many students left university, because Mao had said: 'First make the Revolution.' Kerim had only one pair of worn-out shoes. His family still didn't give him any money. I took a pair of shoes from my father, they were four sizes too big, but he put them on and went on drying the eight-millimetre films with the hairdryer.

I got a part with a touring theatre and travelled to Anatolia. There we slept in a different hotel every night, the rain came through the roofs and in the hotel corridor men who were looking for work hung their wet shoes and jackets on clothes lines over the stove. In long underpants they stood around the stove with me, and we talked about the students who were being hunted everywhere as guerrillas. 'The state didn't give us a helping hand, our hope is the young people.' Then we heard on the radio that Deniz and his friends had kidnapped an American officer, Jimmy Ray Finnley. Finnley's uniform jacket was found at the scene, there were condoms in the jacket pocket. That evening, when we were performing the play, fascists smashed the windows of the hall, and a stone struck my large, fake bosom, which I was wearing for my part. Some members of the audience were bleeding; one wiped away his blood with the evening paper, which said that Deniz and his friends had already released the American officer Jimmy Ray Finnley. Ray had said: 'They treated me well.'

The police got an order to shoot Deniz and two of his friends, Hüseyin and Yusuf, on sight. A young actor was listening to the radio all the time, to find out what was happening to Deniz and his friends. He incorporated a radio into his part and constantly held it to his ear on stage. Once he called out in the middle of his monologue: 'Man, Deniz, Hüseyin and Yusuf have kidnapped four American soldiers in Ankara.' The audience didn't want to go on watching the play, but asked like a chorus: 'What does the radio say? Tell us.' The young actor called out: 'They're demanding a ransom for the four soldiers. Nixon has called the leader of the ruling party, Demirel, and said: "I advise you not to negotiate." The police have arrested two thousand students who blocked traffic between Istanbul and Smyrna.' The director warned the young actor with the radio not to do it again, but four days later the actor interrupted the performance again: 'The four Americans have been released, but Deniz and his friends haven't been caught, don't worry.' The audience applauded, and the director, too, was happy that Deniz and his two friends hadn't killed the hostages. A journalist had interviewed Deniz and his two friends at a secret location about the kidnapping. Everywhere people repeated the details: one of the kidnappers had disguised himself as a Turkish lieutenant and rented an apartment in Ankara. At night they had blocked the street along which the American soldiers always drove to their barracks in a car. It had been cold. Deniz and his friends had worn gloves. They had pulled open the car door, had got in, and one had told the American driver: 'Don't move, man.' They had taken the Americans to the rented apartment in another car. They had all taken off their wet shoes, and Deniz had made tea. One of the American soldiers had been black. Then they had found out that the wives of two soldiers were pregnant. The third had studied literature. The black soldier had related that his grandfather had seen Sitting Bull. The ultimatum had been thirty-six hours, but in the interview Deniz had said: 'We couldn't kill them, we're not fascists, they weren't guilty and no older than we are. The only guilt they bear, perhaps, is that they are American. Nor did they have any weapons, the terms were not equal. Hüseyin couldn't look them in the face, he was afraid he would have to kill them. I, too, put myself in their position and thought of my mother, my father, my brothers and sisters and said no. The Americans had no hope any more and on the third day wrote farewell letters to their families. I took the letter away from one of them, Larry, and read it, he had written his will. I couldn't bear it.' Deniz said: 'We fed them very well, even gave them bananas. We quietly left the apartment. The soldiers didn't even notice that we had gone.'

The police searched one apartment after another, in order to find Deniz, Hüseyin and Yusuf and arrested people who looked like Deniz all over the place. Four days after the American soldiers had been set free, the Turkish army carried out a coup, the leader of the ruling party, Demirel, was removed from office, and the guerrilla organisation issued a declaration: 'The goal has been achieved. The Americanised Demirel and his government have fallen. If the police stop their house searches, we will give ourselves up.' But then overnight the coup leaders removed all the senior officers they suspected of being on the left. In the theatre dressing-room we looked at the photos of the three coup generals. One was an army commander, the second a navy commander, the third an air force commander. To us a navy commander could only be a socialist, because the ocean is large, and a naval officer knows how large the world is. An air force general cannot be a fascist either, we thought, because he sees how wide the world is. We drove on with the bus from town to town, in order to put on our play, no one spoke on the bus, we bought all the newspapers, we almost ate them and searched them for good news and went on hoping that now the navy commander and the air force commander would carry out a socialist coup against the army commander. Early one morning I walked backwards and forwards in a hotel corridor, it was snowing, and the stove in the hotel had not been lit. Through a window I looked on to the street and saw two men talking to one another in the snow, they nodded sadly. I couldn't hear what they were saying, but at that moment I knew that the police had caught Deniz and his friends. In the evening I read it in the newspaper: Yusuf and Deniz had wanted to go by motorbike from Ankara to Anatolia and had repeatedly fallen because of the snow. So on the way they rented a car and wanted to put the motorbike on the roof. The car roof, however, was so icy that the motorbike kept on slipping from the roof and falling into the snow. A nightwatchman had seen them and wanted to take them to the police station. They fired in the air, fled, and during the chase Yusuf was wounded and captured. He was taken to a doctor and laid on a table, but he had still not been recognised. Around his neck Yusuf wore a medallion that he had taken from one of the four American soldiers, it was supposed to protect him from bullets. So at first the police thought they had shot at an American secret agent. Later two policemen disguised as peasants also arrested Deniz.

I returned to Istanbul, because we couldn't perform any more, everywhere we appeared, theatre windows were broken. On the bus to Istanbul I heard on the radio that the composer Stravinsky had died of a heart attack, then there followed a piece of music by Stravinsky. Suddenly the music broke off, the driver had switched off the engine. Soldiers were standing outside who ordered all young men to get off the bus. Some of them, peasants, had sheep with them, which they wanted to sell in the city. While the soldiers searched the bags, the sheep jumped out of the bus and ran across the road. Some of the soldiers now ran after the sheep. When all the men and all the sheep were back on the bus, the driver turned the radio on again, and silently we went on listening to Stravinsky.

In Istanbul I immediately went to my friend the poet. From his window we looked at the sea, in which for days so many sharks had been swimming that the newspapers had reported it. I asked him: 'Do you think the army will hang Deniz, Yusuf and Hüseyin?' – 'Yes,' said the poet, 'they will hang them as an example to the others. In the Ottoman Empire it was said anyone who is involved in politics has two shirts, one for festival days, one for the day he's hanged. Why didn't Deniz and his friends hide in the big city? Even the rats hide in the big cities.' While the sharks lay in the fish shops, the army banned the Workers' Party. The reason was new: propaganda for the Kurds. The trade unions organised more strikes, the workers occupied factories, bombs exploded at the generals' doors. For days people in Istanbul ate sharks, and as they put the fish in their mouths, they heard the bombs exploding, left the fish on the plate and ran to the window or into the street. As a result many fish ended up in the bin, at night I saw cats everywhere, which gathered around the rubbish bins and ate the sharks. The people were banned from the streets. The military banned all films and plays in which topics like theft and kidnapping occurred. They banned trade unions and meetings. If more than three people went into a house together, they were suspect. The police arrested and tortured. The cries were not heard, the walls behind which the torture took place were thick, but weeping mothers and fathers could be heard from many houses. The police searched houses for left-wing books, one of the policemen told the paper: 'I've injured my back from carrying all the communist books.'

In our film commune we were now reading Marx, Engels and Lenin to each other. As in Truffaut's film *Fahrenheit 451* we wanted to learn the books by heart, so that they would go on living.

Leila Khaled, the Palestinian Fatah guerrilla fighter who had hijacked an aeroplane, wore a ring on to which a bullet had been welded. The boy who had made a soup out of pigeons soldered an identical ring for me as a present. I walked to the bazaar wearing the ring, bought fish, and one of the fish sellers laughed and called across to his friend: 'Did you see the ring? She's a guerrilla.' Kerim often said: 'Leave the ring. You'll put us all at risk.' He buried my letters to him under a tree and asked me: 'Do you still have my letters? Take them to your parents and hide them there with the Russian films.' My mother said: 'Take your books here and throw them away. The police have already been to the neighbours.' But I couldn't part from my books and carried them in a bag to my film commune on the European side. The bag was so full that it wouldn't close, people didn't believe their eyes. Kerim saw these books: 'Take them away, bury them, throw them away.' I couldn't do it and hid them under the bed, along with the letters Kerim had sent me from military service. I slept above them, and dreamt that I had rented a house in which I had hidden the student leaders Deniz, Yusuf and Hüseyin. The house had big glass windows and no curtains. I put up clothes lines around the house and hung sheets over them, so that no one could see into the house from the street. Deniz gave me the money from the bank robbery, I was to hide it. Then I sat in a bus and put the money in my vagina, because soldiers were getting on the bus.

I woke up from the creaking of the whores' beds. In court Deniz had declared to the state prosecutor: 'Your indictment has only one purpose – to tear our heads off.' The state prosecutor declared: 'The state never wants a head. The court never tears the head off anyone. Through his deeds the guilty man sticks his head in the noose, and the law merely pulls away the chair beneath his feet.'

In those days a whore who lived above us died. I helped carry the coffin downstairs. Forty whores were waiting down in the street and wanted to walk to the cemetery behind the coffin. Because of the ban on gatherings a policeman came and asked whether the dead woman did not have a father or mother. 'If she had a mother and father, would she have been a whore?' a whore answered him. The police scratched their heads and let us walk behind the coffin.

From time to time I earned money as a dubbing speaker in films by Yilmaz Güney, the greatest Turkish film-maker, who supported our film commune with film stock. One day he sent two Kurdish students to us, whom we were to hide for him. One of the two was wanted by the police, the other carried a pistol, in order to protect him. The streets were full of secret police. To accompany the two students to a safe hiding place, I disguised myself as a whore, put on make-up, put blue marks under one eye and wiggled my bum on the street. One of the two walked behind me, like a man who is following a whore, the second boy, who had the pistol, followed him. I took them to the house of a friend, cooked for them there and in my whore's costume washed their shirts and underwear in a basin. Then we sat together, the boy showed me the pistol and wanted to teach me how to shoot. He had beautiful eyes. I listened to him, then I picked up the pistol, but immediately put it down again. It was heavy, cold.

When I returned to the film commune, a couple of men followed me right away because of my whore's costume.

The wanted men had to change flats every two days. I disguised myself as a wife, turned my Leila Khaled ring round to make it look like a wedding ring, made up a little baby out of bits of cloth, took it in my arm, put aubergines, tomatoes and onions in a shopping net, and walked arm in arm to another flat with one of the two students, while the other one with the pistol followed. Again I washed and cooked for them like a good wife. Then we sat down together to eat, and at one point the boy who was carrying the pistol said: 'Shall I withdraw to the other room? I'll leave the married couple alone and keep an eye on the child.' We laughed.

In the film commune everyone had gathered in the big room. Kerim looked under the easy chairs and in the lamps, in case the police had secretly installed microphones in the flat. Then to be completely sure he switched on the radio to drown out our voices. We made the decision to join the underground movement, to go into the mountains and to film the activities of the guerrillas. But we didn't know the guerrillas, I was instructed to meet a girl who knew a woman guerrilla. Through her I was to arrange a meeting with the guerrillas, and ask her what kind of task they could give us. The next day I bought semolina for the two students and in the film commune disguised myself as a peasant woman with a headscarf and a long coat, in order to take the pair to yet another flat. Suddenly there was a knock at the door. I opened up, and three plainclothes policemen were standing in front of me. They immediately pushed me aside, the bag of semolina fell out of my hand and burst. The policemen ran down the long corridor, I threw my headscarf and the coat into the courtyard. The policemen ran into one room, in which three of us had been sitting. In my room I pulled the Marx and Engels books from under the bed, opened the window, there were pigeons on the windowsill, pecking at dry bread, I put the books among the pigeons and quickly got the letters Kerim had written to me from military service. What should I do with the letters? Should I throw them down? Then I saw a pot of paint, which one boy had recently used to paint all the doors yellow, and put the letters in the yellow paint. I took the yellow-dyed letters, ran into the big room and stuck them down the side of the easy chair. My hands were yellow with paint and the paint was dripping everywhere. Then I quickly ran to the toilet and wanted to pull off my Leila Khaled bullet ring and throw it in the toilet bowl, but it didn't come off. Suddenly I saw our cat running with yellow paws along the corridor and into the room where the three policemen were standing. The three of them followed the cat, saw the yellow paint on my hands and followed the yellow paint to the easy chair which the letters were half sticking out of. They took the letters, and a young policeman opened the window to the courtyard, in front of which the pigeons were cooing. He saw the three Marx and Engels books, picked them up said: 'If you hadn't put them there, we probably wouldn't have taken them so seriously at all.' The pigeons had already shat a little on the books.

The policemen brought me, Kerim, all the boys from the film commune, the shat-upon Marx-Engels books and the yellow-dyed love letters to police headquarters. As we got into the police car, I gave the caretaker the little cat. 'Please, keep it.'

At police headquarters they asked me who the woman in the headscarf and the long coat had been, who had opened the door to them. Then they immediately showed me photos of Deniz and his friends. 'Do you know them?' – 'Yes, from the newspapers. I've seen them in the newspapers for years.' The captain shouted into the next room: 'She knows the bandits.' They wrote down that I knew them, then the captain asked me: 'Do these film boys run all over you? Yes, they sleep with you. I have a daughter your age too,' and spat in my face. – 'They don't sleep with me.' – 'Get this whore away from me.' They released all of us, and I went to the caretaker to get the cat. 'It disappeared.' I looked on the streets for the yellow paint, which the cat had on its paws, but found no trace.

Kerim said: 'I begged you, take my letters to your parents' apartment. They should at least now get rid of the Russian films.' My father didn't know where he should hide the films, went to the Sea of Marmara and threw them in the water. Many people did the same and in the night threw sacks full of left-wing books into the Sea of Marmara, or, one at a time, out of car windows on to the streets. In those days ships and fishing boats sailed on the sea between Marx, Engels, Lenin, Mao and Che Guevara books, and the dolphins went on doing their somersaults. And in the streets buses and cars drove over Lenin, Marx and Engels, the wheels splashed mud on them. The children of the slum quarters collected these books for heating, and the dirty, crushed books lay in piles in front of the slum houses, next to the piles of refuse, rats, cockroaches and lice. Sometimes at night people hung a book on a rope from a tree and wrote in paint on the trunk: 'Murderers, if you hang Deniz, Yusuf and Hüseyin, you hang ideas. They didn't kill anyone.'

Downstairs in the house the sewing machines of the Greek tailor went on working, upstairs the beds of the whores went on creaking at night, and between the two we walked softly through the rooms, we didn't dare steal electricity from the state any more, we wrapped ourselves in our blankets, and walked back and forward in the cold flat. Every time I did so I walked over the yellow splashes of paint. I had endangered Kerim. He said: 'One can't rely on women' and closed the door of the room in which he and the boys were talking about what they would do now. For the first time I was ashamed of being a girl.

I went to the film studios and asked a couple of cameramen whether I could work with them as an assistant. One of the cameramen, a religious man, said yes. I had to carry the camera, it weighed forty pounds, and he showed me how to move close to the face of the star with the zoom. He said: 'You are Turkey's first woman camera assistant.' During the breaks the religious cameraman performed his prayers. At the film studios no one talked about the coup or about the students who had been sentenced to death. Everyone spoke into the camera about love, about betrayal, 'You don't love me any more, I love you,' and at that moment I went close up to her lips with the zoom. But when I sat on a bus after the shooting day, I heard different sentences. 'What are your sons doing?' – 'They're inside.' – 'In which prison?' The toilets were blocked everywhere, because at home the sons and daughters had torn up the left-wing leaflets or letters and thrown them in the toilets. I, too, threw my Leila Khaled pistol ring into the toilet. It came up again every time I flushed, so I threw it into the Sea of Marmara.

One day we shot a karate sex film. The lead actress had to lie in bed with the karate star. It was said she worked as a whore in an expensive brothel. She undressed down to her panties; the director said: 'Please take off your panties as well.' – 'No, Director, it's not in my contract.' We waited. Then the karate star sent his driver to bring cognac and chocolate. He poured cognac into the actress's mouth, then pulled off her panties. At that moment three policemen came into the studio. The director shouted: 'It's not your turn yet.' But they were real policemen, their car was waiting outside in the street, Kerim was in it. The religious cameraman said to the policemen: 'Leave her here until we've stopped shooting, otherwise she won't get any money,' but we drove to police headquarters immediately.

There for two days we sat in an office in which policemen were working. From time to time they snapped their typewriters shut, took their pistols, left the room and came back later: 'Two of the dogs are dead.' After two days they took me and Kerim to another room, in which a woman police captain was sitting. On the table in front of her were the love letters that I had put in the yellow oil paint. The woman captain looked me up and down for a couple of minutes, then she said: 'I wanted to get to know the girl who received such beautiful letters.' Then she congratulated Kerim: 'These are wonderful, very literary letters. But in them you give an analysis of the army. For that you will get at least twenty-five years in prison.' Then we were separated and I was brought back to the office. The policemen typed on their typewriters and went on talking about dogs: 'The dog from the law university', 'The dog who studies philosophy'. Now other women were also sitting in

the room, a worker, a student. The woman worker said to me:
'Why do you let your hair hang down like that? Quick, put it
up, otherwise you'll be treated as a whore.' Then the police took
the student away for interrogation. When she came back, she sat
down silently on her chair. She looked at her white skirt, and hair
fell from her head on to the white material. She had been forced
to listen as her boyfriend was tortured. We were not allowed to go
to the window, so that we didn't commit suicide. There were not
enough political police for all the political detainees, so traffic and
vice police were brought in to help out. At night we were guarded
by traffic police and for them I wrote postcards in German to the
women tourists they had got to know. We were only allowed to go
to the toilet with them. I saw tortured students, two policemen
gripped them under their arms, there were open wounds on their
feet from the beatings. The blood dripped on to the corridors,
and the police walked backwards and forwards over the student
blood. In the toilet I stood in front of the mirror, beside me stood
a well-known guerrilla woman. One policeman held her firmly,
she washed her hands with soap, then she gave me the soap, and
we looked at each other in the mirror. A frozen image. Then they
took me for interrogation, and we went into the interrogation
room with blood on our shoes. Five men were sitting there, they
asked me who had introduced me to the Cinematheque, who
had introduced me to the Workers' Party. I said: 'I read about it
in the newspaper.' – 'Why do you want socialism to come?' I saw
the typewriter on the table, an American make. 'With socialism
I want us to be able to make our own typewriters.' The chief
interrogator said: 'I want that, too.' Then he said to the other four
men: 'You see, gentlemen, the communists always make use of such
beautiful girls. Just look, her eyes, her eyebrows, her aubergine-
coloured hair, her sweet mouth. Just look at this beauty here. Is
it not heartbreaking, that this beauty is exploited by communists
for their aims?' The four men said nothing. The interrogator
suddenly began to sweat, picked up a tissue, that lay beside the
typewriter, and wiped his neck. One of the four men asked me:

'Didn't you recognise me?' He turned to his superior and said: 'You see, major, she doesn't recognise me!' He pushed photographs over to me. 'In Anatolia I followed you every step of the way, when you went to the Iranian–Iraqi border. You told the Kurds in the mountain village they should kill the Turkish policemen.' – 'No, I only brought them medicines.' – 'I was there, you said it.' – 'There were only two women there, they were giving their children milk, and their husband, a horse and three donkeys. Or were you the horse?' The interrogator laughed and then said: 'Gentlemen, let's not waste any time with artistes. Look, my artiste lady, you are very beautiful. You could find a good husband and have children. Why do you want to play at socialism?' I was allowed to leave the room, and the police took me and Kerim to the army on the Asian side of Istanbul. They were to decide what was to be done with us. There a major asked me: 'Why are you here?' The policeman showed him the love letters. The major leafed through them and said: 'They arrested you for this? Just get out of here. Am I supposed to concern myself with your love letters. Get out and I don't ever want to see you here again.' The policemen brought us and the love letters back to police headquarters. From the ferry I saw the Bridge of the Golden Horn through the bars of the police van. Kerim had lost a lot of weight and was unshaven, he was afraid. I held his hand. He said to me: 'Call your father. They must save us. Tell him that I'm your fiancé.' At police headquarters we were separated again, and I sat down on the same chair once more.

I sat on the same chair for another three weeks and at night I played chess and dominoes with the traffic policemen. Again and again new detainees were brought into the room. Once they brought in an Indian woman from the circus as a suspect. She was a snake dancer and came with her boa constrictor. She sat down on a police chair, put the snake around her neck, ordered a half-chicken for us all; the snake hung from her neck and slept drugged with opium. In the night the police chief opened the door, looked at us and asked: 'What are you?' – 'Worker.'

'What are you?' – 'Snake dancer.'

'What are you?' – 'Actress.'

He said: 'A woman worker, an artiste, a snake dancer. May Allah curse you all, you whores.' Then he went away and his shoes left patches of student blood in the room. In the morning, when the police came, they brought packets of salt with them. The people they tortured had afterwards to put their feet in salt water, so that the feet didn't swell up and no traces remained. On the same floor they ran electric current into the students' penises, and when they screamed, the policewomen laughed at them. 'Ooh, is that the THKO hero, then?'

I was allowed to call my father. 'Father, please rescue me and my fiancé from here.' He came immediately with two tubes of toothpaste, two toothbrushes and two towels and wanted to see me. The policemen said to him he should go home, but my father shouted on the stairs, his voice echoed through seven storeys. 'My hair has turned white for this country. I want to see my daughter. What have you done with her?' The policemen said to him: 'Clear off, go away.' My father shouted: 'I want to see my daughter.' The policemen briefly opened the door for him. Suddenly he was silent and said quietly: 'My daughter.' Then he gave me the toothbrush and the towels and said: 'I will rescue you, my daughter.'

Now students without hands came. They had wanted to throw bombs to protest against the death sentence passed on Deniz, Yusuf and Hüseyin, the bombs had exploded in their hands. They sat next to one another on the chairs, and one waved away the flies from the other's face with his stump.

When I was released with Kerim, the fathers of tortured students were standing outside with big shoes in their hands. A father said: 'My son normally wears size forty, but now he needs forty-five. His feet are ruined.' Outside, the blind men were giving the pigeons corn, and the pigeons flew up in front of our feet. We walked across the Bridge of the Golden Horn. We were both forty pounds lighter. The wind blew, I held on to the railings of the bridge and Kerim held on to me. I phoned my parents from a grocer's shop and said: 'We're out.' When I put down the receiver, the shop owner said: 'I wish you a speedy recovery. My son was inside too, but he's out now,' and gave us two apples. We got on the ship and sailed to the Asian side, to my parents. As we were sitting on the ship, I looked at the sea, I saw it as an old blue carpet covering an infinitely large floor. I threw the apples into the sea, the blue moved. At home my parents saw Kerim for the first time and kissed him. My father pointed to his new, thick moustache and asked me: 'Tell me, my daughter, do I look like Stalin?' My mother was talking about a neighbour and suddenly said: 'She is a dependent bourgeois.'

The film commune had broken up, those who had not yet done their military service were called up. Kerim stayed at my parents' for a few days and then moved in with his friend, the poet.

After three days my father said to me: 'You have a letter from Spain.' Jordi, my first love, had sent me a book about stage design and written a long letter. 'My love, I'm afraid. Are you still alive, or have the police already killed you? I go to the Turkish consulate every day and look for your name in the Turkish newspapers.' I wrote him a letter, I had found a bird's feather, I dipped it in ink and wrote with it. In the sea below a couple of dolphins were again leaping between the fishing boats on the water. The ants on the balcony gathered on Jordi's letter, and the sun warmed his words, the ants and my feet. It was as if the ants wanted together to carry Jordi's words to their houses. I closed my eyes. The birds flew past.

> Birds, fly over plains,
> find him
> greet him
> with your thousand wings.

I had taken off my shoes. A couple of jasmine petals from a jasmine tree came flying on the May wind and collected in my shoes. The wind and the smell of jasmine reminded me how young I still was.

While I wrote to Jordi, Deniz, Yusuf and Hüseyin wrote their last letters to their fathers. Yusuf said to his lawyer: 'Tomorrow, after my death, my father will come and take my clothes. Look, I'm wearing rubber shoes. Tell him he shouldn't be sad, that I only had rubber shoes. Tell him he shouldn't be sad. Tell him I also had leather shoes. I just didn't have time to put them on.' The executions began at night, at 1.25 a.m., and took until 5.20 a.m. Soldiers and police brought Deniz to the gallows, and Yusuf, whose turn it was next, had to wait on a chair at the window and watch Deniz being hanged. Then Hüseyin had to watch from the window as Yusuf was hanged. After they had hanged Deniz, and his body was turning on the gallows, all the men in uniform heard a noise. They thought of an attack, all hands reached for the rifles, but it was only a pigeon, its wings beating in the prison yard. Yusuf's father saw his son in the coffin and the wound on his son's neck and three months later got a tumour on his neck. The army didn't allow the three dead men to be buried together, and the imams refused them the last ritual.

The next day people sat on the ship with the newspapers on their knees, no one read them. Big black letters. Just one word: ASILDILAR. ('They have been hanged.') A peasant, illiterate, held the newspaper the wrong way round, wept, his tears remained caught in his beard. A seagull flew into the ship and its head struck the ship's side. Many mothers walked silently, looking at the ground, across the Bridge of the Golden Horn. They didn't say anything, but I heard their voices. 'If one loses one's children, one at first hopes to find them. When one sees that they are not coming back, one gets up every day to die. We go on. We cook, we iron, they have torn our bodies apart. Such young necks, so young, like those of a newborn animal. What does a child think? To be close to paradise, to be far from hell. Now life is a couple of lines on a musty sheet of paper in the pocket of the officials keeping the records. In prisons with weak light bulbs. Bed bugs, generals, rusty beds. In front of or behind the generals, civilians, in their hands packed-up, folded cities. Hence the steps from house to house late at night. The moon, the rifles wet with rain. The black feelings pulled up one over the other around their hips. Revenge under the pillows. The rumbling voices of flies in one's ears, ships bearing sadness. Shivering, shivering. He had eyes, he had hands, his hair wet. His mouth was kissed in the dreams of dreaming girls. How can a gallows pull away the dreams from under the feet of a young man who lives in so many dreams? The doors, the doors, the doors. The closed windows. The clouds cover up the sea. A few shadows by the shore are wet. Shivering. Don't look on his death. He has eyes, he has hands, his hands are still in mortal fear. Sweat. Sons, stay here, stay here. Sweep the darkness into the dark. They weep. They have sung their songs and have gone. They have not got used to the world. Today I was, tomorrow not. Eye beats lashes. A fish rests above the sea. THE MAN GOES. A child dies, a woman weeps, a cat runs along the wall of the house, the smell of wood, alleys, oranges, clouds of linen, children not properly dried, smelling of soap, bird counting its feathers in poverty. With a pair of scissors that can cut off fear. Dream living in the pupils of the eye. City, be silent. Hear our song. We have long been living with the dead who have no grave. Look on our breasts, arms. We want our children living. Living they were taken away. Especially large men, an elite, on horses, have bent down to the alleys, gathered up our children from their horses. There our children still looked as if they gave the spring its colour. Rabies spat in the face of our branches, trees. Rabies doesn't anticipate the love of mothers. Our children still have milk at the breast. Sweet. All the children saw it. All the children wanted to get to them, because they smelt of sweet milk, at her breast. They have buried our children in a bird's beak, which had never thought that it would have to remain silent. They walk in the wind, somewhere. The mountains are like coloured wool, plucked by hand. The sun is folded. Folded dark pieces of cloth. The stars give them their hands. The sea burns. Not the rain that falls, the clouds. Pregnant women look, their hands clapped to their mouths, at children leaving their stomach. They fall down like feathers, as light as sinless deeds. The milk they drank from our breasts came out of their nostrils. Why do our children only come in our dreams? Here we stand on the Bridge of the Golden Horn. With these eyes in this blind world we have seen the Day of Judgement.'

Kerim said to me: 'It is time to gather up bourgeois culture and to read new books and to listen to different music.' We sat at the same table, saw the jasmine leaves falling from the same tree, but he had begun to speak a different language from me. He said: 'Don't talk this slogan language. Take off the green army parka. Dress like a woman.' I didn't want to sleep with Kerim any more. Many are in prison, I thought, and I'm free. When my parents were not at home for a few days, I sold all their furniture. My mother saw the empty apartment; I said: 'It was a petty bourgeois apartment.' – 'I weep for you, because I know that later you will very much regret what you have done,' she said. 'I've become left-wing too, I've read Dostoevsky, read Aitmatov, read Tolstoy. What did the carpets and the few easy chairs do to you? One has to be able to sit down.' My father said: 'My daughter, you have to see the psychiatrist.' My mouth got an allergy, it could be peeled like an orange. I couldn't talk any more, every word hurt my mouth. My father put syrup into my mouth with a spoon and said: 'This is for Marx. This is for Che Guevara. This is for Engels.' I laughed, and that hurt my mouth even more. In the night I heard on the radio that the Chilean president, Allende, had been murdered. My father said: 'Don't weep, my daughter. Look, I'm weeping for both of us.'

Then the Social Democrat Ecevit and the religious party won the elections; the three coup generals now fought with each other to become president of the republic.

The new government declared a general amnesty for all prisoners. Suddenly the streets of Istanbul were full of men with shaven heads. Some had no arms or hands any more. The universities were opened again. Once I was standing alone at a bus stop, there was a police car near by, and I asked the policeman which bus went to the city centre. He said: 'Number sixty-eight', and when the bus came he shouted: 'Hands up. Hands up.' I immediately raised my arms so that he wouldn't shoot at me, but he only wanted me to signal to the bus driver.

Then the Social Democrat Ecevit was forced out of the government, and before the hair on the shaven skulls of the left-wingers had grown, we heard shooting in the night again. The Grey Wolves came on to the buses with rifles, kidnapped left-wingers from houses, from student hostels, and killed them in cemeteries. They came into cafés, in which left-wingers were sitting and killed; I didn't want to sit with my back to the apartment door any more, because they also shot through doors. When I saw pregnant women in the streets, I thought, now the children in their stomachs are afraid. If I was sitting in a car and we took a bend, I became afraid and gripped the driver's hand. If a kettle was boiling for tea, I became afraid. If I saw a cockroach I thought, it may grow bigger during the night. Once I came home and saw a rat running into my parents' cellar. My books were in a couple of big sacks there. I went into the cellar, the pigeons had come through the wooden walls into the cellar and had shat on all the sacks of books. Because of the dampness of the cellar the cloth sacks had come apart in many places, the corners of the books poked out, they were all damp and covered in shit. Karl Marx didn't have an eye any more. I took a book by Bertolt Brecht, a volume of poetry, and leafed through it.

> *Thank the Lord the whole thing's quickly over*
> *All the loving and the sorrow my dear.*
> *Where are the teardrops you wept last evening?*
> *Where are the snows of yesteryear?*

I quietly sang the song in German in the dark night and as I lay in bed at my parents', I thought, I shall go to Berlin and work in the theatre. My heart beat loudly.

The last night, before I went to Berlin, I cried in bed. My mother heard me, came into my room with her rolled-up bed, lay down beside me and said in the dark: 'Flee and live your life. Go, fly.' The next day I packed my suitcase and went to the train. A poor man stood in front of the station and showed the soldiers and whores gathered outside the station a bottle in which lay a small, poor snake. The poor man said: 'How does a snake smoke?' Then he opened the top of the bottle, drew on his cigarette, blew the smoke into the bottle and closed the top again. And the poor snake lay with the smoke in the bottle. 'That's how a snake smokes.' A few yards farther on a man had started a fire, on to which he was throwing newspapers. In one newspaper I read: 'Watergate Scandal: Nixon faces impeachment', and the newspaper went up in flames. This man had a cockerel with him. He asked the people who had gathered there: 'How does a cockerel dance?' and set the cockerel on the burning newspapers, the cockerel's toes burned and it constantly raised its feet, so that they didn't burn up. The man said: 'Look, the cockerel is dancing.' A poor sesame ring vendor watched and drew on his long filter cigarette, it began to rain. The newspaper fire went out, the train whistled, and I sat down in the train to Berlin. From the train window I saw the Bridge of the Golden Horn. Building workers were dismantling it, because a new bridge was to be built. Their hammers echoed as they struck the bridge. The train to Berlin pulled out, from the window I still saw the Bridge of the Golden Horn. A couple of ships drew the bridge parts behind them, and the seagulls flew after them and cried out and the train cried too, for a long time, and went past the Istanbul houses. Opposite me sat a young man about my age. He opened the CUMHURIYET and I read: 'Franco is dead.' It was 21 November 1975. The young man who was reading the paper asked me: 'Do you want a cigarette?'

'Yes.'

# Quotations

p. 36      *I am lovely, o mortals, a stone-fashioned dream,*
              *And my breast, where you bruise yourselves all in your*
              *turn,*
              *Is made so that love will be born in the poet—*
                  Charles Baudelaire: *The Flowers of Evil / Les*
                  *Fleurs du mal*, translated by James McGowan
                  (Oxford, 1983), p. 38.

p. 36      *What will you say, my heart…*
              *To the most beautiful, the best, most dear.*
                  Charles Baudelaire: as above, p. 84.

p. 50      'Hymn of Baal the Great', translated by Peter Tegel.
              Bertolt Brecht: *Collected Plays*, ed. John Willett/
              Ralph Manheim (London, 1970), pp. 3–4.

p. 66      Bertolt Brecht: *The Mother*, translated by Steve
              Gooch (London, 1978) p. 6.

p. 68      Friedrich Engels: *The Origin of the Family, Private*
              *Property and the State*, translated by Alick West,
              (London, 1940).

p. 104–5      *My sister, my child*
                *Imagine how sweet*
                *To live there as lovers do!*
                *To kiss as we choose*
                *To love and to die*

> In that land resembling you!
> The misty suns
> Of shifting skies
> To my spirit are as dear
> As the evasions
> Of your eyes
> That shine behind their tears.

> There all is order and leisure,
> Luxury, beauty and pleasure.
>    Charles Baudelaire: as above, p. 108.

pp. 139 and 255    Bertolt Brecht: *Poems and Songs from Plays*, translated by John Willett (London, 1990), pp 134–5.

pp. 148–9    For the translation of the extracts from: *Recherches sur la sexualité. Janvier 1928–août 1932*, ed. José Pierre, I have relied on Malcolm Imrie's translation, *Investigating Sex. Surrealist Discussions 1928–1932* (London, 1992).

pp. 173–4    Federico García Lorca: 'The Unfaithful Wife', English translation by A. S. Kline, in García Lorca: *Fourteen Poems of Love and Death*, at www.tonykline.free-online.co.uk/Lorca.htm.

p. 175    Federico García Lorca: *Collected Poems*, ed. Christopher Maurer (New York, 1991), p. 510. These lines translated by Alan S. Trueblood.

p. 203    Peter Weiss: *The Persecution and Assassination of Jean-Paul Marat as Performed by the Inmates of the Asylum of Charenton under the Direction of the Marquis de Sade*, tr. Geoffrey Skelton and Adrian Mitchell (New York, 1983), p. 20.

Fiction
Crime
Noir

Culture
Music
Erotica

# dare to read at serpentstail.com

Visit serpentstail.com today to browse and buy
our books, and to sign up for exclusive news and
previews of our books, interviews with our
authors and forthcoming events.

---

| NEWS | cut to the literary chase with all the latest news about our books and authors |

| EVENTS | advance information on forthcoming events, author readings, exhibitions and book festivals |

| EXTRACTS | read the best of the outlaw voices – first chapters, short stories, bite-sized extracts |

| EXCLUSIVES | pre-publication offers, signed copies, discounted books, competitions |

| BROWSE AND BUY | browse our full catalogue, fill up a basket and proceed to our fully secure checkout – our website is your oyster |

---

FREE POSTAGE & PACKING ON ALL ORDERS…
ANYWHERE!

---

## sign up today – join our club